continued . . .

"Plenty of sexy times, nonstop action, well-developed secondary characters, and engaging dialogue all rolled into an excellently crafted plot. I absolutely love where Ms. Ashley appears to be taking this series . . . A fabulous series."

—*Fiction Vixen*

"Jennifer Ashley again proves her skill as a writer."

—*Fresh Fiction*

TIGER MAGIC

"Another enjoyable read from the hardest-working woman in romance . . . Satisfying." —*Fiction Vixen*

"A true paranormal romance that delivers well-developed characters, devious plot lines, steamy romance, and engaging dialogue." —*Smexy Books*

"The Shifters Unbound series just keeps getting better and better . . . Fast-paced action and fascinating subplots round out a fantastic read." —*Night Owl Reviews*

"Nearly perfect . . . It's impossible not to fall in love with Tiger." —*RT Book Reviews*

MATE CLAIMED

"One of my top paranormal romance series, with its complex political and social issues and some intense, hot romances."

—*All Things Urban Fantasy*

"A must-buy series for paranormal romance lovers."

—*Fiction Vixen*

"Another paranormal romance by Ashley is just what the doctor ordered. Her characters are intense and full of passion, and there's plenty of action in this fourth book in the Shifters Unbound series."
—*RT Book Reviews*

WILD CAT

"Danger, desire, and sizzling-hot action! *Wild Cat* is a wild ride. Jennifer Ashley walks the razor's edge of primal passion . . . This is one for the keeper shelf!"
—Alyssa Day, *New York Times* bestselling author of *The Cursed*

"A riveting read, with intriguing characters, page-turning action, and danger lurking around every turn. Ashley's Shifter world is exciting, sexy, and magical."
—Yasmine Galenorn, *New York Times* bestselling author of *Priestess Dreaming*

"Another excellent addition to the series!"
—*RT Book Reviews*

PRIMAL BONDS

"[A] sexually charged and imaginative tale . . . [A] quick pace and smart, skilled writing." —*Publishers Weekly*

"An enjoyable thriller . . . [An] action-packed tale."
—*Midwest Book Review*

"Humor and passion abound in this excellent addition to this series." —*Fresh Fiction*

continued . . .

PRIDE MATES

"With her usual gift for creating imaginative plots fueled by scorchingly sensual chemistry, RITA Award–winning Ashley begins a new sexy paranormal series that neatly combines high-adrenaline suspense with humor." —*Booklist*

"A whole new way to look at shapeshifters . . . Rousing action and sensually charged, MapQuest me the directions for Shifter-town." —*Publishers Weekly*, "Beyond Her Book"

"Absolutely fabulous! . . . I was blown away . . . Paranormal fans will be raving over this one!"
—*The Romance Readers Connection*

SHIFTER MATES

A Shifters Unbound Anthology

JENNIFER ASHLEY

BERKLEY SENSATION, NEW YORK

THE BERKLEY PUBLISHING GROUP
Published by the Penguin Group
Penguin Group (USA) LLC
375 Hudson Street, New York, New York 10014

USA • Canada • UK • Ireland • Australia • New Zealand • India • South Africa • China

penguin.com

A Penguin Random House Company

SHIFTER MATES

A Berkley Sensation Book / published by arrangement with the author

Berkley Sensation Books are published by The Berkley Publishing Group.
BERKLEY SENSATION® is a registered trademark of Penguin Group (USA) LLC.
The "B" design is a trademark of Penguin Group (USA) LLC.

For information, address: The Berkley Publishing Group,
a division of Penguin Group (USA) LLC,
375 Hudson Street, New York, New York 10014.

ISBN: 978-0-425-26694-6

PUBLISHING HISTORY
Berkley Sensation mass-market edition / March 2015

PRINTED IN THE UNITED STATES OF AMERICA

10   9   8   7   6   5   4   3   2   1

Cover art by Tony Mauro.
Interior text design by Laura K. Corless.

CONTENTS

LONE
WOLF

CHAPTER ONE

"Whoa there, little lady."

Maria stopped, scrabbling to hang on to the tray loaded with beer bottles and glasses, to find the asshat who'd been bugging her all night standing in front of her. He was human, annoying, and in the Shifter bar for kicks.

Maria had labeled him *asshat* the second he'd walked in the door, for two reasons. First, he'd strolled in with his friends in his greasy jeans and baseball cap, unshaved whiskers, and attitude. He was human; he was superior—he thought—over these Shifters and the little human Maria who was there to serve him.

Second, Maria called him *asshat,* because Ellison liked that word, and she liked Ellison.

"You bringing those to my table?" the man said, raising his voice over the rollicking country song playing on the old-fashioned jukebox. "None of that Mexican beer crap, right?"

"Your order's coming," Maria said with cool dignity. "This is for them." She jerked her chin at a cluster of Lupine Shifters in the corner, one family—brothers, sisters, father, and mother, all having a good time.

"Don't think so. We're tired of waiting. Take it to our table."

Maria stood her ground. "Not yet."

"You talking back to me, bitch? Someone needs to teach you a lesson."

With a practiced hand, the man banged the tray upward from the bottom. Maria tried to hang on to it, but the tray became a vertical plane, and bottles and glasses slid off to land in a spectacular crash on the floor. Beer fountained over Maria's black leggings, glass skittering past her sneakers. The asshat danced back, laughing . . .

Right into a tall Shifter in jeans and a button-down shirt, with honey-colored hair, wolf-gray eyes, and a body that bulked above the human man's. His large hand, tanned by Texas sun, landed on the human's shoulder.

The music from the jukebox ran down, and the Shifter's slow drawl sounded over the last strains. "I think you need to apologize to the lady, son."

Ellison's grip on the man's shoulder looked loose and relaxed, but Maria saw the asshat flinch, his pale eyes widening. "Stupid clumsy bitch dropped beer all over me."

Ellison's fingers tightened. "Wrong answer," he said in his fine Texas baritone. "You go on over to the bar and pay for what was on that tray, then you and your friends get on out of here."

"Screw you. I ain't paying for that. She dropped it. Take it out of her paycheck."

His stupid trick hadn't angered Maria much, but his last words made her fury rise. She needed every penny of her paycheck and her tips for the goal she'd determined as soon as she'd moved back to the Austin Shiftertown six months ago. Every day she worked for it, saving everything she could, so that one day, she'd not have to put up with asshats like this, or live on the charity of the Shifters who'd rescued her.

Another Shifter, a scary-looking Feline with a shaved head and body full of tattoos, was already coming up behind Ellison. His name was Spike, and when Maria had first seen him, when she'd arrived scared and broken from Mexico, she'd wanted to run the other way.

Asshat didn't notice him, and he didn't notice the tall, black-haired, blue-eyed Shifter who ran the place coming up behind Spike. The man *did* see the Shifter Maria sensed behind her—Ronan, a giant of a man who could turn into a Kodiak bear. Hard to miss Ronan.

The human man paled. Liam Morrissey, the black-haired Shifter, stepped into the man's line of sight. Liam flashed his Irish smile that could melt paint off a building, and the asshat looked uncertain.

Shifters did that—they charmed and terrified you at the same time. They could gaze at their prey with half-closed eyes, like animals dozing in the sun. The next moment, they'd be awake, alert, focused right on you, while your animal brain yelled at you to run, run, run . . .

Shifters might wear Collars, but they weren't tame, and they sure as hell weren't safe.

"Now then, lad." Liam moved around the man with his lanky grace and stopped a foot in front of Maria and a little to her right.

This forced the human man to turn slightly, moving his line of attack away from Maria. Ellison adjusted so that he was now half behind the human and half on his left side, a position from which he could grab said man if he tried to go for Maria. Spike and Ronan moved in to cover any remaining gaps in the circle.

Maria had seen the same tactics during her three years of absolute terror living with a pack of feral Shifters. No, not *living* with them. They'd stolen her from her family and imprisoned her in a warehouse basement with other females.

She'd watched those Shifters form similar circles around intruders or with dissidents within their own pack. They'd surround the victim, not threatening, not attacking. Just intimidating.

Shifters had intimidation down to an art. The Shifters in Mexico had finished their circle of fear by killing the intruders and the dissidents. Maria had never seen the Austin Shifters kill anyone, and they wore Collars made to shock them if they grew violent, but she knew the potential for destruction was there.

Something deep in the asshat's drunken brain knew it too, but he tried to brazen it out. "I'm not paying for shit."

"Nor will you be," Liam said smoothly. His Irish lilt was musical and deep, despite twenty and more years living in Texas. "You'll leave this bar on the moment, and you won't be coming back again. Not ever, I'm thinking."

He smiled when he said it—the smile of a lion who knows the gazelle is within paw's reach. Didn't hurt the lion to be nice to the gazelle.

"You don't own this bar, you piece of Shifter turd," the man said. "You can't throw me out, or my friends."

"It looks like your friends have already left. Fine men they are for deserting you, aren't they?"

The man looked around, blinking when he realized he stood alone, surrounded by Shifters. His friends, who'd been loud and obnoxious in the corner, had quietly walked out when Ronan had left his post.

"Ellison," Liam said, looking over the asshat's head. "See that he gets out, will you? I'll put you in charge of his safety. Spike, go with him."

Ellison's grin flashed. It was a wolf's grin, matching the large gray wolf Ellison became when he shifted. His was a fine-looking beast, with silver gray fur that shone in the moonlight, and a long-legged grace that went with his strong face.

"I'd be happy to." Ellison returned his hand to the human's shoulder. No mistaking the flinch that time. "This way, son."

"Stop calling me *son*."

Ellison laughed, his strong Texas accent booming through the room as he said, "Hey there, Ronan. Why don't you back off and let the man through?"

Ronan—who, Maria had come to know, was one of the gentlest guys in Shiftertown—instead moved to block the doorway, folded his arms, and looked mean. Seven feet tall, he made a formidable barrier, and the rumbling in his throat became a deep, vibrating growl.

"Come on now, Ronan," Ellison said. "Liam says we got to let the man go."

Ronan glared down at the asshat, whose face was now shining with sweat.

Spike—the tall, tattooed biker-looking Shifter—moved past Ellison and leaned his hand on the doorframe. As though he and Ronan went through an unspoken conversation, Ronan finally nodded and turned sideways in the doorway to let Ellison and the man pass.

Ellison, hand on the man's shoulder, steered him between Spike and Ronan. Ronan left barely enough room for them to squeeze through into the glaring lights of the parking lot.

Maria went to the doorway to watch, as did every other Shifter in the bar. Ellison turned the man loose at the edge of the parking lot, halting as the man jogged across the dark street and got himself into a pickup.

"Y'all *don't* come back, now," Ellison called after him. "Hear?"

The truck roared to life. The man peeled out onto the quiet road, squealed around the corner, and was gone.

Ronan laughed, the loud sound filling the bar. Ellison strolled back inside and high-fived first Ronan then Spike. Ellison's laugh joined Ronan's in loud, rich warmth, and Spike added his grin. Liam stood back and watched the three with a fond look an older brother might give mischievous siblings.

Ellison let out a Texas whoop. "Good fun, Liam. You all right, Maria?"

His cowboy boots crunched on the glass in the middle of the room. Maria, shaking from anger, fear, and watching Ellison's eyes soften to warm gray as he looked at her, lost her temper.

The human man had unnerved her, and the Shifters surrounding him like stalking beasts had reminded her too strongly of the Shifters who'd held her captive. Shifters were Shifters, and Maria would never be safe.

She swept a shaking finger and a scowl around the four men, ending at Ellison. "*Locos.* You'll bring the police in here, and then they'll close the bar, and I won't have a job. I *need* this job."

She ended shouting up at Ellison, who blinked his gray eyes then turned up his grin. "Now, sweetheart, it was good fun, and that asshat is too scared to do anything to retaliate. He's gone."

"I could have taken care of him, until you had to step in with all your muscles."

No, no, the term was *muscle in.* That's what they said on TV shows—Maria was learning all her American slang from television.

Ellison started laughing again. "Yeah, me and my muscles to the rescue. Don't leave out Ronan's. His are pretty hefty."

"You gobshite," Maria snapped. Liam was also teaching Maria slang. She retrieved the tray from the floor and held it up like a weapon. "If he tells the owner I made trouble, who will get fired? *Me.* You don't even work here."

"Now, honey . . ."

Said in that Texas drawl, in Ellison's deep voice, the endearment made Maria warm inside, threatening to assuage her anger. Which was why she raised the tray and started for him.

Liam's big hand yanked the tray from her hands. "Take a break, child."

Maria opened her mouth to let her hot temper have its way, but one look in Liam's eyes made her close it again. "I don't need a break," she said. "I'll clean this up and get back to work."

"I'll be cleaning it up," Liam said. He jerked his thumb at the office door in the dark rear of the bar. "You. Break. Now."

No one argued with Liam. Not for long. At least, no one but his wife, his brother, his father, his nephew, and now his little girl, who couldn't even talk yet. Maria raised her chin, turned her back on the Shifters, walked past Ellison, shoes crunching broken glass, and slammed her way into the empty office.

Ellison started after her and found Liam in his way. "Let her go," Liam said in his quiet voice. "Give the lass time to catch her breath."

Ellison eyed the office door between him and Maria, a barrier he needed to break down. That Liam formed another barrier made him growl in irritation.

Maria lived in Shiftertown under the Morrisseys' protection, staying now in Liam's brother Sean's house. She'd been brought here by Liam's dad a year ago after she'd been rescued from the feral Shifters down in Mexico. She'd then gone to stay with her brother, who lived way out in El Paso and who had sponsored her to get her a visa. But the brother had made it clear that he, like her parents still in Mexico, considered Maria ruined goods and a disgrace to the family.

Maria had returned to Shiftertown after six months, and Liam made sure she got hired on at the bar he managed. In her off time, Maria cleaned houses, ran errands, and looked after cubs for Shifters who paid her. She worked nonstop, her energy amazing. Ellison's sister had said, with a laugh, that Maria could be a Shifter with stamina like that.

Liam brought out a broom from behind the bar, then the great alpha Feline, leader of his pride, his clan, and all of Shiftertown, went to work sweeping up the glass. Spike, one of the most formidable fighters in Shiftertown, grabbed a mop and started helping him.

Another Lupine stopped next to Ellison—Broderick, who was in the second wolf pack in Shiftertown. Ellison's pack was very small. Most of his clan had died out in the wild, their immediate family going just before Shifters took the Collar, leaving Ellison, his sister, and his sister's tiny cubs alone. Shiftertown had been good to them, letting the boys, Jackson and Will, grow up unharmed.

"She's ripe," Broderick said. He was watching the office door, behind which Maria rested, his gray eyes intense.

Ellison tightened, the wolf in him tense, readying itself to take down a rival. Ellison kept his voice mild when he said, "I think she smells pretty good."

"I mean she needs to be mated. Soon. Now."

"I know what you meant." *Asshole.* "But she's off-limits." Liam and Dylan had made that clear. "To you, to me, to all Shifters."

"That's bullshit. This is a Shiftertown full of mateless Shifters. And she's fair game."

Ellison didn't bother to answer. *Fair game* was a female without a mate, a clan, a pack or pride. A female whose mate had died and who had no family to return to was considered fair game, as was a female stolen from another clan. Unmated, unprotected. *Shifter leavings* was another term Ellison had heard.

Maria wasn't quite the same. First, she was human, and second, she was definitely under Morrissey protection.

Good thing she was. As soon as Maria had returned to Shiftertown, intending to stay a while, male Shifters had started sniffing around. Maria had formerly been mated to a Shifter, she smelled of Shifters, and Shifters were desperate for mates.

Including Ellison.

"She's off-limits," Ellison repeated with a growl.

Broderick laughed. He was tall and rangy, with a buzz cut and white gray eyes. "And don't you just hate that?"

Ellison did. Maria was lovely, with her black hair, red mouth, and lush hips outlined by the black leggings she wore to waitress, but Ellison saw the bleakness in her eyes. Her life had been destroyed by Shifters, and she was hurt, and she grieved.

He eyed the blank panel of the closed door, knowing Maria was hurting behind it. He wanted to go to her, put his arms around her, and say, *Hey, sweetheart, it will be all right. I'll fix everything for you.*

But he knew he couldn't. The Shifters who'd captured

Maria had sequestered her—Shifters in the wild in ancient times had locked their females away from all others in the same way. She'd been imprisoned against her will, hurt, terrified—nothing that would heal easily, if ever. The best Ellison could do right now was turn Broderick away from the door and let Maria have some peace.

"Ellison." Annie, another waitress, passed Ellison with a tray of drinks to replace the one Maria had lost. "You have a phone call."

Ellison put his hand on the cell phone in his pocket, but it was silent. At the bar, the human bartender briefly held up the house phone, then set it down to pour the next drink.

Ellison didn't want to take his eyes off Broderick, but he knew that neither Liam nor Spike would let anyone into the office with Maria, especially Broderick.

Ellison made his way to the phone, thanked the bartender, and picked up the receiver, wondering who'd call the bar, not his cell phone.

"Yeah?" he drawled.

"Ellison?" the breathless voice of one of his nephews came to him. "You need to get back here. It's Mom. She's gone again."

CHAPTER TWO

Ellison tore away from the bar and sprinted out into the darkness, his nephew's words pounding through his brain. The wolf in him told him he could move faster in animal form, but Ellison didn't want to lose precious minutes stopping to undress and shift.

He ran up the porch steps of his house to find all the lights on inside. Jackson, the older of his nephews, met him at the door.

"We tried to stop her," Jackson said, panicked. "But you know what happens."

"Tell Andrea to come over," Ellison said, pushing past him. Andrea, a wolf Shifter who lived in the house across the street, was a healer. They might need her.

Ellison raced down the hall in the one-story bungalow to his sister's bedroom, finding his second nephew, Will, waiting anxiously in the doorway. Will, twenty-four, the youngest of Denise's cubs, had tears in his gray eyes.

"She's bad this time."

Ellison paused to put his hands on Will's shoulders. "Jackson's getting Andrea over here to help. Don't worry."

Will returned the clasp, slightly comforted by Ellison's touch, but he didn't relax.

Ellison stepped into Deni's bedroom. In the middle of it, facing him, was a huge gray wolf with murder in her eyes.

Deni wasn't as large as Ellison, being female and about forty years younger, but she was a Shifter, and that made her powerful. She snarled at Ellison, no recognition in her expression.

Deni's room was a wreck—furniture overturned, clothing shredded on the floor. The window blind had been half ripped down, the slats tangled as though an animal had seen something through them and had gone for the window, not caring that the blind was in the way.

Deni sniffed, smelling Ellison fresh from the bar, and then snarled again, ears flattening on her head. The Collar around her neck emitted several sparks.

Ellison carefully didn't move. He was Deni's alpha, leader of their tiny pack. Though it broke his heart to see her like this, at the moment he needed to be less worried brother and more alpha wolf.

"Den." He made his voice firm but not harsh.

Deni growled right through the word, an arc of electricity running around her Collar. Ever since whatever foul bastard had run her down on her motorcycle and left her mangled and half-dead, Deni had been having episodes of forgetting who she was, who Ellison was, who her own cubs were.

Each time this happened, she reverted into her wolf and stayed there—threatening like a cornered animal.

Deni's body had healed fairly quickly—Shifters had incredible metabolisms that closed wounds swiftly. Plus, they had Andrea   half Shifter, half Fae—who had Fae healing magic, made greater when she channeled it through her mate, Sean, the Shiftertown Guardian. They'd brought Deni back from death and thought all was well.

Then had come the first episode of Deni's brain more or less shutting off and making her forget everything she was. Human doctors couldn't find anything wrong with her, and Andrea couldn't help.

What Deni needed was a Shifter healer—one stronger than Andrea, well versed in ailments from which Shifters could suffer. The trouble was, Shifter healers weren't thick on the ground, if any even existed these days, and Deni was sick *now*.

"Deni," Ellison said again, making his voice hard with command. "It's Ellison."

Deni snarled one last time, then attacked.

Ellison blocked her leap with arms folded to protect his face. He took the brunt of her weight, sparks from her Collar dancing across his skin, and they went backward together.

Ellison's heightened Shifter senses scented his nephews in the hall, scared and unhappy. He smelled Deni, enraged and terrified, as her wolf untangled herself from him, whirled, and leapt at him again.

Ellison caught her in his arms this time and swung around with her, using the momentum of her impact to toss her away across the room. Deni smashed into a wall, the thud of her contact lost in her growls. She came to her feet with terrible swiftness, her eyes red with rage, her gray coat dusted with plaster that had cracked off the wall.

Deni went for Ellison again, fangs bared. The Collar was taking its toll on her—Deni was a little slower this time, the impact not as strong. Ellison saw pain in her eyes as she landed on him.

This time she clung on with her claws, her jaws snapping at his neck. Ellison changed under her grip, his favorite black cowboy shirt ripping as his massive wolf shoulders burst through it.

His own Collar sparked as he caught Deni's muzzle with his mouth, now a wolf's mouth, turning aside her deadly bite.

Ellison tasted her blood, the blood of his pack, and his feral rage ignited. No wolf attacked the alpha and lived.

The human part inside him knew that this was his sister, lashing out, scared. The wolf in him said it was one of the pack, hurt yes, but she needed to be subdued.

Both entities wove together and knew what to do. Ellison released Deni's muzzle and went for her throat, locking his teeth around loose fur. Deni howled, her Collar sparking wildly as she shook her head to try to tear free.

Ellison held on tighter, carefully not letting his teeth break her skin. He put his large paw on her head and used his weight to bear her to the floor. He landed on top of her, his wolf big enough to cover her and keep her down.

He heard the distinctive footsteps of Andrea and then Glory, Dylan's mate, following his nephews—Andrea sure-footed and graceful, like her wolf; Glory with the click-click of impossibly high heels.

Deni howled, still fighting, but Ellison's hold was strong. Deni growled and snarled, terrified, not understanding.

"I can tranq her," Glory said.

Ellison didn't want Deni tranqed. She'd been given drugs and sedatives, poked and prodded. She didn't need another round of tranquilizers that would leave her groggy and afraid.

But they might not have a choice. Deni was still fighting, weakening, but fighting. She still didn't know who Ellison was—she was lost and scared, afraid to yield to the wolf who pinned her. In the wild, Ellison would have had every right to kill her for the safety of the pack. Deni's wolf, by the look in her eyes, somehow sensed this.

"Mom," Jackson said, voice thick with tears. "Mom, try. Please."

Deni snarled again, trying to dislodge Ellison. Her Collar gave her a barrage of shocks, which shocked Ellison at the same time, hot bites of pain.

Ellison growled, a long, low sound. *Stop. I'm your brother. Those are your cubs. Come* on, *Den.*

Deni snarled again, then she blinked once, twice, and her eyes cleared. She drew a breath through her wolf muzzle, and her Collar went silent.

Ellison snatched his teeth away from her throat as Deni shifted to human, lifting himself away from her before he could hurt her. Tears filled Deni's eyes. "Jackson?"

"Mom."

Jackson fell on his knees beside Deni as Ellison shifted

back to his human form. Ellison's arms went around his
sister, and she relaxed into his strong embrace.

Ellison kissed her hair, holding her, rocking her. Deni
reached for Jackson, who came into the embrace with
them, her son openly crying. Will knelt on Deni's other
side, sliding his arms around his mother's waist.

Ellison didn't get up, knowing that Deni needed his
comfort, his forgiveness, his understanding. Her cubs gave
her love, and Ellison gave her strength.

"So," Glory said. Ellison heard the butt of the tranquilizer rifle click softly on the floor. "We won't be needing
the tranq, then."

"No," Andrea said. "Just me."

She came to kneel beside Ellison, careful not to break
the family huddle. Ellison couldn't have let Deni go for
anything right now, in any case. Andrea reached between
them, laid her hand on Deni's forearm, and let her healing
magic trickle into Deni to soothe her better than any man-
made tranquilizer ever could.

Ellison felt the small pulse of magic flowing into him
through Deni. Though Glory was the leader of the rival
Lupine pack in this Shiftertown—Broderick's pack—and
Andrea her niece, Ellison had nothing but gratitude for them.

Maria finished her shift without any more asshats harassing her, or drinks spilling, or glasses breaking.

Liam had cleaned up the mess by the time she emerged
from his office, the floor pristinely clean. He said nothing
to her about the incident, only winked at her as she walked
back to the bar to fill her next order. The rest of the Shifters had gone back to drinking, laughing, and talking, the
excitement over.

Maria's shift that night finished before the bar closed.
She let Ronan walk her partway home, but he had to get
back to help Liam close, and she told him to go. Shiftertown lay before her, with its small bungalows and neat
yards, quiet under the cool of the night. Summer would hit

soon, with sticky weather that only Austin and its river and creeks could bring.

Ellison had gone before Maria emerged from the office, long gone, Spike told her. Jackson had called, and Ellison had raced home.

Spike, a man of few words, of course hadn't been that effusive. What he'd said was: "Ellison went. Jackson called. While ago."

Maria knew why. Poor Deni, and her poor sons. Jackson and Will were grown men in human terms but still considered cubs to Shifters.

She hoped everything was all right. She'd have to visit Deni tomorrow if all was well, maybe cook her something. Buñuelos. Deni liked those, and they were fairly easy to put together. Sean always kept flour, sugar, and honey around for making his pancakes, and never minded when Maria used the ingredients. Maria helped pay for groceries with her tips from the bar, in any case.

Her tips had been pretty good tonight. Maria's pockets were full of coins and bills, more for her jar of savings.

A shadow rose beside her, and a Shifter fell into step with her. "I liked how you stood up to that human," the Lupine called Broderick said. "Took guts."

"Thank you." Maria kept walking, though her calm had shattered again. Broderick liked to follow her home, to walk too close to her. Though he'd never done anything inappropriate in Shifter terms, he violated her personal space all the time, doing everything but rubbing against her.

"No one would do that to you if you had a mate," Broderick said.

His constant argument. "I don't want a mate," Maria said quickly. She'd been mate-claimed by one of the Lupines in Miguel's Shifter pack, and at first, she'd been stupidly enchanted with Luis, which was how she'd been stolen from home in the first place. She'd learned quickly about the things Miguel expected from females brought in by his feral males.

At first, Maria had blamed herself for falling for tall,

handsome Luis, but she knew now that if she hadn't have
run away with Luis willingly, he'd have kidnapped her.
Miguel and his Shifters had dominated Maria's little town,
and there had been nothing her family or any of the other
townspeople could do.

"Yeah, you keep going on that you don't want anything to
do with Shifters," Broderick said. "But you live here, honey.
You can't be wriggling your ass at us and then telling us we
can't have any. Not when male Shifters are dying to mate."

Maria shivered, and not from the breeze. She was too
alone out here, the first houses of Shiftertown half a block
away. If she tried to run, Broderick would be on her before
she took two steps.

"Maybe someday," Maria said. But not if she could help
it. She had her plan, and she would be free.

"Maybe *now*." Broderick grabbed her arm and leaned
close, breathing into her face. Maria cringed back from the
scent of stale beer. "Maria Ortega, I mate-claim you under
the light of the mother goddess."

Maria tried to break free, but his hand was strong.
"There's no moon tonight, and you have to do it in front of
witnesses." She knew that much.

Broderick's grip bore down. "Then let's go find us some
witnesses."

"Here's one," came a male growl.

Ellison appeared out of nowhere, a mass in the dark,
reaching for Broderick. Ellison's face was bruised, as though
he'd been fighting, his hair a mess. He clamped one hand
around Broderick's neck and yanked him away from Maria.

"You heard me," Broderick managed to say, even with
Ellison's fingers digging into his throat. "I claim this
female in front of a witness."

Ellison snarled, his eyes tinged with red. "Then I Challenge."

CHAPTER THREE

Ellison smelled Maria's fear, a scent that spiraled his protectiveness—already high—skyward. He shook Broderick, hand still around the wolf's throat.

Broderick wrenched himself free but kept to his feet, his Collar sparking as he came back at Ellison.

"Stop!" Maria shouted.

Broderick surprisingly obeyed, his eyes bloodshot with drink and anger. He was fairly high up in the other Shifter-town pack, the one Glory led, and he always behaved as though he had the weight of his pack behind him.

"You can't touch her until the Challenge plays out," Broderick said, rubbing his throat. "Off-limits."

"Then I'll play it out right now."

"*I* name the time and place, as the Challenged."

Ellison waited. Broderick looked Ellison up and down, keeping his sneer but with assessment in his eyes. Ellison's pack might be small, but that didn't mean Ellison had lesser power.

Maria stepped between them. Ellison sensed her panic, a primal fear that had been seared into her by the ferals who'd captured her. She was afraid of Shifters in general, but she bravely stood her ground now and held her hand out in a stopping motion to Broderick. "I can refuse the mate-claim. I know the rules."

"You're fair game, darling," Broderick said. "You need a mate to protect you."

"What I need is for both of you to leave me the hell alone!"

Broderick took a step toward her, but Ellison was around Maria with Shifter speed, blocking his path. "She refused. That's the end."

Broderick glared at Ellison, fists closing. "I'm taking this to Liam. He decides."

"He knows Shifter law."

"I know. He knows pack law too. When Andrea came here, the pack wouldn't accept her until she had a mate. We didn't need her running around making every male fight over her. The same thing applies now."

"Not with a human. She's not part of *any* pack."

"Then what's she doing here? She either follows Shifter law, or she leaves."

Maria already had left. Not being stupid, she was walking swiftly across the vacant lot, heading for the street that would lead to where she lived with Sean and Andrea, Dylan and Glory.

Ellison turned his back on Broderick and strode after her. He heard Broderick mutter something behind him, but Broderick didn't follow. Likely he was going back to the bar to either drown his troubles or whine at Liam.

Ellison quickened his footsteps to reach Maria. Broderick wasn't wrong about male Shifters wanting to fight each other over her. Females were few and far between. Unmated, unprotected females, fewer still. Most of the males were more polite than Broderick, but just barely.

Ellison, who'd watched her across his street every day as she'd lived, first with Liam and family, then with Sean and family, had left her alone. Having heard the story of her rescue from the feral pack by Dylan, Ellison knew Maria was still hurting.

The feral Shifters, led by a Shifter called Miguel—had kept Maria like an animal. What they'd done to her exactly, Ellison wasn't certain, and he'd never asked. She'd never talked about it, just as she'd never spoken about her time with her brother in El Paso. From what Liam had said, though, her brother had treated her as though she had some contagious disease.

Maria had never said a word in complaint. Ellison had watched her square her shoulders, learn English as well as she could, and work hard at any job she could get. She squared her shoulders now, in the white T-shirt she wore for her job at the bar, her black braid hanging down her back.

Ellison caught up to her as she walked down the middle of the quiet street. He knew Maria heard him coming—his boots clicked loudly on the asphalt—but she didn't turn to greet him.

Other Shifters were out, sitting on dark porches or running as their animals in the common yards behind the houses, or doing other things in the shadows that made him growl. Shifters were calm on their home territories, but still dangerous.

"Don't walk home alone," Ellison said harshly. He was too raw with emotion to keep his voice gentle.

"I do as I please," Maria said in a hard tone. Then her voice softened. "I'm sorry. I heard you were called home. Is Deni all right?"

"Yes." The word jerked out. Ellison was still wound up from Deni's relapse, and Broderick being an asshole hadn't helped calm him down.

"I'm really sorry." Her mouth turned down, lovely plump red lips. "Thank you for stopping Broderick."

"You refused him. Too bad. I was ready to kick his ass."

"I'm allowed to turn down mate-claims. Liam said so."

"Liam's right." Ellison moved closer to her. "But you're going to piss off every horny Shifter male by doing it. Fair warning."

"Doesn't matter. I won't live in Shiftertown forever."

Ellison didn't like that. "You can't be planning to move back in with your brother."

Maria stopped, her braid swinging. She turned warm brown eyes up to him, but they held a hint of steel. "Of course not. This is America. I don't have to live with my brother, or with Liam, or Sean. I can live in a place on my own."

"Alone?" Ellison blinked. "Why would you want to?" He couldn't imagine living by himself, without sister, nephews, cubs, parents, pack—*family*.

He was almost alone here, head of a pack of four. No mate of his own, no cubs. *Lone Wolf,* the other Shifters sometimes called him.

"It's different for me," Maria said. "The idea of being alone is . . . *splendid*."

"Lonely."

"Peaceful."

"Boring." Ellison shook his head.

"I wouldn't sit at home and do nothing. I would . . ." Maria bit the corner of her lip then drew a breath. "If I tell you this, will you keep it to yourself? Andrea knows, and Glory. And Connor. No one else."

"Connor?" She named Liam's nephew, younger than Ellison's nephews, all of twenty-one.

"Yes, Connor. He's good at keeping secrets. I want to go to school. I've been saving up for it, and I'm already working on my application and looking for scholarships. Connor's been helping me study for the tests called SATs. I'll be taking them this Saturday."

"Community college, eh? Maybe a good thing. You could drive Connor—the kid's a maniac behind the wheel."

"No, not community college. University. UT Austin."

Ellison whistled. "They don't take everyone—they don't take Shifters at all. Maybe you should start with something smaller, work your way up to it."

Her indignant look could have lit a fire. "There is no reason to start small. If you want something, you go for it. You never know in this life when it will all be taken away."

So true. Maria spoke from her own experience, and look what had happened to Deni.

Maria's anger made her shake. She needed reassurance, cried out for it, though Ellison knew she'd never admit it.

Ellison put a hand on her shoulder. Quietly, like he would for a cub who was upset.

But Maria wasn't a cub. She was a beautiful young woman, alone, unprotected, yet gutsy and strong for what had happened to her.

Ellison's touch of reassurance turned to a caress, the backs of his fingers brushing her skin. "You go for it, Maria. Aim as high as you want." *And if you fall, I'll be here to catch you.*

Maria's expression softened. She had a round face, pretty, ringlets of black hair trickling loose from its binding. Ellison's need to kiss her rose like a newly kindled fire, to press his lips against the soft red ones, to taste the moisture inside her mouth.

"Is everything all right with Deni?" Maria asked.

"Yeah," Ellison said, jerking his gaze from her lips. "She's fine now." Ellison had left her sleeping, Andrea holding her hand.

"I'll go over and see her tomorrow, all right?"

"Yeah, she'd like that. But if she gets . . . you know . . . forgetful, you get out. Dominant female wolves can be very dangerous."

"She won't hurt me." Maria spoke with a confidence Ellison didn't share. Deni had been intent on killing him, her own brother.

They'd reached Sean's house, all quiet within. Ellison's house was dark as well. Maria slowed her steps and stopped with Ellison at the bottom of Sean's front porch. Silence hung between them, and warmth.

"Thank you for rescuing me," Maria said. "Twice."

Ellison reached up to tip the hat he'd left at home when he'd raced out to find her. "Any time, darlin'."

Her smile flashed, beauty in the darkness. The smile went from polite to genuine, hot as the Texas sunshine. "*Hasta luego,*" she said. *See you soon.*

Ellison made himself step away from her. The move was difficult, as though someone had wrapped elastic straps around himself and her to pull them together. "You need any more rescuing, you call me, sweetheart," he said. "Good night."

"Good night." Another flash of smile, and Maria turned, ran up onto the porch, and was gone.

Ellison stayed in the street, watching the closed door. A light went on downstairs, then off, then one upstairs, in the bedroom they'd given Maria. A glow illuminated her as she came to the window, ready to close the blind.

Maria saw Ellison, who remained staring up at her like a love-struck wolf cub. She waved then closed the blind, shutting him out.

"You plan on eating her alive?" a gravelly voice asked him.

Ellison whirled around, fist on his chest. "*Shit.* Spike."

Spike stood two feet away from Ellison, his son on his shoulders, the little boy holding on to his dad's head. Ellison hadn't heard or sensed either of them. Spike was a tracker, one of the best—good at stealth. But Ellison should have scented and sensed the cub, a four-year-old called Jordan.

"Hey, Jordan," Ellison said, trying to force himself to relax. "Taking your dad out for a walk?"

Jordan laughed. "Yeah. It's fun." Spike hadn't known about the kid until last fall, and now the two shared a bond that was like cement.

"Watch Broderick," Spike said. "He's going to try to make the mate-claim and your Challenge stick."

"Damn, word travels fast."

"Broderick went back to the bar and started pissing and moaning to Liam. Ronan got worried about Maria and called me, asking me to check on her. So here I am, checking on her. But I guess you got it covered."

He started to turn away, Spike finished.

"If the Challenge goes down, want to be my second?" Ellison asked him.

Spike called his answer over his shoulder. "Do you have

to ask?" Jordan laughed and waved, and the pair of them faded into the darkness.

Ellison walked up to his front porch. From the quiet inside, everyone had gone to bed—he could hear his nephews snoring in the bedroom they shared, and the quieter breathing of Deni.

Broderick was going to be a problem. Ellison had no worries about kicking his ass, but Maria's fear had been sharp. Getting past that would be more difficult.

Ellison didn't trust Broderick not to try to climb up on Sean's porch and steal Maria out of her bedroom. Broderick would never consider doing that with a Shifter woman—not these days—but humans were regarded as weak, and Maria had already been the victim of a Shifter abduction. Broderick would figure that meant he could do what he wanted with her, and unfortunately, so might other Shifters.

Ellison sat down on one of the chairs on the porch, the chair's wood creaking. He put his feet up on the rail and leaned back, hands behind his head, to watch the square of light that was Maria's window.

The window went dark, Maria seeking her bed. She'd be all cuddled up under the sheets, alone, not wearing much of anything. She'd smell of sweet sleep, damp skin, desire.

Ellison let out a sharp breath. If he kept his thoughts in that line, he'd be climbing up on the roof himself to steal her away. He was as bad as Broderick, and he knew it.

Ellison settled back in the chair, gaze fixed firmly on the dark window. Good thing wolves liked to stay up all night.

Maria opened her eyes in the dark. She smelled them around her, the women, both human and Shifter, who'd been sequestered by the ferals. With them the scents of the kids—scared, defiant, exhausted. Maria didn't need to be Shifter to understand what fear and defeat smelled like.

Her own child lay in her arms. She could feel him, the weight of the little body, the warmth, the beauty of him.

But he'd been born too weak. Maria had begged Luis then Miguel to take her and him to a hospital, to a doctor at least, and Miguel wouldn't. Hours later, her son was dead.

The child in her arms disappeared leaving Maria bereft, empty, grieving. She lay on the cold floor, her sobs coming, dry and broken. A hand touched her hair, the soft brush of a woman called Peigi, trying to comfort her.

There was no comfort. Maria had lost everything—family, her child, herself. She lay in the cold darkness, alone, empty. She'd never see daylight again, never feel warmth, never feel whole. She'd been broken, part of herself taken away.

In the middle of the grief came a hated voice. Peigi's gentle touch vanished, to be replaced by a fierce grip in her hair, pulling her up.

"You're trying again," the voice said in rough Spanish. Maria had never known where Miguel had been born and raised, but he spoke several languages, fluently if not elegantly. "We need cubs that live."

Maria screamed. The scream rang through the huge basement, coming back to her in waves. The kids started to cry, the women to keen.

Miguel pulled her up, and up, and up . . . and Maria was sitting in her bed in Shiftertown, her heart thudding, her breath coming in dry hiccups. She put her hand to her face and found it wet with tears.

Air, she needed air. The little room was stuffy, the nights warming now.

Maria scrambled out of bed, her legs shaking, and stumbled to the window. She cranked up the blind and opened the casement as quietly as possible.

Something moved on the porch across the street. Maria froze, ducking into the shadows of her bedroom before she worked up the courage to peer out again.

She saw a pair of cowboy boots propped up on the porch railing, and long legs going back into shadow. Maria's body relaxed, her racing heart slowing.

She crept across the room to her dresser and found the

pair of binoculars Sean had given her when she'd expressed interest in bird-watching down at the river. Right now she wanted to do a little Shifter-watching.

Maria returned to the window and trained the binoculars onto Ellison Rowe's porch. There he was, leaning back in a wooden porch chair, eyes closed, mouth slightly open. She couldn't hear from here, but she knew soft snores issued from his mouth.

Maria smiled, the fear of the dream vanishing. The grief didn't lessen, and it would never go away, but her emptiness receded a little. The cowboy across the street, who'd come to her rescue twice tonight, was here with her. She wasn't alone.

E llison went inside in the morning, stiff, groggy, and having no idea how he'd fallen asleep in the chair.

All looked normal at Sean's, and at Liam's house next door to it. Kim had tripped off to work, Andrea's boy was wailing with his usual energy, and Connor came out to work on Dylan's truck, along with Tiger, another rescue from captivity.

Tiger glanced over at Ellison but didn't return Ellison's wave of greeting. Not that Ellison expected a Shifter who'd spent his entire life in a cage to know how to respond, or to care.

Tiger hauled up the truck's hood and bent over it, starting to tinker, with Connor's help. Working on vehicles seemed to be the only thing that kept Tiger calm.

Ellison showered, shaved, and came out of his room to see Deni cooking breakfast with Will. Jackson had already left for a job he had with a moving company; Will worked at a furniture warehouse. Shifters were good at lifting and carrying.

Deni looked rested, cheerful even. Ellison put his arm around her as she stirred the mess of eggs and cubed potatoes in the frying pan and kissed her cheek.

"Don't put too much salt in mine," he said.

"Don't backseat cook." Deni smiled at him, and Ellison's heart lightened.

It would lighten even more when he saw Maria. Ellison told Deni he'd be right back, gave Will a brief hug, caught up his hat, and walked out the door.

Running across the street to see how Maria was doing after she'd been badgered last night would be the neighborly thing to do. Right? Ellison could pretend he'd come to get a taste of whatever pancakes Sean was cooking today.

Andrea met him at the door, with little Kenny Morrissey, her firstborn, on her hip.

"Maria? No, she's not here," Andrea said. "She left without a word very early this morning, and I don't know where she is. I was hoping she was with you and Den."

CHAPTER FOUR

Maria. Missing. And Andrea stood there calmly, cuddling her son, like nothing was wrong.

"What do you mean, you don't know where she is?"

Ellison took a broad step forward, his wolf growling all the way.

A mistake—a big mistake. Sean materialized out of the kitchen, holding a pancake turner. His eyes were Shifter white, focused on Ellison, the lion in him responding to a threat to his mate, his cub, his territory.

The Guardian was the last person a Shifter would ever see, the point of the Guardian's sword sending the Shifter's soul to the afterlife. Whatever else Sean might be—friend, mate, tracker—he was also death.

Ellison stepped back, hands up, trying to show Sean that he meant no harm—to Sean's house, mate, cub, or pancakes.

"Why don't you know where she is?" Ellison asked Andrea.

"She was gone when we woke up," Andrea said. "Or at least when I checked on her. I was up early, with Kenny, and I heard the back door close."

Which explained why Ellison hadn't seen Maria go. Or else she'd left while Ellison had been in the shower. *Shit*.

"Did you call her?" Ellison demanded.

"Of course I did," Andrea said. "No answer. Left a voice mail."

Ellison didn't need to ask Andrea for Maria's number. He'd memorized it a while back. "And you don't have any idea where she went?"

Sean stepped in front of Andrea, though the deadly look had faded from his eyes. "Come in and have pancakes, Ellison. I'll make some with pecans. Your favorite."

They were trying to placate him. *Calm the wolf down.*

Kenny was looking at Ellison with round gray eyes, his mouth working on one fist. Shifters of crossed species were born in human form and revealed their Shifter form when they were about two or three. Sean was Feline, Andrea Lupine—Kenny could go either way. From his eyes though, Ellison would bet wolf.

"Thanks, but I'll pass," Ellison said. "Where was Maria planning to go? She say anything to you last night?"

"We don't keep her prisoner," Andrea returned, irritated. "She comes and goes when she wants, wherever she wants. She doesn't have to check with us."

The reasonable part of Ellison knew Andrea was right, but the Shifter part of him didn't give a crap.

"She needs to check in when Shifters are threatening to start their own personal breeding projects with her. Tell you what—she can come and live in my house. I'll look out for her better."

Sean's expression hardened. "Not gonna happen."

Liam's stipulation when Maria had come to Shiftertown was that, while she could take a room with whomever she chose, she couldn't live in the house of an unmated male, for obvious reasons. She'd lived for a time in Liam's house with Connor there, because he hadn't made his Transition yet, and the mating need hadn't yet manifested in him.

But once Tiger had moved in last November, Maria had

to vacate. She'd moved in with Andrea and Sean, Dylan and Glory without fuss, understanding, she said.

That Andrea didn't know where she'd gone bothered Ellison a lot.

"She needs looking after," Ellison growled. "If y'all can't do it, we need to find someone who can."

He swung around and walked off the porch, not slowing down. "Where are you going?" Andrea called worriedly behind him.

"To look for her. Where'd you think?"

The scenario in his head went like this—Maria gets up early, deciding to find Connor and study for her SATs with him. She walks out the back door, and Broderick is lying in wait. Ellison is in the shower, and Broderick drags her off.

Anything human in Ellison disappeared. He'd already claimed Maria, in his head and in his heart. He'd held off, because Dylan had explained exactly what had happened to her down in Mexico. *Give her time*, Dylan had said. *Liam, Sean, and I will protect her until she's ready.*

Ellison was ready. He'd kill Broderick and bounce his head down the sidewalk if the Lupine had touched Maria. Ellison's Collar sparked with his adrenaline, warning him to calm down, but Ellison told his Collar to take a flying leap.

Broderick lived two blocks over and two blocks down. A short distance for wolves who were used to patrolling vast tracts of territory.

Ellison approached the two-story bungalow that housed Broderick, his mother, aunt, and three brothers. Youngest brother was on the porch shoveling food from a plate into his mouth but was on his feet by the time Ellison reached the front steps.

"Stay right there, wolf," the brother, Mason, said.

"Get Broderick out here so I can rip his head off."

Mason set down his plate of eggs and Texas toast and stood up squarely. He was the youngest brother, but he was bigger than any of the others in Broderick's house, probably why they had him stand guard.

"Brod!" Mason yelled over his shoulder. "That dumb-ass Lupine is here."

"I heard him." Broderick came out the door to flank his brother. He folded his arms, the pair of them glaring down at Ellison with identical stares. "What? It's early. Why aren't you holed up with your crazy sister?"

"Where is she?"

Broderick didn't move. "You mean Maria? Not here. Why?"

Ellison leaned toward Broderick and inhaled, too far gone in rage to care that it wasn't good Shifter etiquette to obviously check someone's scent to determine whether he was lying. Especially not on that rival Shifter's territory with his little brother ready to rub Ellison's face into the sidewalk.

Ellison didn't smell a lie on Broderick, but he didn't smell Maria on him either. He caught the brief scent of her from last night, when Broderick had tried to mark her and claim her, but nothing more than that. Scents had layers, fading with time and how many showers the Shifter had taken. Broderick hadn't bathed since last night, but his clothes were clean and contained no scent of Maria.

"What did you do, lose her?" Broderick asked. "Doesn't she live across the street from you?"

"Screw you." Maria wasn't here. If she had been, even if they'd locked her in the most protected part of their basement, Ellison would have scented her and found her.

Ellison spun away from the porch and started down the street again, worry piling on worry. The sky was blue, the sun bright, another beautiful day in Austin. The sunlight would sparkle in Maria's dark hair, dance on her smile.

Footsteps sounded beside him, and then Ellison got a full dose of Broderick's unwashed scent. "So where is she?"

"Would I be here ready to kill you if I knew?"

Broderick didn't answer, but he didn't leave either. "I'm coming with you," he said.

"The fuck you are."

"You aren't doing a very good job of finding her, are you? Two heads are better than one."

"But I want your head on the ground," Ellison growled.

"That's where I want yours. But we find Maria first. Sure she's not with one of the Morrisseys?"

"No. And they don't seem worried."

"Fucked-up Feline bastards."

Ellison ignored Broderick the best he could as he made his way back to Liam's house. Connor and Tiger were still bent over Dylan's truck.

Ellison stopped outside the property line and hauled Broderick back before the man could run up to Connor, likely to close his hand around Connor's neck and demand the cub to tell what he knew.

If Broderick did that, he'd lose his arm, because Tiger was already straightening up from behind the hood and glaring at them with those weird eyes of his. Tiger, though only adopted into Liam's family and clan, was seriously protective of Connor.

Tiger hadn't been born of Shifter parents—he'd been bred in a research facility and raised in a cage by human scientists for about forty years. They'd been trying to create a super-Shifter—one who was better, stronger, faster, and all that shit, than your average Shifter. They were trying to do what the Fae had done a couple thousand years ago, except without the magic and possibly not the maniacal laughter. The single-minded cruelty had been there, though.

The result was Tiger—superstrong, barely controlled, and not happy with people who messed with Connor. He wore a Collar, but Ellison was one of the few who knew the Collar was fake. Liam had tried to put a real one on Tiger and it hadn't worked, so a fake one had to do for now.

The man didn't have a name, either. Tiger didn't know what it was—the humans who'd created him had called him Twenty-Three. The woman who'd rescued him had decreed that Tiger could pick his own name, but so far, he hadn't. So everyone called him Tiger.

Tiger wasn't growling, but he didn't need to. The stare from the yellow eyes was enough.

"Connor," Ellison said.

"Yep?" Connor answered, wiping his hands.

"You take Maria somewhere this morning?"

"Nope. But if you're asking if I've seen her, I did. She came out the back door bright and early, said hi to me, said she was going to help Ronan look after Olaf, and said to tell you she could hear you snoring all the way across the street."

Broderick made a sound that was a cross between a snort and a laugh. Tiger said nothing at all.

"Damn it." Common sense told Ellison he was running around Shiftertown making an idiot of himself, but his hackles still wouldn't go down. Something was wrong—didn't matter if he didn't know what. Didn't matter that everyone else was being logical and unworried.

"Thanks, Connor," he managed to say. "If she comes back, tell her to stay put, will you?"

"Sure thing."

Tiger's gaze remained fixed, the big man with his mixed black and orange hair focused in silence on Ellison.

"We go to Ronan's then?" Broderick asked.

"*I'll* go to Ronan's. You go home."

"Like I'm letting a Lupine from another pack tell me what to do. I don't like wolves from my *own* pack telling me what to do."

Annoying asshole. Ellison tried to ignore him as he plotted a course for Ronan's, and started between the houses to get to the common.

"I will come with you."

Tiger stepped into their path before Ellison saw the guy move. He was about three inches taller than Ellison, as big as a bear Shifter. He'd be great to have on hand if Ellison needed help with a fight. On the other hand, Tiger was unpredictable, stronger than any Shifter he knew, and not quite stable in the head.

"You need to take care of Connor," Ellison said.

Tiger remained in place, a wall Ellison wasn't going to get around. "I will come with you."

"It's all right," Connor said, more to Tiger than Ellison. "I'll be fine."

Tiger nodded once and turned away, starting off in the direction of Ronan's.

Connor stepped to Ellison and spoke in a low voice. "Keep an eye on him. Tiger, I mean. He's usually fine, but when he gets upset . . ."

"Yeah, I know what he does. I'm having a great morning— my girl's missing, and now I'm babysitting a crazy Shifter and a wolf from a rival pack."

"Tiger's not crazy," Connor said. "Just . . . intense."

"Intense. Right."

The way Tiger turned around and stared back at them told Ellison he'd heard every word.

"Don't worry, I'll take care of him." Ellison growled again, ruffled Connor's hair, and walked rapidly after Tiger and Broderick.

O ne of the foster kids at Ronan's—Cherie—told them that Maria had come for Olaf early and the two had gone off together. Cherie was a cub going on twenty-one, with brown and lighter brown hair that marked her as a grizzly. She was yawning, the only one at Ronan's house, and barely awake. Ronan had asked Maria to look after Olaf today, Cherie explained, while everyone else was out. Maria had seemed happy to.

Cherie looked annoyed to be roused out of her sleep-in, but bears were like that. They loved their sleep.

"Where did she take him?" Ellison asked.

"Walking." She shrugged. "I don't know. Maria's trust-worthy, and Olaf likes her. They'll be fine." Cherie looked over the three male Shifters as though they didn't impress her, named a park outside Shiftertown where Olaf liked to go, and retreated with a decisive bang of the door.

The park wasn't far, a good brisk walk out the other side of Shiftertown and down a few streets. The roads were quiet here, with little traffic. No drivers to stare at Ellison, Broderick, and the giant Tiger with his orange and black hair bringing up the rear.

The park lay vast, green, and open, the eastern edge of it running up to a little ridge full of dense trees. A few joggers shuffled around the paths, but kids had already gone to school, and most adults to work. One or two moms pushed kids in strollers, but the park was largely empty.

No sign of Maria's dark hair and lovely body, no woman tugging a ten-year-old boy with white hair with her along the paths.

Ellison made for the ridge on the other side. Something pulled him that way, a sense of wrongness. He walked faster and faster, running by the time he took a path that led over a stream, up some stone steps, into the woods that led up the side of the hill.

Tiger heard her first. He grabbed Ellison by the shoulder and silently pointed a broad finger into deeper shadows, where the hill climbed high.

Ellison let Tiger, with his better hearing and sight, lead. Tiger moved noiselessly, fading into the woods like smoke. If Ellison hadn't kept a sharp eye on him, he'd have quickly lost him.

"Olaf!" Maria's voice came to them before they'd walked another twenty yards. *"Olaf!"*

The word had an echoing quality, as though she'd gone into a cavern or tunnel. Ellison jogged to catch up with Tiger, who quietly led him down another little hill into a tiny valley.

The valley ran between the ridge and another hill on the other side. On top of the second hill was a road shielded by a concrete barrier. Cars raced along it, the drivers paying no attention to what was below them.

A wide culvert opened under the road. Maria stood a few feet inside it, hands around her mouth, calling desperately for Olaf.

CHAPTER FIVE

Maria peered into the darkness, straining to see Olaf. She'd taken two steps into the chilly culvert into which he'd disappeared before she'd frozen, unable to move.

The press of the concrete walls, the cold dampness, the dank smell, very like that in the basement of the warehouse in which she'd been kept, triggered memories too powerful to stop. Her heart constricted, her throat working while she fought down the screams.

Only Olaf's little growls—telling her he'd shifted into his polar bear cub—kept her from running out, back into the sunshine, back to Shiftertown.

"Olaf, please come back." Her voice was shaking, but she knew her pleas would have little impact. Olaf would have decided by now that Maria wouldn't come in there after him.

She heard footsteps behind her, heavy ones, made by the firm strides of Shifters.

In her state, Maria's mind told her they were Miguel's Shifters, come to find her. She clamped her mouth closed over her cries of panic and fled into the tunnel.

"Maria!"

The sound of the warm voice made Maria stop, her breath hurting her. Even with his worry, he kept the Texas drawl.

Ellison. An anchor, shelter from the cold. Maria turned back, something heating in her when she saw his tall silhouette at the tunnel's opening, his big cowboy hat a comforting sight.

She took a few running steps toward Ellison, then stopped again as two other Shifters appeared behind him. One was Broderick—what was *he* doing here? The other was the Tiger man who lived in Liam's house. Maria wasn't afraid of him exactly—Tiger had never paid her much attention—but his bulk was frightening in the darkness of the culvert.

Ellison didn't wait. He came into the tunnel, his long legs bringing him to her in a few strides. "Maria, honey, you all right?"

He slid his arm around her waist. He did it without thought, the most natural thing in the world.

Maria managed a nod. "It's Olaf. He's gone exploring and won't come out."

Ellison was like a rock. His arm steadied her, and his warmth at her side quieted her fears. His hat touched her hair, and then she felt his lips on the top of her head.

"Stay put," he said. "I'll get him. Tiger—look after Maria."

"I'll watch her," Broderick said, too quickly.

"No. You'll come with me."

"Chase bears yourself, Rowe," Broderick said with a growl. "I'll take Maria home."

His arrogance snapped something inside Maria. The fiery temper she'd been ashamed of before her abduction reared up. "You get in there and find Olaf," she said to Broderick, pointing her finger down the tunnel. "If he doesn't come out, or one hair on his pelt is hurt, you can explain to Ronan why you didn't go in after him."

Ellison chuckled, more heat. "I know who my money's on."

Broderick growled again. "You're going to leave her with the crazy?"

Tiger said absolutely nothing, but when his yellow eyes flicked to Broderick, Broderick swallowed.

Maria took a step closer to Tiger. "I'll be fine. Get Olaf."

Broderick made another snarling noise but took off down the tunnel.

"Be right back," Ellison said. He touched his hat brim, gave Maria his big smile, and jogged down the tunnel after Broderick.

The wolf in Ellison didn't like the tunnel of the culvert. Wolves preferred wide meadows, where they could run, or the quiet of woods that flowed for miles. Wild wolves did hole up in dens, but those were shallow caves, not deep tunnels.

The dislike of caves came from racial memory, maybe. The Fae had liked caves, not to live in, but as a place in which to keep their slaves. Slaves meant Shifters; that is, until the Shifters had told the Fae to go fuck themselves and had fought a long, bloody war for their freedom.

Ellison's Lupine Shifter ancestors had been thrilled to be free of the underground, to run in the wild, where they belonged.

Bears, on the other hand . . .

"Why does he want to explore down here?" Broderick asked, a shudder in his voice.

"Bears. Damn things *like* caves."

"But he's a polar bear."

"So maybe he likes ice caves."

"Let's find the shit and get him out of here," Broderick said. "It'll make the woman happy."

The woman. That was how he talked about Maria, the beautiful lady Broderick said he wanted to mate-claim. Dickhead.

Ellison had drunk in the beauty of her, even as he'd

worried for Olaf. She wore form-hugging jeans today and
a tight-fitting shirt, a black elbow-sleeved T with spangled
red and blue flowers on the front, two small buttons holding it closed at the very top. She was a delicious package.
Ellison wanted to find Olaf quickly so he could return and
enjoy it.

"Olaf!" Ellison called, his voice falling against the dead
air of the tunnel. "Where are you?"

If they lost Olaf, it wasn't only Maria he'd have to face.
Ronan loved the kid. Olaf was an orphan of unknown clan
who'd needed a home, and Ronan had volunteered his.
Ronan was always doing things like that, the big, giant softie.

The big, giant softie had foot-long claws, and teeth that
could rip a tree in half.

A trickle of water sounded up ahead, the tunnel built to
carry runoff from creeks when they overflowed. Ellison
always found it fascinating that Austin was crisscrossed by
creeks and wetlands, while other parts of the vast state, not
very far from here even, were bone-dry. Texas and its
amazing diversity went on forever.

Ellison heard Olaf growl. A long, low growl, from a
baby animal throat, at something that had the cub surprised and worried. Olaf was a fairly fearless little guy, so
anything that worried him worried Ellison.

Ellison stripped off his boots, ready to let his wolf come out.

Shifting wasn't always instantaneous. Ellison's body
fought it today, both human and wolf wanting to hurry and
find Olaf and take him out. He willed himself to be wolf—
easier to track, easier to fight in that form.

He shucked his jeans as his legs started to bend to the
wolf's, fur swiftly erasing his human flesh. Once Ellison's
four wolf feet hit the ground, the struggle ceased, and the
wolf took over.

He pinpointed Broderick's rank smell right away and ran
past it, Broderick a smudge in the darkness. Up ahead, Olaf
was still growling, throwing off agitated bear cub smell.

Ellison also scented Tiger and Maria behind him. Tiger
was the musky male at the top of his strength. Maria was

the gentler of the two, like the cinnamon and honey she put on her buñuelos. She smelled of home and things of light, a beacon in the darkness.

Ellison knew she'd hesitated following Olaf because the underground reminded her too much of her captivity. Ellison and she shared that hatred of the close darkness, which represented to both of them imprisonment, slavery, and terror.

Another odor assaulted Ellison's nose and had Broderick growling. Humans. Human men not as afraid of confronting a polar bear Shifter as they should be.

They weren't afraid *yet*. Ellison sped up and charged around a corner into a second culvert.

Three human men stood inside the tunnel, blocking the way to daylight behind them. LED lanterns threw pale shadows on the ceiling and over the polar bear cub who stood defiantly before them. One man had a tranquilizer rifle, pointed at Olaf, and the other two held a large net between them.

Ellison took this in with rapid calculation before he gave in to his wolf's rage. He charged, his Collar sparking hard.

The scent from the men changed to panic. Facing a full-grown Shifter wolf was a different thing from facing a bear cub, though they'd have found Olaf a handful. But the gunman still had the tranq rifle, and he raised it to point it at Ellison.

Ellison let his body hit the ground, under the rifle's aim. He slammed himself at the gunman, sweeping him from his feet. The man yelped as Ellison ran into him, and dropped the rifle, which went off as it spun around, the tranq dart flying. The dart hit nothing, clattering to the floor to be lost in the darkness.

In the next moment, Broderick came running in, in the form of his timber wolf. He hurtled toward the men with the net, his Collar snapping sparks, but Broderick didn't let the Collar slow him down. The net men spun with quick reflexes, ready to snare him.

They'd done this before, Ellison realized. The three men worked as a well-practiced team, the rifleman rolling to pick up the rifle and reload it while the men with the net regrouped. In a second, they'd have the thing over Broderick.

Ellison went for the gunman again. His heavy wolf body crushed the man into the nearest wall, making him drop the rifle once more, and Ellison heard a bone snap.

Sparks zapped Ellison hard, and pain ran like fire through every nerve. Fucking Collar. Ellison could control the Collar when he fought in the rings at the Shifter fight club, because his brain knew then that he didn't really want to kill the Shifter against him.

But these humans had threatened a *cub*, and Ellison wanted them dead. The Collar sensed his need to kill and went to work trying to stop him. The Collars evened the odds, in spite of the gunman's broken wrist, and the net had started to tangle Broderick.

Olaf ran back and forth between the men, growling up a storm, grabbing legs and heels, biting.

"Shoot him!" One of the net men yelled. "Grab that damned bear, and let's get out of here."

"He broke my arm!" the gunman shouted back.

"Sixteen million! Think about sixteen million."

Sixteen million dollars? Did they mean for Olaf?

Screw the Collar. Ellison slammed his body into the human's again, letting his Collar's sparks strike the man's flesh. The man screamed, another bone or two definitely breaking.

Broderick fought and writhed, but the net, which appeared to be barbed in places, had closed around him. One of the men dropped his end of the net and dove for the rifle, coming up with it and the dart full of tranquilizer before Ellison could stop him.

And then the tunnel filled with noise, a roaring sound with death in it. The man who'd grabbed the gun executed a practiced roll, got to his feet, and shot the tranquilizer dart straight at the giant tiger that hurtled in from the darkest end of the tunnel.

The tiger was so big that he broke off pieces of the wall as he charged. The dart hit Tiger in the chest . . .

. . . and didn't slow him a step. The rage in Tiger's eyes escalated to madness as he kept on coming.

The man trying to contain Broderick dropped the net and fled. The first gunman squirmed out from behind Ellison and ran up the tunnel toward daylight, staggering and cradling his broken arm.

The man who'd shot the tranq at Tiger stood frozen in stark terror. Tiger was going to kill him.

Tiger had killed once before, Ellison knew, though the Shifters were keeping it quiet. Not Tiger's fault, Liam had said. Human scientists had created Tiger to be a killing machine, and Tiger didn't yet know how not to be.

But if Tiger were arrested for killing a human, the Shifter Bureau might find out who Tiger was and what he was, and take him away. Back to a lab, or maybe they'd just outright slaughter him. And Liam and the rest of Shiftertown would pay for harboring him.

Ellison morphed back to his human self, landing panting, upright on his feet. "Run, you idiot," he said to the remaining man. "I can't stop him."

The human remained rooted in place, staring in horrified wonder as Tiger unfolded from the giant Bengal and became a giant human, his eyes still yellow with fury. The dart stuck out of Tiger's muscled chest, and Tiger contemptuously yanked it out.

"Leave. The cub. Alone." The words were guttural, harsh, inhuman.

The man blinked, gulped a breath, and finally turned to flee. Ellison grabbed the tranq rifle out of the man's hands as he ran by. Ellison raced after him but stopped inside the shadows of the culvert while the man sprinted after his friends into the bright light of morning.

Ellison watched him scramble into a waiting high-end SUV, a cage obvious in the back. The vehicle squealed away, leaving the faint bite of exhaust in the warm spring breeze.

Tiger ran a few steps past Ellison and stopped, not bothering to keep his large, naked body out of the sunlight. "You let them go." He turned back and bent his angry gaze on Ellison. "They were going to hurt the cub."

"No, they were going to *steal* the cub," Ellison said. He leaned against the cool tunnel wall to catch his breath. "I don't know what that's about."

"I would have killed them first."

"I know." Ellison gathered his courage and reached to place his hand on Tiger's formidable bicep. "If you'd killed any of them, hell would rain down on Shifters, and you'd be captured, and possibly killed and dissected. Connor's trusting me to keep you out of trouble, remember?"

Tiger jerked away from Ellison's touch. "They can't hurt the cubs."

Tiger was ferociously protective of all cubs—he'd lost the only one of his own, the humans wrenching it away from him before he could properly know it or say goodbye. Liam speculated that he transferred that grief into being crazily protective of the cubs in Shiftertown.

Ellison shared that obsessive protectiveness—most Shifters had it—but Tiger took it over the top.

"Trust me, big guy, there are other ways," Ellison said. "We have their equipment, and I got a good look at them and their SUV. We'll find them and persuade them it's a bad idea to mess with us. Kidnapping Shifters is against human law too, and Kim knows cops who are sympathetic to Shifters. We'll get them."

Tiger looked unconvinced. But at least he turned away and went back into the tunnel.

Broderick was just finishing fighting his way out of the net. "Bastards, fucking bastards. Why didn't you kill them?"

Ellison didn't bother explaining a second time. "Where's Maria?"

Olaf, still a bear, was dancing around, growling and beating the air, doing a little victory hop as though he'd chased off the bad guys single-handedly. The joys of being a cub.

"Maria is safe," Tiger said.

As soon as the words left his mouth, Maria's voice came up the tunnel. "Olaf? Is Olaf all right? What is happening?"

Maria followed her voice, her words dying as she ran into the light of the LED lanterns and found herself facing three large, naked Shifters and one cavorting polar bear cub.

Ellison watched her expression turn from concern for Olaf to shock at the three tall Shifters with animal rage in their eyes, and then dissolve to stark, remembered terror. He'd seen the same look on Deni's face last night when she hadn't recognized Ellison, her own brother. Maria was reliving a moment of her captivity.

She shook it off in the next second, grabbed Olaf by the scruff, and started dragging him back down the tunnel the way she'd come. The little bear dug in his feet and wailed in protest, but Maria was relentless.

The heightened senses of Ellison's wolf felt her grief and fear, her fight for sanity. He wanted to find the Shifters who'd hurt Maria and grind them to powder.

He motioned for the other two to stay back, and ran down the tunnel after her.

CHAPTER SIX

Maria didn't stop when she heard Ellison calling her name. She continued walking swiftly, pulling Olaf with her. The bear still protested, but he'd quit fighting her, seeming to understand that she'd won.

Maria didn't halt until she reached the sunlight and the spot where she'd dropped her big shoulder bag to go running inside after Olaf. She leaned against the stone wall outside the culvert, absorbing the warmth of the concrete, and closed her eyes.

Her heart still raced in panic, her breath choking her. She knew, logically, that the Shifters inside the tunnels were her friends—except maybe Broderick—not the evil beasts who'd imprisoned her.

Even Broderick followed Shifter rules whether he liked them or not. He and the other Austin Shifters understood that they had to curb their feral tendencies in order to survive. Miguel and his pack hadn't.

"Maria."

Ellison was there, in front of her. He'd resumed his jeans, but he held his shirt crumpled in one hand.

In spite of her shakes, Maria couldn't help reflecting that Ellison was breathtaking. His jeans rode low on his hips, his liquid, tanned skin smooth over a hard body. A few red abrasions decorated his chest, and he had a solid bruise on his cheek. The worst wound was around his neck, where the Collar had burned his skin.

Her visions of the feral Shifters dissolved as concern replaced fear. "Are you all right?" Maria reached up and touched his Collar. The black and silver entwined metal was cool under her fingertips, but she knew it had been hot and painful a few moments ago.

Ellison's gray eyes went quiet under her touch, his gaze fixing sharply on her. "Yeah, I'm OK. What about you?"

Ellison always mitigated his alpha wolf stare for Maria, but even so, it was hard to take. Maria abruptly pulled her hand away. "I need to go home."

After a few more beats of stare, Ellison picked up the bag she'd left on the ground. "Come on then." He put his hand on her shoulder and steered her toward the path that would lead them back to the park. "Tiger's going to sit on Broderick a while, so you don't need to worry about him."

"I'm not." Maria couldn't explain what she felt, words leaving her, so she just walked.

Having Ellison next to her, warm and tall, comforted her beyond what she could think. His hand on her shoulder held strength, but gentled for her as usual, to reassure rather than frighten.

When Maria had rushed into the culvert, worry for Olaf overriding her fears, Ellison had just finished shifting. His naked body had been beautiful, with the fire of the wolf still in his eyes. Now he was Ellison again, soothing her, helping her.

Olaf, as a bear cub, scampered ahead of them then ran back, circling their legs, enjoying himself. His clothes and things were in Maria's bag, but Olaf showed no sign of wanting to change back to a human boy.

They walked back across the ridge and down to the park, Ellison's hand steadying her. A few humans they passed did a double-take at the polar bear cub romping after butterflies, though most people who used this park knew that it lay close to Shiftertown and had grown used to Maria walking with cubs out here.

Ellison was silent as they wound through the park and walked down the few blocks to Shiftertown. Olaf ran ahead of them through the open gates. He spied another cub in a yard down the street and charged to him, the little wolf rising to meet him.

Maria started a few steps after Olaf, but a Shifter woman came out onto her porch, laughing at the two cubs, and calling a greeting to Olaf. Everyone knew Olaf, and everyone liked him. Olaf and the wolf started a mock wrestling match, Olaf none the worse for his ordeal.

Ellison pulled Maria to a halt in the shade of a tall live oak, the tree screening them from most of the houses. His fingers were warm on her shoulder, but firm. He wanted her to stay there.

"You had a flashback in that culvert, didn't you?" Ellison watched her, knowing the truth, but willing her to tell him.

Maria evaded his gaze. "I don't want to talk about it."

"I think you need to talk about it a little." Ellison touched her chin. "You know you don't need to be afraid anymore, Maria. No one will hurt you, or make you do anything you don't want to. And not just because the Morrisseys say so. *I* won't let anyone hurt you. I'll break all their fingers if they even try."

He meant it. She'd seen how he'd been with Broderick last night—ready to kill the other wolf. But Maria never knew what to say to Ellison when he was being gentle and helpful. The only thing she could think of was, "You are all so kind to me."

"Hey, it's not *kindness*, sweetheart. At least not from me." Ellison's touch went to her cheek, the caress light.

Warmth spread down through her chest. Maria tried to speak, to explain, but her lips couldn't form the words. She still struggled to think in English, and Ellison didn't know much Spanish.

"You're here, Maria. Safe." Ellison traced her cheek, increasing the warmth. "Not in the dark anymore. You don't need to be afraid. And if you are afraid, you come to me."

Maria managed a smile. "And you'll make it all better?"

"I want to."

He leaned closer, and Maria's back met the bole of the big tree. Ellison smelled of sweat and a small bite of blood, and of himself. The feral Shifters—all of them—had always stank. Ellison smelled of warmth and goodness.

Maria turned her face up to him, rising on tiptoe to offer the kiss she wanted to give him. She couldn't think of words, but she could show him with this.

She found herself caught hard against Ellison's bare chest, his hand snaking under her braid, he leaning into her. His mouth fit clumsily to hers, his lips moving before Maria was ready. Their teeth bumped, and Ellison lifted away, laughing a little, his eyes full of heat.

"Shifters don't kiss much," he said. "At least, I don't."

There hadn't been much kissing in the feral pack either. No tenderness, not even between the males and females who'd cared for each other.

"Nuzzling, yes." Ellison leaned to her again, his nose touching her cheek, his breath warm. "I guess when you have a lot of nose, you tend to use it."

Maria wanted to laugh. No, not to laugh. To go quiet while he nuzzled her cheekbone.

"I never kissed much either," she said. When Luis had wooed her in the moonlight, before she'd known he was a Shifter, she hadn't kissed him.

This was new to her, as was Ellison's gentleness. Luis had charmed her with his dangerousness, exciting to a naive and sheltered young woman like Maria. Ellison mitigated his strength for her, showing her he'd never let loose and hurt her.

"We can learn together," Ellison said, breath against her lips.

Maria formed an unpracticed pucker, her blood warming as Ellison responded with light pressure. His hand, shirt still dangling from it, went to the tree, his lips firming against her mouth.

Maria felt the strength of his entire body through the kiss, like a hum in the air between them as Ellison licked softly across her lips. She tasted salt and coffee on him, and a bite of himself.

She clenched her hands at her sides. She could barely breathe, nothing existing but Ellison's lips connecting with hers, his mouth tenderly prying hers open, his fingers working under her braid, loosening it.

Another kiss, another slide of his tongue between her lips. Maria flicked her tongue over his in answer, the velvet heat of it stealing her breath.

She should be afraid. She'd been afraid for such a long time. Ellison stood over her, his body against hers, pinning her with his mouth, his presence, himself. Maria should be afraid and want to duck away from him, to run, but she stayed, letting her hand steal to his chest.

She warmed as she contacted the smooth heat of his bare skin, the wiry curls that dusted his chest. She found his heartbeat, his heart drumming as rapidly as hers.

Maria slid her hand up to his neck, feeling the Collar around his throat, the raw skin it had burned. He'd been hurt, while he'd fought for Olaf, but he hadn't stopped until Olaf was safe. She didn't understand the whole story of what had happened inside the culvert, but she was too full of Ellison's taste and warmth to break away and ask.

He laced his fingers through her hair, caressing her neck as he deepened the kiss. Heat, sunlight, everything that was good and warm—Ellison.

Ellison slid his hand down her neck to her back, the other still supporting him against the tree, the softness of his dangling shirt brushing her shoulder. Maria leaned into his embrace, the sweetness of his kiss unknotting her stomach. She flowed into comfort, into wanting.

A small growl sounded, then air whooshed by her. Ellison broke the kiss, his legs bending as the whirlwind of Olaf smacked the backs of his knees.

"Hey." Ellison turned around, his big hand still steady against Maria. He'd never let her fall.

Olaf shook himself like a dog and rose up into the form of a small boy with white hair and dark eyes. "I'm hungry!"

Maria sucked in a breath, the taste of Ellison lingering and heady. "You already had breakfast, Olaf."

"But I want pancakes. Can we go see Sean? Where's Tiger?"

Olaf rarely spoke much—the poor kid had watched his parents be shot to death. To have three or four sentences in a row come out of his mouth was unusual.

"Tiger's walking Broderick home," Ellison said. He straightened up from the tree, but he didn't take his arm from around Maria. "We'll walk with Maria to Sean's house and hit him up for pancakes. All right?"

"Yay!" Olaf grabbed Maria's hand. "Were those men trying to kidnap me, Uncle Ellison?"

"Kidnap?" Maria's eyes widened, some of the warmth evaporating. "What happened?"

"Some men tried to grab me. I smacked them." Olaf danced back, swatting with his hands as he would his bear paws.

Ellison looked grim. "Guys in an expensive SUV," he said. "Their tranq gun was top of the line too."

Olaf had opened Maria's bag and was pulling out his clothes. "Why were they trying to kidnap *me*?"

"I have some ideas," Ellison said.

Maria bent down to help Olaf pull his shirt over his head. "We need to get him home."

"But Ellison chased them off," Olaf said, his rumpled head appearing through the shirt's neckband. "He fought them with his wolf." He growled again and punched the air, his shirtsleeves flailing. "And then Tiger came. It was awesome."

Maria grabbed Olaf's hands and thrust them inside the sleeves. "Home. *Now*."

She tried to berate herself for stopping to kiss Ellison instead of taking Olaf to safety, but the imprint of Ellison's lips remained on hers. The kiss had opened something inside her, as did the smile Ellison sent her now as he caught Olaf's other hand.

What had started to open, Maria never wanted to close again.

"You got the license number, then?" Dylan Morrissey, who showed his nearly three hundred years of age only by the gray-flecked hair at his temples, gave Ellison his powerful alpha stare.

Dylan was no longer leader of Shiftertown, but he was still one of the strongest Shifters around. As Lupine, Ellison should go into intense defensive mode under Dylan's questioning, but because the Morrisseys had accepted Ellison as friend long ago, and because Ellison worked for Liam as a tracker—bodyguard, investigator, enforcer— Dylan was going easy on him. Ellison pushed his instincts aside and answered.

"License plate number, make of the car, description of the guys. It's all in here." Ellison tapped his head. "Tiger saw them too, but he was in killer mode, so who knows what he remembers."

"Tiger and Ellison kicked butt," Olaf said.

Olaf remained at Dylan and Sean's house. Maria, once she'd heard the full story, insisted that the cub shouldn't go home until Ronan could be there to take care of him. Ronan, alerted by Ellison, was on his way, and he agreed Olaf should stay at Dylan's, one of the safest houses in Shiftertown, until he arrived.

Maria played with snap-together blocks with Olaf, the kid building some kind of robot monster with it. From a movie, but Ellison didn't know which one. The only movies Ellison watched were Westerns. The remake of *3:10 to Yuma* was his current favorite, even though it wasn't set in Texas.

Maria's black braid was mussed from Ellison working his fingers through it. He could still feel the amazing heavy silk of her hair, that and the taste of her. Honey, sweetness, fire. Maria.

She was resilient, protective, defiant, and soft all at the same time. Like a rose—fragile but tough.

Maria helped Olaf build the robot with confident hands. She'd seen the movie, because Maria watched every movie and TV show she could, and read every book she could get her hands on. To learn English, she said. She already spoke better than some Shifters who'd come to America twenty years ago.

"Can Sean do his magic and find out who owns the car?" Ellison asked. He mimed typing on a keyboard. Sean could do amazing things with an old computer and dial-up modem.

"Not really," Sean himself said, coming in from where he'd been cleaning up the kitchen. "I already tried it, and got nothing on the plate numbers. They might be fake. Finding out who owns a dark blue recent-model Escalade is playing needle in a haystack. If they drove a 1952 powder-blue Chevy Fleetline DeLuxe with a dent in the right fender, I might have more luck."

"There could be another way," Dylan said. He had the heaviest Irish accent of his family, and every word had a musical quality to it.

Ellison had the feeling he knew what Dylan meant, and Sean nodded. "You're talking about Pablo Marquez," Sean said.

"Didn't y'all run him out of town?" Ellison asked. "After he nearly got Ronan's mate killed?"

"He's been proving himself a useful man," Dylan answered in his quiet way. "He's got a stranglehold on trade coming into South Texas, and keeps the more dangerous of the lot at bay. He knows what he's doing."

High praise from Dylan Morrissey. Made sense, though, that a man like Pablo, overseer of transactions not exactly legal, would know about anyone else trying to stay under the radar in his town.

"I say we go talk to him," Ellison said.

"Aye," Sean said, a sparkle in his blue eyes. "Be good to intimidate . . . I mean *visit* . . . Pablo again."

"Agree," Ellison said. "Let's get Spike."

Maria rose from the jumble of big white toy blocks. "We'll wait for Ronan first. And then I'll come with you."

"No, you won't," Ellison said at once.

"If this Pablo knows who's trying to take Olaf, I want to ask him questions," Maria said, anger in her eyes. "I know a thing or two about people who snatch other people and take them away. I won't sit at home waiting for you to bother to tell me what's happening."

The thought of Maria anywhere near Marquez made Ellison's wolf start to snarl. "I'll tell you," he said, a growl in his voice. "I won't keep you in the dark. But you wait here—or better yet, go across and stay with Den."

Maria put her hands on her hips. "And wait how long? Besides, maybe I can ask him questions you won't think of."

"*Maria.*"

They were a foot apart, Maria's eyes holding dark fire. She was scared, but not for herself. For Olaf. For the cubs. And that gave her the strength of angels.

"Ellison and Maria were kissing," Olaf announced abruptly. He put another block on his three-foot-high robot then stood up as Sean and Dylan swung around and stared at Ellison. Olaf looked up at Maria, innocence in his dark eyes. "Maria, does that mean you're mates?"

CHAPTER SEVEN

The room went still. Maria watched Sean and Dylan fix their blue gazes on Ellison, waiting for him to respond.

Ellison went as quiet as they did. He was the outsider here, on their territory. He contrasted the Morrisseys with his gray eyes and light-colored hair, his taller body more rangy than the broader-shouldered Felines. He'd resumed his shirt, black cotton stretching over the torso that had been warm and bare in the May sunshine.

The two Felines wanted Ellison to answer, to tell them exactly what he'd been doing with Maria, the woman who was under their protection. The friendly ease in the room changed in an instant to threat and the threatened.

Maria had gone through too many tense situations between Shifters to stay calm about this one. She'd seen Miguel face off often enough against one of his lesser Shifters, looking at him the same way Dylan looked at Ellison now. Then had come violence, more fear.

She stepped in front of Ellison and bravely faced Dylan. "If I decide to kiss Ellison, it's my business."

Dylan looked past her to Ellison. "Are you making a mate-claim then?"

"I wouldn't have accepted if he had," Maria said, raising her chin. She'd decided once she'd climbed out of that basement that she'd never let anyone talk over her again. "It's only kissing."

"Maria." Ellison's voice was low and warning.

"I don't care. You all say it is the woman's choice to accept a mate-claim, and then you talk like it's decided for me. I'm not mating *anyone*."

"Maria," Ellison said again. He put a broad hand on her shoulder. "It's all right. I'm not in their pack. I'm not about to let them bully me."

"Pride," Sean corrected. "Felines have prides. Lupines have packs."

"Well, no shit," Ellison said, his drawl broad.

"That was for Maria's benefit." Sean gave her a half smile, but Maria's heart still pounded with the unspoken threats. "I like that she's choosy. Makes good sense."

Dylan alone remained silent. He was a hundred years older than the others, which made him more careful.

His gaze was for Maria now, not Ellison. Dylan had looked Maria over when she'd first been rescued, when she'd stood on a hot, dry airstrip in Mexico, understanding that she was to go away with more Shifters. Dylan's gaze had been calm, holding the weight of ages. He'd not looked at Maria in hunger, as Luis and Miguel and his Shifters had, but in watchfulness.

Now Dylan's watchfulness returned. But there was something new in his eyes—concern for Maria, and also respect.

She saw the same in Sean. The Morrisseys had watched Maria like the overbearing father and older brothers she no longer had. She was grateful to them for it, but she would not let them browbeat her.

"Are we going to go talk to this Pablo?" she asked.

She felt Ellison tense behind her, his hand still on her shoulder. Dylan, Maria knew, would not get one step closer to her, and neither would Sean.

Dylan looked from Maria to Ellison and back to Maria again. "Yes," Dylan said, giving her a quiet nod. "Sean, fetch Spike, and we'll go."

Ellison's warmth felt fine on Maria's left side as he drove her in his big black pickup the short journey to speak to Mr. Marquez. Maria sat between Ellison and Spike, Spike's tattooed bulk squeezed into the cab with them. Dylan's small white pickup followed with Dylan and Sean and the Sword of the Guardian.

Spike bulged with muscle, his entire body covered with tatts, and he kept his head shaved. In the last six or so months, Spike had relaxed, changing from a man who lived for nothing but fighting to one who had more to love. Discovering he had a four-year-old cub, and finding his mate, Myka, had softened the Feline who'd once been hard as granite.

Ellison drove them to a warehouse district and a large mechanic shop housed in one of the older warehouses. When the two pickups pulled up, Spike and Ellison emerging from one truck, Sean and Dylan from the other, the guys working on cars stopped and slowly straightened. Gazes followed the four Shifters and Maria, with Sean's sword obvious on his back, as they moved toward the entrance.

The man called Pablo Marquez had an office in the back of the warehouse, shut away from the noise of the men working on cars. Pablo had dark hair and eyes, Latino coloring, wore a business suit, and rose smoothly when they came in.

He was also a criminal. Maria sensed that before she took two steps inside. He didn't shout the fact—his clothing was tasteful and he didn't flash jewelry, but she knew. He was too congenial, too courteous, and there weren't enough cars being worked on to pay for this cushy office and his thousand-dollar suit.

"I saw you coming," Pablo said, remaining on his side of the desk. "Which means you wanted me to. How are you, Dylan? Sean. Ellison." He cleared his throat as he looked up at Spike. "Eron."

Spike gave him a nod, not betraying surprise that Pablo called him by his real name. Only Myka called Spike Eron, but Pablo seemed the kind of man who knew everything.

"Drink?" Pablo asked without moving. "I have plenty of cold beer, stronger if you want it."

He carefully didn't look at Maria. Maria saw his curiosity about her, but he was acknowledging that she belonged to the Shifters, and he wouldn't poach.

Not long from now, Maria thought with conviction, *I won't be treated like a possession. By anyone. I'll stand up and tell people like Pablo Marquez what to do with themselves.* She started to smile, imagining it.

Ellison didn't see her smile, because he was standing in front of her, a barricade between her and Pablo, but Sean shot her a puzzled look.

"What did you come to ask me to do?" Pablo said, lacing his fingers together. "And why does it take four Shifters and a civilian to ask it?"

"Ellison," Dylan said.

Ellison described what had happened in the tunnels—how he'd found Olaf about to be abducted by the three men with a net and a tranq rifle, how he'd chased them out of the culvert to see them leap into an SUV. Ellison rattled off the license number, but Pablo held up his hand.

"I don't have to look it up. High-dollar SUV, professional thugs with top-of-the-line equipment, fake plates. That's Clifford Bradley." Pablo shook his head. "He's dangerous. Very dangerous. Even for you, I think."

"If he's so dangerous, why haven't I heard of him?" Dylan asked.

"He's a recent arrival. From Atlanta, but he works the entire country. He also doesn't have his finger in things you'd be involved in—you'll never see him at the Shifter fight club or throwing back a beer at a local bar. He's high dollar. The higher the better. He has clients in New York, Los Angeles, London, Paris . . ."

"Clients for what?" Dylan asked in his quiet voice.

"Drugs mostly. The very expensive kind that fund wars. Weapons. Diamonds. Anything he can move that's sought after by the ultrarich and untouchable. I'm too small-time for him—I don't even think he knows I'm alive. Fine with me. I leave him alone."

"Why would he try to take Olaf?" Maria asked. "Not for ransom, was it?" She knew that kidnapping was a lucrative business in some third-world countries. Even people who couldn't pay much for the return of their loved ones would manage to pay *something*.

On the other hand, though Shifters had more resources than most humans realized, they were perceived to live close to the bone. A man who dealt in diamonds might not believe he'd get much from Shifters.

Pablo spread his hands. "I've heard rumors—and I haven't heard them lately—that some very rich people like to keep captive Shifters, especially when they're young." He swallowed and looked at the Shifters, who were watching him in absolute stillness. "As pets."

Silence descended. Outside the office, the clink, clink of tools went on, a sudden clatter and a swear word in Spanish as someone dropped a wrench.

Ellison was the first to speak, his Texas drawl toned way down. "And you didn't bother to tell us this, because . . . ?"

"I said I hadn't heard of it happening *lately*. Last time was before I ever met you."

Dylan remained in place, standing with the utter stillness of a big cat as he watched prey play not far from him. Entirely his choice whether to remain quiet and not attack, or reach out and take down the unfortunate animal within reach. Sean stood as quietly as his father, and Maria swore she saw the sword's hilt on his back shimmer once.

Ellison and Spike were just as still. Maria stood close enough to Ellison to hear the low growl working up in his throat. Spike's hands balled into fists, the tatts on his arms stretching, while his dark eyes pinned Marquez, who wet his lips.

Maria knew enough about Shifter encounters to know who had all the power in this room. It wasn't Marquez with his guys outside and probably weapons hidden everywhere. Dylan ruled, with Sean, Ellison, and Spike tying for second. Marquez was at the bottom of the food chain, and Maria was neutral, an observer, and protected. If Marquez made any attempt to use her as leverage over the Shifters, he'd die quickly, and by the look on his face, he knew it.

"I want to meet this Bradley," Dylan said.

"No, you really don't," Marquez said quickly. "He has ice in his veins. He doesn't care about family, or life, or even the stuff he buys with his money. It's all about him being in control. He's . . . what do you call those people with no conscience? A sociopath."

"Find out," Dylan said in a hard voice. "I want to know for certain if he's behind the attempted abduction, and where he is now, and then I will meet him. He's made a mistake."

"Yeah, I know." Pablo rubbed his forehead. "Austin's your territory. You said."

Maria had to lean around Ellison to ask her question. "What happens to the cubs when they get too big to handle?"

Pablo shrugged, looking uneasy. "I don't know. They keep them on as bodyguards, maybe as servants? I have no idea."

"You will find out," Dylan said. Not a suggestion.

Maria knew that no grown Shifter would allow him- or herself to live as a servant or bodyguard against his or her will. Even the smallest of cubs could be difficult to manage—she knew how much she struggled to make Olaf mind her, and he was one of the more docile cubs. She watched Spike chase little Jordan around Shiftertown every day, and Spike was . . . Spike.

Cubs went through Transitions to adulthood at some point. Scott, another of Ronan's brood, was going through his Transition—hormones flooding his body and filling him with mating frenzy, which made him crazed and dangerous. And whenever humans thought a Shifter endangered them . . .

"They kill them," Maria said, her mouth stiff. "Don't they?"

"Maybe," Pablo said.

The sword definitely shimmered that time. Dylan fixed Pablo with a gaze that had become white blue. "Find out every single person who's bought a captured Shifter and what happened to that Shifter. I want names and locations. I want them soon."

"I don't work for you," Pablo said. "You know that, right?"

Dylan flicked his gaze up and down Pablo, and Pablo's face lost a little color. "Do it," Dylan said. "As a favor."

"You're asking for a hell of a favor. Does that mean you'll owe me one back?"

Dylan held his gaze a moment longer then turned and walked away in silence, fading into the shadows.

Spike and Sean followed, their rigid backs betraying their barely contained rage. Ellison pivoted but remained as a shield between Maria and Pablo as he started to walk her out.

"You're Maria Ortega, am I right?" Pablo asked in Spanish.

Maria stopped. Ellison did too, turning to face Pablo but again keeping himself a protective barrier for Maria.

"Why?" Maria countered.

"You're the one they brought back from Mexico," Pablo went on, switching to English, which meant he wanted Ellison to know what they were talking about. "From the feral pack. I heard how your brother treated you when you tried to live with him. If you want, I could always explain to him that he needs to be kinder to you."

Maria thought about her brother and his old-fashioned ideas about how women should fit into the family. They were to be pure angels, married off to men of their parents' choice, to produce children to strengthen the line. A ruined woman was of no value at all, except to be unpaid help to her brothers and sisters and their children.

Maria had put up with that at her brother's house until she couldn't anymore, but that didn't mean she hated her brother.

He was caught up in his own life with his wife and children, ignorant of what Maria had truly gone through. She could never make her brother understand, and she knew it.

"No," Maria said sharply.

"He's an officious little bastard," Pablo said. "I could make life very hard for him."

"No," Maria repeated. Pablo wasn't wrong about her brother, but she wouldn't wish harm on him. If she became nasty and vindictive, Miguel would have won. "Please leave him alone."

"You heard the lady," Ellison said, still standing like a pillar between Maria and Pablo. "Touch her family, and I'll make you regret it."

Pablo eyed Ellison a moment, then his severe expression softened into a grin. The smile made him go from hard-ass to almost friendly in an instant. "Yeah, that's what I thought."

Ellison growled then ushered Maria out to the lot where Dylan and the others waited, Pablo chuckling behind them.

Maria paced back and forth on Ellison's porch, the breeze of her passing touching Ellison where he leaned on the porch rail. Deni had joined them, folding herself up in a porch chair, watching Maria work out her distress.

Ellison couldn't stop looking at Maria—her dark hair mussed from the ride home in the open-windowed truck, her body swaying as she walked back and forth, back and forth, her face flushed, her agitation uncontained.

"We need to do something. *I* need to do something." Maria shook out her hands as she walked. "Mr. Marquez can possibly raise an army, and so can Shifters. We go after these men *before* they hurt the cubs."

"We will go after them, sweetheart. Definitely. Dylan's in there planning things." He nodded at the house across the street, to which Dylan and Sean had retreated after they'd returned, and into which Liam had disappeared a few minutes ago. Spike had all but sprinted home when they got back to Shiftertown, worried about Jordan, but he'd walked back to Dylan's house a little later. "They'll come get me, and then we'll go kick some ass."

The only reason Ellison wasn't in with the other Shifters was that he'd wanted to stick with Maria. She was too upset, too horrified. The need to comfort her, to reassure her, overrode everything else.

"I need to do something *now*," Maria said, her dark eyes flashing. "Call Pablo and ask him where we find Bradley's headquarters, and we'll go drag him out."

Ellison pushed himself away from the railing. "I'm as mad as you are, sweetheart, but I know Liam and Dylan will put together a good plan. I'll go with them, and Ronan, and we'll get this guy. Trust me."

Ellison itched to feel Bradley's throat between his hands, wanted to see fear in the man's eyes. After that, he'd explain to the three goons who'd tried to snatch Olaf why that had been a bad idea. He'd explain so hard they'd never get up again.

Killing humans was dangerous for all Shifters, as Ellison had tried to explain to Tiger, but only if the dead were obviously victims of a Shifter attack. Ellison could think of a number of ways to make it not obvious.

On the other hand, Maria wanting to rush up to Bradley and shake her fist in the man's face scared the shit out of Ellison. Maria was crazy-furious enough to try it, and then some goon would try to shoot her. Or grab her and have fun with her.

No one was touching Maria. A growl of feral rage worked up in his throat, and Ellison caught Maria's hand as she skimmed by again. "Come on."

Maria stopped, agitated. "Come on, where?"

"Somewhere you can work this off."

She blinked up at him. "We can't leave Deni alone."

Deni spoke from the shadows. "Since when? I'm not that fragile."

Deni was upset, though, not happy about what Ellison had

told her. Ellison had feared that the news of Bradley kidnapping and selling cubs might trigger another of Deni's violent episodes, but she'd remained cognizant, if distressed.

Now she made a shooing motion. "Will and Jackson will be home soon. They'll take care of me. You do what you need to do."

Ellison tightened his grip on Maria's hand. "We're going."

He half dragged Maria down the porch steps to the motorcycle that waited in the driveway on the side of the house before she could think of more arguments to stop him. Technically, the motorcycle was Deni's, bought by Ellison to replace the one she'd been on when she'd wrecked, but Ellison was the only one who rode it now.

He knew exactly where to take Maria. He got her mounted behind him on the bike, warming to the way she confidently slid her arms around him, started the motorcycle, and slid it onto the street.

CHAPTER EIGHT

Ellison drove out of Shiftertown, and down to the Bastrop Highway to head east. Austin had spread in the last twenty years toward the smaller towns around it, but once past the last strip malls and housing developments, the land rolled into Hill Country. Roads were long, miles into nothing.

A while back, while exploring out here, Ellison had found a dirt road that wound up into hills by the river, the road shielded by a spread of trees that followed the small ridge. Few came this way, a perfect place for Ellison to change to wolf and enjoy loping through woods and up and down the hills. The main roads were distant, and not many knew about this place, not even other Shifters.

Ellison drove the motorcycle out to this road now, not stopping until they were as far from civilization as they could get to in one afternoon. Under the cool shade of trees, he helped Maria off the bike, not letting go as she regained her feet.

Maria looked up at him, her hair tangled from the ride, her eyes still full of fire, stirred by anger and fear. She'd been through so much, this woman, and still she faced down the world, standing up for herself and the weaker, like Olaf.

She drew a breath to say something, but before she could, Ellison wound his arm around her, drew her up into him, and kissed her.

He tasted her agitation and outrage, and liked it. Maria's lips, dusky red and warm, moved on his, her kiss more practiced and confident than the one earlier today. She kissed in anger, seeking him, needing release.

Ellison pulled her closer, fitting her body against his, every curve of her against every hard plane of him. She was warm from the ride, mouth hot, skin damp with sweat, her scent filled with spice and heat. He could drink her all day, here away from the world. Nothing else mattered but this moment, his heart pounding desire through every space of him. Out here, Maria was his.

Maria pushed at his chest, breaking them apart, though she didn't step away. She was breathing hard, the spangled shirt that hugged her breasts rising with her breath, its little buttons beckoning his fingers. "Why would someone do that?" she asked, rage in her eyes. "Try to take the cubs like that?"

"Bradley?" Ellison could barely remember the guy's name after that heated kiss. He barely remembered his *own* name. "For the money. And the power. But we'll teach him, darlin'. Don't you worry about that."

Maria didn't calm. "Why do people like him think they can walk into someone's life and *take* them? Away from everything? Like they own the world and can do whatever they want? They steal a person's whole life." She balled her fists. "*Why?* And why do we let them?"

"Come here." Ellison pulled her rigid body close again, knowing what she was really talking about. "You didn't *let* what happened to you happen, sweetheart. They were feral Shifters. They wanted you—they took you."

"You don't know. You weren't there. I did it to myself. I walked right into it, took my *own* life away from me. And now my family won't forgive me, and I'm alone. With no one. Just me."

"And me." Ellison let his voice go low as he stroked both hands down her back. "And what are you talking about, you did it to yourself? It wasn't your fault, honey."

"Yes, it was. I was stupid. So stupid."

Ellison smoothed her hair, letting the satin warmth of it fill something in him. "Well, once you tell me all about it, love, I'll know too. And I'll keep explaining that Shifters do whatever they want, and ferals don't even bother to be polite about it. Don't keep this inside yourself, Maria. What happened?"

"What I did made my own family turn against me. My brother didn't want me around his little girls, didn't want them influenced by me. That's the main reason I came back here. I could take it if my brother hated me, but he was teaching his kids to be afraid of me."

A red haze of anger rose in Ellison, wolf anger. "Marquez is right. You're brother's a bastard, and I'd like to explain it to him. Now, I want to hear your side of the story, so I can tell you again that it wasn't your fault."

When Maria looked up at him, the heartbreak and anguish in her eyes stabbed pain through Ellison's heart. He understood the loneliness he saw in her—he too had been ripped away from everything he knew and loved when Shifters had been discovered and rounded up twenty years ago.

He'd watched his sister lose her mate to a freak infection, and he'd watched his own parents make a pact to die together rather than submit to the Collars. He and Deni had been left alone, bewildered, with Deni's two little cubs to take care of.

"I fell in love," Maria said, tears of anger in her voice. "No, it wasn't love. I didn't understand what I was feeling. Luis was a stranger, exciting, handsome. And I fell for his lies."

"Luis was the Shifter who kidnapped you, right? And

took you to Miguel?" Dylan had told Ellison what he'd pried out of Maria—that a wolf Shifter had abducted Maria to add to the pack at Miguel's instigation. But Dylan had given Ellison only cursory details, and only after Ellison had badgered him. He'd wanted to know everything about Maria.

"I didn't know Luis was a Shifter, not until later," Maria said. "I was a stupid girl, bored with being a good daughter and with waiting to marry the right man. Luis convinced me to run away with him. And I did it. Because I'm an *idiota*."

The tears finally came. She didn't sob uncontrollably, but beads of tears formed on her lashes then splashed quietly to her cheeks.

"And the asshat Luis turned you over to Miguel." Ellison's anger made his voice harsher than he meant.

"I didn't understand what he wanted. I thought Luis was taking me to a big house, where he would marry me. But then he revealed he was a Shifter, and he took me to the abandoned warehouse. When I saw the other Shifters, I was scared and tried to run away. But they dragged me down into the basement and said I had to stay there with the female Shifters. They locked us in."

Dylan had pretty much related all this, but hearing it in Maria's halting words made Ellison's anger escalate to furnace-level rage. A spark snapped in his Collar, warning, and he stepped away from Maria, the wolf in him ready to kill.

"My family might have forgiven me if I'd been abducted," Maria said. "But I walked away from them. I went with Luis in the middle of the night, and then I thought he'd protect me."

"Maria. Sweetheart." Ellison took a breath, trying to cool himself down, but he was finding it hard. She didn't need a Shifter going kill-crazy in front of her, but Ellison fought the instincts that made him want to race away and find Miguel *now*. "You *didn't* go of your own free will, so stop saying you did. Shifters know how to coerce. Trust me, I've lived with them the past hundred years. They do what they want, Collared or no, and these were crazy-ass ferals. You might have walked out of your house on your own two feet, but you didn't go of your own free will, sweetheart. But even if you had, Luis should have protected you. That's what mates *do*. They protect you from all others. Every evil in the world. He didn't do what he was supposed to." And for that, Ellison wanted to taste his blood.

"Luis did try to protect me." Maria wiped the tears from her face. "Miguel killed him when he tried. And Miguel killed Luis's cub before that, or as good as—he let the cub die. *My* cub."

"Goddess." Ellison's Collar flashed another spark, but his rage negated the pain. "Maria."

In the wild, males who headed a pack or clan sometimes killed the offspring of the other males, but that practice had died out years ago as Shifters became less barbaric, and also realized they needed diverse blood to survive. The instinct to kill a rival's offspring, though, was still there. In a community of Shifters going feral—losing every bit of compassion they had and letting themselves be driven by the needs of the beast—the alpha's instinct to kill another's cubs would be strong.

Ellison hadn't known until now that Maria had lost a cub. She'd never spoken of it, and Dylan hadn't mentioned it—maybe Maria had kept it from everyone. But Ellison should have known from the emptiness in her eyes.

"After that, I didn't care anymore what he did to me," Maria said. "I spent my time planning how I would kill Miguel and escape, but before I could, Cassidy and Diego came and blew up the warehouse. And Dylan brought me here."

Where Maria had been floating ever since, trying to make a life for herself. She now lived in the protection of Shiftertown, in a house with four strong Shifters and a cub, but Maria was alone, and she knew it.

The unmated male Shifters had been told to keep their distance from her, but Shifters like Broderick were tired of keeping their distance, and Broderick wasn't the only one. He and others would swoop soon, and Challenges would come thick and fast. Liam would be forced to tell Maria to choose a mate to keep the peace or go live somewhere else.

Ellison would never let that happen.

He wrapped his arms around her again and pulled her in for an embrace. Shifters needed touch for reassurance, for comfort, and humans, Ellison had discovered, pretty much did too, even if some pretended not to. Maria was stiff, shaking, and Ellison held her tightly against him, not letting her go.

It was hot out here, but Ellison rubbed his warmth into her anyway, hands smoothing her thin shirt, kneading her back. He felt her start to relax into him, but not enough. She was hurting, oceans of pain, and it would take a lot of loving to ease that.

Maria looked up at him, her eyes glistening with tears, her eyelashes damp. Ellison kissed a tear from the corner of her eye then he leaned to kiss her lips.

Her mouth opened under his, her kiss hungry, needy. Ellison tasted her sadness—a mother's loss, Maria's fury, her despair—and the will that drove her to live.

The length of her body moved with his as she kissed him, her breasts soft against his chest. She had strength and gentleness rolled into one package.

Maria pulled away from the kiss, her beautiful face wet. "I'm sorry," she said. "I'm sorry. I can't . . ." She wiped her eyes.

Ellison's breath came fast, his lips tingling from the frenzied kiss. "What the hell are you apologizing for?"

"I don't know . . . I don't trust what I think anymore."

"You've been through hell, Maria. No one can think straight after that. I don't care if it was a year ago. But you can trust *me*."

"Trust you for what?"

"To take care of you." He caught her hand, kissed her fingers, and laid his hand and hers over her heart. "Be my mate," he said swiftly. "Let me protect you."

The look she gave him was stricken. "You don't have to. I've already decided what I'm going to do."

"Go to school, yeah, I know. You can do that and be my

mate at the same time. My sister loves you, my nephews think you're cool, and everyone in Shiftertown likes you."

She nodded and looked away. "Everyone has been good to me, yes."

"Let me be better. Come on, sweetheart. All the pretty ones get snapped up before I have a chance. This time, I'm cutting everyone else out."

"Ellison . . ."

She was scared. Terrified from what had happened to her before. She'd trusted the wolf Luis, and he'd not been able to save her from the worst. Trusting again would not come easy for her.

"It's not the same now," Ellison said. "When I mate-claim you, when we're joined under sun and moon, no one will get to you. Not Broderick, not anyone. I'll be your protector, your first line of defense. And believe me, I'll be a way better fighter than your Luis ever was. I'd never let *anything* happen to you. This, I promise."

She wanted it. Maria felt the pull, the need to lay her head on Ellison's shoulder and let him take her hurting away. His gray eyes were focused on her, unyielding, resolute, his body warm from himself and the Texas sunshine. He hadn't worn his cowboy hat while they rode, stuffing it into the saddlebag instead, and his short hair was ruffled by the wind and gleamed gold. He was a delicious sight.

But Maria had woken up one morning months ago, after many weeks of not wanting to get out of bed at all, realizing that the person who needed to take care of Maria was Maria. Hence her plan to go to school, get a professional degree, find a job, and live in safety the rest of her life.

Becoming a mate of a Shifter had no part in that plan. Never again.

Then again, this was Ellison. With Luis, Maria had been not much older than a schoolgirl, and she'd believed Luis was a dream come true. She'd wanted to get away from her dull life of near poverty, of routine that would last forever. Luis had been handsome, romantic, a means of escape.

Ellison was a friend. The first time Maria had seen him, when Dylan had brought her straight from Mexico to Shift-ertown, she was broken and barely able to speak. Ellison had made her want to laugh even then. He'd been so-over-the-top Texan—with his boots, hat, huge belt buckle, the Texas drawl, the *ma'am*. He'd touched his finger to his hat and called her that, nodding and smiling, his gray eyes warm.

Dylan had intimidated her almost as much as Miguel had, and she'd been afraid that her situation hadn't improved. But Ellison had made Maria laugh from day one—he'd been truly funny, instead of using humor to be derisive and cruel. While she'd not been able to look up at Spike, or even Ronan, she'd raised her head and let Ellison's smile make her feel better.

His smile still made her feel better, and his kisses were even better than that.

Maria reached up and smoothed his hair, liking the wiry silk of it. Ellison's eyes flickered, the Shifter in him responding, but he only closed his eyes briefly, letting her touch.

He didn't want to scare her. From the time she'd met him, Ellison had been trying to calm and reassure her, and to keep others from frightening her. He'd been right there when the asshat human had tried to intimidate her last night; he'd been at her side the moment Broderick had tried to harass her on her way home.

Now he stood in silence, letting her touch him, not grab-bing her or coercing her. She ran her hands up his forearms, feeling every muscle, finding the hollows inside the bend of his elbows, the hard strength of his biceps under his shirt-sleeves. Up to his shoulders, which held the responsibility of his sister, his nephews, Deni's violent episodes.

So strong, and yet carrying so much for others.

Maria's touch went to his face, the rough of unshaved whiskers, the warm satin of his lips. She rose on her tiptoes and pressed a kiss to those lips, while he watched her, his gaze intent. One arm came around her, solid, holding her upright. The strength of him took her breath away.

And Ellison was . . . scxy. The way he danced to the country tunes at Liam's bar revealed his grace, and she felt it now as he held her without effort as she kissed him.

Maria had never touched a man like this. Her experience with sex had been limited to Luis deciding when, where, and how. Luis had done all of the touching, and that hadn't been much.

Ellison was different. He caressed her back, easing her closer, kissed her lower lip then the corner of her mouth.

"I think I'm liking this kissing thing," he said.

"Me too."

Ellison touched his forehead to hers. "I'm not going to mate-claim you right now. Much as I want to. I told Broderick to give you a little space, and I will too. What I'm going to do instead is teach you how to love life."

Maria looked up at him in confusion. "I do like my life now. It's much, much better here than it's ever been."

"No, sweetheart, you're only surviving. Maybe basic surviving is a little easier now, but you're still living in the shadow of all that pain and fear. You want to go to school because—why? It will help you survive better?"

She shook her head. "I want to be a doctor, to take care of people. I can live anywhere if I do that, maybe go back to Mexico and help people who don't have anyone. Or find people here that need the same thing."

"You're kindhearted. But it's still surviving. What you mean is you want a way to take care of yourself, so you don't live under someone else's thumb ever again. Not Shifters, not family, not friends, not anyone."

He understood. Ellison's eyes sparkled gray in the sunlight and were full of knowledge. How he knew exactly what went on in her heart Maria wasn't sure, but he did.

Maria's voice was quiet. "I never want to be enslaved again."

"Neither do I." Ellison's hand went to his Collar. "You know what Shifters know—what we've learned? That it's not enough only to survive. We want to *live*."

"I want to live too. That's all I've ever wanted. But when I tried, I nearly destroyed myself." Maria drew a breath, stifled a new wash of tears that threatened to flow. "So now I'm happy with survival."

"No you're not. But I tell you what, love, any other woman who'd been through what you have would be dead by now, or maybe in constant therapy on happy drugs. You're strong, one of the strongest women I know. Now let me teach you how to use that strength, to grab on to life and make it yours."

She wanted to believe him. Ellison's eyes sparkled with liveliness, the man more *alive* than anyone she knew.

"How?"

Ellison seized her hand in a strong grip, and grinned. It was a wide, warm grin, as big as Texas. "Come on with me, sweetheart, and I'll show you."

They rode. Ellison zoomed the motorcycle down another back highway, the road a black line to the horizon.

Maria threw her head back and let the wind catch her hair. It was warm, the early May heat full of the promise of summer. Fields rushed by, green hills rolling from the river as the Colorado snaked eastward to the Gulf.

After about thirty miles or so, Ellison drove off the highway to another twisting dusty road that led down to the river bottoms, stretches of it overhung with trees. Ellison slowed, and Maria rested her head against his shoulder, ducking low branches and the black swarms of bugs that the little hollows bred.

They came off the winding road to a narrow lane, and a small trailer house set up on cement blocks, under the overhang of stooping trees. The tiny lane ended at this house, and the man standing in front of it with a shotgun.

CHAPTER NINE

Ellison halted the bike a respectful distance away and held up his hands. "Peace, Granger. It's only me."

"Ellison?" The man uncocked and lowered the shotgun, shaking his head. "Shit, you should have called first. I was about to blow your head off."

"Didn't know I was coming." Ellison shut down the bike and tilted it a little so Maria could slide off. He settled the motorcycle in place, pulled his hat out of the saddlebag, and took Maria's hand. "This is my friend, Maria. How's the water?"

The man called Granger chuckled. "Nice." His hair hung in a long dark ponytail, his face bore a coating of unshaved whiskers, and his full muscled arms were covered with tattoos. His eyes, now that they weren't glittering over the barrel of the shotgun, were full of good humor.

"Water?" Maria asked.

"Swimming hole." Ellison winked at her. "Come on."

Granger shouldered the shotgun. "You kids enjoy yourselves, now."

Maria gave Granger a polite smile as Ellison led her past him. "It is nice to meet you."

"Likewise," Granger said.

Ellison led Maria into the trees, pushing aside branches for her, taking her down a steep hill. At the bottom, a wide pond, formed by a rivulet snaking from the main river, spread like a sheet of silver, sparkling under the sun.

The banks of the small lake ran up into the trees, and clumps of bluebonnets spread across every open, sunny space. Birds skimmed across the far side of the water, a wading bird turning its head to watch them approach.

Maria, having grown up in arid lands, always marveled that water could simply *be*. The life water gave—the birds, trees, wildflowers, tall grasses—constantly amazed her. The heat and humidity under the trees had perspiration dripping down her face, but she looked around with wonder.

"Where are we?" she asked.

"Don't really know. I found this place when I was running as wolf one day. Granger tried to shoot me, I dodged the blast and knocked him down, and we became friends. He knows I need the space to run sometimes, and he keeps people away when I do. He's a good guy."

Maria thought about Granger's tattoos, which Spike had taught her about this past year. She suspected Granger had gotten some of them in prison, but she said nothing.

"It's a beautiful place."

"Sure is." Ellison hung his hat on the limb of a bush that stuck out from the trees. He unbuttoned his shirt and shrugged it off, hanging it next to the hat. "Don't always see the bluebonnets either. You need the right amount of rain, the right amount of sunshine. We got lucky."

He wore a tight black T-shirt, which he also shucked, then he got out of his boots. Sunlight touched the liquid warmth of his skin and the butter-colored highlights in his hair.

"You joining me?" he asked. "I'm not swimming alone."

"Swim? In there?"

Flashes came to Maria of herself as a tiny child, her

grandparents taking her to a lake in the mountains, beautiful and cool. She'd splashed around and played, while they spread a picnic lunch of all her favorite foods. Maria had thought she'd never be happier in her life. Come to think of it, she never had been.

Ellison unhooked his belt buckle and skimmed the belt from his jeans. "I don't see you getting undressed."

Maria swallowed. "You're going to swim in there naked?"

"Sure. Get my clothes wet if I don't."

"There will be snakes." The lake in the mountains had been home to plenty of snakes, and so had the warehouse, but Maria had learned at an early age how to avoid them.

"Probably. I'll scare them away."

Ellison unbuttoned and unzipped his jeans and pulled them off, hanging them carefully next to his shirts. His loose boxers came off right after that.

Maria sucked in a breath. She'd seen plenty of Shifters naked, including Ellison—they saw no shame in it, and after shifting, they took their time sliding back into clothes, as though forgetting they needed to. Shifters were casual about nudity, and Maria had stopped noticing them a long time ago.

But Ellison was difficult not to notice. His body had been touched by God, sculpted muscle under skin that moved with liquid grace. The silver and black Collar around his neck only drew attention to the bareness of the rest of his body.

He folded his arms and watched her, all that rippling strength becoming still, waiting. Ellison was a being of sunlight and shadow, but with a hint of the moon in his gray eyes.

Maria wanted to look her fill, to feast her senses on his beauty. She couldn't *not* look at his cock, hanging thick and full between his legs, dark blond hair at its base.

"Ungh" was the only thing that came out of her mouth.

"Come on," Ellison said. "I'm getting hot standing here."

Maria's face heated. He wanted her to strip as naked as he was and then jump into the water with him. A slow smile spread over his face, and her body flushed as hot as her cheeks.

Bareness to her meant vulnerability, fear. She hesitated, heart pounding.

"I told you," Ellison said. "I'm teaching you to live life." He came out of his watchful stance and stepped to her, his body filling her world. "Every bit of it, sucking up every drop."

His hand went to the top of her shirt and undid the two small buttons there. Polite of him, because he could have just yanked the shirt off over her head. And he did, but at least he unbuttoned it so the shirt with its pretty design didn't tear.

Maria stood in her lacy bra that Andrea had bought for her, hugging her arms across her chest. Her low-riding jeans suddenly felt too low.

Ellison came closer. The heat from his body touched her like sunshine. He smelled of musk and dust, sweat and warmth. He slid his hands to her waist and popped open the button of her jeans.

A shiver began deep inside her. Fire rose in Maria's body, slowly surging until it blotted out fear, panic, shame. Need eased through her, tangled with warmth and desire.

Ellison's fingers brushed her abdomen as he felt for the zipper. He tugged it down, more touches to her skin. At the same time, he leaned down and kissed her.

A slow kiss, no more frenzy. Ellison's mouth was all that was good, his lips easing hers open. His tongue slid inside, a flicker, as he skimmed his hands up her back to open her thin bra.

Maria's shiver deepened as she felt the bra loosen. Fetters coming off, freeing her.

Ellison traced across her now-bare back, though he didn't pull the bra the rest of the way off. His touch went around her shoulders, up to her jaw. "Come on and swim with me."

Maria swallowed, licking the taste of Ellison from her lips. "Be right there."

He smiled, slow and fine. Another touch to her chin, and he turned away.

His bare backside was taut, legs lean and strong. Ellison unhooked his cowboy hat from the branch, setting it on his head to complete the devastating picture.

He grinned over his shoulder at her. "Last one in's a rotten egg."

Maria suddenly wanted to laugh. *What in the world did that mean?*

Ellison ran forward, jumped, caught another overhanging tree limb, swung himself out over the water, and dropped in with a magnificent splash.

His hat went flying. Ellison surfaced, swiped his hair out of his face, laughed, and grabbed the hat when it floated past.

"Come on, darlin'!"

Maria didn't give herself time to think. She toed off her sandals, slid out of her jeans, tossed aside her underwear, and ran at the water, whooping all the way.

M aria landed in the water a few yards from Ellison, coming up with her black hair wet. She pushed the hair from her face and opened her eyes, teeth flashing in her big smile.

Ellison made himself start breathing again. He'd sucked in air and held it while her body had come into view, sweet and lush, breasts high and firm, a brush of dark hair between her legs. She'd spread her arms to run in, as though embracing the pond, embracing the world.

The water now hid everything but her lovely face and dark hair, her eyes sparkling like the waters around her.

"Whoo!" she yelled again, and slapped the surface. "I feel like a little child."

"You're supposed to." Ellison swam to her, his hat firmly on his head. He knew it was stupid to swim with his hat, but Maria liked it, so the hat stayed.

Cool water slid under Ellison's arms, twining around his legs as he kicked his way to her. Maria hopped in a circle, taking in the banks, trees, bluebonnets, and the sheet of water. Her head and neck showed above the surface, her hair floating.

Ellison neared her, took off his hat, and sprang high enough out of the water to hang it on an overhanging limb. As he came down, he wrapped his arms around Maria.

Her body floated up to his, breasts moving against his chest in a waft of softness. Her hair was heavy with water over his hands, her lips wet as he drew her up to him to kiss them.

Kissing was the best thing. Ellison rarely kissed, because any Shifter women he'd had the pleasure of bedding had been frenzied and interested in getting the job done. Human women were few and far between. In fact, in the last couple years, anything female had been few and far between.

And now Maria. Maybe the Goddess had made sure all the women who'd ventured to Shiftertown recently—Kim and Andrea, Elizabeth and Myka—had found mates in other Shifters so Ellison would be free when Maria came along. He'd joked that he was never fast enough off the mark, but none of them had touched his heart like Maria.

The Goddess had been good to Ellison. Maria tasted like fire, of woman and wanting.

But she was hurt, like a broken bird, like Deni, who was fighting to regain her life. So much had been taken from Maria, and Ellison wanted to give it back to her, without pain, without fear.

Ellison kissed the corners of her mouth, tasting sweetness. Water droplets lingered on her lips, his tongue finding every one.

Her plump mouth was softness itself. Her lips met Ellison's, her kisses falling on the whiskers above his top lip, the curve of the bottom one.

Maria drew back and gazed at him face-to-face, her smiles gone. Ellison smoothed her hair from her forehead, the laughter leaving him as well. He read desire in her, and also terror so harsh it cut.

He'd have to be slow with her. It might take months, or years, of teaching her that he cared. That he'd never hurt her.

"Maria . . ."

"Shh." Maria touched her fingers to his lips.

She kissed him again, resting her arms on his shoulders. He felt her feet leave the bottom of the lake, balancing on him so she could let her legs come up.

Ellison forced himself to stand easy, though he caught her around the waist, steadying her so she wouldn't slip under the water. He had to let her decide what to do.

Keeping her gaze on him, Maria laced her legs around Ellison's hips, letting his cock, which was hard and vigilant, brush her. It slid between her thighs, seeking her warmth, but Ellison held back. He was on fire, but he couldn't rush her.

He smoothed his hands down her back, satin skin with a little indentation where her bra strap had been. She'd be beautiful in a sarong, one piece of clothing wrapped around her, as Shifter women liked to wear in the summer. One piece, which could come off with the tug of a string.

Maria closed her eyes as she kissed him, then she broke the kiss and looked straight at him. Her eyes were dark like velvet night, the lashes black and thick.

She brushed a lock of Ellison's hair from his forehead, then she adjusted herself on him and slid down onto his cock before Ellison could stop her.

Sensation after sensation poured through his shaking body. Maria was tight against him, her intake of breath loud in the stillness, her eyes widening.

"Maria, sweetheart." His voice was a choked whisper.

She touched his face. "I want this."

"You sure?"

Ellison wanted to hold on, to drive into her in his growing frenzy, to spill his seed and slake his need. A Shifter was built to mate. Nature drove them to sex, to have cubs, to live as hard as they could.

But Maria was shaken and upset, and Ellison couldn't take advantage of her. He told his body that with everything he had, but he still couldn't withdraw, stop her, take her away from here.

"I'm sure." Maria brushed a light kiss to his lips. "With you. Do *you* want it?"

"You think I don't?" Ellison's thoughts started to jumble. "I need to be good to you. I don't want to hurt you."

Maria slid farther down onto him, scattering the last of his thoughts into incoherency. "You won't," she said.

Ellison felt like fire. Need crawled through him, his blood hot and his skin chilled. The water took Maria's weight, making her light in his arms.

He wanted to drive into her, not stopping until he found his deepest pleasure. He wanted to rock into her, fast, faster, find her, know her, feel her close around him, squeezing him.

But Ellison held back. He'd go slow, he'd show her caring, tenderness.

If he *could* hold back. Maria's legs were silken against his tight skin, the depths of her like a wash of flame. Ellison pressed higher into her, holding on, his arms shaking. His toes curled as he braced himself in the mud at the bottom of the little lake, the bluebonnets all around them shimmering in the warm breeze.

"Ellison," Maria said in her low-pitched, and damn sexy, voice. She licked his cheek, hot tongue chasing water droplets. "I need you."

Father God, help me.

The sun, the Father God's symbol, seemed to laugh, kissing Ellison's shoulders with heat. *A blessing,* something inside him whispered. The sunlight, the cool water, this woman in his arms.

Ellison slowly thrust up inside her. She squeezed instinctively, embracing him inside her as she embraced him in her arms.

The sensation rocketed through Ellison's body, engendering another thrust. Up and up again, the water buoying him. Maria kissed his cheek, then across his cheekbone to his ear to nibble his lobe.

It was erotic and tender at the same time. Maria was opening to him when she'd been terrified and closed for so long.

A gift. And Ellison was glad to receive it.

He thrust again, holding her, making love to a beautiful woman in the sunshine. The water cradled them, her breasts crushed to his chest, and she brought her caressing mouth to his lips.

This kiss was slower, less tense, the warm goodness of two people sharing the ultimate intimacy.

Ellison rocked carefully into her. Her body welcomed him, accepted him, held him and didn't let go. He couldn't move as much as he wanted in this position, but it didn't matter. This was their bodies getting to know each other, becoming one.

He'd spill his seed soon. Too soon. Ellison wanted to stay inside Maria forever, closer to her than he ever dreamed he could be.

"Goddess, you're beautiful," he said. "You're the most beautiful thing I ever saw."

He brushed her face with his lips, kissing her eyelids, her cheek, the corner of her mouth. Ellison licked across her cheekbone, then returned to her mouth, sliding his tongue inside as the first of his shudders hit him.

Maria was feeling it too, he knew, her eyes half closed, little sounds of pleasure drifting from her throat. She kissed him back as her body moved with his, her hips rocking to pull him farther inside her.

"*Damn...*" Ellison released, control leaving him. Joy poured over him, every piece of his body aching with pleasure.

It was beautiful. *She* was beautiful. The sun flushed Maria's face, and her eyes were warm, her body welcoming. The Goddess had made her for Ellison, and Maria was embracing him and taking him. Ellison needed her in his life the same way he needed air every second of the day.

Maria gave a little cry, Ellison thrusting now in crazed need. He kissed her, she kissed him, they struggled to hold each other in the slippery water.

"Ellison," she said, her voice stricken.

Ellison held her close. "Shh," he said. "Shh, love." He shivered with release. But he was hot too, inside himself, where they joined, and wherever she touched him.

"Shh," he said again. Maria kissed his cheek, the kiss languid, and Ellison gathered her and held her close.

E llison carried her out of the water. Maria trembled in reaction to her impulsive decision to make love to him and the sudden cold of the breeze on her wet skin.

Ellison set her on her feet on the bank, wrapped his big body around her to cut the chill, and kissed her.

All the heat of the spring day poured from the kiss into her. Maria warmed, though she still shivered. She wanted to stay here forever in this beauty, this feeling.

Fear was gone. She had Ellison, passion, this flood of happiness. She wanted to hold the moment, swathe herself in it, and never leave for the real world again.

Ellison caressed her cheek, his kiss slow with lassitude and lovemaking. His body was as wet as Maria's, but his skin held so much warmth, hotter than any living being's should be.

I'm falling in love with you. The thought came to her unbidden, as natural as the breeze that ruffled the lake. *I'm falling in love with you, Ellison.*

He lifted her hand to his mouth and kissed the backs of her fingers. A cloud slid over the sun, and Maria's shaking increased.

"We'd best get you dressed," Ellison said.

He looked up at the tree from which he'd hung their clothes, and started laughing. Next to his jeans, a couple of blankets dangled in the breeze.

"Good old Granger. Don't worry, he didn't look."

Still chuckling, Ellison yanked down one of the blankets and folded it around Maria. The scratchy wool smelled of smoke and outdoors, but it cut the wind.

When they were dry, they dressed again. Ellison looked

at Maria plenty as she pulled clothes over her damp body, and she didn't pretend not to look at him. He grinned at her again as he picked up his hat, but he didn't set it on his still-wet hair.

The sun was setting by the time they reached the trailer, the long spring day drawing to a close. Granger had a small fire going in his front yard, and was poking at it with a long stick. He invited them in, and Ellison took Maria's hand and led her into the trailer.

Inside was small but cozy. Granger was a bachelor, obviously—no woman's touch in the cluttered interior. Maria sank down on the seat under the window, and Ellison was beside her. His arms went around her, drawing her back into his warm body.

Maria started to drift off to sleep. The smoke from the fire held a strange, sweet odor, the trailer was comfortable, and afterglow from lovemaking made her want to lie here with Ellison and never get up.

Ellison slid his thumb under her jaw and turned her face to his. His kiss was slow, hot, holding the same afterglow.

Granger came noisily in. Ellison broke the kiss and cradled Maria back against him, and she started drifting off again.

"You're gonna get yourself arrested," she heard Ellison say, humor in his voice.

"Nah. The sheriff's deputies around here are my best customers. Hey, I have some errands to run. You guys hang out here as long as you want, and leave when you're ready. There's beer in the fridge and some food. I forget what."

"Sure." Ellison's voice rumbled in his chest.

Maria snuggled up to that rumble. In the pond, she'd given in to her desires, and she didn't regret it one bit. In the water, so close to the strong, caring Ellison, she'd put away fear and acted on new feelings.

Ellison had been tender, gentle, taking it easy. She'd felt him shaking, holding back his incredible strength for her. He hadn't wanted to hurt her or scare her.

Now he held her safely against the darkening day . . .
No, the dark. The window was black now, the fire burned
out, and only a weak light shone in the corner of the room.

Maria should get home. Tomorrow, Connor was to pick
her up early and drive her to where she'd take her SATs.
She had to be ready.

No, she had to stay here with Ellison. He'd get her home
and to bed in time. It was nice to lean on someone, to have
him hold her and keep all the bad things away.

Except that he was gone. Maria woke fully to find herself alone in the trailer, the door moving on its hinges. The
light was out, the night was impenetrably dark, and Ellison
wasn't there.

CHAPTER TEN

Maria got herself up off the bench. She was out in the middle of nowhere, inside a trailer belonging to a man she'd never met before today, and the Shifter protecting her was gone. Ellison might trust this Granger, but who knew what the man could or would do? Maria wasn't given to trust as easily as—well, anyone.

She softly opened the door and stepped outside. Moonlight filtered through the trees and filled the little clearing with white light. The fire had died to a tiny glow, and the smoke had gone, leaving the air clean and fresh.

Maria's thoughts were much clearer now too. She needed to find Ellison and get back to Shiftertown. She had to know what Liam and Dylan were planning for when they went after the man trying to abduct their cubs, and she wanted to be part of it. Ellison had been right to bring her out here to cool her down, but her concern for the cubs' safety rose.

But where to look for him? If she went blundering around in the dark, she'd get lost or maybe fall into the lake or something. Plus snakes would be everywhere. Texas crawled with rattlesnakes, especially after dusk, when they came out of their holes to soak up the last of the day's warmth. In spring hordes of baby rattlers joined them.

Maria sank down onto the front steps and pulled her feet up under her, in case snakes decided to come out from under the house and investigate her ankles. She had her cell phone, but a peek at it told her she was out of range of the rest of the world.

What was she doing? The cubs could be in trouble, and on top of that, she was supposed to take her SAT tests tomorrow. How on earth could she concentrate on those between worry for the cubs and running off into the wilderness with Ellison?

The trouble was, she'd felt more alive today than she had in many, many years—since that day at the lake with her grandparents.

What filled her mind was Ellison, the memory of him pressing inside her, spreading her, breaking apart her defenses. She could still feel his hands hot on her back, his strength holding her, the hard plane of his chest against her breasts. He'd been hard and hot, deep inside her, the feeling glorious.

She'd feared sex, which before had hurt whenever she'd felt anything at all. She'd climbed upon Ellison in a moment of daring, her fears laughing at her.

And now Maria couldn't stop thinking of him. The wild burst of pleasure, the joy of watching his face soften with passion, the water holding them—these things would mark her forever.

A step, nearly soundless, but audible in the stillness, made her raise her head. Maria studied the line of trees circling the trailer, but she saw nothing.

She stared hard at the place from which she thought she heard the noise. The sound came again, barely a whisper of movement against grass.

Then a huge gray wolf stepped out of the woods into the clearing. Moonlight brushed his fur with silver, outlining his large, lithe body and pricked ears. He turned his face to her, his eyes as silver as the moonlight, then he looked away, scanning the woods as Maria had done.

The wolf turned his steps to the trailer, picking his way in silence across the ground, blending into the shadows. He halted when he reached Maria and sank to his haunches beside the narrow steps.

He was huge even sitting down, his body nearly twice the size of a wild wolf's. Maria wasn't afraid. The wolf was beautiful, though she knew he was deadly, but all that deadliness now protected *her*.

Maria stroked his back, shivering at the wild strength of him. His fur was wiry and soft at the same time, and held heat and comfort.

"Everything all right out there?" she whispered.

Ellison turned from scanning the woods and nuzzled her, rubbing his furry face against hers. Then he licked her.

"*Ay*," she said, laughing softly. "No wolf spit."

He made a rumble like laughter. Ellison scanned the woods again, nose working as he tested for scent. Then he rose to his feet and transformed himself with a crackle of bone and flesh to Ellison.

Naked Ellison, towering above Maria, his scent full of spice. The night was warm, sultry, back here in the woods near the lake, the air heavy and damp. It seemed right to be here, alone in this strange place, with only a Shifter to protect her, because that Shifter was Ellison.

Her friend. Her champion. And now, her lover.

Ellison sank down to sit next to Maria on the edge of the step, unworried about his nakedness. He braced his hand behind her, a well-muscled arm against her shoulder.

"We should go." His paused. "Damn, you don't know how much I did not want to say that."

"I don't want to leave either."

They sat in silence a moment, a cool breeze brushing the clearing. Crickets and frogs took that as a cue to start singing for the night.

Ellison let out a sigh. "You got your test tomorrow, right?

And I'm not easy about Bradley and his goons. I want you safe."

"He's abducting Shifter cubs, not small human women," Maria said.

"Yeah, but he knows you take care of Shifter cubs," Ellison countered. "His guys were waiting for Olaf today, knowing you'd go that way. That wasn't coincidence. They were following you."

Maria shivered. "I figured that. You're right, we should go."

Ellison's eyes flashed in what was left of the firelight. They were Shifter eyes, the lightest gray, full of wildness. "Like I said, I don't really want to." His voice held a growl. "I want to stay here, kick out Granger, and hole up with you for as long as I can. I want to claim you, and mate with you, and keep you away from all others. That's the Shifter in me— don't matter about Collars and being civilized and all the rest of it."

The declaration should frighten her. Miguel had captured females then sequestered them and used them when he saw fit, telling the other males in the pack to do the same.

But Maria understood, after living in Austin these past months, that Luis and Miguel had been anomalies. Most Shifter males cherished their mates. She'd seen the women in Shiftertown happy—deliriously so—smiling at their mates, slow-dancing with them at the bar, loving how enclosed they were in their families.

Luis should have taken Maria away and protected her instead of subjecting her to the danger of Miguel and the other feral Shifters. Miguel should have made sure his mates were well taken care of, not miserable prisoners.

Maria had seen how Ellison cared for his sister, keeping her from harm, and how stridently he prevented Maria from being harassed by Broderick and other Shifters who called her fair game. Ellison had protected Maria at every turn, and asked for nothing from her.

Maria put her hand in his broad one. She ran her thumb over the back of his hand. "I'll go back with you."

Ellison closed a hard hand over hers. He said nothing, only looked at her, his chest rising with a sharp breath.

Maria rose and kissed him, letting the kiss linger on his mouth. "With you," she repeated. "It's only ever been you."

Ellison tightened his grip on her hand, fingers biting down, and exhaled. "Thank you."

Maria expected to slip unnoticed into the dark and silent house across from Ellison's after kissing him good-night, but she walked into her bedroom to find Andrea sitting on her bed, waiting for her.

Andrea had Kenny in her arms, the boy with his tuft of unruly black hair sleeping soundly in the crook of Andrea's arm.

"*Worried sick*, I think, is the term," Andrea said, her gray eyes watchful in the light Maria turned on. Those eyes narrowed as Andrea inhaled. "Ah."

Andrea's Shifter nose would smell Ellison all over Maria. Maria slipped off her shoes. "You didn't need to worry at all."

Andrea gave her a nod. "You go well together. Ellison is one of the good guys." She said it with confidence, no doubts that the mating would go through.

"Was everything all right here?" Maria asked. She came to Andrea and brushed her hand over the sleeping Kenny's hair. "No threats to cubs?"

"No." Andrea rocked her son, who slept the limp sleep of an infant secure in his mother's arms. "The cubs are safe in Shiftertown. No one gets in that we don't know about. No one will take them from here."

"But you can't keep them holed up here forever." Maria stroked Kenny's hair again, the down soft on her fingers. "They can't be imprisoned, even if it's for their own safety. That isn't right."

Andrea's look softened. "We'll always be closed off from the rest of the world in some ways. We're Shifters,

Maria. People fear us. We'll always be apart. But we manage together." She smiled. "I should know. I'm half Fae. That has most of Shiftertown still a little wigged out. I'm apart even from other Shifters."

Andrea's Fae blood had never bothered Maria, and she still wasn't certain what being Fae meant. But she'd observed Shifters glance at Andrea with curiosity and even fear. They never said anything, knowing Sean would retaliate against any disrespect to his mate, but the nervousness was there.

"I'm apart too," Maria said. "But I decided I can't hide forever. There's a world out there, and I need to face it. It's a risk, but I will take it."

"And you will. Tomorrow. Your SAT tests. I hope you didn't forget." She smiled, knowing Maria never would. Maria had confided in few people about her dream to enter the university, but Andrea was one of them. She and Connor, Glory, and now Ellison.

"What did Dylan decide to do?" Maria asked. "About Bradley?"

Andrea's look turned evasive. "They'll stop him. Dylan, Liam, and Sean together. No need for you to worry about that."

"Yes, but how? Find the man? Murder him? What happens if they get caught?" Maria looked at Kenny, sleeping so sweetly. The boy had been named for the brother of Sean and Liam who'd been killed by a feral Shifter long ago. Kenny had been Connor's father and much beloved.

A shadow passed through Andrea's eyes, worry for her mate and his family. "If there's a problem in the world Sean, Liam, and Dylan can't take care of, then it's a *bad* problem. Don't worry."

"We have to stop them, Andrea—these people who snatch cubs. Bradley and everyone like him, and the people who hire them. It's terrible."

"I know." Andrea held Kenny closer a moment, protective. Then she handed Kenny up to Maria's outstretched hands and rose, stretching as only a Shifter could stretch, every limb supple. She kissed Maria on the cheek. "But you focus on your tests tomorrow. It will be a big day for you."

Maria enjoyed the warmth of Andrea's hug for a moment, the baby scent of little Kenny. Andrea took Kenny back into her arms, left the room, and Maria turned out the light.

She went to the window and raised the blind enough to let in the moonlight. On the porch across the street, two cowboy boots were crossed on the porch rail, long legs in jeans stretching back into shadows.

Maria smiled, her heart lightened. She undressed, blew a kiss across the street, and got into bed, where she lay awake for a long time.

Thoughts tumbled through her mind—the panic when she'd lost Olaf, her sudden fright inside the culvert, her rage when she discovered that men were trying to kidnap Shifter cubs, the distracting worry about the exams.

Over all of this she relived the water embracing her, Ellison holding her, the heat of him inside her, finding something buried deep inside her and dragging it out into the light.

After a long time, she drifted to sleep to the memory of the warmth of Ellison's touch, the tenderness of his kiss. The image of him running into the water, naked but for his cowboy hat, was a fine one too.

"Here, I found more pencils for you," Olaf held them up on the porch in the early light of morning, yellow pencils nicely sharpened.

Elizabeth—Ronan's mate—and Cherie, Scott, and Rebecca, another Kodiak bear, were with Olaf, Ronan hulking in the background while he talked to Spike and the Morrisseys.

"Thank you, Olaf," Maria said, taking the pencils and putting them into her purse.

"Why did you get up early to take a *test*?" Jordan, Spike's four-year-old cub, asked her. "That's no fun."

"You should write the answers on your hands," Scott said.

A large bear Shifter of about thirty years, he seemed calm this morning, not in the frenzy of his Transition. "Always worked for me."

"It's not that kind of test," Maria said, laughing. "I think they check for that anyway."

"Aw. Too bad." Scott grinned.

"I still don't see why she has to go," Jordan said. "Stay home and play with me, Maria."

Connor, who was waiting impatiently at the bottom of the porch steps, said to Jordan, "You'll understand when you're older, laddie. We need to go."

Difficult to leave when all of Shiftertown—at least this block—had turned out to see her off. Maria had talked about her ambitions to very few, but this morning, so many seemed to know her secret, and they were excited for her. Hard to keep anything quiet in Shiftertown. Maria warmed though, at the send-off.

Spike's mate, Myka, a human woman who trained horses for a living, was also making an early start. Horses liked early, she said. She hugged Maria. "You'll bust chops," she said. "That means you'll do well."

Glory almost lifted Maria off her feet with her hug. "You go, girl. I'm so proud of you."

Andrea had another hug, and this time Kenny was awake and talking to himself in wordless sounds. Maria kissed both him and Andrea.

That made Olaf and Jordan clamor for kisses and hugs before she went. Maria bent down to hug each in turn, having to pry them away from her and promise more hugs when she came home.

The only Shifter missing was Ellison. She kept glancing at his closed house, but she heard nothing from within. Maybe Ellison had simply gone inside and fallen asleep after staying up all night watching her house from his porch. He had to sleep sometime.

Maria swallowed her disappointment and turned to follow Connor to Dylan's pickup, which she and Connor were borrowing. Tiger was tinkering with something under the hood, and he dropped the hood closed, watching Maria quietly with his strange eyes when she and Connor approached.

Ellison still didn't appear as Maria took the keys from Connor and got into the driver's side of the truck.

"You know, I do know how to drive," Connor said, hopping into the passenger seat.

"I know. I've ridden with you. I want to get there in one piece."

Maria looked behind her, but Ellison's house remained quiet, the doors closed. Well, she would go over when she came home. She and Ellison weren't mates or married. Just friends.

And lovers. Maria shivered as the heat of yesterday afternoon slid over her again. She started the truck, smiled at Tiger, who returned her look without changing expression, and pulled onto the street.

Behind her the Morrisseys, Ronan's family, and Spike's family all waved and cheered for her. A warmth spread in Maria's heart. She'd been trying so hard to survive on her own that she hadn't realized she'd created a family for herself right here, without knowing it.

"Test me while we go," Maria said to Connor.

Connor unfolded the sample book he'd had ready in his hands, and started asking her questions. Maria had chosen to take one of the biology subject tests. She'd studied and studied, with Connor's help, for the last six months. She'd learned so much—knew the sample tests back and forth—but knots formed in her stomach. What if she went blank when the actual test lay in front of her? What if she couldn't remember *anything*?

She shouldn't have let Ellison take her out yesterday. She should have broken away from him and shut herself in the house. She was tired now, and so distracted by thoughts of Ellison, bare in the water . . .

"I said, what is found in DNA but not RNA?" Connor asked. "Is it, a) . . ."

"Um. Thymine. Right?"

"Yes, right. Concentrate."

"I'm trying."

Connor shook his head as he turned the page. "That's what mating frenzy does to you. Clouds your brain to everything but mating. At least, that's what I hear. I won't have that joy for a few years yet."

"I don't have mating frenzy," Maria said firmly. "I'm not a Shifter."

"But you had sex with Ellison, you can't stop thinking about it, and you want to do it again. That's mating frenzy."

Maria clutched the steering wheel. "Who told you that? Why can't Shifters mind their own business?"

"Well, that would be boring, wouldn't it, now?" Connor grinned over at her. "And it's true, isn't it? You didn't have to tell me anything. Scent doesn't lie."

Andrea had known too, right away. Maria heaved a sigh. "If I admit that yes, I had sex with Ellison, will you stop talking about it?"

"Nah." Connor laughed. "It's fun to see you blush. So what about it? Ellison's dying for a mate. Sun and moon, eh? We're loving all the mating ceremonies around here. Nice excuse to get drunk and party."

"*Connor.* I have to take my SATs this morning. Can we talk about mating later?"

"Sure. Next question . . ."

Fortunately, the drive to the school that was administering the test didn't take long. Maria parked in the front parking lot, her stomach knotting even more. Connor got out of the truck with her and gave her a long hug.

"You'll do great. And I'll be right here to pour you back into the truck when you're done and take you home. Or out for a drink. I remember when I finished my SATs. I was all wound up, and I wanted to sleep for a week."

"Thanks, Connor." Maria returned the hug. Connor had dark hair and blue eyes like his uncles and grandfather, his body already filling out to their formidable bulks. Girls liked to stare at him, and when Connor finished his Transition years from now, he was going to be in high demand. "You've helped me so much."

"Hey, we have to stick together. I'm not old enough to take my place in the hierarchy yet, so who knows where I fit in? You're trying to figure out your place too. That makes us automatic friends."

He pulled Maria close for another hard embrace. Reassurance, comfort—Shifters knew how to give it. Maria hugged him back, grateful for his unconditional acceptance.

Finally Connor released her, patted her shoulder, and held out his hand. "Cell phone."

Maria turned it over. Cell phones and the like weren't allowed at the test. She had to go alone with her calculator and the host of number 2 pencils Olaf had given her. Connor pocketed the phone, clasped Maria's shoulder again, and sent her off toward the building with a little shove.

Maria looked back as she walked down the curved sidewalk. Connor had climbed into the bed of the truck, leaning back with his feet up, to read a newspaper. He'd wait for her. He'd be here, her anchor.

The kids who'd come to take the test this Saturday morning were all about ten years younger than Maria, excepting a few adults who, like her, were hoping to go to college for the first time. America was a fine place, she thought as she walked. Here, a person of eighty years old could decide it was time to get a college education and go. It cost money, but there were ways to find it and people who would help. Maria had explored every avenue and put together a plan to combine scholarship opportunities with working. It would be tough, but she would do it.

An air of anticipation hung over the building Maria entered. She checked in, following the directions to the room where she'd take her test. Kids who knew each other talked excitedly, hiding their nervousness, while others found seats, eyes wide with anticipation.

The current of anxiousness was palpable. Maybe Maria had lived with Shifters too long, because she picked up every nuance of worry, fear, and excitement.

She chose a desk near windows that overlooked the parking lot. Maria could see Connor lounging in the truck fifty yards from her, the sight of him reassuring. Connor had been such a help to her ever since she arrived. She couldn't imagine surviving this long in Shiftertown without Connor. Or Ellison.

Ellison. No, Maria needed to focus. She'd suck it up, do the test, and then relax on Dylan's porch with her friends, and let thoughts of a bare Ellison run through her head all she wanted. He'd been beautiful as his wolf, his fur itself quivering with his strength. She'd loved stroking him . . .

"You may start," the man who was proctoring the test said.

Maria jumped, watery fear running through her, and opened the test booklet. She looked at the first question with numb eyes, and let out her breath again.

She knew that one. She could do this.

Maria answered a few more questions with confidence, then looked up and out the window to reassure herself with Connor's presence again.

And saw him slumped over in the truck, his body limp. She also saw two men she didn't recognize climb into the front of the truck and drive it away.

CHAPTER ELEVEN

Maria jumped out of her seat. The other test-takers looked up and around in irritation.

"You need to sit down," the proctor said.

Maria remained standing, watching the truck speed up and out of the parking lot. She turned around, blindly afraid, and made for the door.

"You can't leave until the break," the proctor said, rising and following her.

"I have to. This is an emergency."

The man looked annoyed. "If you leave the room, you'll need to turn in your test and forfeit your fee."

Meaning she'd have to reschedule the test for who knew when and save up more money for the fee. But someone was busy abducting Connor, and all thoughts of tests, university, and the rest of her life went away.

"Sorry," she said. She shoved her incomplete test at the proctor and ran out of the room.

Outside she stared at the parking lot from which Connor had disappeared in dismay. He had her cell phone, and she was in a building whose offices were shut up for the day, and the campus was deserted, everyone here today focused on testing. The proctor might have a phone she could borrow, but he'd decidedly locked the door after she'd run out. She needed a phone and needed it now.

An ordinary person might have given up. But Maria had grown up in a tiny town with few luxuries in the middle of a desert, and she'd learned to be resourceful. She started jogging down the street, heart in her throat, wishing Ellison was with her, and knowing she needed to find him.

E llison held down his sister's wolf, growling at her. He was dominant. She needed to *obey*.

Deni snarled and fought. She'd woken up out of a bad dream this morning, confused and forgetful again. She'd charged out of her room in wolf form, attacking Ellison as soon as he'd walked in the front door after standing guard over Maria all night.

Deni and Ellison had fought a silent battle on the floor for a long time before Deni had suddenly gone limp, giving up. Ellison had carried her back to bed and turned to get dressed again to go with Maria and Connor to where she'd take her test, only to discover that Deni had been playing possum.

As soon as Ellison turned to leave Deni's bedroom, Deni had come out of the bed and leapt onto his back. He'd heard Connor and Maria drive away while he'd fought off several hundred pounds of wolf.

Will and Jackson had already left for the day, their jobs starting at first light. Ellison and Deni battled it out alone, she too strong and swift to give him time to call for help.

Ellison pinned her with his large wolf's body, Deni swiping with claws and teeth, a mad light in her eyes. Both their Collars snapped sparks, the pain biting Ellison deeply.

This was insane. And heartbreaking. One day Deni would go too far and seriously injure Ellison or her own cubs, or Ellison would have no choice but to kill her.

The idea sent a wash of pain through him at the same

time he staved off her attack, she trying to rip out her older brother's throat.

The phone pealed into the rumble of growls and snarls. Deni jerked, her attention diverted, but Ellison didn't dare let go of her to answer it.

He knew, though he didn't know how, that the person on the other end was in danger. Jackson and Will were out there, neither wanting to stay home from jobs they liked. Connor was out there too, with Maria . . .

Ellison tried to get up. Deni used his distraction to attack, jaws open, fangs bared.

Ellison caught her as he shifted, hands digging into her fur, swung her around, and threw her across the room.

Deni tumbled, howling, and crashed into the wall. Before she could get herself up again, Ellison dove for the phone.

"Ellison." He heard Maria's panting relief, and his fears skyrocketed.

"Where are you?" he said, his voice guttural. "What's wrong?"

"Connor. I couldn't stop them. I was taking my stupid *test*. He was waiting in the parking lot for me because I was nervous . . ."

"Wait. Stop. Tell me."

Maria drew a long breath and told him in simple words what had happened. "I'm at a convenience store at Congress and Ben White. What are we going to do? We have to *find* him."

"You stay right where you are. I'm on this. Aw, *shit*."

Deni crashed into him, yanking the landline phone out of the wall. The phone went dead, Maria's voice vanishing.

Deni's eyes were red, the feral in her taking over. Her Collar shocked more sparks deep into her, but the pain didn't slow her down.

They fought out of the kitchen and to the living room, Ellison trying desperately to stop her. He'd have to knock her out somehow and get away from her. Connor needed help *now*.

The back door banged open. Ronan charged in, already throwing off his clothes, and became a giant Kodiak bear before he hit the living room.

Seriously hit it—the doorframe broke and a table full of Deni's knickknacks went over. Deni rolled away from Ellison and faced this new threat.

Ronan roared, a colossus enraged. Deni laid her ears back and bared her teeth, ready to fight. Her stance told Ellison that she expected her brother to join her in beating back the intruding bear.

Ronan raised a paw to knock her senseless. Ellison jumped at him, instinctively defending his sister, his pack.

Ellison's leap ended on Ronan's massive paw. The Kodiak tried to pull his punch, but the blow smacked Ellison head over tail to land him on the couch. The couch broke into a pile of wood and stuffing, Ellison's wolf buried in the debris.

In that moment, sanity flooded back into Deni's eyes. She rose and flowed back into human form, her face ashen. "Ellison!"

She rushed to Ellison and put her arms around him, stroking his fur, while Ellison lay stunned, trying to catch his breath. Ronan subsided, watching them both anxiously.

"I did it again, didn't I?" Deni asked, her voice broken. "Ellison, what are we going to do?"

The question was a serious one. Shifters who went mad, and who were aware of their madness, sometimes took what they thought was the easiest way out for themselves and their families.

Deni's hopeless look worried Ellison. At the same time . . . Connor.

Ronan shifted back to his human form, a huge, muscle-bound, naked man. "Sorry, Ellison. You OK?"

Ellison climbed out of the ruined couch, shaking foam rubber out of his fur. Deni rose to her feet, finally noticing the overturned table and broken door. Her expression turned to dismay. *"Ronan."*

Ronan flushed. "Hey, I said I was sorry. I'll fix it. I promise. We need Ellison though. Right now."

"Why?" Deni fell into the nearest chair, folding her arms across her stomach. "What happened?"

Ellison shifted back to human form. "Connor's been taken," he said grimly.

Deni leapt to her feet again, her strength returning. "Oh, Goddess. By that Bradley guy?"

"How did you find out?" Ellison asked Ronan. "He contact you?"

"Maria did. She called Sean when your phone went dead. Sean sent me over here to find out what was up with you."

"Goddess," Deni said again, stricken. "Go, Ellison. Find him. I'll be fine."

"Come with us," Ronan said to her. "We might need you."

Deni hesitated, which made Ellison's heart churn again. A few short months ago, Deni would be the first out the door, ready to fight. It wasn't like his sister to hold back.

"What if I . . ."

"Go insane on the kidnappers' heads?" Ellison asked. "I'm not worried about it. Come on, Den. What if they had Jackson or Will?"

Deni's eyes went flat. "Let them try."

"Good girl."

"Hurry," Ronan said as he grabbed his clothes. "Dylan's waiting, and Liam. They're ready for war."

"Go with them," Ellison said to Deni. He caught his sister in a rough hug then released her. "I'm not coming. I need to find Maria."

Ronan looked worried. "Do I have to tell Dylan that?"

"*I'll* tell him," Deni said. "Ellison's right. Maria will be terrified, and Ellison can't leave his mate stranded. Dylan will have to suck it up."

Ronan ushered Deni, who was pulling on her sweats, out the door. "I dare you to say *suck it up* to Dylan."

"He understands about mates and cubs. They come first."

Ellison dressed as quickly as he could then headed for his motorcycle. Deni, back to herself again, herded Ronan across the street, and Ellison's blood warmed in spite of his worry.

Mates. Deni had recognized the mate bond when she saw it. Ellison knew, that after all this time and so much loneliness, the mate of his heart had found her way to him.

Maria's relief when Ellison dismounted his motorcycle in front of the convenience store made her knees weak. Maria dashed to him, and in an instant, his strong arms were around her, Ellison sweeping her up into his warmth. Maria buried her face in his neck and hung on.

"You all right?" Ellison asked.

"Yes, yes, *I'm* fine. Connor . . . It was awful. They just took him!"

"I know. We're on it."

"But why take him? He's a cub, but not in human terms, not like Olaf."

Ellison went silent, and Maria raised her head to find his gray eyes troubled. "I admit, I don't know. But we'll find him."

His expression was somber, but his arms were strong around her. So good to be able to lay her head on his shoulder, for him to understand her burdens, to share them, to fight with her.

"Hey!" A voice sounded across the convenience store's tiny parking lot. "Shifters aren't allowed here."

Maria turned around, hot words on her lips, but Ellison stopped her. "Never mind. Let's go hunt for Connor."

Maria clamped her mouth shut. She didn't like the convenience store clerk's sneering expression, but now was not the time to fight this battle. After they found Connor, she'd come back here and say rude things to him.

Ellison helped her onto the back of the motorcycle. As she had only yesterday, Maria wrapped her arms around him and let him carry her away.

She realized after Ellison had made a few turns away from the convenience store that they were not going back to Shiftertown. He rode them down to the warehouse area they'd visited yesterday morning, with its empty back lots that might as well be in the middle of nowhere.

Ellison stopped in the open space in front of Pablo Marquez's warehouse. Guys working on two high-end cars gave Maria and Ellison warning looks as they left the bike and went inside.

Pablo Marquez sat at his desk in his office, tapping a laptop's keyboard. "I already talked to Dylan," he said before Ellison reached him. "I don't know where they took Connor, but I suggested some leads. You can go away now. I'm busy."

Ellison walked steadily to the desk and stopped in front of it, doing nothing but standing there. "You know where Clifford Bradley is," he said. "Don't you?"

CHAPTER TWELVE

Pablo made himself not blink. Shifters liked to stare a man down, to intimidate with a steady gaze. Pablo had learned in this last year that showing fear was the worst thing he could do—no matter that the small boy he used to be was quivering inside him in terror.

"Don't mess with Bradley," Pablo said. "Find the cub and then go home. I'm telling you this for your own good."

Ellison leaned his fists on Pablo's desk. "You're working for him, aren't you?"

"No." That was the honest truth. Bradley wasn't paying him.

The wolf Shifter inhaled sharply, testing Pablo's scent, hunting for lies. "But you know," Ellison said. "Tell me everything."

Pablo had always thought of Dylan as the scary one. He knew damn well that at any time, for any reason—or for no reason at all—Dylan could simply kill him and walk away. He had no illusions that the human police would be very bothered about Pablo's death, and Dylan knew that too.

Ellison was different. He was the most laid-back of the trackers, with his cowboy hat and his slow West Texas–style drawl. He, Spike, and Sean did little more than stand as silent pillars behind Dylan when Dylan came to visit, although Ellison might toss in an understated joke or tip his hat on the way out.

Today Ellison had left his hat behind, and the Texas drawl was laced with steel.

Pablo contrasted Ellison in his jeans and button-down shirt with Bradley and his ice-cold eyes and five-thousand-dollar suits. Bradley was dangerous because he was all business, no sentiment. The man had no family, no friends, no warmth in him whatsoever. The Shifters would lose against him, because they were *all* warmth, all emotion. Bradley was a robot.

"If I tell you, I'll get you killed," Pablo said.

The human woman, the cute little thing called Maria, stepped forward. From what Pablo had seen, she was a smart, compact firecracker. If he were fifteen years younger and not in love with his obnoxious, silken-haired hacker girlfriend, he might think about her for himself. But the way Ellison closed in on her protectively . . . Nope, she was spoken for.

"Mr. Marquez," she began. That was sweet, calling him *Mr.* "Think about this. If it was your brother, your son, or your best friend who was missing, what would you do? You'd stop at nothing to go after Mr. Bradley, wouldn't you? You are that kind of person."

"True," Pablo said. "I'd go find Bradley and get my head taken off for my trouble."

"You're not Shifter," Maria said. "Shifters can do amazing things."

"I don't doubt it." Pablo turned the force of his gaze on her, and met brown eyes full of fire. "You want to see him shot down, *chiquita*?" He gestured to Ellison. "With enough firepower to blow him to pieces right in front of you? Bradley and his boys are used to dealing with Shifters. I mean, shit, he steals their cubs."

"Which is why you're going to help us," Maria said. "He took Connor—*while I was watching.* Do you know what that made me feel like?"

"Yeah. Actually, I do." As a teenager, Pablo had seen his best friend dragged off by a rival gang and executed, while he'd hidden in terror, unable to do anything to stop it. From that day to this, he'd vowed to have the power to never have to go through that again. He'd protect his family and friends to his last breath. "I do get it. But sweetheart, let Dylan and his crew handle finding Connor. You go back home and wait."

Ellison spoke again, the Texas accent not as pronounced this time. "Bradley wouldn't have taken Connor to his own house. He'd have a place to stash him until delivery, and that's where you sent Dylan and Liam. Right? What I want is Bradley himself. The body of the hydra. Not its heads."

"Cut one off, two grow back, right?" It had been a long time since Pablo had read a book, but he remembered that story. "Let it go, man. Dylan will obliterate the thugs who did the kidnapping, you'll have the cub back safe and sound, and all your Shifter friends will live."

"And it will happen again," Ellison said. "And again."

"And cubs will have to imprison themselves in Shiftertown," Maria said. "We can't let that happen. *I* won't let that happen. I thought you were a tough guy, Mr. Marquez. Why haven't you eliminated your competition?"

"Because Bradley's not competition. And I don't have a death wish."

"You're a criminal," Maria said. "I'm sure you'd like it if you could remake those stolen cars outside without being bothered. If you help get rid of someone like Bradley, just think how much the cops around here will appreciate you."

"Just think how much every other gang boss *won't* appreciate me. They'll never trust me again. I'll be a dead man walking." Sweat beaded on Pablo's forehead. He didn't want to have to kill Ellison and Maria, because he liked them, but these two were getting crazy.

"No, no," Maria said. "You'll be a hero. I bet your rivals

aren't thrilled with Bradley either. I bet you all have to pay *him*, not the other way around."

She really was too smart. "You know, sweetheart, I like it here," Pablo said. "Austin's a cool town. Great music scene, awesome food. Something for everyone. I don't want to have to leave. Understand?"

"Maybe you won't have to." Maria smiled.

Now Ellison was looking at Maria as though he wanted to yank her out of here and hole her up somewhere safe. Poor guy would have his hands full with her.

"Tell us where he is, and then you can sit here and work on whatever it is you're doing. Otherwise, we'll come back with Ronan and Spike and all the others, plus every cop in town. Maybe some reporters too. That would be fun."

"Don't threaten me, sweetie," Pablo said in a mild voice. "You won't make it out the door."

Ellison didn't move, but Pablo saw the wolf gleam in his eyes. One of Ellison's fists tightened minutely on the desk. "Tell us where he is. No one needs to know where the information came from."

"Right. Shifters visit me, then Shifters go after Bradley. They'll know. Then Bradley steps over your broken bodies and comes after me."

Ellison's fist went even tighter. "You won't have to worry about that. But if you don't help now, you'll have to worry about me. And Ronan. And Spike. That's just for starters. I won't talk about Dylan and Sean, and you don't even want to know what Liam will do to you. The rest of us are Girl Scouts compared with Liam. He's the alpha of the alphas. He does what he has to do, no matter what."

Damn it. He'd known when his little brother had stupidly gotten Shifters pissed off at them last year that Pablo would never get out from under them. He could toss them at Bradley and rid himself of his Shifter problem, but he knew it wouldn't be that easy.

"I don't know," he said. "My girlfriend's niece is a Girl Scout, and they can be pretty vicious when it's cookie time. I always end up buying about fifty boxes."

"I'm sure your men appreciate that," Ellison said, straight-faced. "You give up Bradley before I lose my cool, or you'll wish you were facing an army of little cookie-selling girls in green."

Maria watched Pablo, not Ellison. Pablo held out a moment longer, then one of the most powerful gang leaders in South Texas bent his head, sighed, and said, "I'll see what I can do."

Shiftertown was nearly empty when Ellison and Maria pulled into Ellison's driveway. Ellison helped Maria off the bike, then he walked her across the street to Dylan's house, to find the door locked.

Andrea answered Ellison's knock, looking tense. "I thought you'd be with Dylan and Sean," Andrea said as she let them in. Locking doors was unusual in Shiftertown, and Ellison hoped this wasn't the beginning of a trend.

"Took a detour," Ellison said. He looked around the quiet house. Kenny was sleeping in a bassinet, Liam's daughter, Katriona, playing by herself in a playpen. "Where did they go?"

"I don't know. Sean said he'd keep me posted when he could, but he hasn't checked in yet. Which means he can't. Kim went to talk to the police."

Ellison returned to the porch and looked up and down the empty street. "Leaving Shiftertown deserted when someone's kidnapping cubs isn't the best idea."

"They didn't. Ronan is still here. He's scared for Olaf and Cherie. Broderick is here too, because he won't leave his younger brothers and nephews. And Tiger. Liam wouldn't take him—too afraid he can't control him. Tiger is livid, which is why I've got the kids. I'm not leaving them or this house."

"Good. Maria . . ." Ellison slid his arms around her and leaned down for a brief kiss.

The brief kiss turned into something deep and hot. Ellison felt Andrea's gaze on them as he eased back, but he enclosed Maria in a tight hug.

"Stay here with Andrea until it's safe. And thank you for alerting us. They sure knew how to pick the right moment."

Maria's dark eyes glittered as her brows came down. "I wasn't about to sit and finish my exam when Connor was in danger. I can always take another test."

"I know." Ellison kissed her forehead. "That's why I love you."

He turned away, pretending to ignore Andrea's interested look, left the house, and started across the street.

Maria banged out the screen door and followed him. He should have known she wouldn't stay put.

"You don't think I'm letting you go after Mr. Bradley by yourself, do you?" she demanded as she caught up to him.

"Yes, I do," Ellison said, not turning around. "You're not Shifter; you can't fight."

"You also didn't wait for me to answer," Maria said as Ellison let himself in his front door with his key. Deni had locked up too.

"Answer what?" Ellison tossed his keys to the table and sniffed, scenting that no one was home. He needed to call Jackson and Will, make sure they were still safely at their jobs.

"That I love you too," Maria said.

CHAPTER THIRTEEN

Ellison's body went so still that Maria barely saw his intake of breath.

She'd known he'd thrown out the *That's why I love you,* offhand, Ellison always joking. But he had murder in his eyes, rage so deep that he wouldn't stop to think before he attacked Mr. Bradley.

Maria knew that Pablo wasn't wrong to say that Bradley was untouchable. She might not have another chance to tell Ellison what she felt.

"What?" Ellison asked, his voice deadly quiet.

"You heard me."

Maria started to push past him into the house. Ellison clamped a hand on her shoulder, drawing her back, turning her around. She looked up into gray eyes that held hunger and silent need.

"I know I heard you," he said. "I want you to say it again. Like you mean it."

"I do mean it."

Ellison's eyelids slid down in a slow blink. When he

opened his eyes again, they were lighter gray, the wolf in him coming out. "Say it again, Maria."

Why not? She wasn't ashamed or afraid. Maria drew herself up straight and looked into his eyes. "I think I love you, Ellison Rowe."

His fingers bit down. "You *think*? What, you're not sure?"

"I don't know what real love feels like. I loved my parents and grandparents, but I was a child. I thought I loved Luis, but I never really knew him." She swallowed under Ellison's burning gaze. "All I know is, I can no longer imagine my life without you in it."

Ellison yanked her against him, his hands remaining on her shoulders. His grip held raw power—strength, but not imprisonment. Never that.

"Then mate with me," he said, his voice low, savage. "Let me mate-claim you, and join with me sun and moon. I'll give you . . . everything."

Maria warmed against his body. "Will you stay alive for me? And stay with me?"

Ellison started to smile. "You bet. But I hope you're not gonna ask me to stay home and not go after Bradley."

"No." Maria said. "I want you to get that sucker. We need to, as Spike would say, take him down."

Ellison's eyes narrowed. "Who's *we*? You are staying with Andrea."

"We need to stop him, Ellison," she said.

Ellison stilled again, the laid-back human with the smiles and jokes fading into the Shifter who took care of his family at any cost. "We will. But not with you. I don't want him knowing anything about you."

"He already does. Like you said, he had his men following me with the cubs, and he knew Connor went with me to the test today. He must have planned the abduction by watching me, figuring I wouldn't be able to stop anyone taking Connor."

"Yeah, but to Bradley right now, you're just the human female who lives with Shifters. He's an idiot if he thinks you're nonessential, but I want him to think that, if it means he'll ignore you. You flash yourself in front of him, he'll have you in his sights as a person trying to interfere with his lucrative business."

"If you're so confident you can stop him, it won't matter." Maria balled her fists. "We have to stop him, Ellison. They can't keep trying to hurt us."

Ellison's eyes flickered slightly, and Maria realized she'd said *us*.

Well, she *was* one of them now. She'd lived with the Austin Shifters, laughed with them, helped take care of them, and loved them, for months now. Ellison had imprinted himself on her, and she knew that no matter what else she'd do in life, she'd somehow be bound to him.

"We will stop Bradley," Ellison said, a deadly edge to his voice. "But my way."

"Fine, but I will be with you every step of that way." As Ellison started to turn from her, Maria put herself in front of him. "You know that if you go without me, I'll find a way to follow. Unless you intend to lock me in the basement?"

"No." Ellison's tone was harsh. "I'd never do that." He'd never be like Miguel, he was saying. Never imprisoning her. Never. Then he grinned. "Although, there's a new flatscreen TV down there. Doesn't have cable, but Elizabeth has been smuggling me DVDs."

Maria's eyes widened into a glare. "Are we going or not?"

"Yep." Ellison gripped her shoulder again. "I'm taking you, because I know that if I don't, you'll follow me, and I can't be worried about where you are. So you'll stay with me, and when I tell you to keep out of sight, you do it, all right?"

"Of course I will. I don't have teeth and claws, or a handy weapon, so what could I do?" She looked up at him in all innocence.

Ellison gave her another suspicious look, but he nodded, as though he accepted her words. "Fine. Let's go get backup."

* * *

Backup meant, first, Ronan, who didn't want to come. "Ellison," Ronan said, standing in his front door and filling the entire doorframe. "What if they're waiting for us to empty Shiftertown? Then they come in for the rest of our cubs?"

Olaf peeked out from behind Ronan, and Ellison was aware of Scott and Rebecca in the background. Ellison seethed with impatience.

"An attack on Shiftertown is a different thing from their snatch-and-grab modus," he said. "Rebecca won't let anything happen to the cubs—you know that."

"You got that right," Rebecca said. She was tall, like most Shifter women, but when she shifted to her Kodiak bear, in all of Shiftertown, only Ronan was bigger.

"And I'm not chopped liver," Scott said. "Anyone comes for Cherie and Olaf, and I'll let my craziness come out."

"We need you Ronan," Ellison said.

"And if he's too much of a wuss to go," a voice said behind Ellison. "I'm game."

Broderick. The wolf Shifter stood on the walk between Ronan's house and converted garage, arms folded. "I know you think I'm an asshole," Broderick said before Ellison could speak. "But I have nephews and younger brothers. We cut this off at the source, Ronan."

Ronan stroked Olaf's hair, pushed the lad gently behind him, and closed the door. "Fine. I'm coming." He glared at Broderick. "But I'm going at you at the next fight club. For calling me a wuss."

Broderick looked pained—no one won fights against Ronan, except maybe Dylan. But at least Ronan was coming.

"Can we hurry?" Maria asked, as impatient as Ellison.

"One more," Ellison said.

He'd saved the best for last. He knew that once Tiger joined them, the man wouldn't want to slow down to let Ellison pick up anyone else.

When Andrea unlocked the door for them to Liam and Kim's house, Tiger was nowhere in sight. Ellison scented him, though, and the Tiger-man was not happy.

"He's downstairs," Andrea said. "Comfortable with TV and lots of snacks. Liam didn't want him following."

Ellison faltered a step. "You mean Liam locked him in there?"

"Yes. The basement door's reinforced steel. The only thing that would hold him." Andrea smiled her half-Fae, half-wolf smile and dangled a key from its ring. "Here you go. I'll be at home."

She got herself out of there with amazing swiftness, the back door slamming. Ellison heard her run back to her own house, the cries of Katriona and Kenny welcoming her.

Ellison grasped the key and drew a breath. "Everyone needs to clear a space. Maybe you should all leave the house."

"Nope," Ronan said. "If he attacks, you need us to help pull him off you."

Maria, at least, had the sense to leave the kitchen. She ducked out of the big room to the living room beyond. "Good luck," she said.

Gee, thanks. Ellison approached the door to the basement, tucked near a broom closet in the back of the kitchen, squared his shoulders, and put the key into the lock.

As soon as the key turned, Tiger slammed into the door from the other side, nearly tearing it from its hinges. Ellison had danced aside, knowing what was coming. The door, made to withstand Shifter strength and police battering rams, remained whole, but only just.

Tiger roared and leapt at the first Shifter he saw—Broderick.

"Shit!" Broderick yelled, his feet coming off the floor as Tiger's entire body hit him.

"Tiger!"

The cry came not from Ronan but Maria. Tiger paid no attention. He slammed Broderick into the wall, shoving him halfway to the ceiling.

Ronan and Ellison gripped Tiger on either side and tried to haul him back. Broderick screamed and fought, his half beast emerging in defense.

Maria put herself where she could look into Tiger's crazed face. "Tiger!" she shouted again. "We need you. And Broderick. Do you want the man who captured Connor?"

Tiger halted. He swiveled his yellow gaze to Maria, fixing on her. He stared at her for a few more heartbeats, then he dropped Broderick to the floor and stepped over his prostrate form.

"We get him."

Maria patted Tiger on the arm. Instead of jerking away, Tiger accepted the caress, and then carefully sniffed in her direction. "Mate-claimed," he said, and looked at Ellison.

Broderick climbed from the kitchen floor, accepting Ronan's hand up. "What? Oh, you bastard."

"Challenge me," Ellison said. "*Please.* I'm going to need to work off some steam."

"Later," Ronan growled. "We need to go."

"Yeah, I Challenge," Broderick said. He had his hands on his knees, trying to catch his breath. "In front of witnesses. Eat it, Ellison."

"Fight club," Ellison said. As the Challenged, it was his right to name time and place. "Tonight."

Broderick stared. "Are you nuts? We don't know what will go down today."

"If we survive, fight club. Done?"

"Shit." Broderick gave him a nod. "All right. Done."

Ellison laughed. His fighting blood was up. He was in love, he'd had sex with the most beautiful woman in the world yesterday, and she'd told him she loved him today.

The most beautiful woman in the world started yelling at him in Spanish. Ellison understood only a few words, like *idiota*, but he laughed again. Maria was fiery, she was courageous, and she was his.

Now to find Bradley, kick his ass, kick Broderick's ass, and take Maria into his arms tonight.

* * *

"I can't believe you talked me into this," Pablo said from beside Maria in Ellison's truck.

"Insurance," Ellison said, his voice rumbling pleasantly from Maria's other side as he drove. "In case you decided to go behind us and tell Bradley we were coming."

"Would I do that?" Pablo sounded innocent.

"You would totally do that." Ellison grinned across at him, his drawl becoming pronounced. "So you come with us, my friend."

"And you're bringing your girlfriend? You Shifters are insane."

"Yeah, we are," Ellison said. "No telling what we'll do next."

He stepped on the gas of his black pickup, shooting them down the highway past Bastrop and out into the country. A big fire had devastated this area last year, destroying homes in and around the historic little town. Shifters from Austin and the Hill Country Shiftertowns had gone out to help people evacuate and save what they could, though that detail hadn't been made public.

No one had heard from Dylan or Sean about the search for Connor, and none of the Shifters dared make a call in case a stray cell phone ring endangered the Morrisseys. Maria's heart was cold with fear for them, but she knew they *would* call if they had news. They must be searching, planning what to do—or in the middle of a fight for their lives. Not knowing was hard.

Pablo had said that Bradley had a house east of Bastrop on the river, an estate that encompassed about a hundred acres, surrounded by a fence and a large electronic gate. Bradley didn't do his business there, Pablo said—he conducted business in offices and warehouses around the city. He didn't piss in his own sandbox.

Maria found the phrase strange but apt. If police raided Bradley's house, they'd likely find nothing. Pablo's information, though, meant that Connor probably wouldn't be at the house either.

Ellison drove with one hand, while Maria held Pablo's smart phone with its map of the area. Before they reached the gates of Bradley's house, Ellison pulled onto a side road that had once run off to someone's ranch and now led to a housing development.

Bradley's estate had escaped the fire, but many of the houses in the development had not. New buildings were going up again, workers in large pickups and work trucks swarming the neighborhood.

Good camouflage, Ellison said, parking at the end of the line of work trucks. He slid out of the driver's seat, and Ronan, Tiger, and Broderick crawled out from where they'd been lying low under a tarp in the back.

"Goddess," Broderick snarled as he shook himself out. "I smell like bear and . . . whatever *he* is." He gave Tiger a dark look. "I said I'd help, but don't put me with the crazy again."

Tiger growled at him, but Maria swore there was humor behind it.

"Fine by me," Ellison said to Broderick. "You can scout to the north with Ronan. Tiger and I will cover the south. Take out guards, but *quietly*. Ronan, you'll teach Broderick how to do that, right?"

Ronan grinned, and Broderick made a noise of disgust. "Like I can't be more stealthy than a giant bear," Broderick muttered.

"Take out the guards, make your way to the house, and we'll disable the alarm system." Ellison studied a piece of paper before tucking it into his pocket. Pablo's girlfriend had given them instructions on how to go about bypassing the alarm without triggering it.

More trust on Ellison's part. Pablo could have instructed her to give Ellison bad guidance so he'd trip the alarm instead. Bradley might then reward Pablo. The Shifters were gambling on Pablo being more afraid of them than of Bradley.

Ellison didn't say what they'd do after they got inside. Maria knew, though. They'd corner Bradley, find out where the cubs were, then kill him.

Ellison slid back into the truck. Maria looked at him in surprise, then let out a breath when he enfolded her in his arms. He didn't squeeze, he didn't kiss her; Ellison just held her, his embrace strong.

He'd never let her fall, the hug said. Never let her falter, never let anything hurt her. Maria had been drifting, rudderless, and now, Ellison was her anchor.

He kissed Maria's cheek then her lips, his warm. "Goddess go with you," he said, his voice low. "I'll be back as soon as I can." He transferred his gaze to Pablo, and the loving look turned to ice. "You take care of her. If Maria's hurt in any way, or scared, or pissed off . . . You won't live to regret it."

"I know how to do this," Pablo said, with no sign of anger. "Wipe out Bradley for me, and life will be good. That's worth sitting a couple of hours in a pickup with a nice young woman."

Ellison growled. With his arms still around Maria, feeling him rumble against her was like being held by a giant, purring cat.

Ellison kissed Maria one more time, took and pocketed Pablo's cell phone, and exited the truck. Tiger waited for him with his usual stoic patience, his assessing eyes taking in everything.

Broderick and Ronan walked up the street one way, and Tiger departed with Ellison the other.

Maria turned around to watch Ellison go. His backside in the tight jeans swayed in a fine way as he walked, sun gleaming on his hatless hair. He'd left the cowboy hat in the car, but his boots clicked on the asphalt.

Ellison didn't turn back, but Maria felt a tether between her and him, a line connecting them. She was with him, and he with her.

Pablo pulled a magazine out of his pocket, leaned back, stuck his elbow out the open window, and proceeded to read. Maria glanced over and saw that it was a home decorating magazine, open to a page on makeover ideas.

"Francesca's redoing the kitchen," Pablo said without embarrassment. "She wants me to find ideas I like."

"I've never had a new kitchen," Maria said, before she thought about it.

"No?" Pablo shrugged. "Well, that's why I do what I do, sweetie. So I can live a little better than my parents did, which was in the gutter."

"You're a smart man. You could make a lot of money perfectly legally."

"Most of my business *is* legal. I even pay taxes on it. But I was stupid when I was younger, and did some time. Prison gave me the opportunity to think about how I wanted my life to go, but prison closes a lot of doors for you."

"So does being Shifter."

Pablo lowered his magazine. "Don't let them fool you. Those Shifters might wear Collars and be bound by rules, but I'm here to tell you, they do anything they want."

"So I've seen."

Maria turned around to look after Ellison again and found him gone. He and Tiger had vanished. Though open country rolled from behind the one street of houses, she saw no sign of anyone moving through the tall grasses.

Maria had promised herself she wouldn't worry, but that was a silly promise. Of course she'd worry. Ellison was walking into a well-defended fort, with nothing but his teeth and claws and Pablo's phone—though she felt a little better that he was with Tiger.

But if anything happened to any of the Shifters, she'd have to face Liam and Dylan and tell them. Explain why she hadn't helped, why Pablo hadn't.

They'd blame Pablo for not keeping them safe, and they might kill him. From the way Pablo's fingers shook the slightest bit when he turned the pages of the magazine, he knew it too.

"What can we do?" she asked him.

Pablo didn't look up. "Stay out of it."

"Sit here until we know whether they made it or not?" Maria let out her breath. "I should at least call Andrea or Rebecca and tell them what's going on."

"And risk your call being picked up by someone in Bradley's house? I imagine he keeps his ears open for any threat."

"Can someone do that? Listen in on a cell phone call?"

"Yep. A cell call is nothing but a signal going out through the air. If a signal's out there, you better bet some-one has a gadget that can pick it up. My girlfriend can do it. I bet Bradley has a guy on his permanent staff who does nothing but scan phone calls. The guy's paranoid."

Maria's heart squeezed. "Then why do you think Elli-son can get inside Bradley's house without a problem?"

"I don't. But I wasn't given a choice in helping, was I? Besides, if anyone can do it, it's four stealthy, stubborn, scary-ass Shifters. I bet they get the job done with mini-mum casualties."

"I don't want *any* casualties."

"Not always possible. If you go after something danger-ous, there's always a risk. The bigger the prize, the bigger the risk. You have to decide whether it's worth it."

Worth risking her life to stop men like Bradley stealing children, selling them to people with money who cared nothing for anyone but themselves? It was. After Ellison stopped Bradley, Maria would make it her life's mission to find all the Shifter cubs who had been taken and release them. A good goal, better than her dream of going to school. She could always go to school when the cubs were safe.

"Whoa." Pablo dropped his magazine, staring at some-thing in the side-view mirror. "Start the truck. Get us out of here. But slowly. Don't attract attention."

"What? Why?" Maria looked back, her heart in her throat, even as she slid behind the wheel. "Oh . . ."

She saw it now too. A long black limousine, slowly slid-ing its way up the narrow, dirty street, heading for the unfinished houses. Some of the builders saw it too and glanced up, curious.

Maria started the truck. She put it in gear and drove cautiously forward, her palms sweating. She'd have to go to the end of the cul-de-sac and turn around, no other way out.

The limo crept forward, not speeding up, just driving as though the person inside was looking over the houses being rebuilt. Bradley probably owned them, or maybe this wasn't Bradley at all. In any case, with luck Ellison's dusty truck would look like it belonged to one of the workers, with its owner heading out to find some late lunch or maybe more supplies.

Pablo was fidgeting with impatience, but Maria drove slowly, casually. She made the turn at the cul-de-sac, the tires crackling on loose gravel on the asphalt, and rolled back the way she'd come.

Pablo kept his face bent to the magazine, though he watched from the corner of his eye. The limo came on at its same crawl.

As Maria reached the spot where she'd started, the limo glided smoothly forward, turned its long body, and blocked the road.

Maria slammed on the brakes. Pablo's magazine fell. "Gun it. Get around them."

Maria started to, but she made herself stop. If she hurtled the truck up through a yard and around the limo, they'd chase her, stop her, maybe shoot her and Pablo both. Besides, she had a better idea.

"No," Maria said.

"Shit, woman. That's Bradley."

"I guessed that. Wonder what he's doing here, and not holed up in his house?"

"I don't care. Aw, damn it."

Four men exited the limo. They wore casual clothes, jeans and polo shirts, no business suits in sight. They looked like Texas businessmen out looking at their properties, except that three of the men surrounded the fourth as though they were his bodyguards. All four wore guns in holsters on their belts, no hiding them.

The fourth man was shorter and slimmer of build than

the others, had a thick shock of salt-and-pepper hair, and wore wire-rimmed glasses. He looked innocuous, a Texas man with enough money and confidence that he felt no need to dress to impress, until he turned his head and looked at Maria.

The cold in his eyes made her gasp. At five paces away, the chill of him seeped over her, a man with no remorse, no conscience. He could tell his three bodyguards to open fire on the truck, killing her and Pablo without a word, even in front of the construction workers, and walk away without worry.

Pablo's hand went down his jeans to his ankle holster, but Maria put her hand on his arm. "Wait."

"I can get off at least two shots before they can."

"*Wait.*"

Pablo started muttering in Spanish, asking Mary, the mother of God, to protect him from crazy bitches who thought they were invincible because they ran with Shifters. Maria ignored him, opened the door of the truck, and hopped out. She spread her hands and kept them out to her sides so they'd see she had no weapons.

Even so, two of the bodyguards drew pistols, holding them close by their sides, but definitely training them on her.

"Mr. Bradley?" Maria asked, as though the guns didn't make her nervous. "I'm Maria. I was hoping I could speak with you."

CHAPTER FOURTEEN

"Were you?" Bradley's voice was flat, uninflected. "I don't know you. I know Mr. Marquez there, but not you."

"You know *about* me. I work for the Shifters—well, they make me work for them. Your men have followed me when I'm out with their cubs. I know you took one of them today. I asked Mr. Marquez to bring me to your house so I could tell you I can get you more Shifter cubs if you want them. If you'll pay me, that is. They use me as a babysitter a lot, so I'm left alone with them all the time."

Bradley's gaze remained on Maria while she spoke, then he flicked it to the truck. "If that's true, why are you here and not at my front gate?"

"I was trying to talk Mr. Marquez into it." Maria smiled. "He's afraid of you, you see. He brought me this far, but refused to tell me where to go from here. When he saw you, he wanted us to run away, but I *really* want to talk to you. I need the money, and here's an opportunity."

Bradley assessed Maria without changing expression. Good thing he wasn't Shifter, because he'd scent the deception pouring off her. If she could keep him interested, while

Ellison and the others got into his house, he'd have a nice surprise waiting when he went home.

"I'm willing to hear your suggestions," Bradley said. He gestured to the limo. "Ride with me, and be my guest."

Maria didn't need Pablo to tell her not to get into that car. "Can't we talk here?" *Out in the open, with witnesses.*

"No. There's nothing to be afraid of Ms. . . ."

"Ortega." No sense in lying. He could check.

"Ms. Ortega. We'll talk, we'll have coffee, and you'll go. But only if Mr. Marquez comes with us."

"Of course," Maria said. "He's good at business. He's advising me."

"I see."

Bradley didn't move, but the two bodyguards who'd taken out their pistols went to the truck. One aimed his gun through the door Maria had left open, the other went around. Pablo slid out his side of the truck, and let the goon pat him down and take his weapon.

Pablo's face was a careful blank, but his eyes held molten fury. Bradley waited until Pablo was in the limo, then he ushered Maria ahead of him as he walked to the limo's open door. The bodyguard who'd taken Pablo's gun got into the pickup and started it with the keys Maria had left, waiting to follow.

Maria swallowed her misgivings, climbed inside the leather-seated limo, and sank down next to Pablo. She tried not to flinch when the door slammed shut, enclosing them in a cushy, cigar-scented, dark-windowed prison.

Bradley had four bodyguards surrounding his house today, Ellison noted after he and Tiger had sniffed around then met up with Broderick and Ronan. Four guards, four Shifters. Poor bastards didn't stand a chance.

Ellison was about to give the order to take down the guards when he saw Bradley's limo leave from the semicircle of the drive and roll down the lane to the gate.

"Damn it."

The man hadn't seen them coming—couldn't have. The other guards remained in place, not on alert, not altering their pace. Bradley could be heading down to the nearest convenience store for beer and cigarettes for all Ellison knew.

The limousine turned in the direction of Austin, which meant in the direction of the housing development a couple miles away. No reason Bradley should enter the development, but just in case . . .

"Tiger, run back to Maria and tell her Bradley's out, and to be careful. We'll get inside and wait for him."

"What if he's gone all day?" Broderick asked.

Ronan answered. "Then we wait all day. We'll give him a little welcome-home party." He grinned, his eyes flashing the red of an enraged bear.

Tiger said nothing. He acknowledged Ellison's order by turning around and fading back into the grasses. In a second or two, Ellison could no longer see him.

He'd sent Tiger, because the man was faster than any Shifter he knew, and the guards would never spot him. Tiger would be there and back in five minutes, and not even breathe hard.

"Let's go," Ellison said.

"Now it's three against four," Broderick said. "Four with automatic weapons."

"Four against three Shifters with built-in weapons," Ronan said, never losing his feral smile. He brought up his hand and curled it like claws. "They won't know what hit them."

"We should wait for the crazy," Broderick said, jerking his chin the direction Tiger had disappeared.

"No, because I want this quiet, with limited bloodshed," Ellison countered. He'd save the bloodiness for Bradley. "We don't need every cop in the county bearing down on us when someone reports Shifters rampaging at the big house. I want to get Bradley first."

Broderick let out a breath. "I see your point. Fine. We'll hit them fast and hard, knock them out, take their weapons.

If we're quiet enough, the fourth one won't realize what's happened until too late."

Ellison gave him a nod. "You got it. Ready?"

"More than ready," Ronan growled. "They'll see what happens when they try to take my cub."

"Try not to kill anyone," Ellison said.

"Me?" Ronan touched his chest, brown eyes going wide. "I'm a big teddy bear. With a Collar that keeps me tame. I wouldn't hurt a fly."

"I know." Ellison grinned at him. "I've seen you catch them in your house and release them outside. Just put these guys down, and we'll go from there."

Without further word, the three separated, slinking through the tall grasses toward the house. More bluebonnets, Ellison noted as they went. The Texas state flower, its lupine-like stalks thrusting up toward the sunlight, made the meadow almost shimmer blue. The blossoms weren't as thick here as they'd been on the banks of the pond, but they were still plentiful.

Maria was like these flowers, which could lie dormant for long stretches of time, then burst out with amazing, passionate color. Ellison's thoughts flashed to Maria clinging to him in the pond, her legs wrapping him, the feeling of being inside her, watching the water bead on her skin as her head went back in pleasure.

Once they finished with Bradley, Ellison was carrying her to his bed. Period. They'd talk about mate-claims, and forever, later—after he satisfied himself and her with a long night of sweet, hot lovemaking. Ellison would have to go slow with her, he knew that. Slow goodness would be a fine thing.

The guard on his side of the house passed two steps away, never seeing Ellison crouching in the grass. Ellison rose silently behind him, letting his hands change to his Shifter-beast's. Those hands went around the guard's neck, one jerk cutting off his air, rendering him unconscious.

Ellison lowered the man to the ground, plucked up the

frightening-looking automatic sidearm, and hoped he could figure out if the thing had a safety.

He never heard a footstep, but suddenly Tiger was beside him, appearing in the grasses where Ellison had stood only a moment before.

"He has Maria," Tiger said.

Ellison had opened his mouth to swear, but he sucked in a breath. "What? You mean Bradley?"

"He took her inside the long car and drove her to the house."

Ellison's entire body went cold. He'd never been so cold. Numbness spread from his heart down his spine, paralyzing him.

He has Maria.

"Pablo was supposed to protect her," he said, lips stiff.

Tiger didn't answer. He never did when he knew it was useless. At least he didn't offer any meaningless platitudes.

"He's a dead man," Ellison said. He started forward, ready to stride down the little slope to the house, but Tiger put a hand on his arm.

Ellison registered that Tiger rarely offered his touch, so this was unusual, but the thought was dim. Ellison's body was tight, the feral in him ready to kill.

"Your plan is good," Tiger said. "We stay with your plan."

Ellison struggled to breathe. At that moment, he couldn't remember what the damn plan was. *Bradley had his mate.*

No, Tiger was right. Sneak up on the house, disable the alarm, slip inside, find Bradley, and choke off his empire at the source. They had the guards' guns. No one needed to know that Shifters had been here at all.

Ellison nodded. "Yes," he managed to say. "We stay with the plan."

Tiger released him. He led the way, moving in silence for such a big man, down the slope to rendezvous with Ronan and Broderick.

"That asshole's history," Broderick said when Ellison whispered the news. "No one messes with our females."

For once, Ellison agreed with him. When they played out the Challenge, Ellison would pound Broderick, but right now, Broderick wanted Maria out of there as much as he did.

Ronan had subdued the fourth guard, and he handed Tiger the holstered automatic weapon he'd retrieved. Tiger looked over the gun, and then silently handed it back. Ronan gave him a *whatever* look and buckled the second weapon over his shoulder.

Ellison took the radio from the guard he'd knocked out and the second one Ronan had and tucked both in his belt. He then searched his guy for a cell phone, switched it off, and threw it as hard as he could into the meadow.

"Here comes the car," Broderick said.

They hid, the four peering through brush around the house, animals watching their prey. The black limo pulled to a stop in the semicircular drive, and Ellison's pickup stopped behind it. The back door of the limo opened. Bodyguards emerged first, then a quiet-looking Pablo.

Maria's shapely leg in jeans came out, followed by the rest of her, her white cotton blouse tugged by the breeze. She waited, looking unworried, for the next man, a smaller guy in glasses with graying hair.

The feral in Ellison rose up again. He knew, from the way the others treated him, that this was Bradley. His enemy. His prey. His kill.

The first bodyguard went into the house through the front door, the second signaling Pablo to follow. Pablo stopped, saying something, and the bodyguard pointed a gun at him.

Maria turned around, planting her feet, and started talking to Bradley. And talking and talking. She gesticulated toward Pablo and back to the limo, but she didn't look afraid.

"What's she doing?" Ronan whispered.

"Giving us a window," Ellison said. Goddess bless her. "The bodyguard's turned off the alarm. Let's get inside before it's on again."

* * *

"Pablo's the only one who's ever wanted to help me," Maria said to Bradley as they stood on the wide brick doorstep. The door to Bradley's vast house lay open behind her, the bodyguard who'd opened it waiting impatiently inside it.

"So why don't you leave the Shifters and work for him?" Bradley asked. He sounded mildly curious, not annoyed.

"Because he's a criminal, and you can imagine what he wants women who work for him to do. I must get away from the Shifters, but not with him. I need money to do that. That's why I'm here."

Bradley watched her, again with little change in expression. Pablo had been right to say the man had no emotions.

"Let's go inside, Ms. Ortega. My bodyguards get anxious if I'm out in the open too much. Mr. Marquez will be given something to drink in the living room, while we talk in my office."

Pablo raised his hands, conceding, and walked inside. He'd balked at the doorway, pretending to be too scared to enter, and Maria had taken the cue. If she talked enough, and the door was open long enough, Ellison, if he'd gotten into position, would be able to slip inside. If not . . . well, she was back to hoping Pablo's girlfriend had given them the right codes.

She walked into the house, Bradley came behind her, and the last bodyguard shut the door. The interior was vast, the foyer rising two floors straight up, with a wrought-iron railed balcony encircling the second level. Doors opened out from this balcony, which flowed in a circle around the twisting staircase.

The first and second bodyguards peeled Pablo off to a room beneath the balcony, while the third and fourth bodyguard led Maria upstairs following Bradley. Bradley ushered Maria into a room that faced the rear of the house, its window overlooking a meadow studded with bluebonnets, which were bursting into full spring ecstasy.

Bradley motioned for Maria to sit in front of a long empty desk, and went to a wet bar, where he poured cold bottled water into a glass with ice and brought the bottle and glass to her. The bodyguards took up positions on either side of the doorway.

"All right," Bradley said, resting one hip on his desk. He looked almost congenial, except for the chill nothingness in his eyes. "You say you want to help me obtain Shifter cubs for my clients. How would you do it?"

"They make me watch the brats," Maria said, wincing inwardly at the word, but telling herself to play it out. "I could bring one or two to a location where you could easily pick them up. If I had known you were coming when I was with Olaf yesterday, I would have kept the other Shifters away."

"Hmm," Bradley said. "You could get away with that once, maybe. What happens when the next set of cubs you're supposed to be watching also get taken? They'll be suspicious, don't you think?" His tone held faint scorn.

He didn't believe her. Maria shut her eyes, bunched her fists, and tried to look helpless and desperate. "If you pay me enough, I only need to do it once or twice. Then I can take the money and leave town—leave the country. I can guarantee three, maybe four cubs. The Shifter families don't have that many kids, so you won't get much more than that anyway."

Her heart burned. If those precious cubs were lost, the entire community would be devastated.

"Might work," Bradley conceded. "You'd have to make sure the cubs weren't anywhere near any of the adults."

"I could. They watch me pretty carefully, but they also consider me only a servant."

"They'll punish you if the cubs you're looking after go missing."

"They will." Maria drew a breath and took on a resigned expression. "But they won't kill me. I'd be ready to go after the second drop."

"And you want—what? Maybe ten grand a cub?"

Ten grand. If Bradley was willing to pay her that much

to lure cubs away, how much more must his clients be paying to receive them? She felt sick.

"I think that will work." Now to have him let her and
Pablo out of the house so Ellison could continue with his
plan. She rose. "Adios, Mr. Bradley. I'd better have Pablo
drive me back, before the Shifters punish me for staying
away too long. It's my one day off a month."

"You can go, certainly." Bradley's mouth turned up at
the corners. "But I'll have Mr. Marquez stay a while as my
guest. You give me the first cubs tomorrow, and I'll let him
go home then."

Maria contrived to look worried, then she gave him a
nervous smile. "He won't like that. But all right. I'll do it. I
can . . ."

Shouts cut off her words. The bodyguards came alert and
hurried out the door, and Bradley's half smile vanished.

The cold he'd exhibited before was nothing to the ice-
berg he became. All humanity left his eyes, and he came
off the desk, walked back to the wet bar, and calmly took
out a pistol.

Maria's heart stopped, certain he was about to shoot her
dead.

"Get under the desk," he said in clipped tones, then
walked past her out of the room.

Maria heard the unmistakable snarl of a wolf, then the
roar of a bear and the uncanny, breathy growl of a tiger.
Then shots firing, the chug, chug, chug of a semiautomatic.

Her heart pounded in fear. But the animal snarls only
escalated, and one of the bodyguards cried out. Maria raced
out of the room.

Below the balcony, two wolves fought to tear a gun out
of one bodyguard's hands. Ronan rose to his full Kodiak
bear height, bringing his paw down on a second bodyguard. He didn't even have to use his claws.

The man collapsed, and then a puddle of blood spread
out from under him. Ronan blinked his bear eyes at him in
surprise, then at Pablo, who stepped out from the living
room, a large gun in his hand.

A giant Bengal tiger was flowing up the stairs. One of the bodyguards at the top, face paling, shot him. Once, twice.

Tiger came on. The man stepped back. "Mother fu—"

Then Tiger was on him. The weapon flew wide. The remaining bodyguard brought his gun around to shoot Tiger again, but Maria sprang into him from behind.

She wasn't big enough to take the man down, but he at least misfired. The bullets sprayed into the ceiling, bits of plaster and dust raining down on them.

Tiger opened his mouth, his teeth gigantic, spittle running down them, as he turned to the remaining bodyguard. The light in his yellow eyes wasn't sane.

"Tiger!" Maria yelled. "No!"

Tiger jerked his head up, caught by her voice, but the rage didn't leave his eyes. He snarled once again, but Ellison was there, leaping into him, knocking him away from the man.

Tiger roared in fury, but Ellison growled, and Tiger finally loped away back down the stairs.

Ellison turned to the bodyguard. Ellison's wolf was huge, his hair up along his neck, his ears flat with his red-eyed snarling. The bodyguard dropped his weapon and fell to his knees.

"Please. I got a wife. I got kids," the man said. "I just work here because it pays good."

Ellison stopped his charge an inch from the guy's face, jaws snapping in irritation. Maria reached down and picked up the gun. It was heavy, and she didn't know how to hold it. The danger locked in the firm piece of metal scared her, but she figured it was better she had it than the bodyguard.

"Go home," she said to him. "Hurry. Where's Bradley?"

A second wolf and Ronan came up the stairs, the staircase creaking under the Kodiak's weight. Bradley was nowhere in sight.

"He hasn't come past me," Pablo called from below.

"He has a panic room," the bodyguard said, still on his knees. "Through that door and at the end of the hall." He pointed. "Sealed tight. He holes up there when things get bad."

"Thank you," Maria said. "Go now."

The bodyguard hauled himself to his feet. His face was gray, eyes filled with fear. "Thanks. Thanks." He stuttered the words then turned to go past Ellison, Broderick, and finally Ronan.

Ronan couldn't resist giving a little growl and swatting at him. The former bodyguard hurtled down the stairs, ran past Pablo, who only watched him without interest, and sprinted out of the house.

Maria opened the door the bodyguard had indicated, then felt teeth on her wrist. Ellison had his mouth, ever so gently, on her arm, looking at her with admonishment. *Stay here,* he was saying. Maria sighed and stepped back to let the Shifters go through first.

The hall ended in another innocuous door, but it hung partway open, revealing a steel door behind it. The second door had no handle, only a keypad.

Maria reasoned that a man like Bradley would have been too cautious to use the same code for his panic room as his front door. But the combined might of two Shifter wolves and a Kodiak bear was soon breaking the seal on the door. Tiger stood back, growling under his breath, tail swishing the slightest bit over the hall carpet.

"Tiger, what's wrong?" Maria asked.

Ellison glanced up. Tiger's warning rumble escalated, and then he roared.

Ellison, Ronan, and Broderick sprang away from the door as it gave, the wolves diving flat as Tiger did. Ronan, too big to do anything but back up, knocked over a delicate gilded side table, the trinkets on its top shattering.

The steel door burst open, and two large, sleek wildcats hurtled out, straight into the wolves and Ronan.

Maria screamed. Tiger rose, but instead of rushing to aid the others, he ran at Maria, herding her back onto the foyer's balcony. Once she was there, he turned and sprinted back down the hall.

What was Bradley doing with *Shifters*?

Her chest constricted. Oh, mother of God. *What happens to the cubs when they get too big to handle?* she'd asked Pablo.

The cheetahs had been wearing Collars, so not feral. Stolen, she guessed, from a Shifter family somewhere. How long ago? Had the clients given them back to Bradley once they tired of them? Had they been here all this time? Prisoners? How many more did he have?

The hallway was a confusion of fur and snarling, yelps and roars. She saw Ellison fall, cheetah claws raking across his fur. He was up in a second, wolf maw closing over the cheetah's neck. He could break it in the next moment.

"Ellison!" she shouted. "Ellison, they're cubs!"

CHAPTER FIFTEEN

Ellison showed no sign of hearing, but the second cheetah, squirming away from Ronan, knocked into him. Tiger was roaring, but not fighting. Maybe he understood. Tiger was always so protective of the cubs.

Maria had seen Scott crazed from his Transition, striking out before Ronan or Rebecca could stop him. If these two were going through the same thing . . .

They'd stop at nothing to fight their perceived enemies, their killing instinct wound high.

Bradley must be behind them, in that room. Or was he? Would he have run into a room from which there was no escape?

Maria looked swiftly around, taking in the layout of the hallway relative to the rest of the house. She turned and hurried down the stairs and looked out the front door, the gun awkward in her hands, but she feared discarding it. The other guards were subdued, not dead.

Ellison's pickup remained in the driveway, but the limo was gone. Had the driver fled? Or had he driven around to pick up Bradley, who could have escaped out the back?

Maria moved through the house again, looking around for another way out—faster than trying to run around the vast building and encounter who knew how many walls or other obstacles.

In the rear of the ground floor, Maria found a kitchen, a huge, elegant room with stainless steel appliances and warm wooden cabinetry. Maybe she should show it to Pablo, and have him take photos for his girlfriend.

A door from this led out to a wide area between the house and five-car garage, a building that looked as though it had once been a stables. An iron stairwell snaked down the house next to the kitchen, a fire escape. High above was an ornate door, closed, that led back into the house.

Bradley wasn't on the fire escape. He was running across the yard toward the garage. The limo raced up from the other side of the house, dust flying as the driver headed to help Bradley.

Maria raised the gun. It was not very big, but square, like a machine gun with a very short barrel. She aimed down at the limo's tires and squeezed the trigger.

Three bullets spurted from the weapon, and the kick nearly knocked her off her feet. The shots came nowhere near the tires—they popped into the ground by the limo driver's door and open window.

The limo stopped, the driver staring at Maria with fear on his face. She lifted the gun again, her hands shaking.

The limo jumped forward, swung around, and raised dust roaring off the other way. Bradley glared after it, then at Maria, and ducked inside the garage.

"Ellison!" Maria yelled. "Ronan! Bradley's out here!"

Her shouts brought no one. The man was going to go for whatever car was in there and get away.

Maria aimed the gun again and fired a few shots to ping against the ground in front of the garage doors. The weapon's metal felt hot in her hands, and the gun's kick, though she was ready for it this time, still made her take a few steps backward.

All was silent within the garage. Maybe fear of a young

woman with a gun she obviously couldn't control would keep Bradley in place for a moment.

Maria risked it. She ran back into the house, through the kitchen and out to the staircase hall. The fight had moved to the balcony above, the wolves and cheetahs rolling in a free-for-all, Ronan having backed off as though waiting to find a good opening. Tiger crouched on the stairs, growling, unhappy.

And where had Pablo disappeared to? The man was nowhere in sight, though Ellison's truck was still in front. Pablo hadn't taken it, made good his escape, and stranded them there. But where was he?

The iron railing above her creaked and strained. As Maria looked up, one of the supports snapped. The railing teetered under the weight of the fighting animals, then came down. With it tumbled the wolves and cheetahs— one wolf, Broderick, scrabbling to keep his hold on the balcony until the last minute.

Maria fled out of the way. Ellison hit the stairs on his back, the cheetahs' limbs flailing until they landed on him, claws raking as they struggled to gain their feet. Ellison, still wolf, rolled out from under them, coming to a stand on four paws, panting hard.

Broderick managed to crawl back up to the upper floor, shifting to his half beast to do it. He morphed to fully human as he stood up, trying to catch his breath.

Tiger moved. He came down the stairs almost on his belly, heading for the cheetahs, his ears back, teeth bared. The cheetahs looked at him in uncertainty, then the mad look came back into their eyes, and they charged him, Collars sparking.

At the same time, men poured into the house from the front, the back, all armed. Bradley or one of his guards must have called for backup. A man like Bradley could afford the best, and the men who came in, at least two dozen of them, were large, grim-faced, and hard-muscled—likely ex-military, ex-mercenary, ex-convict. They aimed at the Shifters, who'd be mowed down.

Maria yelled a warning. A few of the hard-eyed men glanced at her then walked on, not seeing her as a threat. She still had the gun, held down and behind her back, but her fingers were slick on the trigger. Could she shoot another human being? And if she started shooting, would they simply train weapons on her and obliterate her in seconds?

Her cry had alerted Ellison. He was moving again, racing up the stairs, Ronan coming down toward him. Tiger saw the men and roared, rising to his full height. He put himself in front of the cheetahs as the first shots were fired, a bullet bloodying his fur.

Ellison turned and leapt over the last curve of staircase, landing on one of the mercenaries before he could get off a shot. His Collar sparked as he rolled over the man, the gun clattering away.

The others split off through the staircase hall, aiming, firing. Tiger herded the cheetahs back upstairs, toward the room with the steel door. Ronan and Broderick had ducked behind walls when the bullets started flying. They were big, tough Shifters, but shots could still kill them.

Ellison fought alone. He bloodied the man, while one of the merc's colleagues tried to get a clear shot at him. The rest were moving up the stairs, or through the house, hunting, searching, shooting.

What could Maria do? Whatever happened, she had to stop Bradley. And save Ellison. As soon as Ellison came up from subduing the man he fought, the second man would shoot him.

If this were one of the many TV shows she watched, she'd come up with some clever way to bring down all the bad guys, who'd obligingly drop weapons and look defeated and disgruntled. Maria had the feeling it wouldn't be that easy in real life. These men were professionals, who would shoot Ellison and the others, get Bradley safely away, and then go have coffee.

Maria ducked into the living room, where Bradley's men had originally taken Pablo, but the room was empty. She plucked a cell phone from the man Pablo had shot in the hall and punched in a number. Bradley had called backup; she could too.

She'd dialed Dylan's phone, but she wanted to cry when Connor answered. "You're all right!" she whispered.

"Yeah. Groggy, but all right. Where are you?"

"Where's Dylan?"

"Driving. Maria, I asked you—where are you?"

"At Bradley's. We need help."

Connor started to speak again, but his words cut off to be replaced by Liam's voice. "Lass, you stay put; make sure Bradley stays put. We're coming. Where to, exactly?"

Maria opened her mouth to answer, then the cell phone was yanked from her hand, and a punch landed across her face. She went down, pain exploding through her, the gun falling from her numb fingers.

Ellison was there in the next moment, the giant gray wolf slamming into the man who'd hit Maria. The merc lost hold of his weapon, sending it sliding across the rug. Ellison landed on him, breaking the arm the man stretched toward the gun. The merc screamed, and then again as Ellison's paws rendered his head a bloody mess.

Another weapon clicked, a second merc with an automatic weapon raised and pointed at Ellison. Maria scrambled to her feet, face aching from the first punch. She launched herself at the man, thinking to grab his arm to train the gun away from Ellison.

Crimson burst over the merc's face, and he fell gurgling. Dead. Maria gaped past him to see Pablo, his small pistol back in his hands, his eyes almost as cold as Bradley's. The bang of the gun filled the room and made Maria's ears ring.

Ellison climbed off the other man he'd knocked down, that merc out. Ellison's wolf sides heaved, his jaw bloody, scratches and blood in his fur. He shook himself, nose wrinkling at the smell of death.

"You're welcome," Pablo said to them. "Where's Bradley? I can't afford to let him live."

"In the garage." Maria's jaw hurt when she spoke, and she worked it. "Last I saw. He could be long gone by now."

"Let's go find out." Pablo had lowered his gun but didn't holster it. "I called my own backup, but if we don't get the hydra, I'm a dead man."

Ellison shifted. He rose onto strong legs, his torso bruised and abraded, his face bloody. He limped to Maria, still breathing hard, and put an arm around her.

"You all right, sweetheart? I'm sorry—I couldn't stop him in time."

Maria rubbed her cheek. "I will be. I've had worse."

She had, when she'd been prisoner of the feral Shifters, but the answer made Ellison's eyes fill with fury. His arm tightened around her, but his touch on her face was tenderness itself.

"They found Connor," Maria said quickly. "I told Liam to come, but I didn't get a chance to tell him where." The cell phone on the floor was cracked and dark.

"My girlfriend will tell him," Pablo said. "She's hacked all the calls in and out of here. From a safe distance—I told her to get the hell out of town until this is over." He gave Ellison an admonishing look, as though Ellison should have done the same with Maria. Not that Maria would have listened.

Pablo led the way out, through another door and around to a back hall. More gunfire sounded, and over it came the roars of Tiger and Ronan. Maria wanted to run and make sure they were all right, but Ellison steered her firmly out.

They had to fight in the kitchen. Ellison shoved Maria down behind a counter and shifted into the state between wolf and human as more of Bradley's mercs opened fire on them. A few of Pablo's men—one of them Maria recognized as a mechanic at Pablo's car shop—were pinned down here, firing back. Pablo joined them, Ellison slinking under their fire to tackle one of Bradley's mercs.

Maria crawled behind the counter to the door, then sprinted out. Another two mercs were down outside, one unmoving, one groaning, both unarmed. Maria hurried past them in time to see one of the garage doors open, a gray Cadillac emerging.

She'd dropped her weapon when the other man had knocked her down, and Pablo had grabbed it on the way out, giving it to one of his men in the kitchen who'd run out of ammo. Now Maria could only stand helplessly and watch the car come out of the garage. Bradley was getting away, but what could she do?

The answer came from a deafening roar behind her. The sound pounded through the house, vibrating it like a small earthquake.

Maria had heard it once before, a lion's roar. The lion Shifter that bounded toward the car was Dylan, black maned, his Collar silent, rage in his white blue eyes. He roared again, an alpha male in his full strength. Behind him came Spike, his naked human form covered with tatts, and another black-maned lion—Sean. Sean was followed by a wolf that looked like Ellison, only a little smaller and finer boned.

The wolf stopped beside Maria, then it froze as the Cadillac accelerated, swerving to avoid the Shifters. Maria saw Bradley behind the wheel, his face still expressionless, his glasses shining.

Beside Maria, the wolf's shape distorted and jerked, a Shifter changing before it wanted to. It rose into the form of Deni, who stared at the car, her face set in horror.

"That's the one," Deni said, her voice barely a whisper. "That's the car that hit me."

Ellison, in his wolf form now, along with Pablo, had run up to Maria's side in time to hear her. Ellison looked at Deni, understanding and rage in his wolf's eyes.

He burst away and charged the the car, slamming into its side and forcing it to turn. Sean ran and leapt, landing on the car's trunk, and Dylan planted himself in front of it, his lion's roar breaking the air.

Bradley jerked the car sideways, tires sliding, choking dust rising high. His hand spun the wheel until the car came out of its skid, and he headed straight for Maria and Deni.

Ellison and Dylan tried to sprint ahead of it, Sean climbing to the roof, his claws leaving long gouges in the car's body.

Deni, motionless, watched the Cadillac come at her. Pablo grabbed both women to yank them out of the way, but Deni came alive.

She snatched the gun out of Pablo's hands, aimed it, and fired three practiced shots through the windshield and into Bradley's head.

The car kept coming. Maria slammed herself into Deni and Pablo, pushing them out of the way. The car rushed past them, Bradley's dead foot still on the gas, and crashed, head-on, into the house.

The car's engine spluttered and died, and all was silent.

CHAPTER SIXTEEN

Ellison stood in the ring at the fight club, naked, flexing his hands, ready to go. His ribs hurt, his torso was streaked with deep scratches, and his neck ached from too many shocks of his Collar, but still he was here.

Shifters filled the vast space of the abandoned hay barn out east of Austin, the darkness broken by trashcan fires, huge flashlights, and LED lanterns. Broderick climbed over the cinder blocks that marked out the ring, a big smile on his face. He had come away from the fight at Bradley's relatively unscathed and exuded confidence he'd win the Challenge.

Fuck that.

Ellison felt the pull of the growing mate bond with Maria, stretching between him and her as she stood outside the ring with Spike and Ronan, Ellison's seconds.

Connor stood next to them, too keyed up to stay home. He'd been restless and hungry after they'd all made it back to Shiftertown, Connor eating everything in sight and insisting he go to the fight club. Cubs weren't technically allowed at the fight club, but Connor was given slack tonight, with the approval of all Shifters. Though he wouldn't fight, Ellison imagined that Connor would find a way to work off his steam. Apparently Bradley had taken him because a woman had asked Bradley to find her a strapping young Shifter for her entertainment. Pablo had related this after he and his girlfriend, restored to Austin, had gone through Bradley's desk and computer.

Maria stood close to Connor, her shoulder touching his. Ellison scented her goodness, her courage and passion.

He also scented that she was very, very angry.

Maria had argued long and hard for Ellison to not meet Broderick tonight. By the time they'd all limped back to Shiftertown, Maria driving, Ellison was sore, tired, clawed all over, and aching from a couple bullets that had grazed his arm.

At the same time, he was buoyant. Maria loved him. The mate bond was forming. He'd had the joy of holding her in his arms, being inside her yesterday in the soothing pond. Tonight, after he battered Broderick until the man begged for mercy, Ellison would carry her home and take her to bed.

That is, if he could still stand up.

Around them, Shifters shouted and laughed. Broderick's pack stood behind him to cheer him on. The air was thick with scents of anticipation, eagerness, and mating frenzy. A Challenge brought out the mating need in Shifters, both male and female.

Pablo had come, betting on the fight in his quiet way. Ellison guessed he'd bet on Broderick. But then, Broderick hadn't fallen from a balcony onto stairs and had two crazed cheetahs in their Transition land on him.

Dylan and Tiger had taken charge of the cheetahs. When they'd turned to human, they'd been two males in their late twenties, twins, who had lived as captives on a wealthy woman's estate in New York. The woman had asked Bradley to take them back when they hit their Transition and became too crazed.

Tiger had been solicitous of the two, and Dylan was arranging for them to be taken into the Austin Shiftertown.

They owed another debt to Pablo. He'd stayed behind after the Shifters had piled into various vehicles to leave, taking care of the remaining mercs and saying he'd make Bradley's death and the torn-up house look like a gang hit. Bradley had made many enemies. Pablo had looked around the house and at the kitchen with approval, and said he'd try to buy the place. Ellison suspected he'd provide jobs for Bradley's mercenaries, now that their boss was dead. The battle today was all to Pablo's gain.

As for Deni . . . she stood straight and tall beside Maria. Shooting Bradley seemed to have released something in her. The haunting worry in her eyes had gone, and her cubs, standing behind her, were there to comfort her. Whether she'd thrown off the episodes of her memory blanking remained to be seen, but Deni now knew exactly what had happened to her, and who had done it.

Bradley might have been trying to capture her—maybe he'd mistaken her for a cub, or maybe someone had asked for a female Shifter the same way the woman had asked for someone Connor's age. Ellison's rage hadn't calmed down about that. Maria had declared her new mission to track down all those who'd purchased Shifters—adult or cub—and release the captives. Ellison agreed. They'd start tomorrow.

Tonight, he needed to take out Broderick.

Two refs stood between the two combatants. They thumped their fists, one over the other, and yelled, "Fight."

The refs scattered, and Ellison went for Broderick. Broderick sidestepped, whirled, and shifted at the same time. Mistake. Broderick landed in Ellison's furred arms, Ellison rising into his half-Shifter beast.

Broderick squirmed away, lithe and strong as his wolf. Ellison followed, the pain in his ribs slowing him down, his Collar going off. Broderick took advantage to shift to his half beast and catch Ellison across the torso with his clawed hands.

Ellison danced back, landing on all fours as a wolf. He launched himself upward, latching his teeth into Broderick's throat.

He found his mouth full of the loose fur as Broderick came down wolf. He snarled and shook, flailing Ellison's body, but Ellison held on.

Broderick finally twisted all the way around, and Ellison's teeth slipped. Blood dripped from the wound in Broderick's neck, the metallic taste winding Ellison into a frenzy.

"No killing!" one of the refs yelled.

Too late. Ellison's rage was up. Broderick wanted to steal his mate. In the wild, males tried to abduct females all the time, until the formal Challenge and its rules had been set up to protect the scarce females. These days, Challenges didn't end in the kill, but Ellison wanted it.

He went for Broderick's throat again. This time, Broderick shifted into his half-wolf beast, catching Ellison, raising him high, and throwing him down.

Ellison landed in a whump of dust, the bruised ribs stabbing him, new wounds opening. His Collar was sparking too, slowing his roll to his feet.

He stood panting, trying to raise his head. Damn Broderick. He needed to go down.

Ellison backed up a few steps, but Broderick charged him. Ellison came up, and the two males met, both wolves now, snarling, biting, clawing.

Broderick chomped on the back of Ellison's neck, and Ellison rolled away, wanting to groan in pain. He scrambled to get his paws under him, the light of the fires in the abandoned hay barn starting to blur. Broderick was a blur too, the noise around him a hum of confusion.

Something brushed past him, something that smelled sweet and good, and of mate.

"Stop!" he heard Maria shout. "Stop the fight!"

Ellison blinked. The lights were still fuzzy around the edges, but he saw Maria clearly, inside the ring, between him and Broderick. The refs were coming for her, shock on their faces.

A big rule of the fight club was that no one, *no one*, stopped a fight once it started. The only stopping was when an opponent yielded, or the refs thought one of them too far gone and needed to be contained.

No one watching was allowed to touch the fighters, and certainly not to enter the ring. Especially a human. Especially a human *female*.

The two refs, big Felines, were heading to grab Maria and drag her out. Ellison put his wolf body between her and them, growling hard.

Outside the ring, Connor said, "Maria, you can't do that."

Tiger stepped over the barrier. Ellison noticed no one tried to stop *him*. "Don't touch her," Tiger said clearly.

The refs halted. Broderick shifted into his human form and put his hands on his hips. Goddess, the man stank.

"You can't stop the Challenge," Broderick said to Maria. "Or he forfeits." He grinned at her. "You don't want that, now do you?"

"He was already hurt before he walked in," Maria said angrily. "You knew that. You should have put it off."

"Hey, he picked the time and place."

Ellison leaned back against Maria, a fine place to be, and she put her arms around his neck. "Do it some other time. You can stop this."

Ellison's body decided to shift. He didn't want to—he felt stronger as wolf—but Maria with her arms around him made him change form back to human male. He ended up with Maria's arms still around him, pulling him close.

"Hey, love," he said, his voice barely working. "You're crazy, you know that?"

"I'm taking you home," Maria said. "I don't want to see you hurting anymore."

Around them, the crowd stopped screaming and booing and moved closer to listen. Shifters could never mind their own business.

"Let me finish this first," Ellison said, the words rasping. "A mate always answers a Challenge."

"Doesn't matter. Even if Broderick wins, I'll refuse him, and come back to you anyway."

Some of Ellison's tension left him, and his breath became less labored. His ribs started to feel better too. The healing touch of the mate. He hadn't quite believed in such a power before—especially when the mate was human— but he did now.

Ellison leaned to her, his forehead against hers. "Look around you. All these males here would want you as mate. They call you fair game, but you're the one who does the choosing. Anyone you want, for the taking."

"I already chose."

Her words poured strength into Ellison's body. Enough strength for him to rise up and kick Broderick's sorry behind? Well, maybe not.

Maria was speaking again, her words flowing, but his heart only heard the peace of her voice. "You told me I should stop surviving and start living. You should too, Ellison. Stop just getting by, and show me how to live. Live life with *me*."

Ellison felt the smile spread over his face. "Oh, sweetheart. You've done it now."

"Done what?"

"Made me know the mate bond is real. I love you, Maria."

Maria took a sharp breath, then her answering smile blossomed. "I love *you*, Ellison Rowe."

Ellison kissed her. This kiss went on . . . and on.

Shifters around them cheered. Or howled, roared, whistled, or made ribald remarks. Damned nosy neighbors.

"Aw, shit." Broderick spit on the ground. "Damn it, I can't compete with this. You're a lucky dickhead, Ellison." He heaved a long and aggrieved sigh. "I withdraw the Challenge."

His family groaned. Deni whooped, and Connor followed suit. Other Shifters said, "Awww," and clapped and cheered.

"You're still an asshole," Broderick growled. But he came forward, holding out his hand.

Ellison turned and put his into it, making sure his grip was as strong as Broderick's. He kept his other arm around Maria so he wouldn't fall down.

"Come on," Broderick said. "Get yourself dressed, and I'll buy you a beer at Liam's place."

"Rain check," Ellison said, warming as he drew Maria to him again. "I'm going home."

Ellison carried Maria into his bedroom at the very back of the house, slamming the door with his cowboy-booted foot.

Maria had never seen his bedroom. In the light from the lamp beside his bed, she saw a large map of Texas on one wall, a red pin in the center marking Austin. The flag of Texas, with its one white and one red stripe, blue field on the left bearing the lone star, hung downward on another wall. Photos of Ellison's sister, nephews, and friends were pinned up over the desk. Ellison was laughing in any snapshot he was in, saluting with a longneck beer, or tipping his cowboy hat in an exaggerated way.

She took all this in before Ellison collapsed with her onto the bed. It was a single bed, narrow, and Maria squashed against him.

"Love." Ellison rolled onto his back, rubbed his hands through his hair, and blew out his breath. "Goddess, what a day."

"It ended well." Maria rose on her elbow and tapped the tip of his nose. "You should sleep. You need to heal."

"Not yet." His voice lost its teasing note, his playfulness dissolving. "Not yet." Ellison skimmed his hand along her side to her breast. "Do you know what went through my mind when you ran into that ring tonight, all fired up?"

"Annoyance?"

Ellison dissolved into laughter. "Man, those refs are

never going to let me hear the end of it. The fight club is all about the rules." He touched her face. "No, I thought you were mighty sexy running in there, telling everyone what to do with themselves. Crazy, but sexy."

"They were going to let you fight when you were already hurt," Maria said indignantly.

"You think I couldn't take Broderick in my rundown state? You wound me."

"Don't be stupid. It should be a fair fight. You have to win with skill and strength, not arrogance." She made a face. "And no way was I going to be Broderick's mate."

"I wasn't about to let you be." Ellison ran the ball of this thumb across her lips. "Then he had to go and do the noble thing, and make all of Shiftertown soft on him. But even an asshole could see that we were meant to be together."

"Broderick was good to step back."

"Nah, he'd be embarrassed if I kicked his ass when I was already hurt." Ellison grinned. "No, you're right. I was halfway down already and Broderick came through. Makes me almost like the guy." He winced and touched his ribs where Broderick had gotten in a blow. "Almost."

"You see? You should rest. We'll talk about being mates in the morning."

"Oh, no." In one quick move, Ellison rolled his body over hers, pinning her with his warm weight. "I've been waiting all day to get my arms around you again. I was thinking about us in the pond all last night and all today, remembering the bluebonnets, the sunshine. You." He skimmed his lips, warm and satin smooth, across her mouth. "Why did you decide to start making love to me, yesterday? Not that I minded."

"I wanted to." Maria slid her hands to the small of his back, his flesh warm through his shirt. "I was worried that when you finally seduced me, I would be afraid. So I thought if I did it fast, without thinking about it, then I'd know if I would be afraid. Does that sound crazy?"

"And were you?" Ellison's voice was quiet. "Afraid?"

"No." Maria dug her hands into his back, pulling him closer. "No, I wasn't. It was . . . so beautiful."

"Yeah, that's a good word for it. *Fucking amazing* is another."

"That's two words."

"Whatever."

Ellison knelt back from her and skimmed her shirt up and off over her head. Cool air touched Maria's breasts, held by her satin bra, the spring breeze from the open window soft.

Ellison reached over and switched off the lamp. In the white moonlight, he unsnapped her bra, slid it off, and tossed it aside, then took time to rest his gaze on her, taking her in.

"Trouble with pond water is it's too muddy," he said. "You can't see what you want through it."

She smiled. "I know."

"Oh, sweetheart, you can make a man hard looking at him like that, and saying that."

"I only said *I know.*"

"Maybe, but it was the way you said it."

Maria started laughing. She loved this man, who made her feel good, and made her laugh, at the same time he spiraled her into wanting. She reached for his belt buckle and popped the big thing open.

"Why do you wear this?" The buckle had an oil well and *Texas* emblazoned on it.

"Because I like Texas. It's big, it's bold, it's not afraid of the world. I like to brag that I'm from the most in-your-face state in the country."

"But you're from Colorado."

Ellison grinned his big Texas grin, then subsided. "You want to know the truth?" He traced a soft pattern on her breast, which slid fire to her heart. "When my sister and I and my nephews were rounded up to be brought here, Collared and registered like cattle, I didn't know what was going to happen to us. By the time we were dumped here, left in front of this house, which was at the time a rundown pile of crap, I'd figured out one thing. Deni and I had left behind a lot of sadness, a hole where our lives used to be. I looked around at this vast place, and I decided Texas would be our new beginning. I left behind my old life and totally embraced the new, every part of it. Got me a big pickup, a flag, a belt buckle, and an accent. The hat and boots I already had, 'cause you know, *real* cowboys come from Colorado."

Maria laughed again. "You have a big ego."

"So I fit right in. But I learned to love everything Texas, my new home, my new life. It saved me."

She nodded, understanding. "Like me trying to learn to be American, and go to school, and live with Shifters."

Ellison drew his fingers up her throat and around her chin, his touch featherlight. "We're both carving out a place for ourselves." His voice went quiet. "How about we do it together?"

Words welled up inside Maria, so many words that she couldn't make them coherent. "Yes," she said softly.

The Shifter wolf flashed into his eyes and out again. "Maria, honey, yesterday, in the water, everything was slow, sensual." He slid his touch to her breast again. "Tonight, I don't know if I can be as sweet."

Maria's heart beat faster, a point of heat curling between her thighs. "I don't want sweet."

"You sure?" Ellison's breath came faster, his body tightening. "I don't want to rush you, or scare you. But if I start . . . I won't be able to stop."

More excitement licked through her. "I'm sure. It's not the same." She laced her fingers through his hair at the nape of his neck. "You're Ellison. You care about me. It's different."

"I do care." Ellison's voice gentled. "I love you, Maria. I've been waiting for you for so long."

Maria had been waiting for him. She hadn't known it those long years, through the misery and the pain. But she'd realized, that day she met him, when he'd touched his hat and said, "Ma'am," that her knight in shining armor had come.

"I can't . . ." Ellison said. "Goddess."

He rolled off her, coming to his feet, his eyes pale gray

in the moonlight. He yanked off his belt and boots, jeans and shirt, emerging bare. Bruises and abrasions were dark across his torso, but they were healing, his Shifter metabolism working on them already.

Ellison leaned down and tugged open the button of Maria's jeans. She tried to help slide them down, but he had them off in a few swift jerks, pulling the panties after them. He left her shoes, slim sandals, on her feet, too impatient to remove them.

Ellison came back onto the bed, his warm bare body over hers, lowering himself without hurting her.

That was the last thing he did gently. He skimmed back her hair from her forehead and took her mouth in a deep, long kiss. His tongue tangled hers, the kiss hot and satisfying.

His kisses fell on her throat, her breasts, her belly, back to her breasts again. Ellison closed his mouth over one nipple, suckling, until Maria arched, the tight little pain bringing out a noise of pleasure.

More kisses, down her abdomen, one pressed to her navel, and the next between her legs. Maria felt his tongue, and she cried out. Ellison licked her there, moving his tongue around her opening, plunging inside it, her hips lifting from the mattress. Maria had never felt such a thing, had never experienced this kind of fine wildness.

Because Ellison did it for pleasure alone. The feral Shifters had cared only for *their* pleasure, and for creating cubs, and hadn't been concerned about Maria.

Ellison was taking the time to show his mate pleasure, joy, how it felt to be treasured. It was loving, caring.

The sensation also had Maria winding toward climax. White fire rippled through her, radiating from Ellison's skilled tongue all the way to her fingertips. She rocked against him, her hand furrowing his hair, pulling him closer, closer.

Ellison lifted his beautiful mouth away and slid his body up hers. He enclosed her in his arms, catching her cries of climax on his lips at the same time he slid straight into her.

Maria's eyes widened. Yesterday in the water, she easing

herself onto him, she'd not had this fullness. He'd filled her, yes, but tonight she had the entire length of him, and it was powerful. Ellison spread her wide, she tight and hot, the place where they joined filled with wonderful ache.

"Ellison," she said, her voice rolling through the room. "I love you!"

"I love you, Maria." His voice was fierce, his body strong. "Mate of my heart. Together. We do this *together*."

"Always." Together in life, in family, in love, *now*.

Maria rose to meet him, Ellison's openmouthed kisses like washes of fire, Maria burning to ash beneath him.

She reached out to brush aside her fear, and found it dissolving under his heat and love, like dust motes over bluebonnets on a Texas spring breeze.

FERAL
HEAT

CHAPTER ONE

The fight club had moved since Jace Warden had last visited the Austin Shiftertown. The Shifters used to meet
for their forbidden bouts in an abandoned hay barn nestled
into folds of a hill, but the land had been purchased, and a
developer had built over it.

On his borrowed Harley, Jace turned from the discreet
plane that had flown him this far and headed down a highway that led to drier country away from the river. The
world had darkened while he'd flown east from Nevada to
land at an airfield that had supposedly been closed.

Dylan Morrissey, the Austin Shiftertown liaison, had
left a message for Jace to meet him at the fights, and he'd
also left the bike for Jace's transportation. Tired and hot,
and having hauled himself halfway across the country at
Dylan's request, the last thing Jace wanted to do was to
ride out to the fight club. But Dylan had summoned him to
work on the problem of getting the Collars off Shifters
once and for all, and had extended his hospitality, so Jace
hid his irritation, thanked the humans who had helped him
get this far, and mounted the motorcycle.

Jace turned off where the directions had instructed, the paved road quickly turning to dirt, the bike bouncing and skidding over gravel and through ruts. The road grew narrower and narrower, until it petered to nothing. Jace continued down a short hill and around a bend, and found the Shifter fight club behind a slight rise that hid it from the road.

He smelled it long before he saw the electric lanterns, fire dancing in garbage cans, and flashlights. Anything that could be quickly doused was being used to illuminate the scene.

Jace would have known it was a place of Shifters, even in the pitch-dark. Shifters working off adrenaline rushes and fighting instincts had a certain interesting—and pungent— odor.

Jace killed the engine of the bike, parking it among the pack of motorcycles, pickups, and smaller cars. He hung the helmet from the seat and made sure his backpack was well stashed in the saddlebag before he approached the fight area. He wasn't worried about Shifters stealing his change of clothes and toothbrush—Shifters didn't steal from one another, because a simple snatch could end up in a fight to the death. Possessions were territory, and territory was respected. But humans also came to the fight clubs, and some liked to abscond with things.

The new fighting arena was a broad slab of concrete about a hundred feet long and just as wide. Probably an old building or an event area of some kind, abandoned by its owners when money ran out. Everything had been pulled away except the slab.

Rings were outlined by concrete blocks, and firelight flickered wildly, making it a scene from hell, complete with demons. But the demons were only Shifters having fun and working off steam; those not fighting were cheering, drinking beer, or finding hook-ups—human or Shifter—and sneaking into the darkness to work off steam a different way.

Jace made his way around cars—a few of them being used for liaisons—and toward the firelight. He didn't worry about locating Dylan in the chaos, because Dylan, a

Feline Shifter who was mostly lion, always made himself known.

What Jace didn't expect was the wolf who sprang out of the shadows in a deserted stretch of the parking area and landed on Jace full force.

Jace swung around with the impact, hands coming up to dig into the wolf's fur and throw him down. The Lupine landed in the dust, his Collar sparking and sizzling. The Collar's shocks didn't slow the wolf much, because he rolled to his feet and charged Jace again.

Jace didn't know who the hell the wolf was. Not that he had much of a chance of identification as the Lupine landed on Jace again, his Collar's sparks burning Jace's skin. The wolf went for Jace's throat, and Jace's hands turned to leopard's paws to rake across the wolf's face. The wolf took the blow, landed on his feet, shook himself, and sprang again.

Jace's Collar hadn't shocked him yet, but he felt the build-up. Collars were made to spike pain into Shifters as soon as they became seriously violent, but Jace had learned techniques to fool the Collar and keep it dormant. It was tough to do, however, especially when he was taken by surprise. Jace had to focus in order to keep the Collar quiet, and right now he was busy trying to keep this bloody Lupine from killing him.

Jace whacked the wolf aside again, spinning around as he shed his denim jacket and half shifted to his wildcat. His shirt split, jeans falling as his back legs elongated into powerful feline haunches. He emerged from his shredding clothes as a fully formed snow leopard—creamy fur, black spots, ice blue eyes—and thoroughly pissed off.

Jace went for the wolf. The wolf was bigger, almost twice Jace's bulk, but leopards hadn't made it to the top of the wildcat pyramid because of size. Leopards might be among the smaller big cats, but they were swift, agile, and smart, and they didn't take shit from anyone.

This wolf wanted to give him shit, though. He came at Jace again, fur up, his canine jowls frothing, his golden eyes filled with rage. The scent that hit Jace reeked of challenge.

This was a wolf who wanted to move up in rank, never mind that Jace was a different species and not even from this Shiftertown. Dominance challenges weren't allowed inside the ring at the fight club; one of the biggest rules was that fights were for recreation and showing off—that, and no killing. Outside the ring was a different story.

Jace got ready to teach him a lesson.

As he drew back to renew his attack, another wolf sprang from the parking lot and hurled itself at the first wolf. A female, Jace scented, one he hadn't met before.

She wasn't rushing to defend the wolf, however. She attacked the Lupine in fury, teeth bared, near madness in her eyes.

The first Lupine swung to meet her, and the two went down in an explosion of fur and snarls. Jace sat back to catch his breath, surprised. The two wolves were evenly matched, the male a bit larger than the female, but the female was plenty strong and agile. Probably dominant to the male too.

Jace let the female get her first anger out of her system, then he waded back in to rescue his rescuer.

The male Lupine had the she-wolf on the ground by now. He pinned the female with one big paw, snarling as he turned to Jace.

Jace gave him a warning growl. The growl said that, up until now, Jace had been holding back; that Jace was dominant in his pride, his clan, and his Shiftertown; and the wolf might want to think about it before continuing the fight.

The Lupine ignored the warning and went for the kill. Jace met him head-on, his lithe body and fast paws taking the wolf down to the ground before the Lupine could use his superior weight to his advantage.

The she-wolf rose behind the male, landed on the wolf's back, and sank her teeth into his neck. Her Collar was sparking frantically, and she got hit by the arcs from the other wolf's Collar, but she kept biting.

Jace drew back his paw and whacked the male wolf

across the throat. The wolf spun with the blow, knocking the female loose. The male Lupine rolled across the dust and dying grass a long way before he was able to stop. He righted himself but stayed down on his belly, panting hard, conceding the fight.

Jace walked to him with a stiff-legged Feline stalk. When he reached the Lupine, he lowered his head to the wolf's eye level and growled again. *Stay the fuck down.*

Whether or not the Lupine understood Feline rumbles and body language, Jace's glare must have gotten the message across. The wolf snarled, teeth bared, but he plastered his ears flat on his head and didn't move.

Jace turned back to the she-wolf. She lay limply on the grass, and Jace went to her, giving her a cat's lick across her face. She growled softly, and Jace licked her again, feeling a need to thank and reassure her.

The need didn't leave him when he shifted back to human. He stroked her head, liking the wiry fur of her wolf.

The female wolf looked up at him in a wash of confusion. She was a gray wolf, with gray eyes. She breathed in Jace's scent, wrinkling her nose, clearly wondering who he was.

Jace gave her head another stroke, wishing she'd turn back to human so he could talk to her. She'd run to his rescue, a Lupine taking the side of a Feline, and Jace wanted to know why.

The she-wolf remained wolf, still growling softly. Jace touched her head one last time and walked back to the male wolf. "New way of greeting guests in Shiftertown?" he asked. "Let me introduce myself. I'm Jace Warden. A guest of Dylan's."

Jace knew he didn't need to explain that his own father was leader of another Shiftertown. The fact that Dylan sanctioned Jace's visit should be enough for this wolf.

The wolf morphed into his human form, a man with short black hair and light gray eyes. "Hey, I saw a strange Feline trying to sneak into the fight club when he wasn't invited, and when no one but regulars are supposed to know about the new place. What did you expect?"

"So you were defending all the Shifters here?" Jace asked with evident skepticism. "Commendable."

"Ask that crazy bitch what *she* was doing," the Lupine said, scowling at the she-wolf. "Nurturing females, my ass. She's all spit and vinegar."

"Let me guess." Jace felt mirth. "She turned down your mate-claim."

The Lupine gave Jace an incredulous look. "I wouldn't mate-claim *her*. Not if she were the last female in Shifter-town. She's out of her mind. You can never tell what she's going to do." The man made a broad gesture in her direction. "You saw her."

"I thought it was nice of her to help me out."

"Nah, she saw a fight, it sparked her loony side, and she dove in. Look at her. She's not even sure what happened."

Jace turned his gaze to the she-wolf again and saw that the man was right. She watched Jace and the Lupine, trembling but trying to hide it with a growl and a glare. Jace saw fear in her eyes along with deep anger—a woman hurting from something and not wanting anyone else to know it.

"I keep trying to tell Liam she should be put down," the Lupine said. "She's a danger to the rest of us."

The she-wolf snarled again. Scent and body language told Jace what he needed to know—the female was dominant but of a different clan than the male wolf; the male was aggressive, cocky, and hated to be bested. The male wolf would be dominant in his clan as well. Jace outranked both of them, though.

Jace looked into the other man's eyes. "Why don't you shut your hole, get dressed, and go the hell home? You're too unstable to be here tonight."

The man tried to meet Jace's gaze. He did pretty well, but in the end had to slide his eyes sideways. "What, you want some privacy with her? Don't say I didn't warn you."

"Just go," Jace said.

The wolf snorted. "Whatever." He climbed to his feet and strolled away, not worried that he was naked.

The fight hadn't attracted any attention. A sudden roar

of voices within the arena told Jace why—there must be an intense match going down. The human voices were accompanied by roars and growls, since half the watchers would be in animal form.

Jace retrieved his torn clothing, grunting in irritation. He'd only brought two changes of clothes, thinking he wouldn't be in Austin that long.

The jeans had escaped the worst of the shredding, and he pulled them on, the ripped seams stretching as he crouched down to look at the she-wolf again.

"You all right?" he asked her. "Who was that asshole?"

The disgust in his question reached past the feral fear in her eyes. He saw clarity return, and then the wolf shifted into a female with a lush, lovely body, close-cut wheat-colored hair, and large gray eyes.

She remained in a crouch, covering herself, but Jace's gaze traced the curve of her ample breasts, his natural need rising. She'd be worth sneaking off into the darkness with, maybe having a bounce with in the bed of a pickup.

No, she'd be worth more than that. This wasn't a lady Jace would use to relieve horniness and then forget. Not with that gorgeous gaze pinning him flat.

"His name's Broderick," she said in a voice Jace wanted to embrace. "He usually wins Asshole of the Month around here."

"No doubt. What did you jump in for? He's right about one thing—it was a crazy thing to do. Two males with their blood up could have hurt you."

"I saw him besting you. No one deserves to be pounded by Broderick for no reason."

"He wasn't besting me," Jace said, giving her a grin. "I had him. And then he started kicking *your* ass."

She frowned. "Oh, please. I was a few bites away from making him crawl away whimpering."

As Jace hoped, his needling made her irritation erase her fear and pain. "Not to mention, your Collar was going off," Jace said. "Are you sure you're all right?"

He placed his hand on the side of her neck, over the Collar

in question. Ordinarily, Jace wouldn't touch uninvited, especially not cross-species, but something in this woman cried out to him. She needed soothing.

Her eyes widened a little, but she didn't jerk away. "What about you? Your Collar *didn't* go off. You can dampen its effect, can't you? Like Liam does?"

Jace let his fingers caress her neck as he chose his words. "That's not supposed to be common knowledge. Need-to-know basis."

"Maybe I need to know. Dylan's trying to teach me, but I can't do it yet."

"In that case, I'll give you some pointers." Jace traced her Collar to the front, pausing when his fingers rested on its Celtic cross lying against her throat. "But I'd better find Dylan and tell him I'm here before the payback for controlling my Collar hits me."

"Dylan's fighting right now," the woman said. "His bouts are always popular. But short. He should be done soon."

Jace placed his hand on hers. He wanted to keep touching this woman for some reason, as though breaking contact with her would lessen him somehow. "Come with me. We'll watch him win together."

"No." The woman started to rise, and Jace unfolded himself and helped her to her feet. She didn't hide herself anymore, a Shifter woman unembarrassed by her body. "I have to go. Are you Jace? You've been to Shiftertown before, haven't you?"

"Yeah, but why haven't I met you?" Jace still didn't want to release her hand. "I've made lots of trips out here, but I don't remember seeing you."

"I've been . . . sick," she said. "I'm Deni. Deni Rowe."

Deni watched him anxiously, as though gauging his reaction to the name. "Ellison Rowe's sister?" Jace asked.

"Yes." Deni still peered at him, waiting.

Jace tightened his hand on hers. "Why do you have to go? Stay with me and watch Dylan kick ass. You can keep other Lupines from jumping me."

Deni didn't smile. She glanced at the arena and the mass

of figures there, and Jace scented her nervousness. "I can't. Sometimes the fighting . . ."

"Calls to the feral in you? Makes you lose control?"

She gave him a startled look. "How did you know that?"

"Because I saw your eyes when you attacked Broderick. You didn't dive into the fight only to rescue me. You did it because watching made you want to fight too. I was like that during my Transition." Jace caressed the hand he hadn't released. "All you have to do is hold on to someone. The touch will calm you and keep you tethered."

Another startled look. "That doesn't work. Even my cubs . . ."

"Bet me," Jace said. "You hang on to a dominant, and he takes the heat and cools you down. Works. That's what dominants are for."

A spark of pride returned to Deni's eyes. "And you're saying you're dominant to me?"

"Yep. It's obvious. You outrank Broderick—I bet you outrank a lot of wolves—but you're not dominant to this Feline." He touched his chest.

She gave him a half smile. "And you're not full of yourself about that."

"Just stating facts." Jace did *not* want to let go of her hand. "Let's find your clothes and go. Unless you want to watch as wolf."

Deni sent him another haughty look that made her eyes beautiful, but she didn't pull away. "I'll find my clothes."

"Good."

Jace left his shredded shirt behind—why bother with it?—but caught up his jacket and followed her into the darkness, her hand on his like a lifeline. A warm, sweet lifeline. He definitely wanted to know this Lupine woman better.

Deni's heart beat swiftly as she pulled on the sarong she'd thrown off to rush into the fight with Broderick. Broderick's scent of arrogance had enraged her, and she'd wanted to pummel him for jumping the other Shifter without challenge.

Then she'd felt her memory slide away, the feral thing inside her taking over. She shivered. Her wildness hadn't receded until Jace had smacked the wolf down himself, and Deni had fallen away from the fight.

Jace hadn't then turned around and kicked her butt, as he'd had a right to for interfering. Instead he'd touched her, licked her with his strange Feline sandpapery tongue, then held her hand after she'd changed back to human.

Deni was still shaky as they entered the fight club's main area. Jace kept hold of her hand. It was a big hand, warm but callused, his grip strong. He was a fighter, a warrior.

If Deni remembered right, Jace Warden was the son of Eric Warden, leader of the Las Vegas Shiftertown. Jace was third in command there, the second in command being Eric's sister. Jace would be in the most dominant Feline clan of his Shiftertown, and in the most dominant Feline pride of that clan. The top of the top.

Alphas usually bugged Deni, because they could be arrogant shits, but only concern and protection flowed from Jace. An alpha interested in taking care of others. What a concept.

The biggest crowd gathered around the central ring—the other two rings were empty. From throats, beast and human, came wild cries, delight in whoever was winning, groaning from those foolish enough not to back Dylan.

Jace moved through the throng to the ring. Shifters moved aside for him, most without noticing they did so. Instinct, Deni guessed—sensing that they should get out of Jace's way before he made it an order.

A large man stood at the perimeter of the ring, arms folded, the Sword of the Guardian on his back. Deni always felt a frisson of dread when she saw the sword, whose purpose was to be driven through the hearts of dead or dying Shifters. The sword pierced the heart, and the Shifter turned to dust, his or her soul following the pathway to the Summerland.

The sword shimmered a little in the flickering light. Other

Shifters gave the Guardian a wide berth, also uncomfortable with him. Kind of hard on Sean, Deni always thought, but Sean had been much less haunted since he'd taken a mate.

A human woman stood next to Sean—not his mate. She was the scrappy woman who'd tied herself to Ronan, a Kodiak bear, who was even now in the ring, fighting Dylan. The woman—Elizabeth—danced on top of the cement blocks, cheering for Ronan at the top of her lungs.

Sean would be standing as second for Dylan, his father. A second's job was to make sure that no one interfered with the fight and that the other side didn't cheat. Dylan and Ronan would go for a fair, straight fight, but other Shifters could be cunning. The seconds were there for a reason.

Dylan was the black-maned lion snarling in the middle of the ring, his paws moving lightning fast as he battled the bigger bulk of the Kodiak. Ronan was fully shifted to bear, his ruff standing up, his eyes alight with fighting fury. Ronan's Collar sparked deep into his fur, but Dylan's was quiet.

"Unfair advantage," Jace said into Deni's ear. "Dylan knows how to keep his Collar from going off."

Deni had to turn her head and stand on tiptoe to answer into Jace's ear. His hand in hers was warm, and she leaned close. "That's why he only fights the strongest: Ronan, or Spike, who's the champion. Sometimes Dylan lets his Collar go off on purpose, to keep things interesting."

"But he usually wins anyway," Jace finished.

He had a rumbling baritone that tickled inside her ear, his hot breath making Deni tingle even more. She squeezed his fingers a little, and was rewarded with an answering squeeze.

Ronan roared. His Collar was sparking, his mate yelling her encouragement, but Deni saw her worry. These matches weren't to the death, but Shifters could be badly hurt in them.

Deni could scent and sense Elizabeth's excitement tinged with fear. She also caught Sean's tenseness as he watched his father battle. If something went wrong, if one of the Shifters was hurt so much the Guardian was needed,

Sean would have to plunge his sword into the heart of either his father or his close friend.

Deni caught his sorrow—Sean had had to send one of his brothers to dust a dozen years ago—which laced through the sorrow in her own heart. Deni wished her cubs were here, her boys, but they were working at their jobs in the city, earning what little money Shifters were allowed to earn.

Dylan backed away from Ronan's onslaught, ears flat on his head. He didn't roar—Dylan's roar could shake apart the town—but his growls filled the space.

The sound caught in Deni's nerves, calling to the feral inside her. All Shifters had the instinct to throw off any polish of civilization, to revert to their wild forms, to return to the time when they'd been bred to fight and hunt. Even after a thousand and more years, Shifters retained the same basic instincts—fight or be killed, hunt or be hunted.

Shifters had come up with strict rules made to tame their inner beasts. To keep themselves from tearing each other apart after they'd fought free of their Fae masters, Shifters had agreed to certain rituals that must be performed in regard to mating, fighting, and even death. Take those away, and they were simply animals who could make themselves look human.

Deni's motorcycle accident last year had robbed her of the veneer of calm Shifters strived to learn. The wreck must have jarred something loose in Deni's brain, because she'd been fighting her instincts ever since, often losing. Knowing the bastard who'd run her down was dead had helped her begin to heal, but she wasn't there yet.

In the midst of the growls, snarls, roars, and cheers, with the scent of blood and sweat pouring from the ring, Deni's thoughts began to tangle. Her scent sense heightened, bringing in the excitement of the Shifters, the bloodlust in Dylan, the singed-fur smell from the sparking Collars, the strong male scent of Jace Warden next to her.

She probably would have been all right with Jace's calming hand in hers, if the fighting Shifters had been anyone else, but Dylan had a powerful Shifter presence. Being alpha didn't simply mean winning fights and scaring Shifters into submission. It was an indefinable something about the Shifter—scent, timbre of voice, subtle compulsion to follow this male. In animal form, it was more apparent, and Dylan was broadcasting his force loud and clear.

Since the accident, Deni had been able to use her animal senses fully in her human form. All Shifters retained some of their superior senses of hearing, scenting, and tracking ability when human, but they were muted, distant, able to be pushed aside so the Shifter could live as human without going crazy.

Not so for Deni. She had to constantly fight herself not to shift, attack, or even kill when she was confused, afraid, or angry. *Going feral* was the term. Her Collar tried to shock sense into her, but that only resulted in more pain, more confusion, more anger.

Deni smelled Dylan's fighting blood, which announced to everyone there he was far stronger and meaner than the giant bear he battled. Ronan continued swinging his enormous paws, landing blows on the smaller lion. Dylan's lithe body moved and flowed with the hits that would have crushed any Shifter who'd stood still and taken them. Dylan's lion's paws moved in a flurry, batting back the bear with the swift, manic strength of a cat.

Deni's wolf howled to life. She wanted to leap into the ring, rush to Dylan's side, and help him fight. He was her alpha—he'd been leader of all Shifters for a long time before conceding his position to his son. Ronan was lesser than Deni, and he dared to confront Dylan. Now Ronan must pay.

Deni clenched her free hand into a fist, jaw so tight it ached. She shouldn't be here—she should have gone home and not let the compelling Jace talk her into watching the battle. She now wanted more than anything to break all the rules of the fight club and run into the ring. Ronan would knock her senseless before he could stop himself, but her wolf didn't care. The bear needed to go down.

Deni started to growl, the sound rising in her throat.

Her Collar snapped a spark into her, but she didn't stop. She *couldn't* stop. And that terrified her most of all.

"Hey," a deep voice in her ear rumbled. "Hold it together."

Jace. His warmth covered her side, his stern command reaching her inner beast and stilling the need to shift. Deni realized her fingers had already changed to wolf claws, and fur ran from her head down her back, which was bared by the sarong.

Jace didn't let go of her hand, though she felt her claws pierce his skin. He ran his other hand, warm and broad-palmed, up and down her back, which returned to human smoothness.

"Want to go?" he asked her.

Deni nodded. She couldn't see much anymore—the fires and lanterns blurred into one whirling light, the shouts and growls blending into a mass of animal sound.

Jace tugged her away, again becoming the lifeline that drew her through the crowd. In the howling, swirling madness, Jace was a constant, his warmth pulling her onward.

He took her into the parking lot, turning her away from the lights. Once the cool night air touched her, darkness erasing the maddening lights, Deni drew a long breath. Her fur and claws receded, leaving her on her human feet, shaking.

"I shouldn't have done that," Jace was saying as they threaded their way through parked vehicles. She heard his voice but didn't pay much attention to the words. "I shouldn't have taken you in there. I didn't realize it was that bad."

"It's bad," Deni said, nodding. She wasn't concentrating on her words either. "I should have stayed home tonight, but I needed . . ." She shivered. "I don't know what I needed."

Not true. Deni had needed escape, life, not hiding in the dark. Her sons had gone to work, Ellison had taken his mate, Maria, out for dinner and probably sex, and the rest of Shiftertown had emptied to attend the fight club. Sit at home and mope or go out and be with her friends and neighbors? She'd been tired of moping, so here she was.

Deni's uncontrolled instincts were punishing her now.

Jace had known to take her out of there before she did something stupid, but the wildness in her didn't calm. It needed release.

Deni's wolf needed to fight, to hunt, to kill. Robbed of that, the she-wolf in her wanted the nearest thing to it.

She swung to Jace, his scent filling her, his strength calling to her. He was solid, strong, alpha, male, and he was here with her in the dark. She couldn't have stopped herself even if she'd wanted to.

Deni slammed both hands to Jace's chest. He caught her with a strong grip but fell against the side of a pickup, carrying her back with him. He had a musky male scent, a little wild, like the woods on a moonlit night. The moon was high and full tonight, always irresistible to a wolf.

Jace's eyes were unusual, jade green, the color heightened by his tanned face and brown black hair he'd buzzed short. He was large too, but agile and athletic.

He watched her, not shoving her away, not angry. Just watching.

Another surge of sound came from the arena, human and animal crying out for blood. Deni snarled, pinned Jace against the truck, and kissed him hard on the mouth.

CHAPTER TWO

Jace found himself with his arms full of gorgeous woman. A *hungry* gorgeous woman. Her kiss pushed him flat against the truck, the ridges of its door digging into his back.

Against his front, he felt nothing but soft woman—breasts, hands, thighs. Deni's mouth was all over his, lips seeking, tongue swiping into his mouth, giving him a taste of spice and wildness.

Jace told himself to push her away, but he cupped her waist and ended up dragging her closer. Another roar came from the arena, galvanizing her, winding up Jace's heat in response.

The sarong bared much of her flesh—the garment clasped at one shoulder and wrapped her hips, leaving Deni's neck, arms, and most of her back bare. Her warm skin was silken under Jace's fingers, curves lush. A full-bodied Shifter woman.

Deni was tall, as Shifter women were, but Jace was taller. He scooped her into him, liking how she fit against him. Her buttocks were a handful, her breasts the best cushions.

He opened his mouth to hers, welcoming her greedy

kisses. She was hot in his arms, she smelled good, and her hair was silken against his skin.

It was exciting and erotic, pulling a woman he'd just met into his arms, the two of them wound up from the fighting, wanting to relieve themselves in the shadows with fervent, hard sex. Her body rubbed his hard-on, tingling raw pleasure through him. Some Shifters were already scratching their itches tonight in this parking lot, with humans or other Shifters. By the sounds and scents, they were at it in cars or in the shadows beyond. Frantic, basic coupling.

Deni groped for the button of his jeans, fingers sliding along the zipper. In a few seconds, she'd have his hot cock in her hands, and he'd be done for.

"Not here," Jace managed to say. He had just enough presence of mind to not want to be caught banging Ellison Rowe's sister up against the side of a Shifter's pickup. A few steps and they'd be in deep shadow, on hard Texas earth.

Deni nodded, her eyes the light gray of her wolf. Jace swung her off her feet and ran with her beyond the circle of light.

He didn't bother trying to find a soft place to lie down in the darkness. Jace could hold the both of them up—he was plenty strong. One tug of strings and the sarong fell, baring her to him. Jace buried his nose in her neck as he nipped her flesh. He loved how she smelled. Feminine, strong, beautiful.

Deni managed to get his jeans open. Jace let them slither down his legs, then his underwear followed. He lifted her, cradling her hips, and she slid straight onto him.

Her eyes widened. Beautiful silver white eyes, moonlight eyes. Jace caught her head with one hand, loving the feel of her hair against his fingers, and he kissed her.

Hot, amazing woman wrapped around him, as hungry as he was. Jace was deep inside her, the penetration satisfying, filling him up as much as he filled her.

Deni moaned a little against his mouth. Jace released her from the kiss, but he wanted to go on kissing her, her mouth hot. Goddess, how lucky was he that she'd run to join in his fight?

Jace thrust what little he could, lifting her with hands under her buttocks and lowering her onto him again in small, swift jerks. They were both making noises now, and not being quiet. Anyone passing would know two Shifters were finding relief out here in the dark.

This was raw, rough sex. No finesse, no romance. Just a man and a woman doing what the Goddess had made them to do. Come together, join, mate, create.

"Jace."

Deni cried his name, then her head went back, passion making her incoherent. Jace held on to her, taking their combined weight on his planted feet, rocking to seek more and more of her.

He gathered her hard against him, feeling his seed build in its need to reach her. Shifters wanted more than anything to make more Shifters, and Jace's body knew it. Instinct, desire, whatever he wanted to call it. It took over, and he couldn't fight it.

"Son of a *bitch*," he whispered as his climax hit him, harder than any he'd had in his life. He felt his seed go and felt her take it, heard his own shouts drowned in hers and another, final victory roar from the arena.

Jace shuddered, whatever the hell he said lost to the night. Deni clung to him, her gasps of pleasure not muffled. She hung on to him until the last thrust, and then Jace simply held her, wondering that he'd found something so beautiful so unexpectedly.

His body was still crazed with need. He felt his cock rise again, not that it had deflated much.

Oh, hell no. Jace was crawling with heat, desire rampaging through his body. He thought he'd be sated with a quick coupling—that both of them would be sated.

But the Shifter in him had other ideas. *Mate. Take. Mine.* "Son of a bitch," he whispered again.

This was *not* the time for mating frenzy—that basic Shifter need to take a mate someplace safe where they could screw for days. And days. Weeks, even months if need be. Not to come out until they were both half-starved and exhausted, and the female was plump with cubs.

Shifters could follow their rituals, ceremonies, laws, protocol—whatever they called it this century—but the truth was that the mating frenzy could still grab them by the balls at any time and not let them go.

The woman in Jace's arms had awakened his frenzy as no other female had before. This was crazy. Jace had only just met her—he hadn't known her more than an hour.

The mating frenzy didn't care.

With effort, Jace made himself loosen his hold on her. At least he could give Deni the chance to run.

Then I can hunt her, the leopard in him said with glee. *Chase her. Catch her. Make her mine.*

He was so screwed.

Deni gasped. Jace hadn't been able to look away from her, her light hair and face a pale smudge in the darkness, but now her eyes were round with fear as she gazed off at something behind him. Jace turned his head to see what had caught her worry, and his own breath constricted.

Across the flat plain behind the arena, about a mile away Jace would guess, came lights. Flashing lights—red and blue—and the white pulses of headlights. A ton of them, sirens blaring, all heading toward the arena.

"*S*hit." Jace snarled and grabbed at his jeans, zipping them as Deni groped for her fallen sarong. She wrapped the cloth around herself, fastening it quickly, her heart pounding.

Human police poured toward them, racing for the Shifters' very illegal fight club. Not good. Not good at all.

Even as Jace pulled on his denim jacket and started at a run for the arena, Deni following, her body thrummed with elation. For a year now, she'd been walking around in a half-aware state, but at this moment, in spite of the imminent danger, she was *alive*.

She was a little embarrassed she'd grabbed Jace like

that, barely able to control her mating urge, but dear God
and Goddess, he'd taken her in a storm. Deni wasn't a
stranger to casual sex—Shifters often needed to burn off
steam—but this encounter went beyond in intensity anything she'd experienced before.

Deni couldn't stop watching Jace's lithe body as he ran,
the grace of his wildcat evident even in his human form.
He smelled of the road, of Texas dust, of himself, and now
of what they'd done together. The combination made Deni
want to catch him, throw him down, and fling herself on top
of him. She was shameless, but he was beautiful, virile, and
strong, and Deni wanted him with a mindlessness that unnerved her. Even the string of lights and sirens couldn't
dampen her need.

Deni sprinted into the arena alongside Jace to find that
Dylan's match had finished, though the noise hadn't much
lessened. Ronan was sitting heavily on a bench, human
again, breathing hard and looking rueful. His mate was
wiping his naked body with a towel, giving him it's-all-
right-I-still-love-you caresses.

Dylan took his triumph in stride, but quietly, without
gloating. His mate, on the other hand, a tall blonde named
Glory, watched Dylan admiringly, her gaze roving Dylan's
honed body. She opened her mouth, probably to boast that
her mate was undefeatable, but Jace's voice cut over the din.

"Cops!" he boomed. "Coming. *Now!*"

The Shifters who'd been celebrating, or grumbling about
Ronan's loss, came alert. Shifters stopped, jerked around, stared
at Jace or gazed beyond him. Stillness, silence, and animal
wariness took over, erasing anything human about them.

Then one of the Shifters yelled, "Go to ground!" and
the arena erupted again into noise.

"No!" Jace bellowed over them all. *"Stop!"*

The power of his voice sent a hush rippling across the
Shifters again. Jace had the compelling presence of a
leader, Deni noted with admiration, the ability to make others stand still and listen, no matter how dire the situation.

Jace had his hands up. "If we run, they chase," he said,

his words carrying across the arena. "The slowest will be caught."

The Shifters' unease didn't lessen, Deni saw, and the smell of fear was high. They wanted to flee, and damn the consequences.

"The lad's right," Dylan said. In spite of his bruised and abraded body, he stood upright, his blue eyes hot. "No one gets taken. We stand."

"Then we all get arrested," someone else shouted.

No one moved, though. They wouldn't ignore Dylan.

"No, we won't," Deni said. She stepped up onto one of the cement blocks, using Jace's shoulder to steady herself. "They're going to find us—no time to get away. But *we* can decide what they find. I have an idea."

In a few brief sentences, Deni outlined what she had in mind. The humans looked bewildered, but Shifter faces began to relax, smiles starting to take the place of fear.

"You're cunning, sweetheart," Jace said. His hand on her back was warm as he slanted her a grin. "Anything you're not good at?"

Deni went hot all over, her face flaming as his eyes sparkled. She wasn't sure what the consequences would be of her crazed mating in the parking lot with Jace, but the look he was giving her made her decide that losing control had been worth it.

"You heard her," Dylan said. "This is what we do."

Shifters broke off, organizing themselves as only Shifters could when the need was upon them. The police cars and lights came nearer, sirens cutting the air. Deni still sensed deep fear, the humans barely containing it, the Shifters striving to suppress it.

The waves of panic caught her, jarring Deni's already-heightened nerves. The wolf in her growled, wanting to shift, to confront her enemies and make them run. To chase them if need be and bring them down.

Deni clenched her hands, shuddering, a bead of sweat running down her back. Damn it. If she lost it now, she'd condemn them all.

A comforting touch warmed her shoulder. "Easy," Jace said, his breath in her ear.

He was leaning close, his body heat wrapping around her, his scent relaxing the tightness inside her. Deni's fear eased before a wash of relief and also desire. Jace put his hand in hers, and she leaned into him, wanting to twine herself around his big body again.

Sean came to them, sword on his back glinting, and took Deni's other hand as the Shifters formed circles. "Smart idea, Deni. I commend you," he said. Then his nostrils widened, taking in her scent combined with Jace's. His gaze sharpened as it moved over Jace's mussed hair and Deni's hastily tied sarong. "Shite," he said to Jace. "You've been in Austin, what, twenty minutes, lad? You didn't even stop for a meal first."

Deni went hot again, though she kept her head up under Sean's scrutiny and made herself meet his gaze.

"Keep it down," Jace said. "Don't embarrass the lady."

"Only if *you* can keep it down." Sean didn't burst into laughter, but his big smile showed amusement enough.

"Shut up, both of you," Deni said, certain her face must be burgundy red. "They're here."

Every law enforcement agency in this county must have answered whatever call had reported Shifters up here. Cars and SUVs surrounded the arena, floodlights glaring over the circles of Shifters, gleaming in eyes, glinting on Collars. Police in bulletproof vests swarmed out of the vehicles and into the arena, carrying guns, chains, nets, and tranq rifles. They'd come prepared to round up all of them.

The cops stopped when they found, not Shifters fighting in primitive frenzy, but Shifters and humans standing in quiet circles. The largest circle, where Deni and Jace stood, outlined the perimeter of the arena floor, with concentric circles inside it, smaller and smaller as they neared the middle of the arena. The circles of Shifters moved slowly, each one in the direction opposite of the one before it, the Shifters walking in a slow, shuffling gait. The smallest circle ringed around Dylan, Glory, and Dylan's grandson, Connor, who stood in front of a trashcan full of fire.

Shifters held hands—or had tails wrapped around hands, if they were still in animal form—and chanted a prayer to the Goddess as they moved. Each Shifter spoke quietly, but the mingling voices reverberated to the starry sky.

Deni clasped Jace's hand tightly on one side, Sean's on the other. Sean should technically be in the innermost circle with his father and nephew, but he'd stopped to make sure Deni was all right and hadn't had time to reach it.

Sean had his gaze on the inner circle and his father, but Jace looked at the ground, his shoulders hunching. The posture made him appear smaller than he was, less challenging, just another Shifter in the bunch. Deni understood why. Jace wasn't supposed to be in Texas at all. If the human police discovered he was from the Las Vegas Shiftertown, here without official permission, he'd be arrested, and things could only go downhill from there.

Shifters weren't allowed to leave the states where their Shiftertowns were located without special permits, and Jace didn't have one. Deni knew that without asking—permission was difficult to obtain and took forever. Jace had been coming and going from the Austin Shiftertown when he pleased for the last year or so, to work with Dylan and Liam on the Collars. Shifters like Jace had figured out how to go where they wanted whenever they wanted, but humans didn't need to know that. If one of the cops realized that Jace wasn't from around here . . .

Deni moved her body so both she and Sean shielded Jace from the cops who stopped closest to them.

The police had halted in uncertainty, but they kept their weapons trained on the Shifters, tranq guns at the ready. The two cops in charge, a man and a woman, pushed their way through the circles of Shifters until they reached Dylan in the center.

"Tell me what the hell is going on here," the man said, his pistol trained on Dylan.

Dylan gave him a cold look. "A Shifter religious ceremony." His words came clearly, and the Shifters stopped chanting and fell silent. "What does it look like?"

"What kind of religious ceremony?" the male cop asked, not impressed. "Explain it to me."

"It's private." Dylan's voice held an edge.

"Keep it together, Dad," Sean whispered next to Deni. His gaze was on Dylan, as though he could will his father to stay calm.

"I can arrest everyone," the cop said to Dylan. "And question each and every one of you. I have the manpower and the time. Or I can arrest you by yourself, Morrissey. Your choice."

Connor spoke up, his voice shrill and sounding a few years younger than he was. "It's a memorial ceremony. For my dad."

A few of the cops moved uneasily, but most of them went more rigid.

"Who's your dad?" the male cop asked.

Dylan answered, "Kenny Morrissey. My son. He died twelve years ago. We're remembering him tonight."

"Remembering him how?"

Dylan shrugged, keeping his voice steady. "Prayers, the circle dance. We usually burn photos or other mementoes." He gestured at the flames in the trashcan next to them. "Kenny was well liked, and his brother is now the Shiftertown leader. Everyone wanted to come."

"What about fights?" the cop asked. "Bouts between humans and Shifters?"

Dylan scowled. "I don't know what shit people have been telling you, but Shifter religious ceremonies are peaceful." That was absolute truth. "No violence in any of them."

"Not what I heard," the cop said. "Cuff him," he told the female cop beside him.

Connor started forward in anguish but both Dylan and Glory stepped in his way. "It's all right, lad," Dylan said. He gave the two cops a nod. "You don't have to cuff me. I'm happy to come with you and explain everything. I bet someone told you a bunch of Shifters had gathered here, and it made your higher-ups nervous."

"Something like that," the cop said, his tone still sharp.

The woman moved forward with the cuffs. Dylan gave her a resigned look and held out his hands. "If I come with you, the others go home."

"You don't have a choice," the male cop said. "But, sure, the others can go home. In fact, they need to go, *now*. My officers will escort them out. If I like what you say downtown, then they can stay home."

Sean released Deni's hand. "I'd better go with them," he said in a low voice. "Dad can scare the shite out of people just by looking at them. I'm more diplomatic." He said it without boasting. "Ronan," he called. "Make sure Connor and Glory get home all right."

"You got it, Sean," Ronan said.

"Ride with me," Jace whispered to Deni as Sean walked away and the Shifters and humans began to disperse. The cops started herding everyone out to the parking lot, Shifters growling and rumbling in annoyance, but not arguing, their human friends walking along quietly.

"I came with Ronan and Elizabeth," Deni said nervously. She knew Jace had ridden in on a motorcycle— she'd heard it when he'd pulled up.

"I need to pretend I didn't come alone. Ronan and Elizabeth will understand."

Deni knew Jace was trying to make himself look as though he belonged in this Shiftertown. If he went off with Deni, as though part of the community, he might escape scrutiny. But that meant Deni would have to climb onto the back of a motorcycle.

"What happened to you?" another cop asked before Deni could answer Jace.

Deni stopped short, but the man wasn't talking to her. He was looking behind them, at Ronan, his tranq rifle pointed at the big man.

Ronan did look bad, his arms cut and bruised, one eye swollen. He'd skimmed on clothes while the cops were closing in, and Elizabeth now had her arm firmly around him. "I'm a bouncer," Ronan said. "At a bar. Humans like to throw punches at me." He shrugged. "I let them."

The cop gave him a look of suspicion, but he didn't pursue it. Instead he stepped in front of Jace and gave him a belligerent scowl. "What about you? You let humans take punches at you too?"

Jace's face, neck, and torso, bared by his open jacket, bore bruises from his fight with Broderick. Deni realized something she hadn't earlier—a few of the marks on Jace's neck were from her fingers, some from her teeth. She flushed.

Jace gave the cop a lazy smile without lifting his head all the way. He draped his arm around Deni and pressed a kiss to her hair. "Religious ceremonies can be boring," he said, his voice slightly slurred. "Found something better to do for a while."

The cop got a knowing look, and Deni blushed harder. Well, Jace wasn't lying. What they'd done in the darkness had been swift, hot, and glorious, not boring at all.

"Yeah, well, keep it at home," the cop said.

"Love to." Jace kept up his careless slouch, leaning on Deni, his arm around her.

The cop, fortunately, left them alone, looking around for others to harass.

"You'll have to drive," Jace said when they reached the bike. Deni thought she recognized it as belonging to Liam, who must have lent it to Jace. "I acted a little drunk so he'd leave us alone, but if he's watching, I don't want to give him an excuse to stop me for DUI." He gave her a grin and dangled the keys in front of her. "So tonight you're my designated driver."

CHAPTER THREE

Deni looked at the keys Jace pressed into her hand, and blind panic washed through her. "I can't." She couldn't draw a breath. "Jace, I'm sorry. I can't."

"Can't?" Jace frowned down at her, his expression a mixture of compassion, curiosity, and the need to hurry. "Why? Never driven a motorcycle before?"

"I have. I own one. Or, I did. It's just . . ." Deni's body was cold, fear pumping through her. "I was in a wreck on my motorcycle," she said in a rush. "A man ran me off the road last year, on purpose. I was badly hurt—took me a long time to recover. I haven't been able to ride a motorcycle since then. Plus I have . . . episodes. I don't know what I'm doing for stretches of time—I've even attacked my own family. I start to go feral. Like tonight, when I fought, and when we—"

"Hey," Jace interrupted her hurried flow of words, his voice warm in the darkness. "Stop. It's all right."

"It's not all right. It's a long way from all right." Deni drew a shuddering breath. "I haven't been able to so much as get *on* a motorcycle, not even to ride with someone else. I panic—I can't do it. Sorry, I should have told you."

"Yeah, well, we didn't get much chance to talk, did we?" Jace's eyes glinted, the teasing light in them making her both embarrassed and relieved.

She handed the keys out to him. "Thanks for understanding."

Jace didn't take them. "I mean, I get that this is hard for you, Den, but you're still going to have to drive the bike. Sorry, sweetheart, I can't risk getting stopped or arrested, or even questioned. If they find out who I am, things could get bad. Not only for me, but my father, Liam, Dylan— maybe all Shifters." He slowed his words, as though sensing Deni's fear escalate again. "You'll be all right. I'll be with you."

The keys were heavy in her hand. "Oh, right. So I won't black out and crash us, because you'll be on the seat behind me?"

"Something like that." Jace brushed his hand over her arm, his fingers blunt and warm.

Deni's fear was too raw to be easily calmed, but she was grateful to him for trying. She knew she had to get on the damned bike and take them out of there—he was right about that—but she couldn't make her feet move.

One of the cops was looking their way. The man waited a beat or two, then started for them.

Jace gave Deni a small shove toward the motorcycle. "We've got to go." Another push, moving her another step. "Only for a few miles. Once we're off their radar, we can switch."

"I can't ride in *this*." Deni gestured to herself, the fabric wrapped around her body. She had, in fact, ridden in a sarong before, but the wind would be cold and chafing. Maybe he'd take pity on her and find someone else to take him to Shiftertown.

Jace slid out of his denim jacket and draped it around her shoulders. That left his torso bare, but he didn't seem the more vulnerable for it. "You can wear this."

The jacket held his body heat and his scent. Deni closed her eyes. She looked for something peaceful inside herself, a place she used to be able to find. Jace would be with her. He'd make sure they reached Shiftertown. She willed herself to believe.

"Now," Jace said in her ear.

Deni jumped, but his voice galvanized her. She took a deep breath and started to swing her leg over the bike.

It got stuck halfway. Deni's heart thumped—*hurry, hurry*—but she couldn't make her leg go over the seat. She clenched her muscles, willing her body to obey, but she was shaking, her breath leaving her.

Jace swarmed onto the bike behind her, shoving her leg all the way over with his. There, she was on, with Jace wrapping his warm, bare arms around her.

The motorcycle was big—Liam, who owned it, was a big man—but Shifter women were tall. Deni could ride it.

Deni trembled all over as she started the bike, her body brushing back against the solid warmth of Jace's. The motorcycle rumbled beneath them, the deep throb of a well-tuned Harley, which let every vehicle near it know what a powerhouse it was.

Jace tightened his arms around her, pretending to have to cling hard because he was drunk, but he turned the hold into a steadying one. Deni relaxed a little, enough to glide the bike forward, lifting her feet smoothly as they went.

The narrow road back to the highway was dark, rutted, and unnerving. The headlight sliced through blackness, the Texas night vast. Far ahead, tiny lights marked where other Shifters were driving away.

Deni started to calm even more. Her body instinctively knew how to balance the bike, how to guide the big machine, even when the road was rough. Her panic lessened, but then, out here, there were no other cars, no city streets, no humans running their vehicles into Shifters and ruining their lives.

Jace's arms around Deni, his warm body at her back, reminded her of their wild coupling, beautiful for all its brutality. Jace had a tall, strong body, one Deni would be willing to climb again. And again. Deni wished she and Jace could be truly alone, racing down the road, nothing on their minds but the wind, stars, and what they'd do together at the journey's end.

They reached the highway, the traffic sparse. Deni swung the bike to the right, heading for the lights of civilization. Austin glowed on the horizon, the city beckoning.

Deni had grown to love Austin and its quirkiness—the music, Sixth Street on a Saturday night, bars that ranged from upscale to shabby honky-tonks, the bats emerging every sunset from the Congress Avenue Bridge, the town's sense of being different from everyplace else in the world, even from the rest of Texas. Deni had found something like happiness settling here, with her brother, Ellison, and her sons, Will and Jackson. Not the greatest existence, living in Shiftertown, but at least they were together.

And then the bastard human, who'd been involved in some nasty business regarding Shifters that Ellison and Deni had helped clear up, had deliberately run down Deni on her motorcycle, robbing her of control and any sense of tranquility. Tonight, coupling with Jace and now having him hold on to her was the closest she'd come to finding peace again.

Deni turned onto the 183 and headed north. She was sure Jace would tell her to pull over any minute so he could take over the driving, but he didn't. Jace kept his arms around her, his body leaning with hers as she made the turn and joined traffic.

Deni started to shake again as traffic thickened, cars and trucks surging around them to head for Austin from points east of San Antonio. Jace's warm hands moved on Deni's belly, as though he knew she needed his reassuring touch. Deni felt a little better, but when they reached Lockhart, she pulled off to a gas station.

"You can take over now," she said, sliding off the helmet.

Jace didn't dismount. "You're doing fine. Keep going."

"Jace, come on. I'm scared. The wreck really messed me up. The guy who did it was trying to grab me—he was kidnapping Shifters."

Jace's eyes narrowed. "I heard about him. He didn't get you though, right?"

"Only because there were too many other people around. He nearly killed me."

"But he's dead now." Jace spoke with conviction. Dylan must have told him some of that story.

"Yes." Deni swallowed, her mouth dry. She wondered if Dylan had told Jace exactly how the man had died, and Deni's part in it. "My mind knows that I'm safe, but my instincts don't. The wolf inside me hasn't fully processed it yet, I guess."

Jace kept frowning. "I see that. But I'm right here with you. Show yourself you can do it. Don't let him win."

Deni wanted to—she truly did. Her brother had given her similar advice: *Don't let the asshole take everything away from you.*

Wise words, but still, it was hard. "What if I black out?"

Jace shot her a grin. "I'll wake you up."

"Jace, I *can't*."

"You're wrong. You can."

Deni grasped the handlebars. She used to love to ride, she and Ellison going all out on the back roads, side by side, racing. She missed it.

She gave Jace a challenging look. "What if I get off right here and refuse to ride?"

Jace shrugged. "Then I take the bike back to Liam and send you a cab. Or you can shift to wolf and go cross-country."

"Oh, thanks."

The grin returned. "Or, you can drive."

He was a shithead. A sexy one. Damn it.

Everything in Deni wanted to do this. Waiting at this gas station for a cab certainly didn't appeal to her, especially not with the few good old boys starting to eye them. Humans and Shifters weren't supposed to tangle, but out in farm and ranch country, in the middle of the night, rules didn't always stop anyone.

Deni slapped the helmet back on her head. She revved the bike and pulled out of the gas station, opening up the engine once she got out of town to make it throb.

Wind rushed past her, the bike rumbled under her, and Jace, hard-bodied and hot, hung on to her. Deni still felt the ache of their rough lovemaking, and knew she carried his seed inside her. What would happen if that seed took root? The thought of having another cub frightened her almost as much as riding did, but it elated her at the same time.

Deni navigated them onto the 130 then off when the 183 split from it again, and kept on straight north for Austin. She was sweating by the time they hit Austin proper, Jace's jacket cutting the bracing wind. The increasing traffic made her panic rise once more, but Jace was there, caressing her, his touch calming.

Excitement hit Deni when she rolled into the mostly deserted streets around Shiftertown and pulled the motorcycle up behind the bar Liam managed. She swung off the bike after Jace dismounted, and yanked off her helmet.

"I did it. Goddess, Jace—I did it!"

"Yeah, you did." Jace swept his arms around her and pulled her against him. "You were great. And you didn't even pass out."

Deni was too buoyed to respond to the remark. She gave him a hard kiss on the mouth, loving the taste of him. Her excitement increased, her need for him not slaked. Jace didn't discourage her. His kiss turned hard, his hands on her back strong.

Deni made herself ease away from him, though he remained holding her a moment, his eyes dark green in the moonlight. Shaking a little, Deni stepped back, slid his jacket off, and handed it back to him, though it was a shame to watch him cover himself.

Jace shrugged the jacket on then took a backpack from one of the saddlebags and slung it over his shoulder. He put his arm around Deni. "Come in and have a beer with me?"

This was Deni's chance to tell him she needed to go home, to wait for her sons to get in from work, her brother and his mate to return from their date. To go back to watching everyone else live, while she sat in the corner and tried to stay sane.

To hell with that. Deni squared her shoulders, slid her hand through Jace's offered arm, and walked in with him through the back door.

They emerged into the loud bar, half full of Shifters. A tall Shifter covered in tatts spied them and stepped in front of Jace.

"Liam wants to see you," he said with his characteristic brevity, then turned around and walked away.

"That's Spike," Deni said. "Man of few words."

"I've met him." Jace took Deni's hand and led her through the crowd, making his way to the black-haired Irishman leaning on the bar. He wasn't tending it—Shifters weren't allowed to serve alcohol. A human barman did that.

Liam Morrissey turned as they approached, as though sensing them come, which he probably had. He wouldn't have been able to hear them over the jukebox, or smell them over the odors of smoke, alcohol, sweaty humans, and Shifters who'd also just returned from the fight club. But Liam had the uncanny knack of knowing where everyone was at all times. Liam was tall, like his brother, Sean, and had the same intense blue eyes. Those eyes took in Jace, then Deni, then Liam leaned forward and pulled Jace into a Shifter welcoming embrace.

Jace dropped his backpack on a barstool and let Liam enfold him. Because the two had met before and liked each other, the hug was more cordial and less wary than many alpha male exchanges. No veiled hint that each would rip out the other's throat if they had half a chance. Just friendship and camaraderie, arms tightening on each other's backs.

Liam released Jace, turned to Deni, and pulled her into his arms as well. This hug was more reassuring, the Shiftertown leader trying to calm one of his own. "Well done," Liam said quietly into her ear, and Deni warmed with pleasure.

Liam released Deni and found Jace right next to him. *Right* next to him, as in slap up against him. Jace's eyes had tightened, and he pinned Liam with a warning stare.

Liam reached past Jace for a half-filled bottle of beer he'd left on the bar and held it without drinking. "Spike and

Ronan told me what happened out there with the cops." He gave Deni a grin. "I see you two already celebrated."

As she had under Sean's scrutiny, Deni flushed, but Jace looked unworried. "Have you heard anything from Dylan?" Jace asked him.

Liam lost his smile. "They took Dad downtown. My mate is with him, and so is Sean. They told me not to come." He nodded, as though he agreed. "Kim knows what she's doing."

Liam's mate was a defense lawyer who now specialized in defending Shifters. Liam was right that she was plenty competent, and Dylan and Sean were good at keeping human attention away from Shifters. Deni saw the tightness in Liam, however, sensed his need to race to the police station and use any means necessary to extract his father.

"Did the police talk to you?" Jace asked him.

"Aye, they did. Came rushing in here, demanding to know about this fight club they'd heard about. Of course, I knew nothing, did I?" Liam, as leader, had decided to look the other way about the fight club, which went against Shifter laws as well as human. Though the fight clubs had rules, they were dangerous, but Liam had acknowledged long ago that he couldn't prevent them. "A detective and half a dozen uniforms came in here the same time the arena was being raided, or I would have warned my dad and Sean." Deni saw the outrage in his eyes that he'd been blindsided.

"Well, they found it somehow," Jace said. "You have a leak. Just to reassure you—it isn't me."

"Didn't think it was, lad."

If Liam *had* thought Jace was the one who'd betrayed the whereabouts of the fight club, Jace wouldn't be standing here speaking calmly to Liam. He'd have been stopped at the door, and Liam would now be disemboweling him in the parking lot.

"Do we lie low?" Jace asked.

Liam answered with one quick shake of his head but no words. Not all Shifters were privy to the work Liam and his family were doing on the Collars. Need to know only.

Most Shifters were trustworthy, but as tonight had proved, leaks happened.

Liam looked at Deni again and started to smile. "A memorial service. Good thinking, lass." He chuckled.

"It was the first logical thing I could think of," Deni said. "I'm sorry I used your family's grief as a distraction."

Liam shook his head, his eyes bright with mirth. "Kenny would have laughed his balls off. He always loved a good joke, did Kenny."

Liam was grinning, but Deni saw the moisture in his eyes, his sorrow for his dead brother never far away.

"Then we'll meet as appointed," Jace broke in. "Unless you wave me off."

"Aye, get some rest." Liam's amusement returned as he turned to Deni again. "*Rest*, mind. Looks like you need it." He gave her a quiet nod. "Like I said, well done, lass."

"Leader's pet," Jace whispered in Deni's ear as he guided her through the crowded bar, his hand on the small of her back. His laugh did warm things to her. "Let's get you home."

W alking Deni home was delayed when Broderick came into the bar, followed by Shifters looking enough like him to be his brothers. Jace felt Deni's rage and worry increase, her body vibrating under his hand.

"We don't like outsiders," one of Broderick's brothers said, stepping in front of Jace. "Don't like them coming in and taking our women."

Deni was around Jace before he saw her move. "Suck on it," Deni said. "I thought I was too crazy for you all, anyway."

Broderick showed his teeth in a smile. "She's got good reflexes, for a nutcase."

Jace pulled Deni back behind him and moved to Broderick, the clear leader of this bunch. "Keep your shit to yourself and your brothers quiet," he said, "or I'll wipe the floor with your ass. Again."

Broderick glanced around Jace to Deni, and his eyes

widened as he realized what other Shifters had been all night—that Jace and Deni had gotten to know each other in the dark out at the fight club. Broderick lifted his hands. "Hey, if you're that frenzied by her, you take her. You'll be doing us all a favor. Hope you can keep her under control."

Jace had Broderick by the throat before Broderick could blink. Jace surprised even himself with the move, and his speed. "What did I just tell you?"

Jace was aware of Shifters turning, watching, stilling. The music pumped on, a loud country song, but the Shifters stopped dancing, talking, and drinking to watch.

Broderick's brother was right about one thing—Jace was an outsider. He was a dominant and sanctioned by Dylan and Liam, but that wouldn't matter if the entire Shifter community didn't want him. A pack, en masse, could kill an alpha and not care.

He felt Deni behind him—close behind him—pressed against his back, but she wasn't trying to soothe him out of his rage or stop him. Jace sensed her excitement, her uncontrolled need to fight. If he followed up his threat on Broderick, Deni would be right beside him, battling it out with him. The thought made him warm, gave him strength.

Liam was still at the bar, watching. Doing nothing. He wanted to see how Jace would handle this.

Letting Broderick go would decrease Jace's standing in this Shiftertown. Not letting him go might get him killed.

A very large hand landed on Jace's shoulder, another on Broderick's. Jace got a whiff of an annoyed Kodiak bear Shifter who hadn't showered since his arena fight.

"Take it out of the bar, boys," Ronan said. "Better idea—Broderick, you stay here and get rat-faced drunk like you do every night, and you . . ." He gave Jace the slightest shake. "You go and sleep it off. You're supposed to be holing up at Dylan's house, but he's off trying to stay out of jail. Take Deni home, and crash on Ellison's couch."

Ronan, as bouncer, was breaking the impasse. Smart. Ronan's intervention let Jace save face, and Broderick didn't get his ass handed to him. Jace had no doubt that

Liam had signaled Ronan somehow, but Liam still watched as though only mildly interested.

Jace eased the pressure of his fingers around Broderick's throat. Broderick's Collar sparked once, jumping electricity into Jace's hand, but Jace didn't jerk away. He opened his fingers slowly and lowered his arm. Broderick remained where he was, not stepping back or rubbing his neck, which was imprinted with Jace's finger marks.

Jace deliberately turned away from him. "Good idea," Jace said to Ronan. "By the way, you fought a good fight out there."

Ronan gave him a brief nod of thanks, but he moved himself solidly between Jace and Broderick. If they decided to go for each other again, they'd have to do it around the wall of Ronan. Jace might outrank Ronan in dominance, but there was no disputing that Ronan was huge.

Jace took a step back, showing he wouldn't push it, and held his hand out to Deni.

He sensed Deni's relief as she took his hand, but also her disappointment that another fight with Broderick wouldn't ensue. She said nothing to Jace, only gave Broderick a final glare, and then Jace led Deni to the door and out into the night.

Deni started walking swiftly once they left the bar, moving faster and faster, until she was nearly dragging Jace across the empty lot and toward the streets of Shiftertown. In the middle of the dusty, weed-choked field, Jace pulled her to a halt.

"Hold up," he said. "Tell me something—what the hell was that?"

Deni's gray eyes gleamed in the darkness. "What the hell was what?"

"You." Jace pointed his finger at her face. "Egging me on in there. Not *Be careful, Jace, you don't want to get yourself into trouble.* More like, *Go on, Jace. Kick his ass!* You wanted to see me get taken down by that whole bar, did you?"

"No." Deni clenched her hands, as though resisting the

urge to nibble the end of his finger. "Broderick just pisses me off. And you wouldn't have been taken down by the whole bar. I saw you fight—they'd have backed off."

"Were you this bloodthirsty before your accident?"

Deni hesitated, her chest rising with her breath. "I don't know."

Jace put his hands on her arms, which were cold. The night was cooling, and her flesh, bared by the sarong, rose in goose bumps. "You said fighting makes you want to fight," he said. "But we weren't fighting in there. Not yet."

"But you wanted to." Deni rested her fingers on Jace's forearms. "I sensed that loud and clear. You were ready to rip out Broderick's throat. I can take his crap, but you couldn't. Are *you* always this bloodthirsty?"

Not until today. He made himself grin. "Everyone at home thinks I'm reasonable and a peacemaker." *Good old Jace. He'll calm everyone down.*

"Yeah? Not sure I'd want to meet your family, then."

"You would. You'd like my dad, and his mate." He rubbed her arms. "Too cold out here. Let's get you home."

Deni shivered, as though realizing how lightly dressed she was. "Fine. Though I'm not sure about you sleeping on the couch. Liam might have room at his house. Or Spike might."

She started to turn away. Jace thought about finding space in a dark house that didn't contain her, and something kicked him in the gut.

Jace dragged her back to him. Deni landed against his chest, her gray eyes going wide. He felt her heart beating rapidly as he scooped her to him, slid his hand to the back of her neck, and pulled her up for a hard kiss.

CHAPTER FOUR

Their mouths met in a frenzy. Deni clung to Jace, her breath hot on his lips, her kisses wild, hungry.

Jace wrapped his arms around her. This woman, this delicious female, was awakening something he'd never felt before—need, primal and intense, which all Shifters possessed, but which Jace had only experienced dimly before this. Even the hormonal craziness of his Transition to adulthood hadn't spiked the intense desire through him that kissing Deni did.

As her strong hands pulled him down to her, Jace realized she needed him in return. Needed *him*, Jace the man, not Jace the Shifter leader's son—she hadn't known who he was when they'd met. Nothing in her behavior, her scent, her voice had told him she cared where he was in the food chain.

She rose on tiptoes, running fingers through his short hair, kissing him as though she couldn't get enough. Jace felt his frenzy reply—*need, mate, don't let go.*

Deni pushed away from him with a suddenness that

robbed him of breath. Cold air filled in where she'd been, and Jace felt suddenly empty.

Deni was staring up at him, her chest rising with her agitation. "Sorry. I can't control—"

Jace's returning breath hurt him. "It's not control I'm looking for."

"I am."

Because of her accident, she meant, her fear it was making her go feral. "I get that," Jace said. He clasped her elbows. "But that's over, Deni. You survived. I won't let you lose it when you're with me—I promise."

She shuddered. "I just wish—"

"Wish what?" Jace drew her closer again, running his hands up her arms to cup her shoulders. "Tell me what you want."

"To be normal again. A year ago, I would have snatched up someone like you, taken you somewhere private, and not come out until we were done enjoying ourselves."

Jace grinned down at her. "Me too. With you, I mean."

"But now." Deni shuddered but she didn't pull away. "I'm afraid to let myself go."

"Yeah," Jace said, his voice quieter. "Me too." That's why they'd sent Jace to Austin to liaise and test the Collar control problem. Jace was trustworthy, dependable. Could keep a secret. Could take pain and not go crazy from it. He didn't need anyone to hold his hand, never had.

He liked to stay in control, be strong. But tonight . . .

"Come on," Deni said. She laced her hand through his, tugging him along with her. "Best I get home."

Jace's heart still thrummed from the kiss—Deni's taste, her scent, the warmth of her body imprinted on his. The feral being deep inside him growled in frustration, wanting out.

Keep it together. He was supposed to be helping Deni stay calm. But as Jace walked behind her, watching her hips sway while her hand was hot in his, he wondered which of them would prove to be the stronger.

* * *

Will and Jackson, Deni's sons, were home. Deni's heart lightened when she saw their pickup in the driveway and the lights glowing in the house. Home. Safety.

Jace's scent like wild sage wrapped around her as she led him up onto the porch. Her idea that he could go sleep at Liam's or Spike's didn't seem as good now. Deni didn't like the thought of him saying good-bye and walking away.

"Sweet ride," Jace said, gesturing at the motorcycle parked next to the pickup. "Yours?"

Deni nodded, her heart squeezing. "Ellison bought it for me after mine was totaled." She glanced at it and turned resolutely away.

"And you haven't ridden it," Jace said. "Shame."

"Isn't it?" Deni jerked open the door to the house. She was *not* going to let Jace talk her into getting on the motorcycle tonight. She'd done well riding Liam's bike home, but she still shook from it. Too much too soon.

Jace followed her inside without further word. Deni entered her haven, filled with the scents of her sons, her brother, and his mate. Soon her brother and mate would have their first cub, and more laughter would fill the house.

"Mom."

Will, her youngest, already twenty-four, came to Deni as she entered the kitchen and wrapped his arms around her. She hugged him back, her beloved son. After a long time, Will lifted his head, looked her up and down, and asked, "What the hell happened to you?"

"Fight," Deni said. "But I'm okay. I rode, Will. Liam's bike—all the way from the fight club."

Will's eyes widened, but Jackson, two years older than Will, said, "And you were at the fight club why?" He came forward, greeting Deni by giving her a hug from the side. Will hadn't moved.

Neither son acknowledged Jace standing quietly near the door. Will and Jackson were still technically cubs, though they were in their twenties—adults in human terms. They hadn't gone through their Transitions yet. They were clinging to Deni as instinctively as they had when they'd been tiny, waiting for her to either tell them the strange Shifter was a friend, or for them to join together to attack him.

Deni also knew they scented Jace on her, and her on him, and knew what they'd done. Before the accident, they'd have started teasing her. Now they waited, uncertain.

"This is Jace Warden," she said. "He's staying with us tonight."

"Oh yeah?" Jackson finally eyed Jace, though he didn't go so far as to pin him with a defiant stare. "Why's that?"

"Dylan invited him out here," Deni said. "But Dylan's been arrested."

As she'd guessed, the announcement made the boys put aside their nervousness and barrage her with questions, starting with *What? Are you serious?*

Jace helped Deni fill them in on the story. Once Will and Jackson were more relaxed with Jace, Deni went to her room, washed up, changed her clothes, then returned to the kitchen and started putting together sandwiches. Big ones. She was *hungry*.

The boys and Jace devoured everything she set down on the table. Deni watched her sons relax even more as Jace talked. He really did have the knack of putting everyone at ease.

The sight of him hulking at the table, shoveling down roast beef, ham, and turkey on three different kinds of bread while Will and Jackson hung on his words made Deni's heart ache again. This is what she should have had with her mate and cubs—a family, laughing, talking, eating, sharing. Deni's mate had died of illness long ago, robbing Deni of the life she'd wanted. Being shoveled into a Shiftertown had been even more bewildering. But they'd made it, she, Ellison, Jackson, and Will.

Here they were, and now Jace seemed to complete the picture.

"Seriously, Mom," Will said, his mouth full. "Why did you go to the fight club? You know what happens . . ."

Deni reached across the table for the butter and slapped some onto her slab of bread. "Because I was tired of sitting at home huddled up in a shawl. Ronan and Elizabeth offered to give me a lift out to the fight club, and I took them up on it. I thought it would do me good to get out and have fun."

"You could have gone to the bar," Jackson said, frowning. "Safer."

"Not really. Too many human groupies looking for a Shifter to grope. Plus, all my friends were at the fights tonight. I wanted to go." Deni gave Jackson a motherly glare, and he shrugged.

"Speaking of groping . . ." Jackson trailed off, deliberately not looking at Jace or Deni. Will snorted as he took another bite.

"None of your business," Deni said.

Jace said nothing at all, only looked amused. He betrayed no shame, no regret for their quick encounter in the darkness.

The boys got their snickering in, but Deni could tell they were relieved. Had they thought their mom was washed-up? Out of life because she sometimes went out of her mind? That maybe no other Shifter would want her?

Jace remained silent, letting them laugh. At one point, he caught Deni's gaze and winked, and Deni's blood started to simmer. It really was dangerous to have him here.

Jackson and Will retreated to their room after the meal to watch videos and sleep. Jace came to Deni where she looked out the window across the street, wondering if Dylan would return tonight, and wrapped his arms around her from behind.

"They love you," he said.

Deni leaned back into his warmth. "They're my cubs."

"It's good to see." Jace let out his breath, heat tickling her ear. "I never knew my mother. She died bringing me in."

Deni heard the sorrow in his words. She pressed her hand over his. "I'm so sorry."

"It's always made me a little touchy, you know?" Jace held her tighter. "Afraid to get too close to anyone. It can happen so fast, losing someone."

So true. "You have your dad," she said. "And the rest of your family." Though she knew no one could ever take the place of a lost loved one.

"I do. And my dad has done some shit that's scared me to death, trust me." Jace gave a little chuckle. "But it's made me careful."

Careful. Deni had learned to be that as well.

His closeness made her nervous, and not because she didn't like it. Deni broke his hold and turned around. "Hope the couch is comfortable. Linens are in the closet in the hall."

His gaze sought hers. "I'm sure it will be." He touched her throat above her Collar, fingertips caressing. His jade green eyes darkened, but he didn't speak. Whatever his thoughts were, he kept them to himself.

"Good night, then." Deni rose on her tiptoes and gently kissed his lips.

Jace slid one arm around her, turning the kiss into something deeper. His mouth was a point of heat in the darkness, their lips meeting in silence.

Jace eased away, taking his hands from Deni and balling them into fists, as though stopping himself from reaching for her again. "Good night," he said.

Deni swallowed, but didn't move. "Good night."

Jace took a step back. "You'd better go."

Good thinking. If Deni stayed, she'd grab him, and they'd go down right here in the living room. Another chance for them both to lose control.

"Sure," she said. "If you need anything . . ."

Jace held up one hand, fingers stiff. "Don't say that. Too dangerous. Good night," he repeated, firmly.

Deni nodded and made herself turn around, walk down the small hallway, and enter her bedroom. She looked back before she closed the door, seeing Jace standing in the living room, rigid, large, solid.

Shutting the door on him was one of the hardest things she'd ever done.

In the middle of the night, Collar payback hit Jace.

He opened his eyes in the dark, sweat rolling down his face, pain smacking him in the gut. He stifled his groans—no use waking up the rest of the house.

Payback happened when a Shifter prevented his Collar from going off while he was fighting. Helped a lot during the fight, but afterward there was always a backlash. The systems relaxed, the Shifter's adrenaline dissipated, and the suppressed pain woke up and said hello.

Jace's nerves were on fire. The pain started at his throat and poured from there into his body. He doubled up, still on the couch, rolling onto his side and silently fighting the agony.

Smooth, cool hands touched his skin. Jace had stripped down to his jeans to sleep but hadn't put on anything else—he'd found enough blankets in the linen cupboard to keep his bare torso comfortably warm.

Deni's touch cut through his pain. She knelt on the floor next to him, the fabric of her long T-shirt brushing his body. She wore a bracelet on her right wrist, a thin gold chain with a small charm that soothed when it touched him. She hadn't been wearing it earlier tonight, but maybe she hadn't wanted to risk it getting lost at the fight club.

Jace took a deep breath, trying to still his racing heartbeat. Deni drew her hands up his chest and across his shoulders. A few hours ago, Jace would have found the touch sexual, invigorating. Same hands, same woman, but now she calmed.

He laid his head on the arm of the sofa, forcing his body to open up from its cramped position. Deni moved her hands down his chest and to his abdomen, her touch firm but caressing.

Jace drew in another breath. Deni left swaths of relief as she pulled her hands across him, paths free from pain.

She leaned down and kissed his chest. Jace wound an arm around her and pulled her closer. It felt so natural to hold her to him like this. Maybe he'd known this woman in another life, perhaps they'd had a love for the ages there. Shifters didn't believe in reincarnation, but Jace's fogged brain liked the idea.

Deni kept kissing his body, kept stroking with her hands. Her lips were soft points on his hot skin, her hands so beautifully skilled. If Jace weren't in so much pain he'd be aroused. He'd love to pull her up to straddle him, to hold her while she found pleasure in him.

He let out a whispered groan. Deni kissed his lips, stifling the small sound.

Jace held her, moving his lips to kiss her back. Wonderful, sweet woman. Her touch unclenched the tightness in him, feathering comfort through his body.

She'd risen from her bed, somehow knowing he was in pain, and had come out here, even after the wary *good night* they'd shared. Jace had made sure he'd been as quiet as possible, but she must have heard him or sensed his pain.

Jace kissed her lips again, stroking her hair. If they had time and freedom, they'd find so much together. He was Feline, she Lupine, he from the Vegas Shiftertown, she from the Austin. Distance, family, and laws kept them apart, but at this moment—who cared?

Deni raised her head. She kissed the tip of Jace's nose and brushed her hands down his chest once more, the gold chain whispering.

"Better?" she asked.

"Much."

"Good." She unfolded to her feet, the hem of her long T-shirt brushing her knees. She leaned down, bathing Jace in her scent, and kissed his lips once more. Then her touch and kiss were gone, Deni moving down the hall to her bedroom.

Jace lay back, the vestiges of his pain fading. "Good night," he whispered, and fell into a deep, untroubled sleep.

* * *

Jace walked out of the house the next morning with Ellison Rowe, Deni's brother. He walked out, even though Deni wasn't up yet, because Ellison escorted him out.

Jace had been sleeping hard after Deni had gone to bed the second time, when he'd been jerked out of slumber by a big Shifter sitting down on him.

Both men had come off the couch with a yell of rage, then they'd faced each other across the living room rug. Ellison's pale hair had gleamed in the moonlight, his big fists clenched, his eyes wolf white. Jace stood barefoot in jeans in another Shifter's house, and for that, this pack leader had a right to tear him up.

Ellison's mate, a small human woman named Maria, had stepped between them and calmly asked Jace what he was doing here. Jace had met her before—the woman had been rescued from a feral Shifter in Mexico and brought here, and Ellison had fallen on his ass in love with her.

Once Jace explained about his visit, Dylan, and the fight club, Ellison had backed off a little. Ellison had heard about Dylan's arrest and conceded that Jace could stay. But the look on his face when he scented Deni on Jace was pure fury.

Deni hadn't woken up during the altercation, but then, they'd conducted most of it after their initial shout in silence, with only a little growling. Jace decided to take a shower, tired of people sniffing him, and by the time he'd come out, the sun was up. Ellison pointedly walked Jace out of the house and started along the street with him.

"My sister," Ellison said, "is going through some shit."

"She told me some of it." Jace hoisted his backpack on his shoulder, reflecting that he'd probably need to find someplace else to stay tonight.

"She's scared and still healing. She doesn't need to be confused."

The pissed-off feral in Jace started rising again. Why did everyone assume he was ready to take advantage of

Deni? They all needed to leave her alone, give her some space.

"I'm not here to confuse her." Jace stopped, forcing Ellison to face him. Ellison had his cowboy hat and boots on—he liked to play the big, bad Texan. "Deni's a good woman."

"I know. I've lived with her all my life." Ellison's gray eyes held worry behind his anger. "Keep it cool. Don't let her . . ."

He trailed off, as though unable to find the words to describe his gut-wrenching fears.

Jace dared to close the space between them, dared even more to put his hand on Ellison's shoulder. "I'd never hurt her," he said. "I can see she's special."

Ellison held Jace's gaze but softened it. "She is."

Jace squeezed his shoulder. "Then we're good."

Ellison gave him another look, then put his hand on Jace's shoulder in return. His squeeze was a little harder than necessary, but he was conceding. Two Shifters agreeing not to fight. At least, not right now.

Ellison walked away from Jace after that, and Jace continued on a few blocks to a house that was set back behind another. Behind *that,* completely hidden from the street, was a brick garage that looked like nothing more than a normal garage. Jace opened the door and walked in, to be greeted by Liam Morrissey and his brother Sean.

"Excellent," Liam said. "Dad sends his regrets . . . obviously. We'll get started."

CHAPTER FIVE

"They still have Dylan?" Jace asked.

The garage he stood in had been converted to a workshop. Two long tables ran the length of the room, flanked by a few stools. Bolted to the benches were a scroll saw, a drill press, and what looked like a router in a stand. At the end of one bench was a jeweler's vise that rotated on a huge ball bearing so the worker could look at a piece from every angle.

The benches also held tools—every style of pliers and vise grips, wire snips, knives, gauges, squares, rulers, and other measuring devices. Boxes holding silver bits and jump links were arranged on the benches, and a soldering iron lay next to a can of flux.

A few half-built pieces of furniture and some trays of jewelry had been set up in the corners of the room, but Jace knew those were for verisimilitude should humans find this workshop. The true projects lay in the boxes of silver pieces. Liam and his family were making fake Collars and also researching how to remove real Collars from Shifters without making said Shifters insane.

Sean nodded to Jace's question. "Dad's still in jail. They wanted to keep him overnight. Kim's working on it."

"She's good, is my mate," Liam said. "She'll make them see reason, or at least shove legalese at them until they choke."

Sean and Liam, in spite of their hopeful words, were worried, Jace saw. Both men had deep shadows under their eyes and moved a bit stiffly. They'd probably been up all night.

"Sure you want to be experimenting on my neck when you've had no sleep?" he asked, only half joking.

"Don't worry, lad. We won't do much today."

Sean unbuckled the Sword of the Guardian from his back, slid the blade out of its leather sheath, and laid the sword on the table. Runes that looked ancient and powerful were traced all over the sword, blade and hilt alike.

Jace had seen the sword belonging to the Guardian in his own Shiftertown, but this one, he knew, was the original. The first, made by Shifter sword maker Niall O'Connell and woven with spells by the Fae woman Alanna, had been passed down through the generations to Sean—the men of the Morrissey family were O'Connell's heirs.

Shifters didn't much go in for magic, but Jace knew the tingle of it when he felt it. There was magic in the sword, and its vibration permeated the air of the room.

"Collars," Liam said, seating himself on one of the stools. "Fae magic and human technology woven together. Cracking that code is the toughest thing."

"How's it going?" Jace asked. "Any progress?"

"Some," Liam continued while Sean sat down, laid a few pieces of silver together on the jeweler's anvil, and clicked on the light of the magnifier above it.

"We can get to the Collar's chip." Liam tapped the round black-and-silver piece that was a Celtic cross resting on his throat. "It's in there, wired up and ready to go. The magic part is in the silver that weaves through the Collar— *most* of the magic is in there, that is. What we haven't figured out is how the magic and technology tie together.

That's important, because what fuses them is also, we think, what fuses the Collar to the Shifter's neck. It bites into our nervous system and stays there. That's why, when the first experimenters simply ripped Collars from necks, the Shifter's adrenaline system kicked into high gear, sending that Shifter feral. It was as though years of instincts being suppressed by the Collars suddenly sprang out, with twenty years of rage fueling them."

Jace had heard about the experiments of a few years ago, done by an idiot who hadn't cared that the Shifters went crazy when the Collars came off. He'd only wanted the Shifters free of Collars and under his thumb. Liam had been caught up in the battle to stop it. Liam, his father, and Sean had taken over the experimenting and were being much more careful about it.

Liam continued, "We have to figure out what it is that makes the Collars work as one piece. What that third element is, so to speak. Magic, technology . . . and something that slides in between."

"And I'm the guinea pig?" Jace asked.

"Only if you want to be, lad. We won't force you."

But this was why Jace had come. He'd learned, slowly over the last year, how to control his Collar. He'd been teaching his father and others in his Shiftertown how to do it, and preparing himself for Collar removal. The Morrisseys had learned to make fake Collars that would fool humans, but only two Shifters thus far wore them—Andrea, Sean's mate, and Tiger, a Shifter who'd been created by humans. Tiger had never worn a Collar before he came to Shiftertown, and when they'd tried to put one on, he'd gone even crazier than he already was. Liam had decided a fake Collar for Tiger was the best solution.

Andrea had worn a real Collar most of her life, but strangely, it had never worked on her. Andrea was half Fae. Sean's theory was that her Fae-ness somehow counteracted the magic inside the Collar. Or else her healing magic did—Andrea was a healer. Andrea's Collar had come off easily, in any case.

The Morrisseys were trying to apply what they'd learned from Andrea to other Shifters, but they still hadn't figured out the details. It was tough to find Shifters stable enough, trustworthy enough, and willing enough to let themselves be lab rats for the Collar experiments. Hence, Jace's trips to Austin.

Jace opened his arms and shrugged. "What do you want me to do?"

Sean picked up a soldering iron. "Be best if you held still."

Jace looked at the pencil-thin device, which hummed a little as Sean turned it on. The tip would be turning brutally hot.

"Seriously?" Jace asked him.

Sean attempted to keep a worried look off his face as he approached, which didn't make Jace feel any better. "We're trying to both find a safe way to remove the Collars and discover their secret at the same time," Sean said. "I volunteered myself, but Dad and Liam won't let me."

"Because you're the Guardian," Jace said as sweat broke out on his face. "If this kills you, ripples will be felt throughout Shiftertown—the Shifter world, even. Kill me, and the ripples will be smaller."

"No killing," Sean said quickly. "We'll stop short of killing."

"Whew." Jace's heart beat faster, but he kept his voice light. "Thank the Goddess for small favors."

"I'd love to tell you this won't hurt," Sean said. He raised the soldering iron.

Liam closed in on Jace's other side. "You going to be all right, lad? No ripping into us, I mean?"

A bead of sweat trickled down Jace's back, and he curled his hands to fists. "Let's find out."

"Dad should be here," Liam said. "But he told us not to wait."

"How did he tell you?" Jace kept his eyes on the hot tip of the iron. "He's in jail."

"He's good at getting messages to us," Sean said. "He wants us to start. He must know something."

"Possibly," Jace said. He clenched his jaw, fists tightening.

Something cold touched the side of Jace's neck. A knife—a very small, delicate one, wielded by Liam. Sean held the iron competently between steady fingers and brought it close to Jace's throat.

"The heat loosens the metal without tearing you," Liam said. His knife nicked Jace's skin, just barely.

"You know this how?" Jace asked. Neither Sean nor Liam answered. Jace didn't want to move his throat by swallowing, but he couldn't help but lick his dry lips. "Ah, so you *don't* know."

"We've done a lot of thinking on this," Liam said. "Someone's got to be the first."

"Sean said you took Andrea's off with a knife alone."

"True, but Andrea's wasn't fused to her nervous system. Trust me, we'll do this slowly. Only a link or two today. More tomorrow if it works."

"*If* it works," Jace repeated. "Your skills at reassurance are terrific, Liam. What a hell of a Shiftertown leader you must make."

"Stop talking," Liam said. "Stay very, very still."

Jace was doing this for the good of all Shifters, he reminded himself. Shifters for years to come would benefit from Jace's sacrifice.

It was that word—*sacrifice*—that Jace was having trouble with at the moment.

The knife blade cut. At the same time, Sean darted in with the iron. Searing heat radiated across Jace's neck and down his spine. He felt a wildcat snarl begin deep inside but he tamped it down as hard as he could. If he shifted now, who the hell knew what would happen to him?

Liam and Sean backed off as swiftly as they'd gone in. Jace opened his eyes and shook his head, the pain easing. He blinked, realizing he viewed the other two through cat's eyes. He relaxed his hands and found he'd gouged his own palms with leopard claws.

He drew a ragged breath, willing all of himself to resume human form. "Is that it?"

Liam shook his head. "Started it. A little bit more, and we'll have a link or two off. Then drinks are on me."

"It's eight in the morning."

"I'm thinking you won't care what time it is when we're done, lad. Plus, you had one hell of a night last night. So did we. Beer is a good thing."

Jace drew in a deep breath through his nose. "All right," he said. He released the breath. "I'm ready."

Sean jammed the iron onto Liam's knife blade, and the searing knife slid under Jace's skin. "Oh, son of a f—" Jace's words became a wildcat snarl. He slammed his eyes shut, not wanting to see the world rock if he shifted.

The process took longer this time. Liam's breath brushed Jace's neck as he leaned close, his lion's scent different enough from the Feline scents Jace had grown up with to make his leopard a little crazy.

After an agonizing stretch of time, Liam stepped back, Sean took away the iron, and the pain, mercifully, let up. Jace opened his eyes again, taking deep breaths until his killing instincts calmed down.

His clothes were drenched with sweat, his body shaking. Jace wiped his face with the back of his hand and moved his fingers toward his neck.

"Careful," Liam said. "That's going to be a little tender."

A little? Jace barely brushed himself and jerked his hand away at the raw pain. "Is it off?"

"A link and a half," Liam said. "Good for today."

"A link and a half?" Jace spun to a grimy mirror over a sink. Sure enough, a link had loosened on the right side of his neck. Beneath it was an angry red mark. "We can't let anyone see this."

"No," Liam agreed, while Sean turned off the iron. "I suggest a scarf or a jacket."

Jacket. Jace had brought a hoodie for cooler nights, and Liam had pulled the link where such a thing could hide the traces.

Jace rummaged in his backpack. The cloth of the jacket,

when it settled against his neck, stung, but the small hurt was nothing to what had gone through him before.

"What now?" Jace asked.

"Beer," Sean said, sliding his sword back into its scabbard. "Lots of it. And trying to spring my dad from jail."

Deni kept busy in her yard after Will and Jackson left for work. Maria had gone off to school, and Ellison was back, snoring in his bedroom, sleeping off his night, leaving Deni relatively alone. She didn't want to sit in the house waiting to see whether Jace would come back—that way led to brooding, then to craziness, and to her feral wolf coming out.

In shorts and a T-shirt, Deni planted new bedding flowers Will had brought home for her. The weather in Austin was usually dry enough and warm enough for her to mix arid climate plants like autumn sage with wetter weather plants like petunias and roses. Many Shifters went in for gardening, keeping their small yards colorful throughout the year. An antidote, Deni figured, to the restlessness that made them want to roam and fight. Nesting as compensation, she supposed.

Deni was straightening up from clipping off a few dead red roses when warmth covered her from behind.

"I prefer a sarong," Jace said, his breath hot in her ear.

"Do you?" Deni nestled back into him. "I'll get you one for yourself, then. Bet you'd look cute in it."

His laugh started all kinds of fires inside her. Deni turned in his arms, still holding her pruning scissors. She started to smile at him, but she broke off, seeing the streak of blood on the side of his neck.

"Are you all right?"

Jace moved the collar of his jacket over the wound. "Price of wisdom. We won't know what removing the Collars will do until we remove them."

"It's still on." Deni pointed at the Celtic cross at the

hollow of his throat. Her bracelet, which she liked to wear as often as she could, clinked lightly against the cross. Deni's mother had left her the bracelet, a reminder of happier days.

"Baby steps. I think the Morrissey boys are through torturing me for the day, or at least the morning."

Deni touched her own Collar. "Do they really think they can get them off? I wonder if . . ."

Jace closed his fingers over her hand as she started to tug at her Collar. "If taking yours off will stop your episodes? I don't want you risking that, Den. What they just did to me hurt like hell. I don't want you going through it until they know what they're doing."

Deni squeezed his hand. "Why are *you* going through it, then? I don't want you hurting like hell either."

Jace shrugged. "Someone needs to go first. Why not me?"

"Why should it be you?" she asked indignantly. "Let Liam and Sean torture themselves."

"Think about it." Jace laced his fingers through Deni's. "Sean's the Guardian. Liam's the Shiftertown leader. Dylan needs to be intact in case Liam needs backup. Connor their nephew is too young for this kind of pain. Liam's trackers—Ronan, Spike, Ellison—are mated now, with little ones, or little ones on the way. I'm a strong enough Shifter to take the experiment, and if something irreversible happens to me, my dad and my aunt Cass are already running our Shiftertown. I'm unmated, have no cubs . . ."

"Meaning you're expendable?" Deni snatched her hand away, anger rising from someplace deep. "No one's expendable, Jace."

Jace gave her a tolerant look. "You're nice to worry about me. Now, how about putting on the sarong?"

Deni made a noise of exasperation and smacked at him with her empty hand. Jace caught her hand again and tugged her closer, up against his hard body.

His face lost its teasing expression, and his grip tightened. "Deni, you make me glad to be alive."

She looked up into his eyes, which held fire, and something in her that she hadn't realized was tight unwound itself.

Deni spread her fingers on his chest. "Don't let them have it all their own way."

Jace gave her a startled look as though surprised at her defense of him. He leaned down and kissed her, drawing the fire that had already begun inside her. He rested his cheek against hers after that, rocking a little as he held her, warmth to warmth.

Jace lifted his head, brushing Deni's hair from her face. "I'm beat. Too bad. I was hoping to do other things this morning."

The light in his eyes was suggestive, but he did look tired. Exhausted. He hadn't had much sleep in the night, and he'd been gone at dawn. Deni was willing to bet he hadn't eaten anything either.

"Take a load off," she said, gesturing to the porch. "Let me finish here, and I'll make a late breakfast. Or early lunch. Whatever you want to call it."

Jace gave her a smile and kissed her forehead, tightening his grip on her again, but finally he let her go. "Liam and Sean went home to consume a boatload of Guinness," he said, moving to the porch. He shook his head. "Irishmen."

He laughed, but Deni grew irritated. Liam expected Jace to sit still while he and Sean poked at him, and then they didn't even bother to feed him.

She jerked on her gardening gloves as the porch swing creaked—Jace let out a sigh as he relaxed on it and went back to her task of spreading mulch around her new plants. A few roses to deadhead, and then she'd go whip up a mountain of eggs and a stack of bacon. Ellison would be up soon too, and she knew how much male Shifters loved to eat.

A small car pulled up across the street. Deni straightened to watch as Kim Morrissey descended in a neat skirt and blouse with low-heeled shoes. Deni sensed other Shifters in yards and on porches down the street coming alert, watching too.

Kim looked over and gave Deni a brief wave, but her

usual smiles were gone, her face set in grim lines. The passenger door had opened as Kim got out, and Dylan emerged.

Deni let out a breath of relief. Dylan was safe. She
sensed the other Shifters relax as well, and saw them turn
back to their morning tasks.

Dylan glanced at Deni then walked swiftly across the
road toward Deni's yard. He paused at the edge of the
browning grass, too much a Shifter to invade Ellison's territory without invitation. He only continued toward Deni
at her flowerbed when she gave him a nod.

Dylan looked terrible. His cheeks were covered with
black stubble, the gray that brushed his temples more prev-
alent this morning. His face was lined with dirt, his hair
lank, his clothes smelling of stale smoke and sweat.

"You all right?" Dylan asked her.

"I should be asking *you* that," Deni said, pulling off her
dirty gloves and dropping them to the ground. Dylan's blue
eyes were always difficult to look into, but Deni met his
gaze for a few beats.

"I'm good," Dylan said, though it was obvious he
wasn't. He put a firm hand on Deni's shoulder and pulled
her into a hug. "You did well last night, lass," he said. His
arms tightened, the alpha giving one of his frightened
Shifters reassurance.

A growl sounded. Low and vicious, it rolled out from
the shadows, its threat clear.

Dylan jerked around, releasing Deni. An answering
growl came from his throat, Dylan too tired to worry about
any kind of protocol. A Shifter threatened him—Dylan
was going to strike him down.

It took Deni a second to realize that the rumble had come
from Jace on the porch. He was still sitting on the porch
swing, but alert, upright, his eyes glinting in the shadows.

Shifters in another's territory were always careful about
what they did—this entire Shiftertown was technically
Morrissey clan territory, though they respected the rights
and privacy of individual families, packs, and prides. But a
Shifter from out of town couldn't threaten, challenge, or

cause any problems when he was an invited guest. It wasn't polite, and it was dangerous besides.

So why the hell was Jace Warden leaning forward, his gaze fast on Dylan, growling with full menace and ready to attack?

CHAPTER SIX

*D*on't touch her, Jace's growl said.

He knew Dylan understood him, because Dylan was staring back at Jace with full comprehension. Dylan was also angry, the short fuse of his temper not helped by his night in jail.

Jace knew he was violating all kinds of protocol, but he didn't give a crap. Dylan had put his hands on Deni, and Jace had seen her first.

A faint, logical voice deep inside Jace told him Dylan's reassurance of Deni was natural, and the intruder in this picture was Jace.

Jace kicked at the voice until it shut up. He knew if he rose from the swing, there'd be a fight, and he wasn't sure he wouldn't welcome it. If Dylan was a good Shifter and went along home, Jace would let him go. Otherwise . . .

Dylan started for the porch. Jace recognized the determination in his stride, having seen it in his own father often enough. Dylan was coming to teach the upstart Jace a lesson.

Jace held his place on the porch swing. The logical voice had just enough volume to tell him that no one in this

Shiftertown would take his side in a fight against Dylan. Not in a real one. This wasn't the fight club—fight club rules didn't apply here.

Dylan was on the steps, moving slowly but menacingly. Jace saw a flash out of the corner of his eye, and then Deni was leaping from the ground, up and over the porch railing with Lupine grace. The fact that she'd crushed one of her newly planted petunias as she made the vault told Jace of her apprehension.

Deni moved swiftly in front of Jace, facing Dylan before he reached the porch floor.

"He's tired and hurt," Deni said to Dylan, words coming fast. "Like you are. Let it go."

True, Jace was. But he was also enraged. A fight with Dylan would be fun. Lion against leopard—brute strength against finesse. Which would prevail?

Dylan looked at Deni, willing her to move. Deni held her ground—good for her. Dylan growled a little, then he looked around Deni to Jace, his blue eyes going Shifter white. "Den is right," Dylan said, every word slow and deliberate. He was holding himself back from throwing Deni aside and going for Jace, and making it clear he was holding back. "We're both exhausted." Dylan's gaze went to Jace's neck, where Jace's jacket had slid back again to reveal the loosened Collar link. "And you're in pain. Eat something. Sleep it off."

"Good advice," Deni said to Dylan. "Take it yourself. Neither of you got much sleep last night."

Jace remained silent, but he gave Dylan a slow nod. Dylan rested his gaze on Jace for a few moments longer, the weight of his stare palpable, before he turned and walked off the porch. He said nothing, not a good-bye or an acknowledgment, only strode away and back across the street to where Kim waited anxiously.

Deni watched Dylan go, her hands on her shapely hips. Jace could reach up and clasp those hips, pulling her back to his lap.

Deni swung around before he could move. "Are you all right? Why in the Goddess's name did you do that?"

Jace shrugged, which rubbed his jacket against his sore neck. "I didn't like the way he touched you."

"He's Shiftertown leader." Deni folded her arms and glared down at him. "It's his job to reassure us all, to make sure everyone's okay."

"He's not leader anymore."

"Not technically, no. But Liam still relies on him pretty heavily to keep the peace. Didn't Dylan invite you here in the first place?"

"He did." Jace knew everything Deni said was true and reasonable. But the mating frenzy only knew *mate* and *stay away from my mate*.

Time to apologize, make amends, tell Dylan he didn't mean to be an idiot. But Jace didn't want to. He still hurt from Liam's knife and Sean's soldering iron, and he needed a break.

Jace pressed his hands to his thighs and rose to his feet. He liked that Deni didn't take a step back but remained in his personal space, as though she belonged there.

"We're both tired," Jace said. "Like you said. Now, about this breakfast. Let's get something started. I'm *starving*."

Deni watched Jace eat. And eat, and eat. She put away a plate of eggs, bacon, and Texas toast herself, but Jace kept shoveling it in. Ellison woke up and joined them, as hungry as Jace.

"I guess no more fight club for a while," Ellison said after they discussed what had happened with the cops. "Damn. Shifters need to work off steam somehow or else we combust."

"You can work off steam by cleaning out the gutters and fixing the roof," Deni said, piling more eggs, cheese, and salsa onto both males' plates. "That will cool you down."

Jace laughed out loud. He was sweet and sexy, filling up the place at the table as though he belonged there.

Ellison grimaced. "Don't be so literal, woman."

"Just giving you an alternative," Deni said, resuming her

seat. Jace closed his hand over hers, squeezing it, before he returned to his food. "I wouldn't want you to burst into flames."

Ellison looked over Jace and Deni, his gray eyes shrewd. He didn't pretend not to notice the signals between them, how comfortable they were sitting close together.

A knock sounded on the back door, and Jace came instantly alert. His hand jerked on Deni's, his eyes losing their deep greenness for a lighter hue.

At the same time a police car went by the house, its black body and white doors sliding past in silence. Ellison went noiselessly for the door and opened it to find a small boy with white hair and black eyes standing on the doorstep.

"Olaf," Ellison said, his body relaxing. "Maria's not home yet." Maria, Ellison's mate, often babysat for eleven-year-old Olaf, who was a polar bear cub, as well as other Shifter kids. She looked after them while their parents—or in Olaf's case, foster parents—worked.

"Ronan sent me to tell you the police are here," Olaf said.

"We see that." Ellison turned to watch a second car go past the front windows.

"They're going door-to-door," Olaf said. "Checking ID." He looked past Ellison and into the kitchen at Jace. "Everyone's ID."

Deni's heartbeat sped in alarm. "Does Ronan know if they're looking for someone in particular?"

Olaf shook his head. "No. They're just asking for ID." He peered at Jace, his small face blank. "What's the matter with him?"

"Nothing," Deni said quickly. "Long night."

Olaf didn't nod. He kept staring at Jace, his brow puckering. "He's not right."

With that declaration, Olaf turned from the door and ran in a loping stride down the porch steps and across the backyard to the next house.

Ronan had been smart to send him as an early warning system, Deni thought as Ellison closed the door. If the police stopped him, all Olaf had to do was look cute and innocent, and charm them senseless. He did that so well.

Ellison came back to the kitchen, his shoulders tight. "Don't we have a new Shifter Bureau liaison to prevent this kind of harassment? I need to have a talk with Tiger."

"Maybe it's coming from a different department," Deni said. "Not our biggest concern at the moment."

Both she and her brother turned to look at Jace.

"Shit," Ellison said. Deni waited, tense. They could help Jace, but only if Ellison agreed.

Jace held up his hands. "I promise not to touch anything."

Ellison went past Deni and into the hall between kitchen, living room, and bedrooms. "Shit," he said again, his Texas accent thickening.

"No choice," Deni said to Ellison as she and Jace followed. "He doesn't have time to get away."

Ellison put his hand on the false wall panel in the middle of the hall. "You know this is a sacred trust," he said to Jace. "Right?"

"I'm familiar with the concept," Jace said impatiently.

"Damn it," Ellison said under his breath. "If I still had a pack, they'd kill me."

"I *am* your pack," Deni said. "And I'll speak for my sons. Jace goes to ground."

Were Jace anyone else, Deni would be as reluctant as Ellison to open the door behind the paneling and let Jace see what was in there. But this was Jace, and she'd let him soothe her in the darkness at the fight club last night. He'd kept her from going feral, had gotten her home safely, and proved she could start going back to her normal life without fear. She owed him.

The opening door revealed a set of cement stairs heading down into darkness. The three of them paused at the top a moment, letting the air from below cool them.

Secret spaces. Every Shifter house had them. Traditionally built below the main house, they held secrets of that Shifter pack or clan, things collected and cherished, the pack's wealth.

Shifters had survived all these centuries because of the things contained in their vaults. Shifters now lived together above-ground in relative peace—different clans and species rubbing elbows, or paws—because they kept this part of themselves, places only close family went, safely underground.

To let an unrelated Shifter see the secret spaces was unthinkable. Jace wasn't family or clan—he wasn't even Lupine.

Another knock came, this one on the front door, and much firmer than Olaf's. "Mr. Rowe?" a man's voice sounded.

Ellison let out a growl and headed for the front. Jace, instead of going down the stairs, spun and started after him, stepping in front of Deni as though protecting her.

"No!" Deni whispered. She grabbed Jace by the jacket and shook him. "Get down there."

Jace swung around and gave her a startled look, as though he'd had no idea he'd gone into his protective stance. His eyes were the light green again, his Shifter rage apparent.

Deni knew he didn't want to go down the stairs without her, to leave her vulnerable. But this wasn't the wild. This was the human world, and at the moment, she and Jace had to play by their rules, or risk everything.

"Down," Deni whispered again.

Jace finally nodded, let her push him to the first stair, and held her gaze as she shut the door on him. Deni had the false panel back in place and was walking out toward the living room by the time two police officers, one armed with a tranq rifle, strode in and demanded to see her and Ellison's IDs.

Jace remained in the stairwell, pressing his fists to the stone wall, dragging in deep breaths. He knew he couldn't risk the police finding him, but the need to keep them away from Deni had risen swiftly, his primal fear for her driving away common sense.

He could hear the police through the thin paneling, talking to Ellison and Deni, asking where Maria was, and about Deni's sons. Human hearing wasn't as good as Shifters', but

Jace knew they might be able to hear any noise he made if he wasn't careful.

In silence, he walked the rest of the way down the stairs, his Feline eyes letting him see in the dark. At the bottom was a door, unlocked. Jace opened it as noiselessly as he could, slipped inside the basement room, and closed the door behind him.

Only then did he flip one of the switches beside the door, only one. A single light came on in the middle of the room.

Jace looked around. *Nice.* The main room held soft-looking furniture and opened to a kitchen larger than the one upstairs, with more upscale appliances. The refrigerator was stocked, he saw when he opened it. A Shifter could live down here comfortably for weeks.

A flat screen TV had been mounted to a wall, and a game console and controls sat under it. Jace smiled. Will and Jackson must have fun down here. Probably Ellison too. Jace thought about Cassidy at his house, and her prowess at the pool table. Deni likely held her own. Why Shifters liked to play RPGs, Jace had never figured out—they were shapeshifters and fighters in real life—but given the opportunity to take a new identity and kick a troll's ass, they couldn't resist.

Games were off-limits right now. Jace couldn't risk that the humans upstairs wouldn't hear. Shifter spaces were usually soundproofed, but soundproofing was only so good.

Jace figured Ellison would want Jace to stand with his eyes closed in the middle of the room and not smell, see, or touch anything. And then somehow wipe his memory of everything the moment he left. He had to smile.

In any other situation, Jace might try to keep clear of the Rowe family's secrets. But this was Deni's place. It held the essence of her, even more than the house upstairs did.

Jace couldn't resist stopping by the tall cabinet that held books and a collection of framed photographs. Family photos. A tall couple Jace didn't recognize must be Ellison and Deni's parents. The photo was old, but kept with care.

Another older photo showed Deni, much younger, probably just past her Transition, with a male Shifter. The Shifter male, who had black hair and gray eyes, was a Lupine, big and rawboned, like most of the wolves. Deni leaned against him, a smile on her face, looking happy. Deni's name was still Rowe, though, Jace mused. She hadn't taken her mate's family's name, which meant her mate had been of lesser dominance than her, probably much less. These days, it was a female's choice which name to take, but in the past, that choice had been made for her by whichever family was dominant. Even now, more dominant families would fight to keep their daughters under their name. Deni had been mated long ago enough that she'd likely gone along with the tradition.

Another picture of Deni showed her holding two wolf cubs, the pair bright-eyed. Will and Jackson, as pups. Deni's mate must have taken the photo, because Deni smiled out of the picture at him, her eyes full of love.

More recent photos showed Deni with Will and Jackson as tall young men, all of them wearing Collars. Then one of Ellison cuddling the small human woman, Maria, both grinning. Ellison wore a more relaxed expression than Jace had ever seen on him.

Another was of Deni alone. The river was in the background, Deni in a bathing suit and wrap, her hair wet, the gold bracelet she liked to wear on her wrist. She smiled with all the animation she'd showed when she'd held her cubs. This was Deni happy, without the haunted look in her eyes. Before the accident, Jace figured.

A sudden savage fury rose up in him, filling his throat with growls. She'd been deliberately run down by a human trying to kidnap her. Though the man had been killed, Jace wanted the culprit in front of him, so he could have the pleasure of ripping his head off.

His rage rose so quickly that he started to shift. Then his Collar shocked him.

The pain was fierce. Jace dug his fist into his mouth to cut off the scream that had welled up, ready to burst out.

Son of a bitch. He closed his eyes, trying to breathe, rapidly repeating the meditation mantra to calm the Collar. The Collar shocked him again, and he balled his hands in agony.

What the fuck?

Jace found himself on the floor, arms curled around his legs as he rocked in pain. Flashes of rage went through him, followed by just as intense flashes of need. Need for Deni.

He needed her touch, her kiss, to breathe her scent. Her body against his. Another time of passion with her, another time when he'd bury himself inside her and be, for once in his life, complete.

"Shit," he said out loud. This wasn't mating frenzy. Or maybe it partly was. But Jace recognized his symptoms from seeing them in an unfortunate few. Rabid hunger. Intense need for sex. Quick to anger, ready to kill, especially to protect what was his.

Only two links of his Collar had been pulled away, not even that, but it had triggered the feral in him.

Shouldn't surprise him, he reflected. Liam had said taking off the Collars made the instincts suppressed by years of wearing them burst out in a volcanic flare. The trick would be figuring out how to negate the effect.

For now, Jace had to control himself. Somehow. The police upstairs were interrogating the woman he wanted . . . but he couldn't think about that. If he did, he'd rush up there and destroy them all.

Keep it together.

Funny, it had been easy to tell Deni to keep herself calm. Difficult to convince himself to do so now.

Jace yanked open the door of the cabinet—he stopped himself from simply smashing the glass and putting his hand through it. He took out the photo of Deni by herself, smiling cheerfully out at him.

He touched her face with his fingers, drawing a deep breath. Looking at Deni kept him cool, but barely.

Jace had to know what was happening upstairs. Were they taking away Deni in a patrol car, arresting her for whatever reason?

He clutched the picture to his chest, trying to still his

need to run up the stairs and drag Deni to safety. He had to *think*.

Jace was smart—he'd designed most of the underground space and its gadgets in the house he shared with his dad and family in the Vegas Shiftertown. He'd been recruited to design the spaces in the new houses being built out there as well. What had he done to make sure they wouldn't get trapped in their own hiding places, without knowing what was going on in the outside world?

He moved to the TV, made sure the sound was all the way down, and clicked it on. A little button pushing on the remote . . . yes, they'd done it too. Or maybe they'd followed Jace's design, which Eric liked to brag about.

One of the TV channels monitored the upstairs. Ellison must have put cameras in the big living room and one on the front porch. They focused now, showing Deni standing next to Ellison, both she and her brother upright but easy, without defiance.

Four cops barred their way out of the room, the female one with the tranq rifle talking to them. Ellison and Deni answered, standing casually, trying not to betray nervousness through body language. Humans were not as good at reading nonverbal signals as Shifters, but some could be good at it, especially the police sent to deal with Shifters.

Jace inched up the volume, but the sound was too muffled for him to make out what they were saying. No one was lunging to put Ellison or Deni in cuffs, fortunately. Just cops talking to citizens, citizens who happened to be Shifters.

Jace sat down on the couch, unwilling to look away. He hugged Deni's picture to him almost without realizing it. He was still hugging it when the cops finally left the house and Deni came downstairs to find him.

Jace was off the couch and at the bottom of the stairs as soon as Deni stepped off them. Deni found herself caught in a hard hug, Jace lifting her from her feet.

"It's all right, Jace," she said quickly. "I'm all right."

Jace growled and buried his face in her neck. Deni held him, the solidness of his body against hers slowing her racing heart.

"You touched stuff," Ellison said, half joking. He went past Jace, snatched the remote off the couch, and clicked off the television. He started to close the cabinet door and stopped. "You touched more stuff."

Deni took the framed photo of herself from Jace's hand. She had to tug at it before he blinked and let it go, as though he'd forgotten he was clutching it so tightly. Deni handed it to Ellison, who restored it to the cabinet, not before giving Jace a sharp look.

"Did you hear what they said?" Deni asked.

"Not well." Jace released her from the hug and took a firm hold of her hand. "I only saw they didn't arrest you, thank the Goddess. What happened?"

"They're interested in what Shifters have been up to lately," Ellison said. "*Very* interested. Looking at identification, asking where we're working, what we're doing when we're not."

"Have to wonder why they're asking all the sudden," Jace said. "Right after I arrived. I don't believe in coincidences."

"Neither do I." Ellison and Jace shared a grim look. "I hate to say this, but you'd better stay down here awhile. They're roving Shiftertown, and probably won't be leaving soon."

Deni saw the flash in Jace's eyes, the wild look she saw in herself sometimes. *Trapped.*

She touched his arm. "I'll stay here with you."

Jace's look changed in an instant to something hungry and raw, his eyes going very light green. "You shouldn't."

"You're hurting." Deni put her fingers to the red marks around his Collar but she didn't touch them. "Because of this?"

"I don't know." Jace's hand was sweating, slick against hers. "I think so."

"I knew Liam was crazy," Ellison said. "Going on about releasing us from Collars. I'm going to go get Dylan, have him look in on you."

"Be careful," Deni said.

Ellison tipped an imaginary cowboy hat. "I'm always careful, ma'am," he drawled, then went past them and up the stairs.

"Let's sit down." Deni started to lead Jace to the sofa, but he didn't budge. His body was strong, a boulder she couldn't move.

"Den, you should get out of here." His grip was tight, his hand hot.

Deni's heart beat faster as she touched his wrist and found his pulse banging beneath her fingers. "I think I should stay. Ellison will be right back."

"No, *go!*" Jace pushed at her, his breath coming fast. "If you stay, I don't know what I'll do. I want you—last night wasn't enough. I want it hard, and I want it now. Don't let me take it from you."

Deni let go of his hand, but she remained squarely in front of him. A Shifter going feral and feeling mating frenzy was a dangerous thing. Jace could do anything, even kill her, if he was crazed enough. She understood that.

On the other hand, in mating frenzy, only the mate kept a Shifter from completely losing his mind. She thought of Jace behind her on the motorcycle, warming her and giving her the strength to cut through her fears and get them home. He'd been with her every second, and he'd held her in victory when she'd made it. When Jace had to hide down here, Deni had reasoned that she owed him. She still believed that.

"I'm not leaving," she said.

Jace's eyes turned all the way white. He grabbed Deni by the wrists and hauled her against him.

CHAPTER SEVEN

Deni landed against Jace's chest, his skin hot through his thin shirt. His jacket's zipper rubbed Deni's arms, the friction of it releasing the heat in her own body.

Jace's kiss was hard, opening her mouth, his grip on her wrists crushing. But Deni was strong, had always been strong. She could not have endured so much without strength. She rose on her tiptoes, kissing him back, her body fitting to his.

Jace raised his head, breaking the kiss. His lips were parted, the moisture inside his mouth beckoning her. Deni knew his taste now and craved more. She also knew what he felt like inside her, and she wanted that again. She wanted his firm body on top of hers, wanted the heat of his thrusts to fill her. Deni reached for the button of his jeans and slid it open.

Jace tightened his fingers on her wrist again. "Don't play with fire."

"I'm cold." Deni said in a low voice. "Warm me up."

Jace was struggling with coherence. "Ellison will be back soon, you said."

She gave him a hot smile. "Then we should hurry."

"Bloody hell."

Deni unzipped his jeans. He hadn't bothered with underwear this morning, she found as she dipped her hand inside. His cock, hard and hot, tumbled into her hand.

Jace let out a groan. He jerked Deni against him, his arm solidly behind her as she lightly stroked him. "Gods, woman."

"You woke me up, Jace," she said. "I want to thank you for that."

"In the middle of last night, you mean?" His words were strained. "I was feeling payback from the fight. Tried to keep it quiet."

"You know I don't mean that." Deni squeezed his cock until he let out another noise of pleasure.

"*Damn.*" Jace tugged her hand from him but only to lift her into his arms, kissing her with a ferocity that tasted of fire.

The sofa was near. Jace tipped Deni back over its arm until they both fell onto its cushions, arms and legs bumping and tangling in each other's. Deni laughed.

The laughter probably saved her, she thought later. Jace shook his head slightly as though clearing his mind, and his eyes took on a jade hue again. He slowed his kisses to something tender, lips soft on Deni's. She ran her fingers through the short ends of his hair, liking the warm brush of it.

Jace unbuttoned her shorts, tugging them down and off with a contortion of bodies that had them laughing again. His jeans landed on the floor on top of the shorts, and then they were body to body. Deni took handfuls of his jacket, but before she could start to coax it off, Jace slid inside her.

All the way in. Last night had been wild and fast, a raw coupling at the edge of a parking lot. Now everything stopped. Jace looked into Deni's eyes, the feral Shifter softening into a man, hard-faced but warm-eyed.

He filled her, his breath slowing as he lay on her, touching her face. The pressure of him inside her loosened her

entire body, and Deni wrapped herself around him, drawing him in.

Jace closed his eyes, letting out another soft moan. He
kissed her mouth, giving a nip to the corner of it.

After a moment, he opened his eyes again and started to
move. Slow thrusts, intensity building as each one completed. Jace held her gaze, his eyes a dark green now. The
frenzied animal had calmed. Now it was just Deni and
Jace.

Deni arched under him, Jace's thrusts coming faster.
Her back pressed into the sofa's soft foam cushions, all the
way down to the springs. She held him close, laughing into
his hair as the springs started to squeak.

"Goddess, you are beautiful," Jace whispered, feathering kisses over her face. "I came here to find you; I know
I did."

He'd been to this Shiftertown before, but Deni knew
what he meant. They'd been ready to meet last night.

The soft fleece of Jace's jacket felt good to Deni's hands,
the zipper rough against her palms. As he kissed her, she
could again see where one link of his Collar and part of
another had been taken off, his skin angry red beneath.

He'd been ready to kill Dylan on the porch, and the
police when they'd knocked on the door. The loosening
Collar was letting out his feral instincts, she guessed. Liam
had explained to her when she'd first considered trying to
take her Collar off that such a thing might happen. But for
now, Jace gentled himself, loving her without madness.

He kept thrusting, and Deni moved under him, meeting
those thrusts. His jacket held his heat, and she slid her
hands into it, finding his hard back beneath. Jace's honed
body was sleek under her touch, the lithe dance of his muscles exciting.

They were both breathing hard, uttering little groans,
holding on to each other when heavy footsteps sounded on
the other side of the couch.

A pair of brawny fists jammed to the back of the sofa, and

Deni looked up in time to see Ellison spin away in half disgust, half irritation. "Are you kidding me?" Ellison growled.

Jace said, "Shit," and the feral whiteness returned to his
eyes. He was up off the sofa, his jacket falling, but it wasn't
long enough to hide his privates. Deni saw his cock, still
dark and hard from what they'd been doing, black hair
crisp at its base.

Deni knew Dylan was upstairs, away from their basement sanctuary, of course. Ellison kept his back squarely
turned. That back was quivering, but Deni couldn't tell
whether from rage or laughter. A little of both, probably.

"Goddess, Den, he's a *Feline*," Ellison said. He shook
his head without turning around, the overhead light gleaming in his blond hair. "Both of you get your asses upstairs.
After you've covered them."

He gave one more shake of his head and started for the
steps. His cowboy boots grated on the cement stairs, then
he was gone.

Deni swallowed, tamping down her need to burst into
hysterical laughter. "I guess he was faster than I thought
he'd be."

Jace didn't smile. "He needs to respect you."

Deni sat up, pushing her hair from her face. "He just
caught you making the beast with two backs with his little
sister. Give him a break."

Jace growled again, then he reached down and helped
Deni to her feet. As she came off the couch, he pulled her
against him. "You all right?"

"Yes." Deni truly was. She should be embarrassed at
being caught by her brother—at being reckless like this.
But she wasn't. It seemed natural to be coupling with Jace.
Shifters celebrated sex, because it meant life, cubs, con-
tinuance. She wouldn't apologize for it.

"What about you?" Deni asked. Jace was shaking, but
his hold on her was strong.

"I'll be okay." Jace took a long breath and pulled her
into a tighter hug. His bare cock touched her abdomen. "I

get it now—what you must go through when you start losing track of who you are. I shouldn't have made light of it."

Deni looked up at him in alarm. "Are you losing track of who you are?"

"Not quite." Jace kissed her hair and rested his cheek on the top of her head. "But almost. You keep reminding me who I am, though, all right?"

"They're looking for someone," Dylan said when they emerged upstairs.

They spoke in the kitchen, where the windows were high, small, curtained, and looked out to the backyard. The wide windows of the bungalow's living room were out of bounds.

Jace didn't like human police roving Shiftertown, but right now, his body hummed from the nearness of Deni, and the remembered joy of being in her one more time.

He loved the sweetness of her scent, today coupled with fresh earth from her digging in the dirt. The taste of her filled him like heady wine. He was imprinted with her now, the feel of her soft thighs against his legs, the way she squeezed him when he pressed inside her.

"Jace?" Deni said.

She wasn't trying to get his attention, he realized after a heartbeat. She was asking Dylan if Jace was the Shifter the police were looking for.

"They didn't say," Dylan answered. "I don't even know if they're looking for a Shifter. They had a tip-off, I got one of the officers to tell me, about the fight club. I told them there's always rumors of a Shifter fight club, because humans find it titillating. Same as rumors of Shifter hookers."

Shifter women never sold sex, never had. But Shifter women could be promiscuous, because Shifters didn't find sex shameful. As long as a Shifter was unmated, they could have as many partners as they wanted. Not all liked to go roaming, but some Shifter women spread it around. Humans confused that with the sex trade; hence, the rumors.

"Tip-off from a human?" Ellison asked.

"They wouldn't tell me that." Dylan's eyes glinted. "What Shifter would betray us?"

Ellison shrugged. "One pissed off for some reason. At other Shifters, or at you. Broderick springs to mind."

"He sprang to my mind too. I'll be having a talk with him." Dylan's Irish accent made the words sound casual, but Jace heard the steel behind them.

"If they're going door-to-door, what about the workshop?" Jace asked.

Dylan shook his head. "They haven't found it yet. Lie low here, and I'll send for you when it's clear. If it is." Dylan looked Jace up and down. "We might want to stop the experiment anyway. It's affecting you."

"Agreed," Deni said quickly.

Jace shook his head. "No, we'll never get the Collars off by being afraid to have them off. I want to keep at it." It was tempting to turn his back on the agony, and Sean with his soldering iron, and run for home, but learning all they could about the Collars was too important. Besides, Deni was here.

"We'll see." Dylan gave him another hard look. Jace knew his display on the porch had not won him any favors from Dylan, but Jace had definitely not liked Dylan touching Deni, even innocently.

"Why did you want me to meet you at the fight club?" Jace asked him. "I could have come to Shiftertown and waited for you."

Dylan's face shuttered. "For reasons that are no longer important. Don't leave this house until I let you know it's all right. Catch up on sleep or something." Dylan glanced from Jace to Deni. "I mean real sleep."

Jace didn't bother to answer. Deni went pink, but only because Ellison was rolling his eyes.

Ellison agreed that Jace could stay downstairs until Dylan gave the all clear. Safer, he said, in case the cops tried to surprise them. Police had been known to walk right into Shifter houses, the rules about warrants being a little relaxed when Shifters were concerned.

Deni was glad Ellison shared her worry for Jace, though Ellison was a bit grumpy about it. Finding Jace and Deni in flagrante hadn't been the highlight of his day, he said.

"It's not like I've never come home to you and Maria in the living room," Deni reminded him.

Ellison gave her an innocent look. "That's different."

"My ass," Deni said, sending him a smile.

"I know it was, and I don't want to see it again," Ellison said. "Or Jace's. Yetch."

At least he was teasing now, even if he was annoyed.

When Will and Jackson returned home—Jackson worked for a moving company and Will at a warehouse; humans liked Shifter strength—Ellison apprised them of the situation. Maria, now growing plump with Ellison's first cub, was home by that time too. She was taking classes at a community college in preparation for entering the university next year and spent the rest of her day taking care of Shifter cubs. Maria had lost the haunted look she'd worn since she'd been rescued, and Ellison had lost his look of deep loneliness. Now if Deni could just lose hers.

They played video games in the basement, Jace proving to be very good at them. Will, who was turning out to be a computer genius, had a hard time keeping up with him.

Deni worried that the games might start drawing out Jace's feral anger, but they didn't. Maybe knowing it wasn't real, only pixels on a screen, made a difference. Deni was never upset by the games either. But then, games had no scent, no texture. Shifters were more stimulated by things that assaulted all the senses at once.

By the time Will and Jackson went to bed, they'd expressed more respect for Jace. He might be twenty years older, but his knowledge of games and computer programming helped him rise in their estimation.

Before Deni could start arguing with Ellison that she wanted to stay downstairs and sleep with Jace, Sean arrived at the back door to tell them the police had gone, had been for several hours.

"But we wanted to wait until we were certain," Sean said, lounging against the kitchen doorframe, his sword gleaming under the porch light. "Didn't want them doubling back and saying *just fooling*." He glanced at Jace, who stood behind Ellison, Jace conceding Ellison's place to guard the house. "You ready for more torture, lad?"

"You're not going to do more tonight, are you?" Deni asked sharply. "Leave Jace alone. He needs to rest."

"Liam wants to continue under cover of darkness," Sean said. "We'll leave sleeping for the day. Felines are mostly nocturnal anyway, lass."

"It's all right," Jace said. "I want to finish this." He looked less crazed—maybe gaming did have a good effect on the mind. "Liam's waiting there?"

"Liam's at the bar, as usual, in case whoever is calling in tip-offs reports any out-of-the-ordinary activity. Me and Dad will be working on you tonight. Plus a little extra help." Sean looked at Ellison. "Liam says you and Maria are to go to the bar. Laugh it up, talk to your friends, have fun. You too, Deni."

"Nope." Deni took a step closer to Jace. "I'm going with him. You Morrisseys are too eager to dig knives into him. Someone needs to be there who's on his side."

Sean lifted both hands and didn't argue. Of the two Morrissey brothers—much alike with their dark hair and blue eyes—Sean was the more easygoing. If Deni wanted to throw her lot in with Jace, Sean was saying, who was he to stop her?

Ellison wasn't happy to let Deni go to the workshop, but Maria took Deni's side, saying she wouldn't let Ellison go alone if she had to make the same kind of choice. The ladies prevailed, to Deni's satisfaction.

They left the house together, Ellison and Maria breaking away to walk to the bar, Ellison's arm firmly around Maria's waist. Sean and Deni put Jace between them, with

Jace walking in the hunched manner he'd been taking on, the hood of his jacket up to hide most of his face.

Deni caught a whiff of a strange scent when they approached the workshop's door, one that had her hackles rising. The wolf in her was growling, and she felt the bite of nausea that was a prelude to her losing herself. She clutched Jace's arm, and he stepped away from Sean to her.

"What is it, sweetheart?"

"There's someone . . ."

"I know," Jace said. "I smell it."

It was an acrid odor, one ripe with ancestral memory. Sean said, "No worries. That will be the father-in-law," and he ushered them inside.

CHAPTER EIGHT

Jace stepped into the room and faced a strange apparition. A tall man, so tall he looked stretched, turned toward them, a metallic whisper sounding as he moved. He was dressed in chain mail, which was covered with a cloak so black it was like an opening into darkness. The man's hair, in contrast, was pale white, and fell in dozens of braids past his waist, but the effect wasn't effeminate, nor was he elderly. The man's face was sharp, his dark eyes rivaling his cloak for the deepest hue of black. He wore a broadsword on his back, one larger than the Sword of the Guardian, its hilt sticking up above his head.

Deni was still growling, and Jace's snarls filled his throat. An ancient enemy stood before them, and though Jace had seen this man before on other trips to Austin, the shock of him being here made his wildcat a little crazy.

"You remember Fionn," Sean was saying. He eyed Jace warily, as though ready to stop Jace's attack. "My mate's true father."

Andrea Morrissey, Sean's mate, appeared on the other side of the Fae, flanking him in a protective move. Andrea's dark head was up, her gray eyes daring Jace and Deni to do anything against Fionn.

Andrea was half Fae, half Shifter. Fionn, Jace had been told, had come to the human world forty or so years ago, seeking refuge during some unknown Fae war. He'd met and fallen in love with a Shifter woman, a Lupine, who'd then borne Andrea. For complicated Fae reasons, he hadn't been able to stay, and Andrea had been raised by her mother and a Shifter stepfather. Andrea had had it tough as a half Fae growing up among Shifters and hadn't met her true father until a few years ago. Now Andrea was mate to the Guardian, and no one hassled her about her origins. Not to her face, anyway, and never within Sean's hearing.

Fionn had proved himself to be on the Shifters' side in many cases, but the sight of a Fae still made Jace want to shift, fight, and kill. The Fae had created the first Shifters many centuries ago, breeding them to be fighting slaves. The Shifters had finally broken away from their Fae captors, staying in the human world while the Fae retreated permanently to Faerie. The Shifter-Fae war had ended seven hundred years ago, but still Shifters had a tough time even looking at a Fae.

Jace cleared his throat. "I assume you came to help with the Collars?"

Fionn curled his lip—Fae were always prone to sneering. "No, I came for a barbeque. Haven't got my fill of Texas ribs." He turned his disdainful dark eyes to Sean. "Why you think I can help, I don't know. I'm a warrior, not a magician. I don't know anything about the Fae magic in these Collars."

Andrea put her hand on Fionn's arm. Fionn softened as he turned to his daughter—the only person Jace had ever seen Fionn be nice to. "But you might have some insight into their construction," Andrea said. "It's Fae technology as well as Fae magic."

Fionn patted her hand. "We've had this discussion before. I don't know anything about what Fae did with Shifters. Shifters were out of Faerie, never to return, before I was born. I can see where Shifters would have been useful in battle, but I for one wouldn't want to put up with them between wars. I'd have to cage them up to keep them from killing me, and they'd cost a fortune to feed."

Deni made a growling noise in her throat. "Good thing we won the Shifter-Fae war, then," she said.

"Yes, good thing," Fionn answered. "Saved me a lot of bother."

Andrea shot Fionn a frown. "Sorry, my father enjoys baiting Shifters. He thinks it's *fun*."

"I may be looking for amusement in the situation, but I also speak the truth," Fionn said.

From what Jace understood, Fionn was a formidable warrior in his world, leading the armies of his clan in victory over other Fae, and possessing a lot of power. Other Fae had learned not to mess with him. Jace noted that Fionn kept his eye on everything in the room, including all the exits, the high windows, and anything that could become a weapon. He might be here to help, but he couldn't stop being a fighter by instinct.

Dylan opened a locked cabinet and removed a silver and black chain. Jace recoiled inside, and he felt Deni move closer to him. Even Sean shivered. This was a true Collar, and Dylan carried it to Fionn.

"We're looking for the third element," Dylan said. "Fae magic, computer chips, and something else."

Fionn took the Collar gingerly between his fingers, held it up to his eye level, and scanned it. The small circle of the Celtic cross glittered in the harsh light of bare bulbs.

"Interesting." Fionn ran a fingertip down the links. "Silver and black silver, which is a Fae metal. No iron." If it had contained iron, Fionn couldn't have held it—iron made Fae sick, could even kill them if they had too much contact with it. Fionn looked the Collar over again, frowning. "Sorry, I don't know. My experience with metals is confined to swords and other bladed weapons. Not jewelry."

"Well," Sean said, letting out a disappointed sigh as Dylan took the Collar back, "let's see what we can do tonight."

He unsheathed the Sword of the Guardian again and laid it on the table. Jace thought Fionn would walk out, back to the circle of trees that took him to Faerie, but Fionn settled himself against the wall near Andrea and folded his arms, ready to watch.

"You did that before," Jace said to Sean, sitting on a stool and trying to stem his nervousness. "Took out the sword before we started. Why?"

Sean shrugged. "I thought the magic in it might help figure out the magic in the Collars. Magic vibrations or something. The sword has done some interesting things." He glanced at Andrea, who nodded. The two together had performed amazing bouts of healing, when both of them had been touching the sword.

"Ready?" Sean asked Jace.

"No. But let's do this."

Dylan held the knife Liam had used, plus an electric probe, while Sean stuck with the soldering iron. Jace balled his fists, setting his teeth against the coming pain.

A soothing coolness cut through the heat in his body, originating at a point on his wrist. Opening eyes he hadn't realized he'd closed, Jace saw Deni's hand, tanned from Texas sun, resting on his forearm. She looked at him, giving him a little nod and smile, her gray eyes warm. An answering warmth stirred in Jace's heart, wrapping around his nerves and breaking through his fear of the pain.

"Hurry up, Sean," Jace said without taking his gaze from Deni. "Other things I want to do tonight."

"You got it, lad." Sean brought the soldering iron closer as Dylan touched the electric probe to Jace's Collar.

A vibrating buzz went around the chain, and then Jace felt the nick of the knife. The iron heated the silver, and the second link Liam had already loosened came free. Dylan quickly lifted a third, then a fourth.

The pain was there, but not as intense as last time. That is, until Dylan tried to loosen a fifth link. The Collar snapped back a huge arc that jolted Dylan backward and shocked hot pain into Jace. Deni jumped as well, caught in the current, but she didn't let go of Jace.

Jace tried to clench his teeth over his yell, to keep quiet, but his body had taken over. Darkness clamped his brain, and through it he saw the Collar, a white band around his neck, every nerve outlined with fire.

His yell turned to a scream. The Collar didn't want to let go of him. It clung tighter to Jace's neck, the link Dylan had just pulled off fusing again to his skin.

Jace fell from the stool to the floor, landing on his knees, brutal pain the only thing in his world. Every nerve was crackling, cold washing through him followed by heat so powerful he burned from the inside out. He started to shift, but every bit of fur emerging from his skin hurt, doubling his agony.

"Jace." Deni's voice cut through the fog. Her touch fell like cool water on his burning skin. "Hold on."

Jace heard other voices, too faint and faraway to bother with.

"Shit." "Andrea, can you help him, lass?" "Have you killed him?" came Fionn's disdain. "Well done, Shifters."

The only important words were breathed in Deni's voice. "I'm here, Jace. Hang on."

Jace clung to her voice, needing its warm cadence. His brain couldn't form the syllables of her name, but it didn't matter. He knew her touch, her warmth as she put her arms around him, on her knees too. He knew her scent, the low sweetness of her voice, the soft gray of her eyes, which went a lighter gray when he made love to her. Jace took a long breath, taking in the goodness of her.

The hurting eased the slightest bit. Underneath the pain, the tightness in Jace's chest radiated a different kind of tingling— it still hurt, but without the brutal sharpness of the Collar.

Jace held his breath, wondering if the second pressure was what he thought it was. Through pain came amazing happiness and at the same time dismay. *Not now. Not here. Wrong time. Wrong place.*

"Jace." The word cut through his agony.

Deni. She was Deni, lithe, beautiful. And a *Lupine*, for crying out loud. Their kids wouldn't know whether to bark or meow.

"Help me," he croaked.

Deni's warmth covered him, her breasts soft against his burning chest. "Hold on to me."

She had both his hands between hers, her head on his shoulder. The Collar kept sparking, biting into her as well. She took up the dregs of the pain, jumping a little as the sparks bit deep.

Another female hand touched Jace, this one inflicting a new kind of pain. His nerves balled into one place of fire, Jace shouting with it, then slowly, it eased.

Jace drew a long breath and opened his eyes.

He found himself flat on his back in the middle of a circle of faces—Andrea, Sean, Dylan, Fionn, Deni. Andrea had one hand on the blade of the Sword of the Guardian, which was humming. Fionn's long, thin braids brushed Jace's legs, Fionn's concern mixed with curiosity and fascination.

Deni raised her head and touched Jace's face, her little bracelet making a faint jingling noise. She exhaled in relief.

"Sorry, Jace," Sean said, his voice rumbling with sympathy. "You all right, lad?"

Jace opened his mouth to say he'd live, but nothing came out. He dropped his head back in exhaustion.

"Leave him be," Deni said, suddenly brisk. "Sean, hand me that blanket. You all have tortured him enough tonight."

Sweet of her to take care of him. Jace didn't move—mostly because he couldn't—and let himself enjoy Deni draping a thick blanket over him and lifting his head in her competent hand to slide a cushion underneath it.

She started to get her feet again, but Jace grabbed her hand. *No. Stay.*

Deni caught his gaze, her own filled with pain and worry. She gave him a nod and sank down beside him, folding her lovely legs under her.

"We need to find the link," Dylan said. "No use half killing him trying to pull any more off tonight."

"Agreed," Sean said, sounding relieved.

"If you pull it off all at once, he goes feral?" Fionn asked, sounding interested. The lilting accent in his voice, different from any Jace had ever heard, made him start to growl.

"Aye, that's what happens," Sean said. "Have seen it myself. If the Shifter is too far gone, he can't come back. Best you can do is kill the poor bugger."

Jace growled again. Deni held him tighter and kissed his lower lip. "I won't let them," she said.

Jace remained still. He didn't trust himself not to attack everyone in the room if he moved, with the exception of Deni. He might even go for Andrea, but only after he smacked down the Fae who stank up the place.

"Jace needs to rest," Deni said. "Leave him be."

"I know," Sean said, putting a hand on Jace's shoulder. He quickly took it away as Jace's growl turned to a snarl. "You take as long as you need, lad. We won't start again until you're ready."

"No, you'll find yourselves another victim," Deni said sharply. She sat up, but kept herself between Jace and the others.

"Not victim," Sean said. "Volunteer."

"I know what I said." Deni glared at them, Lupine defiance in the face of powerful Felines. What a sweetheart. "Leave him alone and figure out your problem with someone else. Like me, for instance. I'm already half crazy, so I might not notice the difference."

"No!" Jace came up off the floor to fold himself protectively around Deni. "No." He still had to think about how to form words. "Won't let you. Too much pain."

Deni gave him a startled look, then a stubborn one. "Well, I won't let them put *you* in too much pain either." She switched her anger back to Sean and Dylan. "He's not expendable."

Both Sean and Dylan took a step away, as though sensing something had changed about Deni, and about Jace. Andrea unfolded to her feet and turned to the sink to run some water. The Sword of the Guardian had cut her hand. Brave woman, saying nothing.

"Interesting how the female defends the male," Fionn said. "Fae women, on the other hand, can turn on their men in a heartbeat, running them through and joining their enemies if they find it expedient. Shifter females, I note, will stick with their mates even when the mate is defeated. She'll die for him."

"Isn't that what attracted you to my mother?" Andrea asked from the sink.

Fionn went silent a moment, and when he spoke again, the arrogance had gone from his voice and a sad note entered it. "Yes. One of the many things."

"Jace and Deni aren't mated," Sean said. He slid the Sword of the Guardian back into its scabbard and moved to Andrea as though drawn to her.

Fionn's arrogance returned. "And I'm constantly amazed at how dense Shifters are about their own kind."

"That's enough, Father," Andrea said firmly.

Jace pulled Deni back to him. He didn't care anymore about the Collars, about freeing Shifters, about helping Liam. He wanted Deni—wanted to bury himself in her and not come out. Whether she felt the same about him, Jace didn't know, but he would find out. If she didn't care about him, if he'd simply been a way for her to defuse pressure, he'd let her go.

The thought of letting Deni go made his feral side want to burst out again. Jace kissed her shoulder, drawing in her scent until it calmed him a bit.

This was the wrong time and place for a mate-claim. He wanted it to be special, right, with his family present, and hers as well. They were from two different Shifter-towns, which would be a problem, but they could work it out somehow.

After they figured out this stupid Collar situation, Jace would get official permission to visit and mate-claim Deni. Deni could always turn him down, her choice, but Jace would take some time to persuade her.

He was busy thinking of fun ways to do the persuading when the workshop door slammed open to admit Connor Morrissey, agitated and out of breath.

"They're back," Connor said. "The cops. Liam says to shut down the workshop, and for the Goddess's sake, hide Jace."

CHAPTER NINE

Another thing Shifters could do, if Fionn was so interested, was galvanize themselves to move swiftly when need be. Dylan and Sean slid Collars and tools into hiding places with the smoothness of long practice, quickly placing the half-finished woodworking projects on the tables, scattering about tools and used sandpaper as though a woodworker had absently thrown them down.

Sean and Andrea departed without much of a good-bye, heading to wherever they'd prefer to be found. Deni helped Jace up from the floor, her touch the only thing keeping him from rushing out the door to confront the cops and keep them away from her.

"Where are they, Connor?" Deni was asking. "I need to get Jace back to my house."

Connor shook his head. "No time. Too many cops between here and there."

"I can hide the Shifter," Fionn said. He was the calmest of all, as though the situation was one more interesting tidbit in his observation of humans and Shifters. "I don't want humans to find me either."

"Hide me how?" Jace asked, every nerve a line of fire. "I don't trust Fae."

"Very wise of you," Fionn said. "Fae are treacherous bastards, every single one of us. I should know. Come with me now, or end up in a cage to be poked at by humans. Your choice."

"Go." Deni kissed his cheek. "Dylan will take care of me."

Dylan, the powerful alpha Feline who liked to hug Deni. Jace would rather cave in Dylan's face and pull Deni with him to wherever the Fae was taking him. But putting Deni under the Fae's power wasn't what he wanted either. Jace hugged his arms over his chest, his instincts tearing through him, warring with his common sense. It was hell going feral.

"Now," Fionn said. He didn't touch Jace, as though he knew Jace would attack him if he did, but his voice galvanized. Jace could well believe this man was a general.

Jace caught Deni around the waist. Her gray eyes were large, filled with fear, but behind the fear, Jace saw her mating frenzy answering his. He kissed her, savoring the taste of her warm lips, then he cupped her cheek, pulled on his jacket again, and followed Fionn into the night.

"A nd you are?" the female police officer asked Deni. The woman wore a bulletproof vest and a riot helmet and carried two pistols, while her male counterpart had a pistol and a tranq rifle. They'd come prepared to do battle against Shifters if need be. They found most Shifters peacefully cooking out, as Sean was doing behind Liam's house.

"Deni Rowe." Deni handed the female cop her ID card, which each Shifter had to update every year. "Same as last time," she couldn't help adding. Both these officers had been in the group that had come to Deni's and Ellison's house.

"Hmm." The female officer peered at Deni's ID, shining a black light on it, pretending she wasn't nervous. Dylan stood behind Deni, not wanting her to face the cops alone. Dylan said nothing and didn't try to interfere, but Dylan could unnerve most humans—not to mention most Shifters—simply by standing there. Both the male and female officer were sweating under his scrutiny.

"Seems okay." The female officer handed the card back to Deni. "Nice bracelet," she said, glancing at the gold chain on Deni's wrist.

"It was my mother's," Deni said. She tucked the ID into the back pocket of her shorts.

"Looks expensive." Shifters weren't allowed to wear costly jewelry, and shouldn't be able to afford to buy it.

"Handed down through the family," Deni answered. "I have photos of my mother and my grandmother wearing it, if you want to see them."

"Hmm." Another skeptical sound. "Where's the other guy? The one I saw you with before?"

Deni prayed these two weren't good at reading body language as she answered nonchalantly, "Ellison? He's my brother. He's at the bar with his mate."

"I mean the other one. The drunk one you were with at the . . . ceremony."

Damn it. "I don't know," Deni said. She took a step back to Dylan, putting herself into the radius of his warmth. "I'm with Dylan tonight."

Deni smiled at the female cop, as though willing her to understand. If humans liked to believe Shifter women were promiscuous, Deni would use it to her advantage. The female officer's look turned to disgust, but Deni didn't care what this woman thought of her as long as Jace was safe.

Both cops looked Dylan and Deni over and exchanged knowing smirks. They'd seen Dylan with Glory at the fight club. They must think Shiftertown was one big sex fest.

Dylan put his arm around Deni and dared them to say anything. The cops all but snickered as they moved off toward another set of Shifters walking on the dark street.

"Sorry," Deni said in a low voice to Dylan.

Dylan squeezed her shoulder. "You're good at thinking

on your feet. Nothing to be sorry about." Another squeeze
of reassurance, then he let her go. "But let's don't mention
this to Glory."

Deni smiled. "No fear."

"She would understand eventually, but it's the 'eventually' that would be uncomfortable." Dylan sent her one of
his rare smiles. "Let's go have some barbeque."

They had to, to keep up the verisimilitude. Deni only
hoped Jace was safe, and that the half-crazed wolf inside her
wouldn't make her break away from Dylan and race around
Shiftertown until she could find and protect him again.

"So this is Faerie?" Jace wrinkled his nose at the smell.
"I don't like it."

"As my daughter would say . . . Suck it up."

Shifters had left Faerie forever seven hundred years
ago, not that they'd ever embraced it as home. Though
they'd been created here, Shifters had cultivated a healthy
loathing of the place.

Jace had followed Fionn to a grove of trees between the
backyards of Shifter houses. In the glow of the few street-
lights, he'd seen police officers walking from house to
house, and patrol cars and vans creeping along the streets.

The darkness in the grove of trees had been deep, inky.
A mist rose from nowhere in the middle of the ring of
trees, one that smelled acrid to Jace. A tingling had begun
in Jace's brain that had him snarling, his claws coming out,
before Fionn had grabbed him and shoved him into the
middle of the mist.

Jace had blinked, the tingling dying, and found himself
in another ring of trees, these old, towering, and damp. His
boots squished in mud covered with gray green weeds and
dead leaves. The thick trees ran as far as Jace could see,
the land wet, dank, and muddy.

"Boring," Jace said. "No wonder my ancestors chose to
live in the human world."

Fionn made an impatient noise. "This is only one tiny

corner of one woods in Faerie. I live miles from here in a valley that would put anything found in your world to shame. Mountains reaching to the skies, snowcaps burnished by the sun, meadows of grass so green it makes you weep, and packed with wildflowers in every color. My garden is designed to run right into the meadows, so it's as though I step into paradise every time I walk out my door. My manor house has marble floors, and walls veined with Fae gold, which humans have never seen—and never will. Fae gold is rare even for the Fae. Humans would kill each other—and Fae—over it."

"Walls veined with gold," Jace said. "No overkill there."

Fionn started walking into the trees, ignoring him. "When I come to this area, however, I live rough in a tent. This way."

"Wait a minute." Jace jogged to catch up with him. The Fae-man was *fast*. "How do you know where the gateway, or whatever that was, is? All these trees look alike—and smell alike—to me."

Fionn didn't look back. "Then you'd better stick with me, hadn't you?"

Great. "How do I know you're not leading me to Fae warriors with big swords who'd love a Shifter snow leopard head decorating their fireplace?"

"You don't," Fionn said. "You have to trust me."

"Thanks. I feel so much better."

It was then that Jace noticed he *did* feel better. The feral restlessness had eased from him, the pain of his Collar lessening. When he put his hand to his neck, he still felt the soreness—did he ever—but the certainty he'd drop dead any second had gone.

Fionn led him around three gigantic trees growing close together and stopped in front of a pavilion. *Tent*, Fionn had called it. *Ballroom-sized living space*, Jace would term it instead.

He followed Fionn inside, though his Shifter instincts did not want him to. The interior of the pavilion was as lavish as the exterior. It had been divided into rooms by tapestries hung from solid rods, and carpeted with rugs that looked as though they were made of woven silk. Low couches, chairs, and tables were scattered everywhere, and a large brazier burned with a fire that cut the damp.

"You call *this* living rough?" Jace asked, turning in a circle. Everywhere he saw light, color, and shimmering texture.

"You've been living in human rejects too long. This is what you could have in Faerie, and much better than this."

"Not as a Shifter slave I couldn't," Jace pointed out.

"Possibly not. Though I don't keep slaves. Any Shifters who lived in my realm would be free to come and go as they pleased."

A fair-minded Fae? "Good to know," Jace said.

"I can't speak for other Fae, though," Fionn said. "So if you went outside my territory, yes, you'd probably end up a slave or a mantelpiece decoration."

"You're so comforting."

"Wine?" Fionn poured a golden, smoothly trickling liquid into a cup. "Best I can get out here. The good stuff doesn't transport well."

Never drink anything offered by a Fae. The old tales about Fae, passed down by Shifters, rang in Jace's head. His dad used to tell him the stories, as had Aunt Cass. Jace said nothing, but couldn't stop himself from taking a step back.

Fionn laughed. "You're superstitious. But probably wise. I know Fae who try to drug, poison, or spell everyone they meet. You're lucky I'm not interested. If I want someone under my thrall, I'll take over their territory and let them choose between following me or being put to the sword."

"What a nice guy," Jace said dryly. Fionn held out the cup, but Jace shook his head. Even if Fionn proved to be trustworthy, Jace couldn't be certain what Fae wine would do to his system, especially as traumatized as it had been lately. Fionn shrugged, lifted the wine cup to his lips, and drained its contents.

Jace looked around the lush living quarters, again reflecting that he felt much better. He was afraid to pursue why. If living in Faerie was the only way to stop Shifters who had their Collars removed from going feral, he'd rather take his chances being feral.

"So tell me," Jace said, as Fionn poured himself more wine. "If this is more or less the armpit of Faerie, why do you come out here?"

Fionn lowered his cup. When he spoke, his voice was softer. "To be near my daughter."

"Oh."

Fionn raised his brows and drank deeply again. "Yes, I am that maudlin. But I had to give up Andrea for more than forty years. I want to spend as much time with her as I possibly can. And my grandson."

"I get that."

The hard-faced warrior suddenly looked much older and more vulnerable. "That's why I conquered this part of Faerie. So I could see her without anyone being the wiser. I'm alone now, but Andrea makes life worth living."

"You old softie," Jace said, grinning.

"I am. I admit it without shame. Make yourself comfortable, Shifter. This might take some time. Dylan will send word when the way is safe."

D eni didn't want to eat, but she managed to choke down a burger Sean prepared for her, made with sautéed mushrooms and Havarti cheese, which Deni loved. Mouthwatering goodness, but tonight, Deni had no appetite.

The police still roamed Shiftertown. They'd interrogated the Shifters in Liam's yard—including Deni, again—and now they wandered the blocks.

Deni noticed that they'd left the cubs who'd gathered at Liam's alone. A large number of cubs had found their way here, sent by their parents for safety, and now they sat on the porch and its steps, devouring Sean's burgers. Spike's cub, Jordan; Olaf the polar bear; the older bear girl named Cherie; Liam and Kim's little girl, sitting on Kim's lap;

and others from around the town. Andrea carried her son and helped Kim look after the kids, but mostly the cubs had been sent here because of Tiger.

The police hadn't talked to Tiger much, leaving him and Tiger's mate, Carly, pretty much alone. They hadn't gone near the cubs at all, because Tiger had positioned himself between the police officers and the cubs on the porch. The officers, after taking one look at Tiger, had seemed to tacitly agree to stop even looking at the kids.

The cops might have the badges, armor, guns, and authority, Deni reflected, but in this corner of Shiftertown, Tiger had the power. The police seemed to know it, just as small animals knew they were prey for the cat that strolled by, even if the cat wasn't attacking. They'd feel better once the cat was gone, and they could duck inside their holes again for safety.

Even after the police finally left the yard, Tiger remained on guard. The huge man with black and orange hair unnerved even the Shifters. The only adult truly comfortable with him was Carly, a Texas girl with honey brown hair who wrapped her hands around Tiger's big arm and smiled up at him. She was just beginning to show her pregnancy, and the look Tiger gave her warmed Deni's heart. Those two had found love. Knowing what Tiger and Carly had gone through, Deni felt a lick of hope that she too could find happiness—even with the Feline Shifter who was right now hiding out in Faerie, and who couldn't legally be in her Shiftertown.

"He'll have to go," Dylan said to Sean not two feet away from Deni.

Deni turned to them, not bothering to pretend not to listen. If they hadn't wanted her to hear, Dylan wouldn't have said anything while she was standing so close.

Sean, turning burgers with tongs, nodded. "We'll have to try again later."

They were going to send Jace home, while he was half-crazed with the partially removed Collar, and wait for who knew how long. She opened her mouth to argue, but Dylan shook his head.

"You know I'm right, Den," Dylan said. "We can't risk that the cops won't start taking roll call in all Shiftertowns. I'll get him home as soon as I'm able."

Deni nodded. True, Jace would be safer at his own Shiftertown, where he had his father and family to take care of him. But Deni's heart felt like a stone in her chest, and her food tasted like dust.

She set the plate down, nodded at Sean and Dylan, and walked in a daze toward the porch and the cubs. Deni wished Ellison and her sons were here—she needed to wrap herself in her family to ease the sudden pain.

Andrea seemed to sense her need. She handed her little boy to Kim and met Deni in the yard, pulling her into a hug.

"I know," Andrea said. "I saw it in your eyes when you looked at him tonight. Don't worry. I'll tell Liam, and we'll make it so you can see him again."

Andrea was sweet; she truly was. Andrea herself had been given special permission to move from a Colorado Shiftertown to this one, which proved it could be done, but she'd had to jump through many hoops to do it. Deni knew she could see Jace again, but it would be tough, and both Liam and Jace's father would have to be convinced that it was necessary for either Jace or Deni to move permanently.

Andrea released Deni, giving her a reassuring smile, and returned to the porch to lift her cub from Kim's lap. The look of joy she turned on her son squeezed Deni's heart.

"Don't let him go."

Deni jumped and swung around, her wolf's senses sending her into a defensive crouch. Tiger had moved to her side in that stealthy way he had, and now he stood right next to her, alone, his bulk filling the space Andrea had vacated.

"Tiger." Deni straightened up and clenched her hands. "Don't *do* that."

"You should not let Jace go home," Tiger said. "Keep him with you."

"I can't," Deni said. "He doesn't belong here, and if they catch him . . ."

Tiger shook his head. He reached out his hand, carefully, and touched the air in front of Deni's chest, as though he saw something there. Deni felt the warmth inside her, the tingling need she'd been pretending not to notice. "You have it, don't you?" Tiger said. "Don't let it go."

Deni swallowed. If she admitted the mate bond right now, she'd fall in a crumpled heap and begin weeping. "I—"

"Tiger, honey," Carly strolled to him and laced her hands around his arm again. "Don't scare her. She's been through a lot."

Tiger only looked at Deni with his intense yellow eyes, as though willing her to understand and obey. He let Carly lead him away, but he glanced at Deni over his shoulder, his gaze penetrating Deni to the most frightened part of her.

CHAPTER TEN

When Jace emerged from Faerie into the grove of trees in Shiftertown, it was dawn. Shiftertown was quiet, the nocturnal Shifters having turned in to sleep, the ones who lived by human schedules not up yet.

Dylan met him. Dylan's face was covered with new-growth beard, and lines had deepened about his eyes. He hadn't slept all night.

Time moved differently in Faerie, Fionn had told Jace, sometimes slower, sometimes faster. Jace had spent twice as many hours there as the time had moved here. Scary. What if he popped into Faerie one day, lived a week, and came out to find everyone long dead? Or he aged in Faerie while Deni had lived only one day? Too weird to contemplate. The solution was not to go to Faerie again, which was fine with Jace.

He still felt better, even with the Collar's loose links chafing him. He'd have to figure out why he seemed to have recovered from his need to go feral, and if whatever he discovered could help with removing the Collars.

The police had given up harassing the Shifters and gone

again, Dylan said, but there was no telling when they'd
be back. Best Jace go home, to his own Shiftertown. Jace
couldn't argue with his reasoning, though leaving meant
leaving Deni, and that thought threatened to make his feral
rage return.

Fionn hadn't accompanied Jace. Dylan told Jace to wait
for him there, while he arranged transportation to the airstrip. He walked away, leaving Jace alone.

Not for long. As soon as Dylan left the grove, Deni hurried into it.

Jace said nothing, only opened his arms, and Deni ran
straight into them. Jace caught her up, turning around with
her, holding her hard, breathing in her warmth, her scent.

"I don't want you to go," Deni said. She curled her hands
against Jace's chest, where his heart was pounding.

"I don't want to go either."

Their mouths met, locking together, heat joining heat.
Jace drank her hungrily, imbibing her spice. He licked the
corner of her mouth, and moved one hand to her lush breast.

"Den," he said savagely, "I haven't . . . Finding you . . ."

Is all the world to me, Deni finished inside her head. *I
was drowning, far from shore. And then you came.*

"Tiger told me not to let you go," she whispered.

Jace lifted his head, his green eyes dark. "I have to. If
they find me, it will be bad for everyone here, not only me."

"I know. I know."

"I can't let you get hurt because of me." Jace traced her
cheek with a firm thumb. "But I'll fix this. I'll find a way to
come back as soon as I can."

Deni nodded, tears filling her eyes. No reason to cry,
she told herself. This was smart, and he'd just promised to
come back for her.

She heard Tiger's gruff voice in her head. *Don't let
him go.*

Everyone knew Tiger was a little nuts, but he'd looked at
Deni as though he could see the threads of the mate bond
around her heart. He was telling her to latch on to the bond
and not let go, damn the consequences. But Deni needed to

be sensible. If they did everything by the book, asking for official permission for Jace to move here, or she and her sons to go with him, then the humans couldn't legally keep them apart. But permission was difficult to obtain—the human government might deny it for any number of reasons, and then it would be more difficult for Jace or Deni to sneak away to be together.

"You could always hide here until they get tired of looking," Deni said, though without much hope.

Jace shook his head, pressing her closer. "Dylan's right. The police might start checking the other Shiftertowns. My dad can't cover for me for long."

"I know." His words made sense, but Deni's heart ached. She tried to smile. "The next time you come, we'll take my motorcycle out on one of the back roads and see what it can do. We'll open it up—just us and the wind."

"Yeah." Jace cupped her cheek. "That sounds good."

They kissed again, mouths seeking, needy, each of them holding on tight. Deni memorized Jace's scent and his goodness, his taste, his hard body against hers. He was large, strong, whole, the answer to her emptiness.

From beyond them, Dylan cleared his throat, the sound rolling from the edge of the grove. Jace broke the kiss, lifting slowly away from Deni. His green eyes held anguish. "I have to go."

"Wait." Deni fumbled with the catch of her bracelet, an old-fashioned clasp. The bracelet had been in her family for so long, no one remembered where it had come from. She took off the bracelet and pressed it into Jace's hand. "Keep this for me. Bring it back to me."

Jace started to shake his head. "It's special to you, I can tell."

"It is. But if I know you have it, that will be special too."

Jace hesitated another moment, then he closed his fingers around it. "I'll keep it safe. I promise."

Deni nodded. She stepped back from him and clasped her hands. "The Goddess go with you."

"No." Jace reached for her once more, his arms coming

hard around her. "That's what you say to someone you'll never see again."

His kiss was fierce, wild. Deni held on to Jace and kissed him back with as much force, her heart pounding and aching.

At last Jace eased away, and Deni made herself let him go. Jace laid his hand on her chest, between her breasts.

"Be well, my heart," he said, then he turned and walked away, following Dylan into the Texas dawn.

There was no question of Deni coming with Jace to the plane. Jace understood—the fewer Shifters who left Shiftertown the better.

Jace hunkered down with a bunch of junk in the bed of Dylan's small pickup, and Dylan tied a tarp over it all. Then Dylan drove out of Shiftertown without ceremony, heading east along the Bastrop Highway.

After a long time, Dylan took a turn off the main road, pulled over, and lifted the tarp. The road was deserted, and Jace climbed out, stretching his cramped limbs. Dylan would leave Jace here to wait for a human man to come by who would take him the rest of the way to the airstrip— they'd done this on Jace's previous trips as well. Safer for all concerned if a Shifter wasn't spotted driving out to an abandoned airfield.

"Be well," Dylan said, clasping Jace in a brief but tight hug. "I'll work on things from here."

Jace nodded his thanks, jogged into the tall grasses, and crouched down, hiding himself, to wait. Dylan got back into his truck and drove smoothly away before any other vehicles came down the road.

Jace didn't wait long, though it felt like forever as he lay in the dew-laden grass. Another pickup, which was driven by one of the men he'd seen this trip at the landing strip, slowed down and waited for Jace to climb inside the cab.

Fifteen minutes and an unpaved road later, Jace was back at the airstrip, boarding the small, old cargo plane a man named Marlo flew. Marlo had long ago worked for very bad men, transporting things for them from Mexico, but had given it up. Now he smuggled Shifters anywhere in the country they wanted to go.

"Let's get up in the air," Marlo said, ushering Jace up the little stair into the body of the plane. "The wind is getting bad. Want to get out of this system."

To Jace, the sky was clear and beautiful, only a little breeze stirring the grasses around them. But pilots spoke a different language. Jace stowed his backpack, then took the copilot's seat in the cockpit. He didn't know how to fly, but Marlo tended to talk a lot on the trips, and Jace always felt better if Marlo faced forward, looking at his instruments, than if he constantly turned around to yell at Jace in the back.

Marlo did his checks, started up, checked some more instruments, waved at the ground crew, and taxied out to the grown-over airstrip. The two men at the tiny shed waved back, then returned to the pickup that had brought Jace and drove away.

Marlo sped the plane down the little runway, bouncing over ruts, then lifted off without much of a bump. The plane flopped around a little as they climbed, buffeted by the winds Marlo had mentioned, but soon they were running in a fairly smooth layer of air. The city of Austin spread out to the north of them, hugging the river and its hills, the river country receding to a streak of vivid green in the otherwise dry Texas brown.

Jace opened his hand and studied the bracelet resting in his palm. Delicate, yet strong, like Deni was. He rubbed his thumb over the smooth gold, determined to see her smile at him when he brought it back to her.

He growled. Jace already missed her like crazy, and the wildcat in him snarled at him for walking away. The torn skin on his neck hurt again, the soreness making his beast that much angrier. Whatever mitigating effects being in Faerie had given him must be wearing off.

Interesting about that. Jace let the bracelet trickle over

his hand as he thought. Maybe they should try taking off the Collars inside Faerie. Then again, what if inside Faerie Shifters behaved normally and then went insane when they walked out once more?

Jace let out a sigh. He'd been full of enthusiasm about removing the Collars when he'd come to Austin, but things had changed. He no longer wanted to risk himself for what might be. He had something to lose now. If the Morrisseys wanted to experiment with the Collars so much, they could, as Fionn might say, suck it up, and test it on themselves.

His gaze returned to the bracelet, and he imagined it still warm from Deni's wrist . . .

The plane bounced once, hard, as though it had hit some kind of airborne speed bump. Marlo shouted, "Whoa!" and grabbed for the stick as dials started spinning.

"Whoa, *what?*" Jace yelled over the engines that had started to roar. "You can fix that, right?"

"Shit," Marlo said. He added quickly, "Nothing to worry about—this has happened before. I need to set down. Help me look for a place."

"Nothing to worry about?" The plane was heading downward, leaving Jace's stomach behind, everything in back banging and clattering. Another bump shook the plane, which nosed harder downward. The small airplane gave a profound rattle and smoke poured out the left-side engine, flames licking the wing. "The engine's on fire!" Jace shouted. "You call that nothing to worry about?"

"The wind will put it out. Help me look!"

"Aw, crap on a crutch," Jace snarled.

He wrapped his hand around the bracelet and held it hard, as though it were a link to Deni herself. *Goddess, Goddess, great and good,* Jace began the ritual prayer, then gave up trying to remember the words. *Help me. Let me be with Deni again. I feel the mate bond, for crying out loud.*

The warmth in his heart he'd told himself he didn't yet have time to think about, now suffused his body. Saying good-bye to Deni had been one of the hardest things Jace had ever done. Jace had been ripping out his heart and walking away bleeding, but he'd made himself do it, believing leaving was the right thing to do.

The mate bond meant you gave yourself to that other person, body and soul. You protected them; they healed you, and you healed them while they protected you. Jace didn't know if Deni felt the mate bond for him—sometimes both parties didn't share it—but he remembered the look in her gray eyes before he'd left her.

She had to feel it. They'd grown from acquaintances to lovers to mates rapidly, but it often happened like that with Shifters. Shifters formed the mate bond, *then* they got to know each other—throughout their long, happy lives.

And now, with Marlo fighting this tiny bird, fire whipping around the wing, and the flat ground of West Texas coming up fast, Jace might never move beyond knowing the mate bond had settled in his heart.

Tiger told me not to let you go.

Tiger, damn his crazy, striped ass, had been right. He might not have predicted *this*, specifically, but he'd known Jace should have made sure he stayed next to Deni and figured things out from there.

Something cut his palm. Jace opened his hand and saw he'd clutched the gold bracelet so hard it had pressed into his skin.

Jace clenched the bracelet again and shook his fist at Marlo, the ends of the chains dancing. "Fix this damned thing. I'm taking this back to her."

"You are fucking crazy, Shifter. I need a landing strip, or I'm not fixing anything ever again."

"Shit," Jace said. He'd been scanning the ground, but what did he know about good places to put down a plane? Then he saw it, a flat stretch of land, unbroken, a dirt road without an oil well at the end of it. They were low enough now that he could see the way wasn't full of rocks or hidden washes. "What about that?"

"Good enough for me."

The plane was rattling with bone-jarring intensity, something popping in the back like a row of fireworks. Jace prayed it wasn't really fireworks.

The road came at them, Marlo desperately pulling at the stick to lift the nose enough. The wheels were down, at least, because Marlo had never pulled them up.

"Hang on!" Marlo yelled.

To what? Jace braced himself on the instrument panel, trying not to look at the dials going around and around.

They hit the road with an upward burst of dust, grinding it so thick it coated the windows, blocking their visibility. That was fine, because grass and whatever huge weeds this part of the state grew came up out of the ground and bashed into them, winding around the burning engine and spewing the flame higher.

The plane hit something and skidded sideways, throwing Marlo on top of Jace, and whipping Jace into the window. The window cracked, and flame raced inside.

At the last minute, Jace yanked off his seat belt, hauled himself out of the chair, threw the already unconscious Marlo to the bottom of the plane, and landed on top of him. A roar of explosion met Jace's ears, and then nothing.

CHAPTER ELEVEN

Deni was restless all morning. She tried to work in the yard, neatening her garden, but she found herself stabbing the trowel into the dirt again and again for no reason. Deni threw down the trowel and stripped off her gloves, dropping them as well.

Her arm felt bare and strange without the bracelet she wore all the time. She touched her skin there but smiled. The bracelet was safe with Jace. He'd come back to her.

Still, she was growling by the time she reached the house. Jackson hadn't been scheduled to work today, but Will now gave Deni a good-bye hug and went off to the warehouse.

"You all right, Mom?" Jackson said, peering at Deni after they waved off Will.

Jackson looked so much like his father, his hair dark instead of light like hers and Ellison's, his eyes a lighter shade of gray. Deni pulled him into a hug, feeling a flood of love for him. But she remembered when her mate had been dying, how the mate bond had pulled at her and sickened her . . . as it was doing now.

A reaction to Jace leaving so abruptly, she told herself. *Nothing is wrong . . .*

"I'm fine," she said.

"It's just that you look at little bit, you know . . ." Jackson frowned in worry. "Like you do when you start to go feral . . ."

He trailed off, and nausea bit Deni, the world spinning. She gripped Jackson's shoulder. "No, don't let me . . ." *Forget who everyone is, try to attack my own children. Goddess, please!*

She smelled a strong, male smell, one different enough from other Shifters to make her wolf's hackles rise. Deni growled and spun around, instinctively stepping in front of Jackson, protecting.

Tiger stood at the edge of the yard, having suddenly appeared as he usually did. Deni took a deep breath, willing herself to calm.

"You let him go," Tiger said.

Deni shook her head, the nausea still churning. "I didn't have a choice."

He waited until she came to him, not violating Ellison's territory. Deni felt herself drawn to him, though, as though she needed to go to him. Unnerving.

Tiger let his hand hover a few inches from her chest, as he'd done last night. "Something is wrong."

Fear washed cold through her. "How do you know?"

"The mate bond." Tiger closed his fingers over empty air. "It's telling you."

The logical Deni wanted to argue, to deny. The feral beast inside Deni knew. Jace was in danger.

Tiger pinned her with his yellow stare, then turned around and walked away. Deni's heart beat faster, and she almost snarled when she felt Jackson's warmth suddenly behind her.

She blinked, Jackson's worried face coming back into focus. "I'm all right," she said to him, drawing a deep breath. "I need to make a phone call." She hurried into the house, found her cell phone, and rushed across the street after Tiger to ask for the phone number of Eric Warden and his son, Jace.

The snow leopard choked on the black smoke, paws scrabbling at the hole in the fuselage to find air, any air. He burned himself on the hot metal and snarled, but he needed to get his nose out of the plane and breathe.

More scrambling, using Shifter wildcat strength and huge claws to tear into the metal. His cat brain reflected that having someone like Ronan the Kodiak bear around would be very useful right now, then he went back to the task at hand. Human thought fled, and animal ones took over.

Hole wider. Heave from back legs, wriggle spine, pull with shoulders, scramble *out*. Jace landed on top of the wreckage— on the side of the plane that had tipped over—and tried to take a deep breath. Too much smoke. He had to get away.

The engine was burning merrily, and Jace's cat nose smelled fuel. He needed to run, *now*.

A groan made him turn back, his claws raking against metal. A human lay in the wreckage, a lean man with a scraggly beard who was a little bit smelly. *Marlo,* his brain reminded him.

Jace was Shifter. He didn't need a human slowing him down and returning him to captivity. Now was his chance to run, to be free, to find a place where humans would never hunt him down. He'd get word to his mate somehow, she'd come to him, and they'd live in blissful solitude forever.

Another groan. Jace's ears went flat on his head, his cat instincts telling him to run and not stop. But he turned and lowered his body back into the wreck.

He found Marlo trapped under a pile of metal and junk, barely alive. Jace shoved at the debris, trying to reach him. Something in Jace's brain told him to shift back to human so he could lift Marlo, but his body wouldn't obey. Being animal was the best way to survive, so animal he stayed.

Fire flared high, and the temperature in the wreck doubled.

The smoke thickened. Jace couldn't breathe, couldn't cough, could no longer see. He put his mouth around the back of Marlo's neck and heaved.

The trouble with humans was they had no scruff. If Jace bit down too hard, he'd sever the man's spine and kill him. Not enough, and he wouldn't be able to carry him.

Jace finally got a decent hold on Marlo's neck and shirt, and dragged him out from under the debris. With the last breath in his lungs, Jace clawed his way up through the hole again, weighted down by the extra body. He dropped Marlo on top of the plane, seeing that he'd cut gashes into the man's neck.

Out here Jace could get his breath, but it was still tainted with the heavy smoke. Marlo lay unmoving, and Jace couldn't tell whether he was breathing.

He got his jaws around the man's shirt and neck again and scrambled off the wreckage to the ground. Once he felt the dirt under his feet, he ran, loping almost sideways as he dragged Marlo with him. Marlo's feet bump-bumped over the dry Texas grasses.

When they were about fifty feet from the plane, the fire caught the fuel's fumes and exploded. Fire washed over Jace, who threw himself on top of Marlo. Jace smelled his fur burning and drew in a lungful of volcanic air. Burning metal rained around them, sparking on the dry grass, which obligingly caught fire.

Jace hauled himself up, knowing he was on fire, and dragged Marlo down into the sparse rocks that lined a shallow wash. The wash was dry, no water under the blank blue sky, but it might protect them from the flames.

Jace dropped Marlo and rolled over the rocks, writhing desperately to grind out the fire in his fur. Marlo lay unmoving, bloody and burned, but he didn't smell dead.

Now that he wasn't burning alive and could breathe, Jace noticed all the hurts in his body, cuts from crawling out of the plane, abrasions and rawness from shielding Marlo. His left paw hurt like hell, a stinging pain that meant he'd cut himself deeply.

Jace rose stiffly from his crouch in the wash and looked around. The plane burned by itself in the middle of nothing. West Texas sprawled around them, empty as far as Jace's leopard eyes could see. Someone likely owned this land, maybe it was part of a gigantic ranch, but out here, entire counties might have only a handful of houses in them.

Jace shook himself, aching all over, but he considered himself lucky. He hadn't broken anything as far as he could tell, and though chunks of his fur had burned off and his skin smarted, he would heal.

His left paw hurt like hell, though. The last thing he remembered was clutching Deni's bracelet as the plane hit the earth. Jace flexed the pads of his empty paw and looked back at the burning wreck. He'd dropped the bracelet. Deni's bracelet, which he'd promised to keep safe for her. *No.*

He started to run back toward the plane before his leopard brain stopped him. *Let it go.* The mate bond wrapping him whimpered. That bracelet had been part of her, and she'd entrusted it to him.

Let it go. Think. Survive.

Flee.

Jace was free. No one knew where he was. When humans came to find the plane, they wouldn't even know he'd been in it. He'd been smuggled goods. Shifters, including Deni and his family, would think him dead inside it. Deni would cry. So would his dad.

Grief bit at Jace, but in his cat form, survival came first. He scanned the ground again. The first thing he noticed was a coyote, thin-legged and mangy, waiting to see if the two from the wreck would die. Easier pickings than rabbits the coyote had to chase.

Dark specks appeared in the sky as well, circling higher as they spotted Jace looking at them. Turkey buzzards, big and black, they also waiting to see whether they'd feast today. This was the kill-or-be-killed wild out here, no rules in sight.

Jace snarled and rushed at the coyote. The flea-bitten beast snarled in response but fled. Not far, though. Out of reach of Jace's charge, the coyote stopped and waited.

Jace growled his challenge. In spite of being half-burned and thrown around a wreck, Jace felt strong, more so than he had in a long time. The pain of his Collar was completely gone, and in fact, he couldn't even feel the Collar biting into him anymore. He shook himself again and sat down to let his back paw reach up to his neck to scratch.

He stopped. His delicate back toes didn't find a chain, burned or loose, or tight and whole. He swiped his neck with a front paw, with the same result.

Jace told himself to shift, to make sure, and he would—when he could remember how to. The leopard wanted to stay in this form, so Jace was staying in this form.

He writhed around, trying to find the Collar with each of his paws in turn, probably to the amusement of the coyote. Actually, the coyote didn't care—he was simply waiting to see whether Jace would be food or danger.

No, wait—the coyote had vanished. Damn him, he'd been sneaking up on Marlo while Jace went through his contortions. The coyote darted in, ready to drag Marlo—or pieces of him—away to his pack.

Jace went for the coyote. Ears up, paws moving in perfect rhythm, Jace rushed the scavenger. He didn't snarl or make any noise—he didn't have to.

The coyote barely got away from Jace's striking paw. Jace caught his tail with a claw, causing the coyote to yelp and run. Jace chased him, the leopard rejoicing in the hunt, until he realized that the buzzards had taken the opportunity to land near Marlo and see if there were any good pickings.

Jace turned and barreled toward the birds, who flapped away with slow disdain. He snarled this time, making his fur stand up so he'd be large and menacing.

He knew for certain that his Collar was gone when he finally stopped and planted himself near Marlo. He'd been ready to kill the coyote and savage its body, and the Collar hadn't tried to stop him. Jace had mastered the meditation technique, yes, but out here, chasing away scavengers while trying to stay away from a burning plane, he hadn't exactly been meditating.

The Collar was gone. Completely. It must have fallen off in the wreckage or while Jace had been dragging Marlo away from it.

That meant that somehow in the burning mess that had been Marlo's airplane, Jace's Collar had slipped off, every link of it, without hurting him and without making the world spin into insanity.

Jace sat, blinking, even his leopard realizing the enormity of it. Now, if he could shift back to human, find his way home, and try to figure out exactly how it had happened, all Shifters would benefit.

Or he could stay in the wild. For the first time in twenty years, Jace was *free*. No more Collar, no more rules, no more Shiftertowns, just wind, earth, sky, and small-brained predators.

Free, he repeated.

The only thing that kept his triumphant wildcat from taking over and erasing his human thoughts completely was one word: *Deni*.

Jace would find her and free her too. Then he'd live out his life with her, the mate of his heart. No one in this wide wilderness would be able to prevail against a wolf and a snow leopard. He and Deni would be free to be alone together, mates in the wild, as Shifters were meant to be.

Even in this vast place, someone would have reported a crashing plane by now. The humans would be coming. Jace didn't intend to let them find him here.

He grabbed Marlo by the shirt, dragged him closer to the burning wreckage, which would keep the scavengers away for a while, then turned and loped off into the tall Texas grasses. His paw still hurt him, but that was a minor inconvenience.

Eric hadn't heard from his son all day, he told Deni, and Jace likely had his cell phone off. Eric was worried too, but Marlo's plane was old and slow. It wouldn't land in Las Vegas until late in the evening, but Eric would keep his ear out. He sounded plenty anxious, but tried to calm Deni's fears, as a good Shifter alpha should.

Liam too reassured her. Flying under the radar took time, Marlo often stopped to refuel or lie low for a few hours. Marlo had a cell phone, but he wasn't answering either, and he didn't always.

After Liam left to open the bar in the afternoon, Deni paced, snapped at everyone, and got nothing done. Any pats on the back or calming words only irritated her. Eric and Liam were probably right—but Tiger's words about seeing something wrong with the mate bond, plus the tightness in Deni's chest made her half crazy.

Ellison left for the bar after Liam, telling Deni and his mate that Liam had called a tracker meeting. That meant trackers only—the Shifters who worked for Liam as bodyguards, investigators, or peacekeepers as need be. Ronan, Ellison, Spike, Sean, Tiger, and Dylan made their way there, leaving Deni restless and barely in control of herself.

At five, she couldn't stand it anymore. Deni walked out of the house and down the block, making her way to the bar on the edge of Shiftertown.

The parking lot was already full. This bar was a popular stop on the way home from work for humans who liked Shifters. Groupies were already there, lounging about suggestively, waiting for Shifters to come looking. With the fight club shut down for a while, the groupies had decided to pile on here, it seemed.

The human bartender shot Deni a sharp look when she walked in. The other Shifters already there were cagey, but when Deni asked why, they didn't have an answer. They knew something was up, but they didn't know what. The trackers had gone into Liam's office and shut the door, they told her, then all except Liam and Dylan had come out and left the bar. Where the trackers, including Ellison, had gone, no one knew.

Deni had no business confronting Liam, who wasn't in

her family and held plenty of rank over her. His tracker meeting might have nothing to do with her or Jace, or the police. Shit involving Shifters and Shiftertown happened all the time.

One of the groupie girls sat in a booth by herself, talking on her phone. And talking and talking. She'd look around, and then start talking again. If she wasn't talking, she was texting.

The young woman didn't look much different from the other groupies. She wore a short, skintight pink dress with mile-high black heels, had short dyed-black hair that had been cut into cute wisps, and she'd painted her face with cat's eyes and whiskers. Her outfit shouted, *Come and get me, Shifter, I like to purr,* but her looks and actions spoke of extreme nerves.

After Deni had watched her covertly for a time, she realized another thing that made this woman different. The other groupies were eyeing Shifters hungrily, or sashaying up to them without shame. Most groupies were female, as many of the Shifters here were male, but some young male groupies were eyeing the male Shifters—and Deni—with the same kind of interest.

The young woman in the booth was doing her best *not* to catch any Shifter's attention. Which made no sense if she dressed like a groupie and hung out in a Shifter bar.

Deni picked up the bottle of beer the bartender had slid to her and carried it with her to the booth. Deni plunked the bottle onto the table and sat down opposite the young woman.

The young woman jumped as though struck by sparks. Deni held her gaze, the girl trying to evade her eyes.

"That Shifter over there." Deni pointed. "Broderick. He's looking for some action."

Whether Broderick was or not, Deni didn't know, but the young woman's reaction was telling. She flinched and didn't look where Deni indicated. In fact, she moved a little so Deni would block Broderick's line of sight from her.

"I'm waiting for someone," the young woman mumbled. "Leave me alone, Shifter."

"Yeah? Who are you waiting for?"

The woman stared at her. She had light blue eyes and smelled strongly of fear, and even more of anger.

"None of your business." She had defiance in her words and eyes, but her voice shook.

"Interesting," Deni said. She snatched the woman's cell phone from her hand and stood up.

The girl shrieked. "Hey, give that back!"

Deni stepped away from her reaching hands and scrolled down her list of recent calls. Only one had been made today, much earlier this afternoon, which meant shc'd been faking talking to someone. Stalling. She'd made plenty of calls yesterday, though, and the day before that, and on into the previous week. All to the City of Austin police.

"Don't think so," Deni said.

Broderick turned around, scowling, not liking to have his beer drinking with his brothers interrupted. "Who the hell is making all the noise?" Broderick growled.

Deni ignored him. She swung away from the groupie lunging for her phone and went for Liam's office door. This was too important for respecting Liam's privacy. "Broderick, don't let her leave," Deni said, then was through the door and into the office.

Liam was on the phone at his desk, Dylan hovering next to him, listening. Usually Liam sat back here with his feet up, casually going over billing, invoices, payroll, and the like, but today he sat straight up in his chair, his hand over his eyes, and he was speaking rapidly into the phone.

"Have you pinpointed where?" he asked whoever was on the other end. "Well, damn it, *find* it."

"Find what?" Cold washed through Deni, triggering the dizziness she'd been fighting all day. "Liam?"

Dylan came quickly around Deni and closed the door. "Keep it down, lass. We can't let the world know."

"Know what? Damn it, *tell me*."

Liam glanced up at her, his face strained as he listened

to the stream of words coming from his phone. He shot a look at his father and nodded.

Dylan took Deni's hand between his, pressing warmth into it. "We didn't want you to know until we were sure, Den. Marlo's plane went down, somewhere in West Texas. We don't know where yet, and we don't know who survived."

CHAPTER TWELVE

Deni's world stopped—or maybe it kept spinning, whirling out of control while she froze in one place. She could barely see Dylan as she stared at him, only the blue of his eyes as he held her gaze.

Shock and then panic swept through her, and her wolf started to howl, a grief-stricken, wild howl that only happened with the death of a mate.

"Deni," Dylan's voice cut through the noise. "Keep looking at me."

The voice that came out of Deni's mouth was snarling and wrong. "Where is he?"

"South of the I-10," Liam said. "Somewhere between here and Fort Stockton. Great," he said into the phone. "Covers a hell of a lot of ground."

Deni heard a voice on the other end—Ronan, she thought, from the deep timbre. "That's all we know," Ronan said. "We can't ask too many questions."

"Ask," Deni snarled. "Find him."

"Lass," Dylan said.

"Don't 'lass' me. Find him. He's my *mate*."

Both Dylan and Liam focused on her, as the truth of it filled Deni, hurting her and elating her at the same time. *My mate. Hurt. Lost. Find!*

Deni was growling again, the edges of her world going concave as her eyes changed to her wolf's. Dylan pried the cell phone she'd taken from the girl out of her hand, which Deni had clamped down on so hard the plastic was starting to crack.

"Where did you get this?" Dylan asked, looking at the smart phone, which no Shifter would carry.

"Spy," Deni said, forcing out the word. "Broderick has."

Dylan's eyes moved as he read the phone numbers, then he gave a furious snarl and shoved his way past Deni, banging out of the office.

Deni yanked Liam's phone from his hands. "Ronan. You tell me where he is."

"Deni?" Ronan's tone softened. "Yeah, thought so. Sean's hacking as fast as he can. He's trying to pin down the location based on reports."

"Where are you?"

"Don't know." Ronan turned away from the phone, exchanging questions with others. "Looks like we're about where the 55 runs into the 277, wherever that is. A little west of that. Ellison says don't you dare come out here."

"Tell Ellison . . ."

Deni's coherence left her. She didn't remember dropping the phone or saying anything to Liam. She only knew she was walking out through the bar, past Dylan, who had the pseudo-groupie pinned between himself and Broderick, ignoring them when they tried to stop her. She walked and walked until she found herself in front of her own house, pulling out the new motorcycle Ellison had bought her and mounting it.

Deni must have found the keys, put on her helmet, jeans, and boots. She didn't remember. In a few minutes, she was pulling out of Shiftertown, skimming through traffic to the roads that led west out of town.

Deni didn't know Texas like Ellison did, but she knew

how to get from Austin across Hill Country west, heading through Fredericksburg toward the 10. At the onramp to the interstate, she paused, debating whether to go north or south. She picked north, turning again after about thirty miles to the 377 and cutting south.

Not until she was well down the highway, heading south and west as fast as she could, did she realize she was riding her motorcycle.

Alone. Out on the road, under the sky, through the flat Texas lands and dust. On her own. No one with her, no Jace holding her and telling her she could do it.

She'd navigated traffic that moved thickly to Fredericksburg and then the speeding trucks on the 10, and now the open highway without any fear except that which filled her about Jace.

The sun was still high, though evening was coming on. Not much traffic out here now. Deni opened the bike up all the way, the high-powered machine taking her swiftly down the road. Shifters weren't allowed to buy new vehicles, but Deni always thought Harleys were better once they were broken in. Ellison had tinkered with this one until it purred like a lion, or maybe a snow leopard.

Deni ran it so fast she almost missed the 55, which jogged from this road west and a little north. She sped down it, squinting against the bright sun, nice and hot still in late July.

The 55 ended in a T junction with the 277, one leg of the T going north, the other going south. Deni stopped at a little pulloff at the crossroads and looked around. One truck rumbled past south, and a car sped north, its headlights turned on against the gathering twilight. No road went west from here except for a dirt track that headed off into the wilderness.

But Ronan had said they were *west* of this intersection, and so that was where they were.

Deni waited until the road was clear, then she glided the bike across the highway and onto the faint dirt path that led into nothing. Her wolf senses kicked in as she rode. She'd taken off her helmet at the crossroads, and now she could see, hear, and smell as a Shifter while her human body navigated the bike.

As the sky darkened, the huge arch of it brushed with stars, Deni saw a tiny orange light far to her left. The narrow dirt road bent to her right, taking her away from it, and she had no way of knowing whether the track would curve around again to where she wanted to go.

Deni shut off the bike, stripped off her clothes, stretched her limbs, and changed to her wolf.

Once in wolf form, she smelled the greasy smoke from faraway burning fuel, the scent making her gag. Deni trotted into the empty land, homing in on the fire. She passed oil wells, stark metal giants against the twilit sky, their heads moving up and down, clanking as they pumped. But they were insignificant, an affectation of humans. Deni was wolf now, nothing more, and the night flowed to her.

After a long time of unceasing trotting, she made it to what she now saw was the smoldering wreck of a small airplane. Inside the perimeter of the fire's light, she saw the hulking forms of Ronan and Tiger and the tall one of Spike bending over a heap on the ground.

Jace? Deni's heart pounded as she sped up. No, Deni saw and scented as she neared the others. The man on the ground was human, probably the pilot, Marlo. She smelled no stench of death, so Marlo was still alive. Ronan and Spike were lashing him onto a stretcher, preparing to load him into a pickup that was parked nearby. Tiger saw her and gave her a long look then he turned back to helping with Marlo.

Another wolf ran out of the darkness and straight to Deni—Ellison, large and gray, his wolf's eyes meeting hers. Ellison showed sorrow but also anger.

What the hell are you doing here? his body language said. *What part of 'don't you dare come out here' didn't you understand?*

Where's Jace? Deni snapped back, stopping herself from throwing herself at him and howling in anguish.

Don't know. Lost his scent.

Deni growled and rushed past him. She heard Ellison snarl a curse behind her and follow.

Deni dashed into the firelight, earning a startled look from the Shifters there. Sean, sword on his back, started to step in front of her, but Deni ran around him to Tiger. *You're supposed to be so good at search and rescue,* she growled up at Tiger. *Where is he?* Deni glared at him, willing him to understand, but she was a wolf, and he a tiger, and who knew what got through?

Tiger watched her, his brows furrowed over his golden eyes. "You have to find him," he said.

Why haven't you?

Tiger kept staring at her. "*You* have to."

"Tiger, a little help here," Ronan called to him.

Tiger locked gazes with Deni a beat longer then he turned away to where Ronan was doing something near the burning debris, Deni had no idea what. Deni growled in frustration and ran from the firelight, searching the perimeter of the crash site for Jace's scent.

She picked it up a little way beyond the wreck, when the wind blew the smoke from her face—Jace, loud and clear. She started off after him.

Already tried that, came Ellison's growl. *Lost it pretty quick.*

Deni wasn't listening. Each species of Shifter had an advantage over the others. Felines could see brilliantly in the dark, and they were *fast*. Bears had great strength and also stamina, probably because they slept so much, Deni had always privately thought.

But wolves beat both bears and Felines in the ability to follow scent. No Shifter could outdo a Lupine on a scent trail. A wolf's second prowess was communication. Wolves howled from hill to hill, passing information, warning, claiming territory. Their nonverbal skills were the best of any Shifter.

Right now, Deni needed only scent. Let Ellison howl at her—she had a mate to find.

She lost Jace's trail fairly soon, as Ellison had warned her, near another oil well, this one capped. The metallic stench of old oil and rusting machinery cancelled out the warmer scent of Shifter, and Deni sat down on her haunches, bereft.

Jace had come this way, though, that was certain. Whether he'd doubled back, or was lying hurt somewhere, Deni couldn't tell.

But Jace was her *mate*. They shared the mate bond—no doubt about it. Deni felt it inside her, its warmth around her heart, filling her with strength.

Deni's accident had robbed her of most of her confidence. She'd gone through episodes where she'd forgotten who she was and didn't know anyone around her—she'd attacked Ellison, and she'd turned on her friends and sometimes her own cubs. Terrified of hurting those she loved, she'd locked herself into a tiny world, where she went out little, and kept herself from fighting, or even enjoying herself too much. She'd not been able to ride a motorcycle, even behind someone else, as she'd explained to Jace, after she'd been run down, growing terrified even at the thought. Seeing the dangerous man who'd hurt her die had helped her begin to find closure, but the lingering fears died hard.

The loss of control—the feral rising up in her and taking over—bothered her the most. But in this place, in the darkness, Deni realized that the only way she would find her mate would be to surrender to the beast inside her.

She moved away from the oil well, then sat down and closed her eyes. Deni drew long breaths, scenting past the barrier of the oil and the fire, searching the night.

She remembered what had gone through her when she'd seen Broderick attack Jace at the fight club. She hadn't known Jace was her mate then, but something in Deni had made her attack Broderick, to fight alongside Jace and protect him.

Deni brought to life the rage that had washed over her then, remembering the feel and taste of it. She let go of all rational thought, and let the beast come.

Her Collar sparked once, but her coherence left her, and instinct took over.

The wolf put her head down and sniffed the ground, walking at first, then moving faster. She crisscrossed back and forth over open earth and then down a rocky wash.

She found nothing, but Deni's wolf wouldn't let her grow frustrated. Tracking by scent took patience and time. She climbed up the other side of the wash, continuing to hunt, covering every inch of ground she could. She moved farther and farther from the wreck, leaving the other Shifters far behind. Still she found nothing. Either Jace had left some other way than his own feet, or he'd hidden himself well.

Deni sat down in the darkness, hearing the slither of snakes in the dried grass, they giving her a wide berth. She could scent nothing but the night now—the grains of dust on the wind, the coolness of water far away, the wild dryness of Texas, unchanged for centuries. No wildcats, except those at the wreck behind her, no Shifters at all.

Maybe scent wasn't what she should be following, the dim thought came. Deni contemplated that in her quiet wolf way, then she closed her eyes, wrapped herself around the mate bond, and sent it outward.

There. An answering tug, far to the west and south of where she stood. Jace was there. False scents could be laid, and scents could be covered, but nothing could disguise the almost painful tug of the mate bond.

Deni loped back the way she'd come, across the wash, and started running, drawn to Jace with surety.

She heard Ellison howl in frustration somewhere behind her. He'd lost her scent and couldn't find her in the darkness. No matter. Deni would find her mate and bring him home, and all would be well.

J ace sensed her coming. The snow leopard stopped in midrun, pulled up short as though someone had snapped a tether on him and yanked him to a halt.

He'd been running, putting as much distance between himself and the wreck as he possibly could. Whoever found him—Shifter or human—would want to drag him back to captivity, Collars, and rules. Shifters taming themselves, Jace was realizing, didn't mean safety. It meant submission.

But his mate was coming.

Jace stopped on a little rise, a rare thing in this flat world. He sat down, panting, wrapping his cat tail around him as he waited for her.

Deni raced out of the dry grasses, her body a streak of gray under the moonlight. She came fast, running up the rise, not stopping. She let out a joyful yip and barreled into Jace so hard they rolled together down the other side of the little hill and ended up in a heap on the bottom.

Deni shifted into her human form, naked, her body outlined by starlight. Tears streaked her face.

"I found you." She wrapped her arms around Jace's leopard, who huffed and nuzzled her. "I found you."

Jace licked her face, tasting her tears, and Deni laughed as his rough tongue nearly pushed her over. *Come with me, my love,* Jace urged. *Into the wild, where we belong.*

Deni pulled back, studying him. "Are you all right? It looks like they're taking Marlo to a hospital. You should get looked at too."

For answer, Jace jumped on her, knocking her to the ground. Deni's mouth curved to laughter as she held an armful of fur. "Seriously, Jace. I was worried about you. Everyone is. I thought you were dead."

The tears returned. Jace licked them away again, this time being gentle.

"I was so scared for you that I jumped on my motorcycle and rode away without realizing it. Did you hear me? I rode. *My motorcycle.* By myself. And I wasn't afraid!"

Jace licked her again. *I'm glad, my heart. You are healing.*

"Ride back with me. That will be even better."

Nope. Not going back.

"Jace." Deni stroked his head, and Jace wanted to purr. "I don't speak Feline very well. Change and talk to me."

Jace didn't want to change. He'd stay cat, she'd stay wolf,

and they'd make a den somewhere. They were smart enough to hunt and evade hunters, and to teach their cubs to do the same. He loved her scent, which was stirring his mating frenzy.

"What's wrong?" Deni asked him, stroking him again. "I let go of my biggest fear just now—losing control of myself—to let my wolf take over so I could find you. And you know what? I'm fine. Look." She spread her arms. "I didn't go feral. I found you, and I didn't lose myself. I don't have to be afraid anymore." She held Jace again, his mate strong and warm. "The crash must have been horrible. But don't lose yourself, Jace. Please. Come back to me."

There was nothing wrong with Jace. He was free, and Collarless. But it was dark and Deni hadn't touched his neck. She didn't understand yet.

"Please, Jace. I need you."

Tears trickled from her eyes again, tugging Jace out of his animal focus. He shifted, not as smoothly as he usually did, but jerking and groaning with the pain of it. His cat did *not* want to let go.

"It came off," Jace said, the words bearing a Feline growl. "Look. The Collar. Gone."

He took Deni's hand and put it to his neck.

Deni's eyes widened. She brushed Jace's bare neck, which didn't hurt at all, skimming her fingers around to his throat. "What happened?"

"Don't know. Was out of the wreck before I realized. Maybe the fire. Maybe it takes intense heat to melt them off."

Jace touched Deni's face, his need for her kicking him hard. Deni moved to his touch, then she grabbed his hand and stared at it. "What is *that?*"

Jace glanced at his palm. It still hurt, and now he saw why. His palm was burned but crossed by a gold streak, which he realized was Deni's bracelet. The slender gold band had been fused into his skin.

CHAPTER THIRTEEN

"Hurts," Jace said. And *itched* too.

Deni kissed his palm, her lips cool. "I can see that. What happened?"

"It must have heated and melted," Jace said. "Sorry, Den. I promised I'd bring it back to you."

"You did." Deni touched his face and gave him a smile that tightened the bond around his heart. "Let's go home."

"We are home." Deni was under him, her body soft, her scent and warmth making him forget pain. "Stay here with me."

She looked worried again. "We need to go back. You have friends and family who love you, and they're afraid for you."

Jace nuzzled her. "But I'm free of everything. I'm done with being used, hurt, experimented on. I'm finished being easygoing Jace, in the background. I have my mate, my life. I have *you*."

Deni's expression softened. "Yes."

The mating frenzy was kicking in with her too; Jace

saw it in her eyes. Her fingers were hot as she brushed his face, finding his hurts.

The touch of the mate healed. Jace closed his eyes and knew his wounds were closing, his burns easing, his Shifter metabolism helped by the gentle caress of his true mate.

"Jace, stay with me."

Jace opened his eyes, realizing he'd started to revert to his leopard. He forced himself into human shape again. He needed to stay human right now, because he wanted to have her.

He growled low in his throat. Deni recognized the sound, her eyes becoming darker, filled with need. She ran her hands up his back and to his neck.

Jace knew that once he started kissing her, he'd not be able to stop, and he didn't care. He slanted his mouth over hers, tasting her heat, her frenzy. It built and grew, calling to his own frenzy, which answered.

The kisses turned fierce. Jace bit down on Deni's lower lip, eliciting a gasp from her but also laughter. She arched against him while she laughed, her body moving in wonderful ways.

Jace held her down with a strong hand and entered her. As he slid inside, his world changed.

The selfish wildness that had infused him when he'd realized he'd lost the Collar whirled into one tight focus. *Deni.* She alone mattered. He wanted to be with her—forever—and nowhere else. Even if he had to return to Shiftertown with her, to still be a captive, it didn't matter anymore. Jace would find a way to be with her, he vowed this. And with Deni, he'd always be free.

He fit into her as though she'd been made for him. Jace kissed her lips, her face, her lips again as he drew back then stroked inside her even deeper.

Deni sucked in her breath and then she smiled, her eyes darkening in pleasure. She touched his cheek as she liked to, her fingertips a soft counterpart to the crazed need inside him.

Jace rocked into her, her body squeezing down on him

and turning him wild. Raw need flooded him, relieved
only by the wonderful feeling of thrusting into her. Stroke
after stroke, loving her, cradling her body with one arm so
the hard dirt wouldn't cut into her.

"My mate," he whispered. "I saw you, and never wanted
to be without you."

Deni shook her head, fingers threading through his
hair. "Jace."

"Be mine," Jace said. "Say it. Always mine."

Deni smiled. *"Mine."*

He returned the smile, his fierce. "Forever."

"Yes."

The word turned into a groan. Deni's grip bit into his
shoulders, and she held him while she shuddered and cried
his name, her thrusts meeting his. Jace bent his head and
nipped her neck, tasting the metallic tang of her Collar.

He'd have it off her—he'd figure out how. And she'd be
free, with him. The pain would be gone, and Deni would
heal. He'd be with her, next to her, helping her all the way.

"Jace."

Deni's groan filled him with frenzy. His thrusts grew
faster, his growls deeper. He'd go to ground with her, and
they'd do this all day long and into the night. She'd smile at
him, beautiful and sensual, and wrap her arms around
him, wanting to do it again.

"Deni. *Goddess.*" Jace lost his seed into her, pumping
his hips while she laughed to the stars.

Jace raised his head, his body slick with sweat, and
kissed her lips, her mouth hot with afterglow. "I love you,"
he said, his heart in every word.

"I love you too, Jace. Always my mate."

Jace was still hard, pulsing with need for her. He gave
her a feral smile as he thrust into her again, beginning the
rhythm once more.

Deni gave him a startled look, and then she laughed. The
laughter soon turned to groans, and they gave themselves
over to the frenzy, their cries ringing against the millions of
bright stars.

* * *

Ellison found Jace and Deni where they lay together in the warm Texas night. Of course he did—Deni knew they'd given him plenty of time to find their scent, and they must have been throwing off pheromones like crazy, providing an easy trail to follow.

Ellison came trotting up as his wolf, then shifted to human and groaned. "Not *again*. I swear, I can't come near you two without finding you tangled together." His voice held relief though, even rejoicing.

Jace helped Deni to her feet and put her behind his warm body, but when he faced Ellison, he wasn't defensive and angry—he showed his open hands, a posture of peace.

"Congratulate us, Ellison," Jace rumbled. "I'm mate-claiming your sister, Deni Rowe, under the light of the moon, the Goddess, and in front of a witness—you. I plan to ask Liam or my dad to perform the mating rituals as soon as they can."

Ellison stopped, moonlight gleaming on his light hair and wolf-gray eyes. He was Deni's alpha, the leader of her small pack, but answering the mate-claim was Deni's choice. "You good with that, Den?" Ellison asked, his voice going soft.

"Yeah." Deni slid her arms around Jace from behind, loving the tall solidness of his body, his warm scent, the feel of his skin as she kissed his shoulder. "I'm good with that. I accept the mate-claim. Jace?" She heard the shaking in her voice. "You ready to go home? To my home I mean—it's closer right now. We can call your dad from there. I bet he's worried sick."

Deni held her breath, waiting for Jace to want to return to the leopard, to insist Deni come with him into the wild, or leave on his own if she wouldn't. He wore no Collar now—there was nothing to stop him.

Even so, life in the wild was dangerous. Jace could be found, hunted, killed. And he could still go feral—Shifters who lived on their own, letting their beasts take over, often did go feral. The Shifters Ellison's mate, Maria, had been rescued from had refused to take Collars, hidden out, and become feral and cruel. Collars, for their pain, and the Shifter laws, for their restrictions, at least worked to help keep Shifters sane.

Jace turned in Deni's arms and looked down at her, his face in shadow. Ellison waited behind him, tense, uncertain.

Deni's heart ached, both with the bond and with worry. Jace looked better, his burns pale streaks in the moonlight. He looked stronger too, and more at ease, any uncertainty he might have felt for his place in the world gone.

Then he smiled. Every bit of love was in the smile, every bit of tenderness. He brushed back a lock of Deni's hair, his fingers warm.

"We'll want to tell your cubs you accepted my mate-claim," Jace said. "So yeah. Let's go home."

A Shifter meeting was called in Liam's house the next day, after Jace and Deni had rested from the long drive back to Austin—well, Deni remembered with a blush—they'd done more than just rest. The meeting included Eric Warden, Jace's father.

Deni's heart squeezed as Eric strode across the house to meet Jace when he came in, father enfolding son in a long, hard embrace. Eric's mate, Iona, who was heavy with Eric's child, also hugged Jace, wiping away her tears when she released him.

Jace reached for Deni, who'd hung back from the family greeting, and pulled her forward. "You remember Deni Rowe, Ellison's sister."

Eric understood their connection as soon as he looked at Deni, and Iona caught on a second later. Eric gazed at Deni with eyes the same color as his son's, then he put his big arms around Deni and pulled her into an embrace equally as tight as the one he'd shared with Jace.

"Thank you, child," Eric said, his voice rumbling into her ear. "Welcome to the family."

He stood Deni back and studied her, a satisfied look in his eyes. Iona slid past Eric and hugged Deni herself.

"Congratulations, you two." Iona winked at Deni as she stepped away from her. "Jace is a sweetheart. A keeper."

Deni smiled her agreement. "I think so."

"And now Collar-free," Eric said. "Thank the Goddess."

Deni understood Eric was thanking the Goddess for more than Jace's Collar being off. A shudder went through Eric, which Deni recognized as a father's relief that his cub was safe and whole.

"Jace has a theory about that," Liam said from where he lounged on a window seat in the living room. He held his black-haired daughter in the curve of his arm, little Katriona watching the adults with interest. "Carry on, lad."

Jace held up his hand, which bore a red streak. Last night, when they'd returned to the Austin Shiftertown and after Sean and Dylan had gotten Marlo to a hospital—the resilient man was on the mend—Sean and Jace had painfully dug the remnants of the gold chain from Jace's hand. Andrea had quickly done a healing on him, then Deni had completed the healing in the privacy of the Rowe family's secret basement.

"Fionn saw the bracelet last night when he was visiting Andrea," Jace said. "Andrea told me this morning that Fionn told her that this bracelet is made of Fae gold. Passed down through the female line of many generations of Deni's mother's family. Shifters used to live in Faerie—why couldn't one of them have had access to Fae gold?" Jace slid his arm around Deni. "I was holding the bracelet, which Deni gave me as a keepsake, when the plane went down. I went through hell, nearly burned alive. The heat must have melted it into me, where it entered my nervous system or bloodstream, or skin cells, or something. I haven't figured that part out. But somehow, my Collar loosened and fell away, without hurting me. Though maybe I didn't notice the pain while my fur was being fried off."

"The third element," Sean said. He dangled a Collar from his hand, Jace's Collar, which Sean had found in the wreckage. "Silver and human technology, fused together by Fae gold. Whether the gold is already in the Collar or only put into it when the Collar goes on the Shifter's neck, we don't know yet."

"Or how to use that knowledge to get the Collars off," Jace said.

Sean studied Jace's Collar, which looked remarkably intact for its time in the crucible the plane had become. "Maybe a syringe of the liquid gold carefully injected into the Shifter will loosen it? Or simply rubbed on the skin? Will be tricky, this, since Fae gold's pretty hard to find, according to Fionn. Fionn says he'll help us, but even he says it's very rare."

"He claims he has it in the walls in his house," Jace said. "Tell him to dig it out for us."

"He explained that to me," Sean said, without smiling. "He said when it was all chipped away it would only be an ounce or so. But we'll work on finding a source. And start trying out techniques. It might still be very painful."

Jace touched the fake Collar around his neck, put there courtesy of Liam and Dylan this morning. "Well, you can try it on someone not me. I'm done messing with Collars."

Sean nodded in understanding. "You've got it, lad. Volunteers only. But I'm thinking some will put up with a little hot gold on their skin to be free of these bloody devices."

"Me," Deni said. "You can try it first on me. Use whatever is left in the bracelet. I'm sure my mother would be fine with me using it to free myself and my mate."

Jace's hold on her tightened. "No. Not until they know what they're doing."

"Sean will figure it out." Deni leaned into Jace, feeling warm and protected. "I want this damned Collar off. I want to heal all the way. With you, and without the Collar."

Jace growled, but she saw sympathy in his eyes. "All right, but I'm with you every step of the way. Every second. And if Sean hurts you more than necessary, he answers to me."

"Oh, good," Sean said. "No pressure. Don't worry, lass. I'll be trying these ideas on meself as well. I have a mate who can make us all better if I screw up."

"I *hope* I can," Andrea said. She held her son close, his gray eyes so much like his mother's.

"I'm just feeling better about this all the time," Sean said.

"We can do volunteers from our Shiftertown too," Eric said. "Those who would most benefit. If there proves to be so little Fae gold, the weaker Shifters should be released first, those whose Collars hurt them the most. Those of us who can control the Collars' effects—we'll suck it up for a while."

"Speaking of your Shiftertown," Deni said, and Eric focused on her.

"Don't worry—I'll make sure Jace can move here officially," Eric said. "And have leave to visit me and bring you with him as often as possible." Eric swallowed, the light in his eyes dimming. "I'll miss him, but I know what a mate bond is like." His hand drifted to Iona's, and his mate rose on tiptoe and kissed his cheek.

Another thing Jace was doing for her, Deni reflected. Traditionally, Shifter women moved into the homes of their mates, leaving their own families behind. But it would be difficult to obtain permission to move Deni *and* her two cubs to the Las Vegas Shiftertown, and it would also mean leaving Ellison. To prevent Deni having to leave her sons behind, Jace had volunteered to move here instead. A break with tradition, but a kind one.

"Well," Liam said, pushing himself from the window seat and handing Katriona to Kim. "I'm looking forward to conducting yet another mating ceremony. Unless Eric fights me for the honor. But we have other business at hand. Tiger."

Tiger unfolded his big arms and moved to the basement door—the door to the true basement, not the Morrisseys' secret space. The Shifters at this meeting were Liam and family and Liam's trackers, plus Eric and Iona. Liam had asked for Eric's advice on the sticky problem Deni had uncovered at the Shifter bar.

Tiger unlocked and opened the door to reveal the young woman Deni had caught with the phone that showed she'd made many calls to the police. She'd washed off the Shifter groupie makeup but stared around at the Shifters with defiance in her eyes. Broderick, who'd insisted on guarding her, brought her up the last of the stairs with his hand lightly on her shoulder. Broderick's gray eyes swept the trackers, and he looked almost as defiant as the young woman.

"This is Joanne Greene," Liam said. "She's been following Shifters around and reporting things to the police—the fight club, what Shifters do at the bar—and asking the cops to talk to Shifters and watch them . . ."

Deni had wondered what Liam would do with the young woman. Dylan now went to her, and the woman's defiance dissolved into terror. Dylan stopped a foot in front of her, in her personal space. "Tell my son what you told me," Dylan said.

Her chin came up. "Why should I?"

She was young, even for a human. In her midtwenties, Deni guessed, if that. Connor, who was only a little younger than Joanne, shook his head. "I'd tell him. If you think Grandda's scary, wait 'til you face Uncle Liam."

Broderick squeezed her shoulder. "Best get it over with." He sounded sympathetic, interestingly enough.

Joanne took a deep breath. "Because you took my sister," she said.

Liam blinked in surprise, and so did most of the Shifters present. "Your sister?"

"My sister, Nancy," Joanne said. "She's the true Shifter groupie. Loves to chase Shifters. She was here, in Shiftertown. Then she disappeared. What did you do with her?"

Liam gave her a blank look. "We didn't do anything with her, lass. Where was she last? With what Shifter?"

"I don't know." Joanne's eyes flashed anger. "Does it matter what Shifter? She was at your bar, then she went to your fight club. That was a few weeks ago. She hasn't come home since."

"And the human police agree with you that a Shifter must have taken her?" Deni couldn't help asking.

Joanne looked even angrier. "They say they have no evidence of harm. They think she ran off on her own."

Dylan didn't move any closer to Joanne, but his look of menace was hard. "And so you stir up trouble for all Shifters, endangering us, our mates, our cubs, without coming to us and asking about her first?"

Joanne stepped back in fear, bumping into Broderick, but she spoke in a clear voice. "Come to you? Why should I come to *you*?"

Dylan started to answer, but Broderick took a step sideways, putting himself in a position where he could defend Joanne against the others if need be. "Go easy on her," he said to Dylan. "She's afraid for her sister. Don't tell me you wouldn't do the same thing if you lost track of someone you loved inside another Shiftertown."

Dylan's expression hardened. "No, what I would do is find the right culprit and shake him until he coughed up what he knew. And *then* decide whether to let him live."

"She's been telling me about it," Broderick said, as Joanne gazed at Dylan in fear. "I don't think a Shifter took her sister, but it looks like *something* happened around a Shifter event. You and Liam have all kinds of resources. Help her."

Liam gave Broderick a thoughtful look. "Maybe we will. Dad."

Dylan looked over Broderick and Joanne, then he turned away. Without a word, he walked out of the living room and then out the front door with an even stride. The bang of the door in his wake was loud, and for a moment, no one said anything. Dylan often did such things—keeping his own council and walking away to solve problems on his own. He was older than most Shifters in Shiftertown, and had experience and wisdom no one else had. The Shifters had learned to tolerate his abruptness.

Liam cleared his throat. "Since you like her so much,

Broderick, you're in charge of her," he said. "I don't want her talking to the police, or going anywhere or doing anything without me knowing. Got it?"

"Sure," Broderick said. "Lighten up, Liam."

Liam blinked again. Deni saw Liam deliberately let Broderick's admonition go before he gave Joanne a slow nod. "We're going to help you find out what happened to your sister. But you behave—understand?"

Joanne was bewildered—she must have thought the Shifters would kill her, or at least imprison her and do terrible things to her—but she nodded. Broderick stayed protectively in front of her, and Liam ended the meeting.

"I think he's smitten," Deni said to Jace as they walked back to her house across the street. "Broderick, I mean."

They mounted the porch steps of Deni's house, and Jace pushed Deni against a porch post. "So am I. Smitten is a good word for it."

His kiss stirred fires that hadn't gone out. Deni wound her arms around his neck and enjoyed him for a moment.

"I meant what I said," she murmured as their mouths drew apart. "About the Collar. I'll let Sean do what he needs to. I want it off."

"I do too." Jace touched the chain on her neck. "I'll be with you, Den. And when you're free, we'll do some celebrating."

"Why wait?" Deni smiled into his face, and Jace's serious look dissolved into a wicked grin.

"Wild woman," Jace said.

"Always."

Jace led her into the empty house and to the basement, the two of them laughing as they stumbled down the stairs. Jace kicked the door closed at the bottom as he kissed her again. They waltzed their way into the bedroom they'd been using, hands stripping off each other's clothes while their mouths locked into long, hot kisses.

"I love you, Jace Warden," Deni said as they went down onto the bed.

"I love you too, Deni Rowe. So much." Jace drew her up to him, stoking the fires inside her. "Thank you for finding me."

"You found *me*," Deni said. "Healed me too."

"Mmm." Jace closed his eyes as he slid inside her. His voice went low. "You healed me. We healed each other." He put his hand on hers, the streak where the bracelet had burned him already closed to a red scar. Their fingers touched, spread. "You and me. One."

Jace laced his fingers through hers, and Deni closed their hands together. "One," she said, then she let out a cry as Jace thrust into her with a firmer stroke. "Always."

"Always," Jace said, and then there was nothing but the sounds of lovemaking, and happiness.

Sorrow fled, and Deni proved to herself what a beautiful thing it was losing control in the arms of the Shifter she loved.

EPILOGUE

Deni and Jace were mated in the full-sun ceremony the next day, bringing down the blessings of the Father God on the union. The full-moon ceremony, the final sealing of the mates, happened a few nights later, after Deni had had her Collar removed, at her insistence.

It was severely painful, and how Sean got the remaining gold from the bracelet to blend with the Collar and loosen it, Deni wasn't quite sure. She only knew that the Collar had come off, link by slow link. It had hurt, yes, but Deni knew her release had come with nowhere near the agony that had suffused Jace when they'd tried to take his Collar off him. She'd also not felt the need to shift to her beast to give in to her feral instincts, as Jace had. The Fae gold made the difference.

Jace had been there, right next to her, snarling at a nervous Sean every minute. When Sean had lifted the Collar free and Deni took a long breath, Jace had pulled her hard into his arms, his eyes wet.

Deni, now fitted with a fake silver Collar, stood with Jace in the grove behind the houses under the moonlight, with Eric and Liam in front of them. Both had decided they'd jointly perform the full-moon ceremony—Liam because it was his Shiftertown and he was fond of Deni; Eric because Jace was his son.

Shifters gathered in circles, the chanting already beginning. So was the drinking and partying. Ellison stood next to Deni, proud and grinning, Maria on his arm smiling her sweet smile. Behind Deni were Jackson and Will, deliriously happy for their mother, but plenty willing to tease both her and Jace.

Iona had come, standing next to Eric, with Eric's sister, Cassidy, and her mate, a human named Diego, next to her. Marlo, recovered from his bang-up but lamenting about the loss of his beloved plane, had also come.

So had the young woman called Joanne, who was being looked after by Broderick and his brothers. She'd relaxed a bit around Shifters, at least around Broderick's gruff family. She was still worried about her sister, but Dylan already had things in motion. They'd find her.

As the moon rose, its cool light flooding the clearing, Liam held up his hands for silence. He and Eric stepped forward, Eric smiling in his warm way.

"By the light of the Mother Goddess," Liam began.

"I acknowledge this mating," Eric finished. "The blessings of the Goddess go with you, Son." He put his arms around Jace. "And Daughter." Eric turned and embraced Deni, Jace's hand on Deni's back as she hugged Eric in return.

And then there was laughter, many more hugs, with Deni almost squashed by the enthusiastic ones her sons gave her. Ronan's giant bear hug competed with Will's and Jackson's for force. Tiger even hugged her, then gave her a nod, as though satisfied she'd finally wised up and done the right thing, bringing Jace home.

Shifters whooped, howled, screamed. The mating ceremony was a fertility feast, and Shiftertown would be fertile tonight.

Deni hadn't felt the dizziness or beginnings of nausea that had triggered her episodes of near-madness since Jace had been brought home safely to Shiftertown. She'd made a break-through, she thought, out in the wild, choosing to give in to her instincts, which had helped her find her mate. The fact that she'd been able to pull herself out of the instinctive state once she'd found Jace, and hadn't gone insane, had restored some of her confidence. The mate bond also helped erase her fear, and so had the removal of the Collar. Deni didn't know exactly when she'd been healed, but she knew the process had begun when she'd met Jace that night at the fight club.

Music poured into the night. Deni danced with her sons, then Ellison, Liam, and Eric, with a circle of girls—Andrea, Kim, Iona, Glory, Elizabeth, Myka, Carly. The cubs ran around, undisciplined, shouting and screaming in their own games.

Finally, Deni ended up with Jace again. He tugged her close, his eyes going pale green with barely contained mating frenzy.

"Remember how this started?" he asked.

"You getting your ass kicked?" Deni answered, laughing.

"Me *saving* your ass," Jace said. "And then having it."

"Don't you wish."

"I do." Jace leaned close. "I wanted you again and again, Deni. I went through a lot to keep you by my side, didn't I?"

Deni nodded. "I'm glad you did."

Jace kissed her again, his smiles gone. "It's dark out here tonight. No one would miss us."

She gave him a teasing smile. "Maybe we should be more civilized about it, now that we're mated."

"Screw that." Jace's hold tightened, his hand warming the small of her back. "I like being wild with you, Den. My heart."

"Mmm." Deni kissed him, then wrenched herself out of his arms. "Let's be wild, then." She took the garland from her head and threw it, spinning, away from her. Shifter women shouted laughter and scrambled after it.

"Catch me if you can, Feline," Deni said to Jace, and she swung away, dashing into the night.

She heard a growl of frustrated wildcat, then another one of determination. Deni ran, but she knew she'd never outdistance a leopard who'd do anything to bring down his prey. She did try, though, so Jace would have a challenge.

But when his strong arms came around her in the darkness beyond the bonfires, Jace's kisses frantically falling on her flesh, Deni knew she'd never been so happy to be caught.

Dear Reader,

I hope you are enjoying the Shifters Unbound series! This anthology pulls together two shorter works that were originally published as e-book editions.

"Lone Wolf" tells the story of Ellison, a wolf Shifter who works as a tracker for the Austin Shiftertown leader. Ellison is first introduced in Book 1 of the series, Pride Mates.

"Feral Heat" is Jace and Deni's story—Jace is the son of Eric of Mate Claimed, *and Deni is Ellison's sister.*

Where do these stories fall into the Shifters Unbound chronology?

"Lone Wolf" takes place in Austin, after the events in Mate Claimed, *and before* Tiger Magic.

"Feral Heat" also takes place in Austin, and its events fall between Tiger Magic *and* Wild Wolf.

For the entire chronology and reading order of Shifters Unbound, visit my website, jenniferashley.com, click Jennifer's Books, and then click Shifters Unbound.

Keep reading for a sneak peek at the first chapter of Mate Bond, *the next book in the Shifters Unbound series.*

Best wishes,
Jennifer Ashley

The Shifter groupie was new.

Kenzie had never seen her before, anyway. The woman stood with a knot of friends who'd clumped together for reassurance but turned excited gazes toward the male Shifters roaming the roadhouse tonight.

Kenzie watched Bowman size up the woman while he appeared to be merely leaning on the bar talking to his friends. She saw him conclude, as Kenzie had, that the new girl wasn't a real groupie.

No one but Kenzie would have known, given Bowman's posture, that he'd even noticed the woman. He rested both elbows on the bar as he conversed with Cade on one side of him, Jamie on the other. Even as they laughed and joked, Cade, his second, and Jamie, one of his trackers, kept a little space between themselves and their leader. Bowman dominated the whole damn place without even standing upright.

His casual position stretched his jeans over his great ass, outlining narrow hips and strong legs, one knee bent as he rested his motorcycle-booted foot on the lower rail of the bar. His black T-shirt was smoothed over his broad shoulders, outlining every muscle from neck to shoulder blades and all the way down his spine.

Kenzie couldn't take her eyes off him. She absently held an untasted bottle of beer, half listening to two of her female cousins chatter. Bowman turned his head to say something to Cade, giving Kenzie a glimpse of his strong, square jaw and the nose he considered too large for his face but Kenzie thought just right. He was a wolf, after all.

Bowman's gray eyes flashed at something Cade said, a quick ripple of a smile tipping his mouth. A strong mouth, equally good at snarling orders or kissing.

He was going to teach the fake groupie, whoever she was, a lesson, Kenzie deduced from his quick glance in the woman's direction. Would be fun to watch . . . and painful too.

Bowman pushed himself off the bar, giving a nod to those around him. Cade, a big grizzly Shifter, acknowledged it without moving. Cade and Bowman, in spite of being different species, were so wired to each other that they communicated without words or even gestures.

Kenzie's heart squeezed as she watched Bowman walk in a slow, even pace to the new young woman. The fake ears the girl wore were wolf instead of cat—a signal she was into Lupines—and both she and one of her friends had wolf tails fastened to their backsides. When the friend saw Bowman coming over, she started excitedly patting the new girl's arm.

Bowman could charm. Didn't Kenzie know it? Just by walking toward them, he had the cluster of young women smiling, beaming, melting at his feet, before he even spoke.

The new young woman imitated her friends, but there was something calculating in her eyes, watchful. She might be a reporter, come to dish the dirt on the Shifter groupie scene, or she could be an informer for the human police.

When Bowman gave the new girl a jerk of his chin to follow him, the true groupies dissolved into excited laughter mixed with looks of furious envy.

Kenzie knew how they felt. She set down her beer, told her cousin Bianca she was using the ladies'—alone—and walked away.

She knew she wasn't fooling them. The other two Shifter women exchanged knowing looks and let her go. They knew way too much about Kenzie—everyone in Shiftertown did.

Bowman and the groupie had reached the darkest part of the parking lot by the time Kenzie emerged. It was cold; a North Carolina winter at its peak. The roadhouse was ten miles from Shiftertown, halfway between Asheville and the Tennessee border, popular on a Saturday night.

Kenzie heard the two before she saw them. Bowman's voice, imprinted on her heart, came to her from a deep shadow between the generator-run lights. "So you want to be with a Shifter, do you?" He was growling, and it was not really a question.

The woman answered nervously, her high-pitched voice grating on Kenzie's nerves. Kenzie didn't pay much attention to her actual words—the woman's tone said she was afraid of Bowman but determined to get her story, whatever that story happened to be.

Kenzie edged close enough to be in scent range of Bowman, which meant the woman's cloying perfume came to her loud and clear. Why did human women douse themselves like that? Made Kenzie want to sneeze.

She knew Bowman would be able scent Kenzie skulking in the darkness, even over the perfume. She also knew Bowman wouldn't care that she was there. Those thoughts hurt, but Kenzie remained in the shadows, watching.

"Shifters are dangerous, sweetheart," Bowman was saying. He leaned against the back of a dusty SUV and stretched out his long legs, crossing them at the ankles. Bowman's arms were folded, both shutting himself off and giving the groupie and Kenzie a view of his sculpted muscles. He hadn't bothered with a coat—Bowman often didn't. "Better be sure you know what you're getting into."

He was angry, even if his slow drawl didn't betray it. He

hated anyone spying on his Shifters, and with good reason.
The young woman couldn't scent his fury as Kenzie did,
but some instinct inside her knew to be worried.

"I've always wanted to do a Lupine." The pseudo-
groupie was trying to sound as though she stalked Shifters
to have sex with them all the time, but Kenzie—and Bowman—knew better.

Bowman remained silent and motionless for a long
moment, while the girl grew more and more nervous. Then
Bowman moved—the movement was slow and casual, but
all the more devastating for that.

He reached down and undid his belt, the clink of it coming to Kenzie. Next, she heard the whisper of his jeans'
zipper.

Kenzie froze, riveted in place, as Bowman languidly
slid his jeans and underwear halfway down his thighs and
leaned back again on the SUV.

Kenzie couldn't breathe. His half-lifted shirt showed a
slice of hard abdomen, and his large Shifter cock stood
straight up between his strong, sun-bronzed legs. The brush
of dark hair that cradled his shaft was lost in shadow, but
Kenzie knew exactly what he looked like.

The young woman made a strangled sound that Kenzie
wanted to echo. Bowman erect was a beautiful sight.

"Come on, sweetheart," Bowman said impatiently. "I
haven't got all night."

The young woman opened and closed her mouth a couple times and took a few shaky steps backward. "I don't . . .
I don't know."

Bowman came off the SUV with a suddenness only a
Shifter could manage. One moment he was reclining,
ready, and the next he was nearly on top of the woman, his
big hands on her shoulders.

"Here's what I know," he said in a fierce voice. "You came
to look at Shifters, for whatever reason. So here I am. We
look human, but we aren't—not even close." His jeans were
still around his knees, his tight backside bare under the lights
of the parking lot. But he didn't look ridiculous—Bowman

never could. He was as decadent and enticing as ever. Kenzie's mating need, never very far away, flared.

The groupie's words choked in her throat, her nervousness turning to full-blown fear. "I wanted . . . I just wanted to talk . . ."

Bowman shoved her away. "I know what you wanted." He leaned down and pulled up his jeans, taking his time. "You wanted to come here and get all up in our shit and go tell the world about it. I don't know if you're a reporter or a detective or a do-gooder, but I want you out of here, away from my Shifters."

The pseudo-groupie had the presence of mind to point out the obvious. "You don't own this place. This isn't Shiftertown. You can't tell me to leave."

Her breathless groupie eagerness had gone, replaced by the hard, nasally voice of a woman who liked having her own way. Bowman wasn't impressed. His hands clamped down on her shoulders again, and a very wolf growl came out of his throat.

"I might not own the bar." His voice went low, as it did when he was truly angry. "But I know the owner, and he doesn't like people coming here and giving Shifters trouble. Let me give you a tip—I'm way nicer than he is. So get out, or I'll let him and his bouncers take you off the property in a more forceful way."

"Now you're threatening me?"

Bowman said nothing. He only looked at the pseudo-groupie, and Kenzie scented the wolf in him getting ready to come out. Bowman was careful, but he was still pretty close to wild, and he didn't like his authority challenged in any way.

He hadn't said so—the woman wouldn't understand—but Bowman considered this roadhouse to be part of his territory. Humans might have confined Shifters to Shiftertowns and restricted them from owning places like this bar, but true Shifter territory stretched from one Shiftertown to the next. There was another Shiftertown far to the west of them in the middle of Tennessee, and Bowman considered that his territory ended about fifty miles from that, where the other leader's territory began.

By Shifter thinking, Bowman had a perfect right to sling this woman out. Humans wouldn't see it that way though.

The woman started to reach for something in her purse. Pepper spray? A gun? Bowman caught her hand, his growl rumbling across the empty parking lot, vibrating the ground.

Shit. If Bowman hurt the woman, or even scared her bad enough, the human cops would be all over this place in a heartbeat. Bowman would be dragged away in cuffs spelled to contain Shifters, and probably every Shifter in the roadhouse would be arrested along with him.

Only one thing to do. Kenzie hurried out of the shadows, making for the two of them. At the last minute, she slowed and pretended to be out for a nonchalant stroll. She put a sway in her hips as she eased herself up to Bowman and draped her arm around his neck.

The heat of him came to her, along with his wild scent. The strength of him quivering under her touch made Kenzie flush with warmth.

Bowman's entire body went rigid. No one touched an alpha when he was at the height of his anger, especially not when he was this close to shifting.

No one but his mate.

"Hey, Bowman," Kenzie said, letting her voice drawl in a sultry way. "You seeing someone else now? I'm going to get jealous."

JENNIFER ASHLEY

MATE BOND

A SHIFTERS UNBOUND NOVEL

To cement the leadership of his North Carolina Shiftertown, Bowman O'Donnell agreed to a "mating of convenience." Two powerful wolf Shifters, he and Kenzie keep the pack in order and are adored by all. But as strong as their attachment is, they still haven't formed the elusive mate bond—the almost magical joining of true mates.

Now with a monster threatening the Shiftertown community, Bowman and Kenzie will have to rely on their instinctive trust in each other to save their Shifters—and the ensuing battle will either destroy them or give them the chance to seize the love they've always craved.

"Danger, desire, and sizzling-hot action!"
—Alyssa Day, *New York Times* bestselling author

jennifersromances.com
facebook.com/ProjectParanormalBooks
penguin.com

FROM *NEW YORK TIMES* BESTSELLING AUTHOR

JENNIFER ASHLEY

SHIFTERS UNBOUND

PRIDE MATES

PRIMAL BONDS

BODYGUARD

WILD CAT

HARD MATED

MATE CLAIMED

LONE WOLF

TIGER MAGIC

FERAL HEAT

WILD WOLF

BEAR ATTRACTION

"Sexually charged and imaginative . . .
Smart, skilled writing."
—*Publishers Weekly*

"Exciting, sexy, and magical."
—Yasmine Galenorn, *New York Times* bestselling author

jennifersromances.com
facebook.com/ProjectParanormalBooks
penguin.com